RAISING THE BAR

by

Terry Belleville

Copyright@2017 by Terry Belleville
The Factory Inc., Canada
All rights reserved.

ISBN 978-0-9949469-4-2

Available from amazon.com,
amazon.ca, Createspace.com, and
other retail outlets.

terrybelleville.com

Dedication

To all the family and friends in Australia
who told me stories, shared a laugh, bought
me a beer, and stayed true, thank you.
This novel, along with everything else
I try to do, would not be possible without
the tireless support and encouragement
of my wife, Donna Belleville, our sons,
Jason and Ryan, and our daughters-in-law,
Carla, and Jenn. Their zest for life and
their love of laughter keep me young.

And many thanks to Doug Reid,
a wonderful writer and friend, for his
endless enthusiasm and support,
his sharp eye for detail, and his refined
appreciation of good beverages.

RAISING THE BAR

RAISING THE BAR

Meet Paddy and Molly. My parents.
They are the heart of this story.
One day I was in a pub listening to family
and friends retelling tales about them. There
was a lot of laughter and a lot of joy shared.
Someone should write this down, I thought.
So, I did. It's hard to know now what's real and
what isn't any more, but does that really matter?
Although Raising the Bar is ultimately a work
of fiction inspired by the facts, fables, and
folklores that coloured life, the heart, heartbreak,
and humour of Paddy and Molly is very real.

Chapter One

A brown and cream 1930s' cable tram clattered to a stop outside a chemist shop on Brunswick Street, Fitzroy, one of Melbourne's inner suburbs. Paddy Brennan, the grip man, jumped down, crossed the street, and walked toward the chemist shop. Neville Bishop, the tram's conductor, looked at Paddy for some explanation. Paddy pointed at his head, which further confused his conductor. Their six passengers sat patiently in their places expecting to resume their journeys very shortly.

Hilda, a pleasant woman in her fifties, beamed at Paddy as he entered the shop. She always had an eye for him. He was a tall man, thirty years of age with dark brown hair, and a lean, sinewy body. 'Built like a drover's dog, he is,' she used to say. "Hello Mr Brennan," she said, as Paddy approached. "How are you, today?"

"Pretty good, thanks," he said, as he made his way toward the back of the shop. "You're looking lovely as always, Hilda, you're going to lead me astray one day if I'm not careful."

"Oh, I think you'd be the one leading me astray," she said with a flutter.

Greg, Paddy's brother, was dispensing medicine. "G'day, Paddy. To what do I owe the pleasure?"

"Got a terrible bloody headache, thought you could fix me up."

Greg was three years younger than Paddy, slighter of frame and balding prematurely. He was constantly pleasant and even-tempered. When a saner point of view was called for, Greg was the man. While the other brothers stayed with farming, worked in local industries or hotels, Greg became a chemist. His shop was the oldest continuing pharmacy in Melbourne and its proximity to St. Vincent's Hospital made more than a small contribution to its continued success.

One dubious skill he had was his ability to keep a cigarette with a perilously long ash in his mouth while he worked and talked and laughed. Defying all laws of gravity and logic, the ash was unshakable until Greg so willed it.

"There you go, Paddy," said Greg as he handed his brother a bottle of aspirin. "Got time for a cup of tea?"

"No, I should get going," said Paddy as he filled a glass at the sink.

"Just fresh." Greg indicated the pot of tea steeping on the end of the counter.

"No, thanks."

Back on the tram, there were general murmurs of discontent. "Possibly there has been an accident," was the offering of a fat man in a tweed coat. "Can't you do something?" he said to the conductor. Neville Bishop was a small, thin man in his late thirties. Projecting confidence or assurance that everything was under control was not his strong suit. "Sorry," he said. "I'm just the conductor. I can't run the tram."

"Then what can you do?" said the fat man. Neville help up his ticket punch as a sad token of his very limited powers.

"Ridiculous!" said a middle-aged woman in a smart felt hat. "I could walk there faster than this." She gathered up her parcels, gave a menacing gesture to approaching motorists and set off on foot in the direction of the city proper.

Paddy had taken his medicine, finished his water and complained about the weather. "I should get going, don't want to leave Neville out there on his own for too long."

"Who's Neville?"

"He's my conductor."

"On your tram?"

"That's right."

"You're on duty?" Greg asked, somewhat taken aback by Paddy's casual approach.

"You bet. I'm on 'til ten o'clock tonight," said Paddy.

Greg shook his head in mild despair. "You can't keep doing this, Paddy."

"What?" The defiance in Paddy's eyes was at odds with the innocence he projected.

"Come on, you know exactly what I mean. Do you want to get the sack again? Is that what you really want?"

"You're making more out of this than you should, Greg," he said as he attempted to shrug off his brother's concern. "It's not important."

"Yes, it is, Paddy." It was clear Greg was not going to let the matter rest. "I'm amazed you keep getting jobs. At some point you've got to hang on to one of them."

"Give it a rest, will you. I came here to get rid of a headache, not get one," said Paddy.

"Mum worries about you, you know that don't you?"

Paddy was not about to be drawn into that conversation. He glanced at his watch. "I'm off. Got a job to do haven't I. Thanks for the aspirin."

Greg called out after him. "We're going to Mum's for dinner next week. Don't forget."

"No worries!" He gave Hilda a wink and a wave on his way out of the shop. When he arrived back at his tram, Neville was standing in the front dummy car looking lonely and forgotten. "Something wrong?" Neville asked.

"Had a bit of a headache but feeling better now, thanks Nev."

Neville had worked with Paddy for a week; long enough to know he was erratic. That particular day, however, had proven to be more challenging than he had expected. Paddy inspected the enclosed passenger car. He seemed undisturbed that all his former passengers had deserted him, save only the small, frail old woman who had been with him for most of the journey.

"You're still here are you?" said Paddy to the woman.

"It's starting to rain," she said.

"Yeah," replied Paddy. "Weather's bloody awful."

"I've got to catch a train," she said.

"I'll get you there, I promise. Hang on."

Paddy returned to the front car, worked the levers, and engaged the cable. The tram lurched forward. Rain teemed down around them. When they reached the corner of Brunswick Street and Victoria Parade, Paddy brought the tram to a halt, this time at a legitimate stop. He returned to his sole, surviving passenger. "You look cold," he said.

"I am cold," she replied as she pulled her cloth coat around her. "I got cold back there sitting, waiting."

"Come on," Paddy helped her to her feet and escorted her to the door of the tram. There was mischief in his eyes. "We need to warm you up," he said with a smile.

"Ooh! Where are you taking me?" she said, her eyes growing ever wider as the charming man took off his coat and held it over her head to protect her from the rain.

"Hurry up, darlin', the bloody pub will be closed by the time we get there if we don't move it." He turned to Neville who looked sadly resigned to what could only be a tragic outcome to the day. "You coming? My shout?" Neville shook his head and watching them scurry into the crowded bar of the Eastern Hills Hotel.

That lynchpin of Australian culture, the six o'clock swill, was looming. Glasses hit the bar and were refilled at an amazing rate. Pubs of the day were obliged to stop serving at 6:00 p.m.; drinks ordered before that time had to be out of the glass and into the patron no later than 6:15 p.m. The volumes of beer consumed in those fifteen-minute periods were staggering. That antediluvian imposition did little to curb the Aussie affection for beer but merely served to unleash a disproportionate number of drunks in the middle of rush hour.

Paddy had settled his passenger into the Lady's Lounge with a brandy, and had sought out his brother in the Public Bar. Bill was firing beer into glasses with uncanny precision as he chatted with Paddy. He placed a glass of beer in front of his brother and Paddy downed it in short order. "Who's your friend?" asked Bill as he glanced over at the woman Paddy had brought into the bar.

"Don't know, really. She's a passenger and I couldn't just leave her out there alone."

Bill shook his head at Paddy's gall. "You still at that are you?"

"Can't say I like driving trams much, but I reckon I'm pretty good at it." He spotted the old woman in the adjacent bar and gave her a wave. "I start on time and I finish on time, most of the time, and I'm good to my passengers, except for the ones that piss me off." The old woman raised her glass of brandy in a salute to her host and driver. Paddy responded with the scant remnants of his beer.

Bill laughed. "I'm surprised you're still at it. I was sure they would have been on to you within the week," said Bill.

"Don't start on me, Bill, don't need that tonight." Bill was very aware of Paddy's demons. He returned to that seemingly relentless task of refilling glasses but kept one eye on his brother.

"You're coming to Mum's next week, right?"

"Yeah, I'll be there," said Paddy.

Bill leaned across the counter to speak quietly to his brother. "Just a word, Paddy. That young woman, can't remember her name, the one you brought home last time."

"What about her?" Paddy knew what Bill was about to say.

"She really bothered Mum."

"I know," said Paddy.

"Tell me you're not bringing her again." Bill managed to sustain his duties behind the bar without ever fully releasing Paddy from the issue at hand.

"She's not a bad person, a bit rough around the edges but..."

"A bit rough?" said Bill.

"Yeah, well, I didn't take her out for conversation."

Bill just looked at Paddy. It was a silent but clear reprimand.

"Don't worry," said Paddy. "We parted ways about a week ago. She said something about me being a moody bastard, didn't show her a good time, she had a list," said Paddy. Bill became even busier as the clock ticked ever closer to six. "Gotta get going," said Paddy. He offered a wave to his charge; she acknowledged Paddy's signal and drained her glass. He once again shielded her from the rain as they hurried back to the tram.

"Can we go now?" said Neville as they climbed on board. "Had a lot of people wanted to get on while you were away. I told them we'd broken down."

"Yeah, well, sort of true," said Paddy as he launched the tram into motion. He kept his promise to his drinking partner; she didn't miss her train.

While the dummy and enclosed cars were being reversed at the depot, Neville approached Paddy. He glanced around to assure himself that he wasn't being overheard. It was obvious to Paddy that his workmate was uncomfortable.

"What's up, Nev?" he said.

Neville hesitated for a moment still a little unsure of how to say what had to be said. "I don't want to lose this job, Paddy."

"No, of course not," was Paddy's immediate response. Neville's concern about his position was not a casual comment: it was a clear message to Paddy that his behaviour could have disastrous implications. Paddy understood that. As long as Neville's welfare had been playing itself out in the background, he could continue to defer considering the consequences. Neville's simple, honest statement of concern had made Paddy face the fact that he had been inconsiderate and selfish in his actions and that had to stop. He genuinely liked Neville, and didn't ever want to see him hurt. "I hear you, mate," he said. "Sorry you got drawn into this but don't worry, I won't let you take the fall for the dumb things I do."

"Thanks," said Neville. He was relieved that he'd found the courage to speak up but, despite Paddy's pledge, he still felt unsure of what the immediate future may hold. The two men smoked and watched the cars being coupled for the next run.

"You like doing this, working on the trams?" asked Paddy.

"I don't know," said Neville. Nobody had ever asked him that before. "No, that's not true. I don't like it at all. It's not something I ever wanted. I was trained to do bookkeeping, accounting, that sort of thing."

"And you liked that did you, keeping books and all that?"

"Yes, I did. And I was good at it, too."

"Then how'd you end up doing something you hate?"

"How do you think?" said Neville, without hesitation. "It's a job. It's the only job I could get. I've got a wife and two little ones

13

at home that have to be clothed and fed." Neville dropped his cigarette to the ground and stepped on it. "I don't have a choice, Paddy." Neville had become impatient with Paddy's line of questioning. "What's your excuse?" he asked.

"Me?

"Yes, you. Why are you here? And don't tell me you love it."

Paddy had a few glib comments up his sleeve that he used to blunt any further questions if the subject of him driving trams came up but Neville deserved something more honest. In some ways he envied Neville. Like Paddy, he wasn't where he wanted to be, but unlike Paddy his choices were clear and articulate, his work on the trams had a defined purpose. In the past few years Paddy had made a number of choices, most of them vague, indecisive ones that he had hoped would help fill a void. And there he was, driving a tram, and secretly hating it, but not having a plan to change things.

"What do you want to do?" asked Neville.

"What do I want to do?" Paddy took one last drag of his smoke and butted it one the ground. "Dunno, exactly. "I'd like to have a business of my own, I think. Maybe a pub." The more he thought of that the better it sounded. "Yeah, that's what I think I'd like to do."

"So, why are you driving a tram?" asked Neville.

"Bloody good question," said Paddy. Before he could find an answer the tram was ready to head out. It was on the last run of the night and proved to be a quiet one. On the return sector, Paddy stopped the tram outside the Eastern Hills Hotel. There were no passengers either on board or waiting at the stop. He paused briefly, started to move away and then slammed on the brakes and came to an abrupt stop. Paddy walked briskly back into the enclosed car to where Neville was sitting. "I have to do this, mate. I won't be long, I promise," he said.

Neville didn't contest the decision; he knew there was no point. "We can't be late," said Neville as Paddy left the tram.

"We won't be," said Paddy. "I'll get you home on time, don't worry." Doors of the Eastern Hills Hotel had been locked for hours but that didn't deter the regulars. Inside the hotel, the bar bustled with life. There was an after-hours ritual that had to be observed. Before any after-hours' drinks touched lips, pens had to touch paper, registering the drinkers as legitimate guests of the hotel; a legal semantic that thwarted any overly zealous licensing cop who felt the need to raid the premises.

Esme Pratt, a large-breasted woman on the other side of fifty who wore a wig that was forever just slightly askew, opened the door and beamed when she saw it was Paddy. "Come on in, dear. Someone pour this nice man a beer," she called out as she took Paddy's hand and led him into the hotel.

He really didn't want the beer but before he could protest it was in his hand. "Cheers," he said and quaffed it back. "Look, can't stay," he said to Mrs Pratt. "Just needed to ask you something

"Yes, dear, what is it?"

"I heard you were looking for a new barman."

"Yes, I was, dear, but I just hired someone today. Why? Were you interested?"

"Yes," said Paddy.

"Well, that's too bad, isn't it. I didn't know you were interested in being on the other side of the bar." Paddy was obviously disappointed. "I'll keep my eyes and ears open and if I hear of something, I'll let you know, dear."

"Thanks," he said. "I should go."

"So sorry, dear, you should have let me know."

"You're right, I should have said something. I just didn't think of it before."

"I wish I had a spot for you, love, I think you'd be a terrific barman."

"Yeah?"

"Absolutely. Could be a good future for you behind the bar."

"Thanks, Mrs Pratt," said Paddy. "That means a lot. I've been thinking that one day down the road I'd like to have my own pub."

"Look at you." She chuckled. "Wants a pub of his own already. Good for you, love, but you've got to crawl before you can walk."

"You might have a good point there, Mrs Pratt," said Paddy, "but I think I'd rather walk than crawl, if it's all the same to you."

"Let me get you another drink, love."

"No, I've got to go, I'm still on duty till ten."

"You silly bugger." She cackled and glanced at her lapel watch. "You'd better get a move on then because it's a quarter to ten now. Tell you what I'll do," she said as she led him to the door. "I know this chap named Griffith. He buys and sells pubs and businesses and the likes. He's always looking for the right people, as he likes to call them. You may have to be inventive to impress him, if you catch my drift, but it could be time well spent. I'll give him a shout if you like."

"I'd appreciate that," said Paddy. "Means a lots. I gotta go."

Paddy ran across the street and jumped onto the tram. Everything okay?" asked Neville.

"Yes, mate, good." Without further delay the tram lurched forward heading home. "Could be real good." Paddy said to himself. It felt good to inch his way forward toward something he may have actually wanted.

Once hotels closed and shops were shuttered, the city rapidly fell quiet. Saturday night was no exception. If there were performances at Her Majesty's or the Comedy Theatres, there would be a flurry of activity but on that night the city felt deserted.

Beer can be insidious. You can drink and drink and feel nothing. Then, almost without warning, you have to pee. The further Paddy drove the more uncomfortable he became. The rough, rolling ride of the tram just made things worse.

Maybe it was in response to the Australian affection for beer or maybe it was for more benign reasons, but almost every park and public venue had public toilets. These conveniences were accessible at all hours of the day and night. Needless to say, however, on that occasion there was nary a toilet to be found.

By the time he reached Albert Street, he couldn't hang on any longer. The tram screeched to a grinding halt and fell silent.

"Not another stop? Come on, Paddy," said Neville.

"Only take a second."

The world around the tram was deathly still. The only sound to break the silence was the splash of urine hitting pavement, followed by an extended and audible sigh. Then, once everything was neatly tucked away and pants were re-buttoned, the tram was on its way again.

Watching Paddy's progress from their vantage point across the street outside the 'Smart Frocks' storefront were Mrs Edna Harding, Mrs Dorothy Kent-Hughes and Mrs Olivia Deluca. The three snowy-haired women stood there wide-eyed and stunned by the events that had transpired before them.

When Paddy reached the top of the Collins Street hill, he glanced at his watch. "Bloody hell," he said as he released the grip on the cable and, untethered, the tram began to pick up speed. It was the wildest ride outside of Luna Park. Faster and faster it raced down the hill. Through Paddy's heroic efforts and a total disregard for intersections, he rolled into the South Melbourne depot with a minute to spare. He gave Neville a wink as they left the tram. "Told you we wouldn't be late," he said.

"It's a bloody miracle," said Neville. That was the first time Paddy had heard him swear.

Chapter Two

The Melbourne and Metropolitan Tramways Board offices were housed in a narrow Victorian building on Russell Street. There were four metal chairs in the hall outside the office of Commissioner Andrew Murphy. Neville sat in the first chair.

"What are you doing here?" said Paddy.

"Same as you, I guess," said Neville. "Someone filed a report about the other night."

"Shit." Paddy took a seat beside him. "Sorry I got you into all this, mate." The two men sat there briefly without saying anything. Paddy indicated the door. "You been in there yet?" Neville acknowledged he had. "They're not blaming you are they?" said Paddy. That would be wrong, it was all my doing. I'll make sure they know that."

"No." Neville shook his head. "No, it's okay, I'm in the clear. It's just they had this report and they wanted another account of what happened, that sort of thing." He paused to consider what came next. "I had to tell the truth, I'm sorry."

"Don't be. You did the right thing. It's not the truth that bites you in the arse Nev, it's the lie you tell."

"You're not upset then?" said Neville.

Paddy just smiled. "No, mate. Had to happen sometime I suppose." It was not the first time Paddy had jettisoned his future.

From the very first day on the trams he knew it wouldn't work. His actions merely accelerated the inevitable, confirming that his first impression was the right one.

"There is one thing though you should know, Paddy?"

"What's that?"

"He kept asking me if you'd been drinking. It came up a number of times. I got a feeling he was hoping charges could be laid, driving under the influence, that sort of thing."

The drinking had been risky. Paddy knew that. "So, what did you tell them?"

"I told them the only thing I could tell them, the truth. That's why I stayed here, waiting for you. I thought it was important for you to know that." Neville stood up to leave. "I told them that, in the entire time we'd worked together, I had never seen a drink pass your lips. And that's the truth. So, if it should come up in there, and I reckon it will, he doesn't know any more than what I told him. Just remember that. "

Paddy held out his hand. Neville took it and they shook hands firmly.

"Thanks," said Paddy. "Sorry I dragged you into this."

"Well what's done is done. I must say though there were times you scared the hell out of me." Paddy couldn't help but smile. "It was also the most exciting week I have ever had on a tram." Neville nodded a few times for emphasis. "I think you're slightly mad, Paddy Brennan, and I know we won't be on the tram together ever again. I'm sure of that, but I hope things work out for you." He turned and walked away down the narrow hallway.

A humourless woman in a grey wool suit came out of the room beside the chairs.

"Mr Brennan?" Paddy smiled. She didn't. "You can go in now."

Paddy smoothed out his hair, straightened his tie and knocked on the door. "Come in," said the commissioner. Morning light streamed in the windows and brightened the mahogany walls. Paddy looked around the room. Commissioner Murphy sat behind a large wooden desk. Paddy offered his hand "Paddy Brennan," he said.

"Sit down!" was the curt response. Murphy didn't look up. He read from an open file on his desk. "Mr Brennan, sometime shortly before 10:00 p.m. you were driving Tram Number 66 down Collins Street from Spring Street. Is that correct?"

"That could be right," said Paddy.

The commissioner returned to his notes. "What's more, it says you were driving in an irresponsible and reckless manner. What do you have to say for yourself?"

"I think reckless is a little strong," said Paddy.

"For heaven's sake, you could have caused serious injury to anyone in your path?"

"That's not true."

"And why not?"

"There wasn't anyone in my path."

"That is hardly the point!" said Murphy

"Of course it's the point," said Paddy.

"No, my good man, that is not the point!" The Commissioner had become increasingly impatient. "The point is the you were oblivious to the safety of anyone on the street."

"There wasn't anybody on the street, for Christ's sake. That's what I'm trying to tell you."

"Didn't your tram roar past a car and then race straight across Swanson Street without stopping?" Murphy's face was flushed; saliva was attempting to escape from the side of his mouth. His index finger stabbed the file on his desk. "I checked your records," he said. "You've been here just one week yet there are more infractions cited in your records than most people accrue in a lifetime. You've barely managed to be on schedule once. Not once. Unbelievable. And now, you've been discovered careening down the hill with total disregard for anyone's personal safety."

"Nobody got hurt," said Paddy. "Middle of the night, not a soul around."

"Oh you think not?" Murphy rose and tracked back and forth between window and desk. "What about the three women who witnessed your appalling actions?"

"What women?"

"What women, indeed?" Murphy picked up a typed page from the file and waved it in the air. "Three innocent women who had stayed late decorating the altar at St. Patrick's Cathedral. They saw you expose yourself to the world."

"No, that's not true," said Paddy.

"Do you deny it? Do you take me for a fool, sir?"

"I didn't expose myself. I wouldn't do that."

"They think you did. I think you did!"

"Nature called. Very different thing," said Paddy.

"Then you admit it...you did expose yourself!"

"Well, I don't know how you take a leak, mate, but when I do, I have to whip it out. If there is another way that's better I'd be happy to hear about it."

"You are a disgrace, sir, an absolute disgrace!" Murphy reached for another sheet of paper. "I also have reason to believe you had been drinking."

"No, you don't. You have no reason to believe that. None. And quite frankly I am shocked at the implication." Paddy rose to his feet. "I'm sorry, but you leave me no option: I quit."

"Quit? You're fired! Now, get out of my office." A vein pulsed in Commissioner Murphy's neck. He shook with rage.

And the deed was done. Paddy's days as a brakeman were over. And that was an immense relief to both him and the Tramways Board.

Chapter Three

Thirty-five Taylor Street was a post-Victorian, pre-federation bungalow of red brick. An ornate, oak front door with stained-glass inserts opened onto a side hall that led past the living room and bedrooms and into a dining area next to the large eat-in kitchen. Dinner was being prepared. Bill and Greg's wives, Elsie and Millie, were in the throes of setting the dining room table. Bill stood in the open doorway leading to the yard, having a cigarette; smoking was not something Mrs Brennan tolerated inside the house. Paddy sat at the kitchen table opposite Greg. The men were having a cleansing ale before the meal.

Mrs Brennan lifted the lid on the steaming pot. "I hear you lost your job," she said as she punished the potatoes with a fork.

"Where'd you hear that?" Paddy looked accusingly at Bill who shrugged in innocence.

"Never mind, is it true?"

"Yes, something like that," said Paddy. "You seem to have trouble holding on to a job, Paddy. What's the problem?" asked his mother.

"Look at these, will ya," said Vince as he returned from the vegetable garden with two hands full of tomatoes. "Can't believe how they've grown in the last week." He immediately sensed there were bigger issues on the table than tomatoes. "Right. I'm gonna join Bill outside for a smoke."

Mrs Brennan added some butter and milk to her potatoes. "Listen to me son, that twinkle in your eye and your handsome smile seems to get you opportunities, there's no arguing that. Some say you could charm a snake out of its skin but that's not enough. Once the getting it is done and the holding on takes over, then the troubles begin."

Greg interceded on his brother's behalf. "I don't think Paddy was too happy driving trams, Mum."

"He wasn't happy? Tell me something I don't know." She put the top on the potatoes, wiped her hands on her apron and sat opposite Paddy.

"You haven't been happy for some time son, and that saddens me more than I can tell you. I'm not happy mashing these potatoes but it's got to get done. If you can do what you have to do and still be happy too then that's good. Your poor father, God rest his soul, he knew what had to be done and he did it every day. That's what made him happy, not the work, the taking care of us."

"Can I say something?" asked Greg.

"No, I'm not finished. Oh, without doubt this job business troubles me, but we both know it's more than that, and it's time we faced a thing or two. What day is it, today?"

"What day is it?" asked Greg.

"I'm not talking to you, I'm talking to your brother." Mrs Brennan's attention was clearly directed toward Paddy. "What day is it, dear?"

Paddy was clearly uncomfortable with the question. He shrugged. "I dunno."

"Of course you do," said his mother. "It's the tenth day of April, that's what it is." Nobody in the room except for Paddy and Mrs Brennan found importance in the date. "It's exactly four years to the day since Tesa died." The room became very quiet. Everyone looked to Paddy, who sat very still with his head slightly bowed. "You know what I'm saying, don't you." Paddy didn't speak. He didn't have to. Every year on that date his mother had a mass said for Theresa. Paddy went to the first one, but couldn't go again. "Four years," his mother said softly. "That's long enough, son. You can't go on living with death; you have to start living with life again. She's gone, Paddy, God bless her, she's gone." She wrapped her hand around his.

Theresa Winifred Riley was a memorable young woman: diminutive of stature, with compelling blue eyes and waves of ash blonde hair. Her smile was luminous; her manner was constantly gracious, sincere. Everybody loved Tesa but nobody loved her more than Paddy.

She watched him play football. He took her on long walks. They laughed a lot together. Three months after the wedding, Theresa felt unwell, constantly weary. Many assumed that it had to be good news, that she was pregnant. How wrong they were, how tragically wrong. The true cause of Theresa's fatigue was leukaemia, acute lymphoblastic leukaemia. Nothing could stop its onslaught. Three months later, almost exactly six months from the day they took their vows, Theresa died.

Paddy was devastated. At first he didn't speak. He couldn't. Weeks passed and then, one day, quite abruptly he became his old self. "No worries," he said. No worries, indeed. It was all a posture, pretence, a way to cope. The real pain festered inside him.

"When Tesa died you just gave up," said his mother. "I can't blame you for that but you can't stay that way. She wouldn't want that. She wouldn't want you to be lost, just wandering through the days. She'd want you to find someone to love to share life with." Paddy wanted to interject but his mother was not about to let that happen. "I loved that girl and I knew her, even in the short time God shared her with us. I know she'd want you to find something worth fighting for. Do you hear me, son?"

"I hear you, mum." Paddy knew she was right. That need inside him to find some purpose had been growing stronger every day.

"Right then," said Elsie sensing it was time to lighten the moment. "Let's feed these men before they all faint away." She took the potatoes Mrs Brennan had mashed and transferred them to a serving dish. "Come along everyone," she said. "It's time to eat. Vince, I see you didn't get around to cutting up the tomatoes like I asked. I swear if the women walked out of this house you'd all starve to death, you know that."

Any further conversation of consequence was deferred until everyone settled at the dining room table, grace had been said, and food had hit the plates. Mrs Brennan quietly sipped the tea she had brought to the table.

"Can I tell you something now?" asked Greg.

"If you have something worth saying, you can."

"I think Bill has a good idea"

"Right," said Bill. "Well Mrs Pratt told me...."

"I never cared for that woman," said Mrs Brennan.

"Mum, please can I tell you this or not?" said Bill.

"I find she's a little bit common but we won't get into that now, I suppose. Go on."

"Mrs Pratt told me about this company that handles hotels going into receivership. Some they close down, some they try to revive."

"Why you're telling me this? What's the good idea?" she said.

"We were thinking about Paddy," said Greg. "Maybe he could get in with these people, see if he could take on one of the places, run it till it picks up."

"Tell me something, Bill," she said as she trimmed the fat off a piece of lamb. "Tell me why these friends of that woman should hire a man to run a hotel who couldn't even keep a job driving a tram. Tell me that, Bill."

"As explained to me," said Bill, "there's a shortage of blokes who are willing and able to take this on. It's no sure thing, no guarantee of steady pay or some times any pay at all."

"Seems to me there are people out there lining up to get any sort of job these days," said Mrs Brennan.

"That's true. But it's real tough getting anyone on board who has experience."

"Well, Paddy doesn't have any experience doing that," said Mrs Brennan.

"I think Paddy's a natural for the job, Mum," said Greg.

She always considered Greg brought more insight to the table on account of him being successful in business. "But Greg, surely they'll be needing more skills than the ability to down a glass of beer."

"Fair go, Mum," said Greg. "He's smart, he can learn quickly and you can't deny he's spent enough time in pubs to know what goes on."

"Well, he certainly has done that," she conceded. Mrs Brennan turned her attention to Paddy who had been quiet through all of this. "And what do you think?"

"I'll give it a whirl," said Paddy.

"A whirl? You'll give it a whirl, you say? This isn't a ride on a merry-go-round, Paddy.

"I know that, Mum."

"You can't just sing a song or tell a story if the going gets rough."

"Right, Mum, I know."

"And no more fighting."

"Fair go. It's been a while since I..."

"You have to take things a bit more seriously," she said.

"I do, Mum."

"It's not a merry-go-round," said Mrs Brennan.

"You already said that, Mum."

"You can't just jump on and go round a couple of times in circles and then jump off." She took off her wire-rimmed glasses and slowly cleaned them with the corner of her apron. She only did this when she thought she might cry and needed a small diversion or if the glasses were very dirty. The glasses weren't dirty. "Now finish your dinner before it gets cold."

General conversation flowed over the table as food was enthusiastically consumed. Millie had shopping stories to tell; Elsie had made a new soup she felt was newsworthy; Bill, Greg and Vince got into heated conversations about football.

Paddy looked up and caught his mother's eye. Nothing was said but the slight smile on his mother's lips and the gentle nod of the head assured him that, no matter what, she would be there for him. Neither Paddy nor Mrs Brennan was drawn into the incidental conversations. That evening after dinner plates had been cleared, washed and stacked away, and another fresh pot of tea had been shared, they sat around the kitchen and talked about things that had been, and things that might be, and Mrs Brennan sat beside Paddy and held her son's hand tightly in her own.

Chapter Four

The afternoon was closing in as Molly walked along
Chapel Street. The skies, which had been muddy all day, dissolved
in a light mist. From the pocket of her woollen coat she took a
small piece of paper. Junction Hotel, 358 Chapel Street, Prahan.
The previous day her sister Margaret had jotted down the address
when she had seen a help-wanted sign in the window.

It had been three weeks since Molly had moved to the city.
Every day she had looked for work. Every day had proven
frustrating. The pain of the Great Depression lingered and
revitalization under the conservative United Australia Party was
excruciatingly slow. Unemployment in Melbourne had shrunk
from the harrowing national rate of thirty-two per cent that was
reached in mid 1932, but even though some subtle signs of
optimism were beginning to surface on city streets, it was still a
tough slog.

In country towns, like Yarragon, where Molly had spent all
her life, any spores of recovery from the depression were washed
away in floods that devastated the area in 1934.

Molly's mother was a widow. Her father was a widower.
One had nine children; the other had eight. Add Molly, the only
child by this late union, and there were a total of eighteen children
looking for clean clothes and food on the table. There was an

abundance of love, but nobody was lavished with praise because they had milked cows, washed clothes, cleaned fireplaces or chopped wood. That was what was expected. The exception for Molly's grandmother had her own point of view. For Nana, Molly was always her baby, the one who sat in her grandmother's lap and listened to stories that the other children had all heard before.

By the age of thirteen Molly was a relatively tall girl; she was a hair over five feet eight inches and quickly became self-conscious of her height. "Stand up straight, girl. Be proud of who you are," her grandmother would say to her when she caught Molly stooping. "You have to stand up straight so you can look people in the eye, that's how you get to know who's worth knowing," she would say.

Molly grew into an attractive young woman with long dark brown hair and deep hazel eyes. The gawkiness of teenage year had matured into a more fluid grace. She had a quiet nature and abhorred mindless prattling. She preferred to speak only when she had something to say. She listened to what was said, looked everyone in the eye and made many judgments that were never spoken. But if you impinged upon her rights or legitimate needs and it became a battle worth fighting, you'd hear from her.

Some of her siblings, determined to wring out a life in the country, persevered; a few of the girls found husbands, most left for the city. As the numbers dwindled, Molly felt under some obligation to stay and help on the farm and around the house. She loved her family, but longed to be outside its confines. It was her grandmother who finally prompted her to make the move. "Molly," she said, "it's time, dear." Although christened Mary and labelled Bub by parents and siblings, her grandmother had decided Molly suited her best. "There's no-one here for you dear. If there was a man worth anything more than a sheep's hide within a hundred miles of here, a lovely young woman like you would have been married by now."

The subject of Molly's marriage, or the lack thereof, was a popular topic. The word spinster had crept into conversations more than once. She resented the haste with which people's fates were ordained. She knew she didn't want to just get married to some man, make babies, and milk cows for the rest of my life.

"Then you need to get out of here," said Nana. "I can guarantee you, my dear, that tomorrow morning when you look out that window it will all be the same as it was today and yesterday. Go to the city. Give that a try. Do something."

She knew she could stay with her sister, Margaret, and the idea of earning a wage and establishing some level of independence finally persuaded her to take the leap.

By the time she arrived at the hotel she had walked over twelve blocks from the train station on Toorak Road. She examined herself in the window. She remembered her grandmother's words and held herself tall. She looked younger than her twenty-five years. Her pale, smooth skin was a gift of her Irish heritage; her cheeks were flushed by the wind and anticipation. Although her clothes were very conservative and a little old fashioned, and she wore no more than a hint of lipstick, there was evidence in her bright eyes and the line of her mouth that there was a very attractive woman waiting to fully emerge.

She opened the door to the hotel residence. Uncertain what to do she simply waited for someone to appear. The combination of loud conversation from the back of the building mixed with the voices of children assured Molly that someone was indeed there. "Hello?" she called. "Anyone home?"

The sounds from the other room abated briefly, and a woman with a shock of grey and black hair appeared through a door. "What you want?" she asked. He voice was heavily accented and loud.

"I came about the position. The sign in the window."

31

"You wait." The woman left Molly standing in the corridor. Some time passed until a man in his fifties approached. He was dressed in a pair of grey slacks and a white shirt with the sleeves rolled up.

"Who are you?" he asked.

"Molly Donahue," she replied.

"What do you want?"

"Yes, I'm sorry, I didn't catch your name."

"Lombardi. Mario Lombardi, What do you want?"

"Hello, Mr Lombardi, I came about the job, the one you have posted in the window."

"You cook?"

"Oh yes, I'm a very good cook." The extent of Molly's cooking had been on the farm. It was simple food but good food and she knew how to cook for large crowds.

"It may not be permanent, maybe only for a couple of months? If business doesn't pick up I'll have to let you go."

Molly nodded. "That's fine."

Lombardi headed toward the back of the hotel. "Well, come with me, I'll show you the kitchen." He paused in the doorway. "You've done this sort of thing before?

"Well, not in a hotel, Mr Lombardi" Molly replied. "But I can cook and I can clean too. We had a very large family."

"Not the same thing." His dismissive tone bothered Molly.

"No, I am sure it isn't, but it's all just about hard work and hard work never bothered me," she said. "I can cook for small and large numbers and I promise you the place will be clean."

He studied her for a moment. She seemed an unlikely candidate. "You sure you want to do this?"

"I need a job, Mr Lombardi."

He was not totally convinced. He knew he could wait and there would be more people applying, but she was here and she was cleaner than the other women who had applied.

"Okay, this way," he said. "You start tomorrow. Nine o'clock." He walked away down the corridor and shut the door behind him.

She wasn't sure she would be happy there, but she had work. That was all that mattered. Her brother, Jack, had use of a car and had promised to take her home on the following Sunday. She wasn't sure she would be happy working at the Junction Hotel but it was a job in the city and that was all that mattered.

She remembered standing on the side of the road and looking back at her home in Yarragon, that small grey timber house nestled in the gully. She marvelled how they ever survived. Moving away gave everything context, and some of the older sisters to whom she had never felt truly close, were now at the core of her life.

Chapter Five

Molly had worked at the Junction Hotel for two weeks. There had been a lot of shouting in other rooms but very little conversation. The hotel kitchen lacked both light and ventilation. Molly took a large cut of beef from the ice chest. She smelt it and carried it over to the small window to examine at it more thoroughly. She turned it over and smelled it again. Then, reluctantly, she threw it away. Waste was something they couldn't tolerate on the farm.

Lombardi entered the kitchen. The pungency of his cigar prefaced his entrance. "The food was better tonight," he said. "We can't afford to loose any houseguests because of bad cooking," he said, puffing smoke into the static air of the kitchen.

"Have you done that, lost guests because of the food?" said Molly. "Because if you have, nobody told me." There had only been guests one night and they weren't real hotel guests, just extended family. The food served in the bar was never an issue.

The persistent drone of mother and children fighting in the room above them grew even louder. Lombardi crossed to the doorway and yelled up the stairs for them to shut up. This was returned by a hostile retort in Italian from Mrs Lombardi. They traded another volley of insults and he slammed the door.

35

"Excuse me, Mr Lombardi." Her voice stopped him from leaving the kitchen.

"If I could suggest something."

"What?'

"Regarding the food in the kitchen, if I could do my own shopping it would be better." She put down her dishcloth and dried her hands. "There's too much waste."

"What waste?" This was not something he wanted to hear.

"Some of the cuts are so big. If I could do something with the leftovers."

"This is a first-class hotel. We don't serve leftovers."

"I could make some lovely meat pies for instance."

"I don't serve bloody meat pies. This is a first-class hotel."

"It would just be better if I planned menus and did my own shopping," she said.

"Who made you a bloody expert?"

"I'm not saying that," said Molly.

"You come in here with your airs and graces!"

"No, that's not true," she said. "It's just that when you come from a big family you learn to make the most of things."

"I don't want to hear about your bloody family. I'm sick of you and your family. You serve my customers not your family, you hear me!" He turned to leave. "I know more about running a hotel than you ever will. Make sure this is clean before you leave."

Molly desperately wanted to say that only thing people didn't complain about in that hotel was her cooking. All the other services were chaotic. She bit her lip and vented her frustration scrubbing a pot. She wanted to believe he was not just a totally unpleasant human being, but that the stress of an ailing hotel exacerbated his ill humour. It was not easy to believe he was anything but a rude bully but she was determined to try.

Chapter Six

Seeing a glistening new Ford gliding down the street was enough to draw attention at any time of day. It appeared the depression hadn't been bad on everyone, especially those in the business of harvesting companies that just didn't quite handle the fall. James Griffith's low-key demeanour and gentlemanly manners didn't truly represent the hard-nosed opportunist he was at heart.

There were so many businesses on the cusp that it was a challenge to find enough people to manage or at least sustain them until the emerging markets nursed them back to profitability. One of the biggest challenges was finding qualified people who were willing and able to step into such tenuous situations. Paddy came through the door with the right attitude, more than a modicum of confidence and a stated history of actually running a pub. Griffith immediately knew there was a place for him.

As they drove along Bourke Street, Paddy fancied that one day soon he, too, would have a car like this, a gleaming black symbol of affluence and influence.

"You do understand, don't you, Paddy? The job will last just as long as you can manage to keep the place from collapsing altogether," said Griffith.

"No worries, I'll get it back on track," said Paddy, both excited that this unanticipated opportunity was materializing and anxious because he really didn't know what he was getting himself into."

"How big was this hotel you managed in Watchem?" said Griffith. Watchem, Paddy's hometown, was a very small community in the heart of Victoria's wheat growing district.

"Aw, it wasn't huge," said Paddy, improvising, "but I think the principles of running a pub are the same everywhere." Paddy considered his deceit a minor lie. He had spent enough time in the Watchem Hotel to grasp some sense of the operation. "I tell you Mr Griffith, it's all about making people feel comfortable, giving them the feeling that their pub's a home away from home."

"You enjoy working with people?" asked Griffith.

"The people are everything," said Paddy. "They're the heart of the business." Sometimes Paddy's need to elaborate allowed words to flow before thoughts were properly formed. "I admit I may not do everything according to the book, but I always take good care of my passengers."

"Passengers? I've never heard it phrased quite like that before, but there you are. I would say we are all passengers aren't we? Travelling through life, as it were. Are you a religious man, Paddy?"

"Yes, as matter of fact I am," said Paddy. "Somebody once asked me if I'd consider serving God. I told him yes I would. If he's got the price of a drink, I'd definitely serve him."

By the time the car reached the Junction Hotel in Prahan, Lombardi was hauling two large suitcases out of the hotel. His wife was attempting to force five children into the back seat of the old sedan.

Molly stood in the doorway silently watching the farce accelerate. Griffith approached Lombardi; Paddy followed a respectful distance behind. "I'm sorry it had to end this way, Mr Lombardi," said Griffith.

"You bastard!" shouted Lombardi. "Every day you hope things get worse for me so you can steal my hotel away from me."

"That's not true, Mr Lombardi." Griffith's position was firm, rational and unflinching. "You have had more then ample time to reconcile the debt, but I'm afraid the problem just gets worse."

"Problem! You're the bloody problem!" The frustrated Italian stormed over to Griffith, his sweaty face flushed with rage. Mrs Lombardi had lost patience with the children, the youngest of whom was now wailing loudly, and she repeatedly shrieked at them to get into the car. Paddy was a little stunned at the scene.

"How many times I ask you just a little more time? Huh? How many times? Another week or two could make it all different. But no, you want to squeeze us out. You've got no fucking heart!" Lombardi shouted and inched even closer. Griffith was not going to be intimidated, he had suffered similar such tirades before.

"It's unfortunate you feel that way, Mr Lombardi. May I have the keys, please?" said Griffith.

Lombardi fumbled through pockets, found the keys and hurled them at Griffith's feet.

"There, take your fucking keys!" said Lombardi.

As Griffith bent over to pick up the keys, Lombardi suddenly leapt forward and stuck him on the back of his head. Griffith gasped and crumbled. Lombardi unleashed a string of Italian invectives. He kicked the fallen man in the stomach. Mrs Lombardi shrieked, the older children incited their father to further violence; the younger ones cried.

"Oh, my God, stop it!" Molly rushed forward from the doorway and called out to Paddy to restrain the man. Paddy stalled for a moment, still shocked by the sudden turn in events. "Go on!" shouted Molly. Paddy immediately moved into the fray and took hold of Lombardi, putting the angry man into a neck-hold.

"Okay, that'll do," said Paddy. Lombardi swung his arms wildly. "I said that'll do!" Paddy tightened his hold and Lombardi gasped for air. "You gonna behave now?" Lombardi grabbed Paddy's arm to ease the pressure.

"Let him go, he's choking," said Molly.

"Good," said Paddy. Lombardi stopped resisting and slumped in front of Paddy. The moment Paddy released his grip Lombardi stumbled to his feet and thrust his knee into Paddy's groin. With Paddy doubled over in pain, Lombardi set his sights on Griffith again.

"Get away from me," cried Griffith as Lombardi chased him around the car full of screaming, crying, cursing children. At the end of the first circuit, Paddy grabbed Lombardi and slammed him against the car.

"Now, you've done it!" said Paddy. He abruptly introduced his knee to Lombardi's testicles. The man yelped and crumpled. As Paddy took hold of him, Lombardi uncoiled and backhanded Paddy across the face.

"Fucking wop!" Paddy grabbed him by the shoulders and threw him against the bonnet of the car. He grabbed Lombardi's chin and slammed the back of his head hard against the metal. There was a thudding, hollow sound.

Molly yelled. "Stop it! Stop!" She ran to the side of the car and attempted to physically restrain Paddy.

"You saw what he did!" said Paddy.

"Yes, yes I did. But please. His children are watching."

Paddy looked into the car. The children had fallen silent and the whole family's attention was fixed on the fight in front of them. Molly tugged tighter on Paddy's arm.

"Please, please, leave him with something."

Paddy dragged Lombardi to the driver's side, opened the door, and stuffed him inside.

"Get out of here! Dago bastard. You don't belong here. You should be laying bricks somewhere not trying to run a pub, for God's sake!" said Paddy as he kicked the door of the car shut. Satisfied the father was not about to be further beaten, Mrs Lombardi and the five children returned to sobbing and shrieking at each other and at Paddy as the car lurched forward.

Paddy's attention turned back to Griffith who had his feet back under him and was standing by the entrance to the hotel.

"You all right?" asked Paddy.

"Yes, yes, I'm fine." He rubbed the dirt out of his dark grey suit. "Apologies about that. You can see he wasn't an easy man to deal with."

He turned to enter the hotel.

"Just who do you think you are?" Molly's verbal assault stopped Griffith in his tracks. "Who do you think you are to walk in here and throw a family onto the street?"

"I beg your pardon?" said Griffith somewhat affronted by this challenge. "You don't know anything about this."

"I know enough to see that there is very little respect for human dignity here."

"You know nothing!" said Griffith harshly. He'd had enough of this rancour and wanted to move on.

"I know more than you think," said Molly.

"Who are you?" said Griffith, staring Molly in the eye.

"I'm Molly Donahue and I work here."

"You think so, do you? Well, Paddy, looks like she's your problem." He turned away and disappeared into the darkness of the hotel doorway.

Paddy stared at Molly. Any other time his first thought would have been what a nice looking woman she was. Right now all he saw was her flash of anger and it actually frightened him a little.

"You really work here?" he said.

"Yes, I do. And I won't be thrown out like yesterday's newspaper."

"Great, great and it's lovely to meet you, too," said Paddy. "I guess I'll see you inside."

Paddy stopped briefly to look at the elaborate red brickwork on the façade of this old hotel. It was grubby but gracious. He knew this wasn't about to be his, not in any real sense, but it would do for now. Griffith called from inside. "Paddy!"

"Be right with you." He turned back to Molly. "You all right?'

"Yes," was the automatic and slightly defensive response.

"You sure?"

She looked at him and saw a glimpse of a man who was perhaps less of a gruff bully and more of a man with some measure of compassion. "Yes, thank you for asking." She was very shaken by this episode but she needed that job and was not about to let strangers take it away. She took a deep breath, crossed herself and re-entered the Junction Hotel.

Chapter Seven

By 5:00 p.m. the bar was getting busy. It was nothing like rush hour at the Eastern Hills where they'd be three or four deep but for Paddy it was more than enough. He poured beers as fast as he could while still trying to project a calm demeanour.

"Where's the other bloke?" the customers asked. "He had to leave suddenly," replied Paddy, "but you got lucky, you got me."

"Well, we'll see about that," said the burly man in the overalls. "How long do I have to wait to get a beer here?"

"Coming right up, mate, and this one's on me."

Paddy lined up the beers and dashed to the doorway. "Molly! Molly, you there?" He scurried back to the bar as more customers flowed through the doors.

"I hear there's a new bloke, that you?" said one man. "Yeah," replied another. "There was a huge bloody fight before," said an old codger at the bar. "You should've seen them goin' at it." He said it with such conviction that you'd swear he had personally witnessed it, which of course he hadn't.

Paddy filled the orders and then called out once more. "Molly, I need you here, now."

Molly arrived at the entrance to the bar. "Whatever's the matter?"

"I need you up here!" He was starting to panic.

"I don't like being yelled at,"

Paddy turned back to the bar and Molly watched him as he tended to the next round of beers. He was doing his best but demand rapidly outpaced supply.

"For Christ's sake," he said in a forced whisper. "I'm dying here, help me."

"What about Jack?"

"He's gone. I'm on my own here. Please. Please give us a hand." Paddy turned his attention back to the bar, "All right, gentlemen, what can we do for you?"

Word of the scuffle earlier had been broadcast through the neighbourhood and locals wanted to inspect the site firsthand. It had been a long time since that many men had stepped into to the bar of the Junction Hotel.

Molly looked at the horde of thirsty, rowdy men. She removed her apron, folded it over a chair, took a deep breath and entered the mêlée. She started by clearing away unwanted glasses and generally getting the place into some semblance of order. It was instantly clear, however, that the real need was for someone to serve beer. She studied Paddy's form as he filled glasses with the tap, taking the glass, holding it as just the right angle as the beer gushed into the glass and then adroitly straightening the glass as the beer reached the rim. The head on the glass had to be precise. It might not be as important as finding a cure for malaria but in the eye of the drinker, it was bloody close. It was also critical that the integrity of the glass be maintained: no new-glass-for-every-drink pedantry, the glass in which you drank your first beer should be the glass in which you drank your last.

"Right," said Molly. "Here we go then. "Her first effort was a predictable disaster. In the blink of an eye the glass frothed with foam: all head, no beer.

"Bloody hell," said the largest of the men in the blue coveralls whom, according to the tattered embroidery, was named Bruce.

"I'll get you a fresh glass," said Molly.

"No, you won't," said Bruce. "Just let it sit a bit. Try his." He pointed to his mate's glass.

"Right," said Molly. She took a deep breath, put his mate's glass under the spout, turned the handle. Same results but and even faster that time. To prove it wasn't a fluke she did it twice more. She shook her head in despair. "Sorry."

"Who taught you how to pull a beer anyway?" asked Bruce.

"Matter of fact, nobody, that was my first try," said Molly.

"All right, here's what you got to do," said Bruce. "Pour that mess out, we'll start again."

Paddy had kept an eye on Molly's progress and made his way over. "How we doing here? Can I help you out a little?" said Paddy.

"Bit late for that, mate," said Bruce. "You should have thought about that before you threw the little lady in at the deep end."

"Bloody right," said one of his mates. The other two sternly echoed his sentiment.

"We're doing fine here, don't need you," said Bruce. This rebuttal came as something of a shock to Paddy.

"Bugger off, so we can get on with it," said the short, swarthy bloke in the front.

Molly could only shrug and laugh a little. She smiled at Paddy and indicated the other end of the bar where people were waiting to be served.

"Okay love, what's your name?" asked Bruce.

"It's Molly."

"Okay Molly, now pick up the first glass." Thus began the coaching of Molly. The four men patiently and wisely dispensed tips on how to pour a beer. Before long, the words of encouragement evolved into cheers.

"Look at that! Just look at that!" said one of the coaches as he held up a 'perfect' glass of beer. There was a general round of applause and shouts of 'good on ya, love' and the likes. Molly was the hit of the day and she was enjoying every moment of it. Soon other patrons made their way to her end of the bar just to have her pour a 'perfect' beer for them. That day, the bar was ebullient. Everyone left very happy, a little in love with Molly and more than a little pissed.

Paddy leaned back against the door once it was finally closed. He was exhilarated but tired. He glanced at Molly but she didn't acknowledge him, she was busy gathering glasses and cleaning the bar.

"Well, that was something," he said and smiled. Molly looked at him and politely returned the smile. "You wouldn't like to pour me one would you?" he asked.

"Not really," said Molly, "I've got enough to do."

"I just thought you might like to show off your skills," he said. "You want one? You've earned it."

"No, thank you," said Molly. She walked past him to collect some more glasses.

"You really don't like me, do you?" said Paddy.

Molly put down the glasses and turned to face him. "Why'd you fire Jack?"

"I didn't fire him. He walked out," said Paddy.

"Why would he do that, just walk out?" Molly was still unconvinced of Paddy's motives.

"He was one of the most miserable buggers I've ever met. I told him to smile, make a joke or two and just stop arguing with the customers. Then, when the crowds arrived and he realized he'd

46

have to work, he mumbled something about 'I don't have to take this,' and a few other things I can't repeat in front of a lady and he was off."

"Where did those people come from anyway?" Molly resumed gathering glasses.

"Some of them work at the factories down the street. I dropped in at lunch before Jack left asked them why they didn't come to the pub. They said they didn't like the publican and I said, you don't know him. I'm in charge now. I said that if they'd give me a shot, I'd shout them the first beer. I think some just came because they heard about Lombardi getting chucked out. Had no idea we'd get so busy"

Molly went about her chores.

"I think you did a terrific job today,' said Paddy.

"I didn't much care for the way you spoke to Mr Lombardi," said Molly.

"He hit me!" said Paddy.

"He was losing everything he had in the world. I think you could have been more understanding." She looked at the clock on the wall. "I have to go."

She left the bar and headed back to the kitchen to collect her coat and handbag. She splashed a little water on her face and leant against the sink. She was tired. It had, indeed, been a long day. Paddy appeared in the doorway.

"You'll be back tomorrow, won't you?" asked Paddy.

"I suppose so but I wasn't hired to do this." She indicated the bar.

"Fair enough, but I need you in the bar. I'll get someone else to do the cleaning."

Molly slipped on her coat and propped herself against the table to consider the offer. She did find certain exhilaration in the day but was not convinced it was what she wanted to do every day. "I don't know," she said.

"I can pay you a little more money if that makes a difference," said Paddy.

Molly considered the offer. "Same as Jack?" she asked.

"Aw, I don't know about that," he said, thinking that her notion overly ambitious.

"Excuse me Mr Brennan but wouldn't I be doing basically the same work?

"Paddy. Call me Paddy," he said. "Yeah, pretty much I guess but there's only so much I can do, after all."

"I'm sorry Mr Brennan I don't quite understand. You told me I did a great job today. You thought Jack was a waste of time and he walked out on you. Now it seems to me that if I'm not worth at least as much as him, then something is very wrong," she said. "If you want me to work in the bar, something I never wanted to do, you have to make it worthwhile for me. Fair enough?"

Paddy sensed her implacability. "Okay, same as Jack. Will you do it?"

"And you'll get someone else to do the cleaning and cooking?"

"For sure, First thing tomorrow."

"We had a couple of women in looking for work last week. Shall I go ahead and ring one of them?" she asked.

"Absolutely, that'd be great," said Paddy. Molly was looking at him. He could tell she anticipated something more. "Thank you," he said.

"I have to go," she said. Molly gathered up her things and walked to the door.

"There's a lot to do to set up for tomorrow," said Paddy, wishing she would stay.

"Yes, there is," said Molly. "I have a train to catch. Good night." She left and a moment later re-entered. "If you like, I'll come in an hour early tomorrow to help."

"That'd be much appreciated, Molly," said Paddy. "Thank you." He walked back into the bar and surveyed the remnants of the day. "What a bloody mess," he said and poured himself another beer.

Chapter Eight

Yesterday seemed so far away to Paddy as he rode the taxi back to the hotel the following morning. The night before, he managed to do some cleaning, turn off lights and lock the door but that was it. Tomorrow, he had hoped, things would fall into place. When they pulled up the taxi driver asked, "You work here."

"No," replied Paddy, "I run the place."

"You gonna buy me a beer then?" asked the driver.

"No, I'm not," replied Paddy.

"You're a cheap bastard aren't you?"

"Piss off!" said Paddy.

He turned the key in the front door, released the latch and opened door a fraction. He stood there for a moment wondering what lay ahead. It was so much easier musing about the possibilities of having a pub than it was unscrambled the realities. The truth was, he didn't have a clue what he was doing. Oh, he could pull a beer but that didn't begin to answer the many other questions. He had two choices: relock the door and just walk away, or go inside and face the madness.

Morning light betrayed the confidence of the previous night. What Paddy thought was a passable job of cleaning the previous evening was revealed to be nothing more than a smeared, streaky mess that demanded to be mopped and washed far more thoroughly before doors were opened. It was discouraging to say the least.

When Molly arrived Paddy was in the bar washing the counter.

"What are you doing?" she asked him.

"What does it look like I'm doing?" he said.

"It looks like you're just moving the dirt around but not much more than that. Where did you get those rags?

"Under the sink."

Molly picked up the rag from the counter with her fingertips. "Oh, my! That is disgusting. How could you even pick it up?" She was amazed at the depth of his ambition and the shallowness of his skills. "You need a clean rag for a start, some hot water and a dash of vinegar. Let me do that, please and you get on with the rest of it."

"Right," said Paddy. He managed to shuffle around the bar and look busy while Molly made things shine. "Molly, could I ask you something?" he said.

"What is it?" said Molly without losing momentum.

"Well, I was just wondering, you see I have all the receipts here from yesterday and I'll have to...." His voice trailed off. "I was wondering, you know, how Lombardi set up for the day. How much money in the till to get started? Things like that."

Molly put down the cleaning materials and dried her hands as she studied Paddy. "You don't know?" she asked.

"Well, every pub's different, you know," he said, blustering a little.

"Yes, I am sure it is," She continued to look at him and watched him become increasingly uncomfortable. "You've never done this before have you?" she said.

Paddy just stared back at her. There was nothing he could say; no level of obfuscation could save him. She had him pegged.

"If you tell Griffith that when he comes this morning, I'll be out on my bum. You know that don't you?

"You shouldn't have lied," she said.

"I know I shouldn't have but I did. Not a lot of choices here. What should I have done? Say hello, you don't know me, I've never run a pub, in fact I've never actually worked in one either, but people like me and I want to give it a shot. They'd laugh at me out of the place." He couldn't look at her for a moment. He felt embarrassed, naked, trapped. "I need this Molly, I really do. I need a fresh start. If they sense I don't know...." He shook his head and walked to the far end of the bar. "I'm sorry, this is my problem, not yours."

Molly considered his words carefully while she washed her hands and dried them on a clean cloth. "When I first came down to Melbourne, I saw they wanted someone to work at a dairy. I thought I've milked cows, that's dairy. So when they asked me if I had any experience, I said sure, lots. I didn't know anyone who'd milked more cows than me." She reflected on the moment briefly. "Do you know how many cows there were in the dairy? None, just machines. It was awful. I knew if I stayed I'd be fired before the end of the day so I lied. I said I was coming down with an infection. They told me to go home and I never went back," she said. "We're sort of a pair, I guess." She contemplated their respective situations. "Look, Mr Brennan..."

Paddy turned to face her. "Please, call me Paddy," he said.

"All right, Paddy. I've done the books for him a few times so I know how that works and I could probably set up the tills. If you want I could do that."

"Thank you," he said, enormously relieved.

"I have no idea how to set up the barrels, you'll have to work that one out. Jack used to take care of it. If you get the bar and the bottle shop stocked, I'll look after the rest, for today anyway. Then we can talk about what happens tomorrow."

"Thanks very much," said Paddy. In his heart he wanted to explain about trams and his other misadventures but, instead, just stood there looking at Molly.

"You can't daydream there, Paddy," she said, "there's much too much to do. Your Mr Griffith could turn up anytime," she said.

"Right," said Paddy and he swung into action.

"Make no mistake, Paddy, I want it to work out, too. After all you're paying me what Jack made, remember. Mind you, I never thought he earned enough so I may be looking for a raise pretty soon."

Paddy wasn't too sure how to take that. "You're kidding, right?"

"You think so?" said Molly. "You'd better get a move on if you want to look like you know what you're doing."

"Right," said Paddy.

"And once you set the barrels, you'll need to check the bottle shop and restock it. I'm sure the beer will be low and you won't have time to duck downstairs once the rush starts. Be sure to check the spirits. I know they sold a lot of whisky lately."

"Right." Paddy knew he was brought on side to run this pub. He was the boss, no doubt about it. But right then it didn't feel that way.

Chapter Nine

The ensuing days merged into weeks and then months.
The turnaround of the hotel was dramatic. Paddy convinced
Griffith to agree to a series of short-term leases. For Paddy, it was a
chance to establish himself as the publican he'd always hoped to
be. The lease gave him a greater sense of ownership and noticeably
improved his margins; there was a serious incentive to keep those
men at the factory coming back.

It had become obvious that his conviviality and bonding
with the blokes had brought the pub to where it was in a
remarkably short time. It was also obvious that he wasn't the only
key asset. Bruce and his mates glommed onto one end of the bar
every day after work. Coincidentally, it was the end Molly worked.
"Gimme four 'perfect' beers, love," never failed to elicit a response
from the men. Oh, they liked Paddy well enough but there was a
healthy percentage for whom Molly was their patron's saint.

Payday was traditionally the busiest day of the week. To
cope with the rush in business Paddy recruited Alice Monahan,
principally to work the Lady's Lounge. Alice was Molly's older
sister and had three or four years experience under her belt.

As the pre-six o'clock crush loomed, a fracas which had
been fermenting in the corner had become a real problem. An
inordinate amount of shouting and shoving caught Paddy's

attention. Standing on the edge of the crowd was Larry, the neighbourhood bookie. Nobody knew if he had a last name. Nobody knew where he lived but he was always there when you needed to lay a bet and he was always there when a payout was due. Paddy beckoned him closer. "What's up?" he asked.

"It's that bloke," said Larry, indicating a ferret of a man in a grubby fedora. "He says I can't take bets around here any more without his permission, says he's takin' all the bets on Saturdays now, says I can do the country meets but have to give him a percentage."

"Bullshit," said Paddy. "Who does he think he is?"

"Says he knows people and I'll get the shit beaten out of me if I don't."

"Tell him to piss off," said Paddy.

"You tell him," said Larry.

Paddy worked his way around the bar toward the clutch of men who had become increasingly agitated. "Listen, you dumb bastards, you want to place a bet, I'm the man you deal with!" said the ferret in the hat. "Larry works for me now."

"Okay, what's the problem here?" said Paddy.

"It's him!" shouted one of the men, pointing his finger accusingly at the stranger. "Says he's in charge now." Other men joined in the chorus. Some didn't give a damn as long as they could place a bet when they wanted to; some resented the change in routine; some just generally needed to vent.

"Who the hell are you?" said Paddy.

The man in question elbowed his way toward Paddy. He was small and skinny and mean and he wasn't even slightly intimidated by Paddy's advantage in height and bulk.

"I'm gonna do the business here, you got that?" said the man. "As long was you don't fuck with me, we'll get along fine."

"Okay," said Paddy, in a surprisingly restrained and conciliatory manner. "Couple of things though, you gotta watch your language in here. There are ladies behind the bar and you have to respect that." The man scoffed at Paddy's admonishment. "And another thing," said Paddy. "Larry's been the bookie here ever since God first placed a bet and that's not about to change."

The man issued his challenge. "Do you know who I am?"

"No, I don't and what's more I don't care," said Paddy.

"I warn you mate, you don't want to fuck with me," said the arrogant little man.

"Okay, that's it," said Paddy. He clutched the man with one hand on the front of his jacket and the other on his throat. The man thrashed violently and Paddy hurled him backward against the wall; the man fell like a broken toy. The crowd from the other end of the bar pressed hard to catch a glimpse of the action. Alice had ventured closer to the skirmish. Molly held her ground back toward the cash register.

"Watch out, Paddy, he might have a gun," came a warning from the crowd. Alice blessed herself for protection. "He's a bad one," called a voice near the door.

Showing no respect for the warnings, Paddy grabbed the offender by the scruff of his neck and the seat of his pants and carried him toward the door. One of the patrons opened the door and Paddy hurled the shabby figure into the street.

The man shouted when he hit the footpath; he rolled onto his side and looked up. "I'm gonna get you," he hissed. "I'll fucking kill you!" The nostrils flared on his scarlet face. Blood ran down his fingers from his skinned knuckles; his hand reached for something inside his jacket pocket.

Paddy made a sharp move toward him and his foot squashed the injured hand. The man yelped, clumsily found his feet and backed away. "Don't you fucking touch me," he shouted as he tucked his bloody hand under his arm. "You're a dead man, you hear me." Threats continued to spit out as he shuffled down the street, stopping every few yards to empty his venom.

It was not the first time Paddy had chucked someone out the bar. This time though there was a sense of foreboding, a feeling that he hadn't seen the last of the mean, little man.

"You all right?" Molly asked quietly as he passed. Paddy nodded. The event had shaken him but he was not about to display any vulnerability.

"Okay, enough of that," he said loudly, "who needs a beer?" The mention of beer was all it took to dispel the disruption. Paddy summarily dismissed any attempt to recap the incident by simply saying, "Don't want to talk about that. It was enough to spoil a man's thirst." All accepted his jovial summation. Larry was, however, still reluctant to take any bets. "What's the matter with you, Larry?" said Paddy.

"Oh, nothing, Paddy," replied Larry.

"These blokes here," Paddy indicated three of the regulars at the bar, "they want to place a bet and they tell me you're not cooperating. What's up?"

"Nothing, no, it's nothing, Paddy" said Larry.

"You're taking the bets then, right?" sail Paddy.

"Look Paddy, I've heard about that bloke, his name's Jackie Dyson. Remember them shootin's in Barclay Street, Carlton about ten years ago; they say that was him, him and his hooligan mates. And the Bulleen Road murder, that taxi driver they shot dead, they reckon that was Dyson's doing too. There's lots more."

One of the men from the factory down the street spoke up. "I was in Pentridge for six months, just petty shit, but he was in there running all sorts of business from inside. Larry's right, Paddy, he's no good that one. You should keep an eye out."

"So what am I to do, Paddy?" said Larry. "I don't wanna get shot."

"I don't want you to get shot either," said Paddy. "Take the bets."

"Aw jeez, Paddy."

"Take the bets, Larry, or clear out. Cause if you don't, he wins."

"Who's gonna watch my back," asked Larry

"Same person who's gonna watch mine," said Paddy as he poured Larry a drink. "There you go, mate. My shout. Steady your nerves."

Molly was still standing by the till through all of this. "Should we call the police or something? What if he comes back?"

"Why don't you let me worry about that?" said Paddy.

"What are we supposed to do now?" said Molly.

"We do what we're here to do," said Paddy. "We take care of our customers."

And so they did, until the last one was swept out the door a scant two minutes after the six-fifteen curfew. The place fell silent. Molly did the tills and recorded entries in her ledger. Alice combed her hair and applied some rouge and lipstick. Her red hair had earned her the nickname Copper when she was a child. Alice loved the wrong men, cigarettes, and Jesus: the latter two being unfiltered. She was a perfect fit at the pub; she now lived onsite, as did Paddy. It was better in so many ways to have the place occupied. Molly elected to return to Ascot Vale every evening, an inner suburb where she lived with Margaret and Anne, two of her other sisters.

More often then not, Alice would be on the tram into the city within fifteen minutes of the pub closing. Twenty-five minutes after that, she'd be on her knees in the second row of pews at St. Francis Church on Lonsdale Street in the heart of the city. The oldest Catholic Church in Victoria, having been built in 1841, it was Alice's second home and first love. The venerable sandstone building, like the Catholic Church itself, was old and implacable.

Paddy leaned back against the bar and folded his arms; his eyes were shut.

"I'm going to leave you both to it, I have to go," said Alice as she gathered up her possessions.

"Say one for me," said Paddy.

"After today, I'll pray for all of us," said Alice. "You look tired," she said to Paddy.

"I am, I'm bloody tired, I'll admit that," said Paddy.

"I'm not surprised," said Alice as she pulled on her coat.

"Just by the way, Copper, your boyfriend, Jack was asking after you today," said Paddy.

"He wasn't. And he's not my boyfriend, thank you. Where did I put my gloves?" Alice rummaged through her bag and pockets.

"Oh, I think you've got Jack Murphy all hot to trot, Copper," said Paddy.

"Don't listen to him. He's just teasing you," said Molly.

"He was rubbing up against the bar and muttering your name. He's like a little fox terrier in heat."

"Paddy, that's enough," said Molly.

Alice stopped at the door and turned to Paddy "I was going to ask Jesus to save you. Paddy Brennan." She snapped her purse shut. "But I think it's too much to ask of anyone."

Chapter Ten

It was almost ten o'clock when Molly rushed through the door the following morning. A long shaft of morning light preceded her into the bar. "Sorry, I'm so late," she said as she deposited a string bag on the counter and proceeded to unpack bread and a few other staples. "There was an accident on the bridge over the river and everything was backed up. It was terrible. Some people just got out and left their cars in the street, I swear they did. It's going to take forever to get things running properly. I had to walk across the bridge to get the tram on the other side. I think I got everything on the list."

"Did you get The Sun?" asked Alice. She always enjoyed the paper with her morning tea.

"No, sorry, Alice," said Molly, "but I did get a copy of The Age."

"Oh that's just fine, thanks Bub," said Alice with a smile. Alice took the paper off the counter and headed for a table where she had her morning tea and her smokes. She hummed lightly as she crossed the room.

"You seem in a good mood this morning," said Molly. "What's up?"

"Nothing's up," replied Alice, "its just a lovely sunny day, isn't that enough?

"Where's Paddy?" asked Molly.

"Not sure, think he was in the cellar," said Alice as she spread the paper before her, smoothed it out with the palms of her hands, lit an unfiltered Turf cigarette, drew the thick smoke deep inside her and then tilted her head back slightly allowing the spent smoke to drift into the air. A sip of hot tea with milk and sugar, one more languid, sensual draw on her smoke and the day could begin in earnest.

Molly was in the kitchen and Paddy in the cellar when the cry went out. "Jesus, Mary and Joseph!" shouted Alice. "Paddy! Molly! Quick!"

"What the hell?" Paddy put down the cases of beer he was carrying and rushed into the lounge.

Molly entered drying her hands on a tea towel. "What is it Alice, what's wrong?"

Alice just looked at them, her mouth trying to find the right sounds. Finally she blurted out, "It's him. Look. It's him, I tell you." She stabbed at the front page of the paper. Molly picked up the paper and there on the front page was a photo of the ferret in the fedora. The headline shouted "Police officer shot! Dyson escapes!"

Molly took the paper and read out loud. "Wanted for a string of robberies across Victoria, notorious convict, Jackie Dyson, was finally apprehended by the police. A phone call led police officers to the King's Arms Hotel on Chapel Street...that's just down the street from us."

"Go, on" said Paddy, "what else does it say?"

"Well, it says that he came into the King's Arms yesterday afternoon at about....he must have gone there just after he left here....says his hand was wrapped in a blood-soaked handkerchief and...oh my...."

"What?" said Paddy, "Go on!"

Molly quickly scanned the story. "He threatened the people in the bar. Pulled out a gun, waved it around, said if anyone gave him a hard time he'd be back once he'd taken care of business up the street." She looked at Paddy. "Business up the street? Oh, my. Do you think he's talking about here?"

Alice gasped, crossed herself and quickly lit another cigarette.

Paddy sat beside her. "Bloody hell," he said.

"Seems someone there went outside and managed to flag the police," said Molly. One of the officers got shot. He's going to live. It says that the policeman winged him, but Dyson slipped away and now they don't know where he is." Molly sat at the table with them. Nobody spoke. Nobody had to. They all felt the same chill. Molly reached across the table and put her hand on Paddy's hand. "You all right?"

Paddy grasped her hand briefly but firmly. "Oh yeah, for sure, no worries." He rose and headed toward the cellar. "I should get the rest of the bottles up."

"Alice and I could handle the bar today you know," said Molly.

"Yeah, I'm sure you could," said Paddy. "But I think, considering what's happened there, all the customers will be looking for me today and I have to be here. Right?"

Molly nodded "Of course," she said. "Besides, they're on to him now, they'll get him. He won't come back here, he knows they'll be watching."

The two women sat silently at the table. Alice finished one more cigarette and declared she had to lie down for a few minutes. Molly said that would be fine. It was almost time to open the door but Molly wasn't in any hurry to do so. She would have been happier to close everything up, turn off the lights and go home. She prayed the day would be benign, nothing more than the bar flies and locals, please.

She got her wish. The day was thoroughly uneventful. Everyone who came through the doors had their own version of the previous day's events and in turn described how they put their very lives on the line for their mates. The storytelling soon gave way to the mundane repetition of bar room chat and they all went home happy.

Alice had gone on her pilgrimage. Molly was doing the books. Paddy came to a halt in the centre of the bar and, from overhead, took down an envelope.

"Did you see this?" he asked Molly, holding it in his hand. She looked at it for a minute trying to make out what it was then shook her head and went back to the books.

"It's an invitation," said Paddy hoping to evoke a response. He opened it and read it as if it was the first time he'd seen it. "There's a publican's ball in a couple of weeks. Very smart affair. Black tie." He looked at her again. Nothing. "You interested?"

She looked up "I'm sorry, what?"

"The Publican's Ball!" Paddy delivered the line as if it had huge importance. Molly just didn't see the significance but smiled anyway. "Very elegant affair," said Paddy. "It's at the town hall in Prahan this year. Just down the street. You could walk there from here. Of course you wouldn't, walk that is. Should be quite the event," said Paddy.

"Really?" said Molly feigning interest.

"Oh yeah. Quite the event. You interested?" he asked casually.

"Am I interested?"

"Yeah."

"In the publican's ball?" she said.

"Yeah," said Paddy.

"Not really. Why would I be interested in that?" she said.

"I dunno. Just thought you might like to get out for the night. There'll be a band, dancing and the likes," he said.

"Oh," said Molly, totally unsure of where to take the conversation.

"I think you'd enjoy it," said Paddy. "It's quite a function. Very impressive."

Molly felt the best defence was to busy herself in her work and so retreated to the pages of her accounting book. Paddy matched her enterprise by taking down liquor bottles and putting them back in exactly the same order as he had found them. Some minutes passed before Paddy had the courage to re-enter the topic.

"You like that? Dancing? You know, getting all dressed up and going out like that?"

Molly had to think about the question for a while. "I don't know. I don't think I've ever done something quite like that."

"Oh, you should," said Paddy. "You should go to the ball."

Molly was amused by the idea of her at a gala event. "How would I get there?"

"Well, I suppose I could take you?" Paddy carefully threw the line away as casually as he could, giving it marginally less emphasis than he would if he were talking about an impending football practice,

"I don't think so," she said quickly. It wasn't that Molly hadn't considered the possibility that Paddy was heading in that direction but the actual articulation took her by surprise.

"Right," said Paddy, looking for a new tack. "I just thought since you said you'd like to go…"

"I don't think I said that."

"I thought you did."

"Not exactly, no," said Molly.

"Right," said Paddy.

Molly flipped a page and tallied numbers. Paddy took six bottles down, straightened them and put them back on the shelf. He moved to the next six bottles and repeated the process. Molly regretted the speed with which she had declined. She knew she was inept at handling such moments and hated herself for it. The idea of going to a ball both excited and terrified her. She observed Paddy doing the dance of the half dozen bottles and realized if the moment was to be salvaged it was now up to her. "I just wouldn't be comfortable. I wouldn't know anyone," she said.

"You'd know me!" Paddy immediately leapt in.

"What would I wear?" said Molly.

"I don't know. I'm sure you've got something that would be suitable."

"What do women wear to these function?" said Molly.

Now Paddy felt cornered. How was he to answer that? He didn't want to seem an insensitive bore who couldn't distinguish between satin and hopsack but in the reaches of living memory he had never before been asked to describe what a woman wore.

"Well," he said thoughtfully. "A nice dress," was his best offer.

"You're not much help," said Molly. "What will you wear?"

That was an easy one for Paddy. "Black tie and tails," he said.

"Right," said Molly. She didn't have one thing suitable for such an occasion. She had stood outside the Melbourne Town Hall on a few occasions to watch guests arrive. Men looking uniformly impressive in black and women resplendent in ruched, pastel satin gowns replete with corsages of orchids or gardenias. Some had satin shawls; some wore furs; some had sparking jewels; some wore pearls; all of them wore long gloves; none looked like they'd ever milked a cow. It was impossible.

"Thank you for asking me, but I don't think so," she said. The calm, assured delivery of the line belied the emotions behind it.

"Right, okay," said Paddy matching her casual tone. "Not a problem. It's not until the end of next month anyway so no need to make final decisions yet. I'll check back with you a little closer to the night and we'll see how things stand then, Okay?"

"Yes, fine," said Molly. "I should get going. Good night."

"Good night," said Paddy. He watched her gather up her possessions and head out of the bar toward the front door. He elected to try one more shot. "Promise me you'll think about it, all right?" He threw it into the air hoping she was still there. There was an uncertain moment of silence.

"Yes, all right," came the reply from around the corner. The door slammed and she was gone.

Chapter Eleven

Paddy picked up his tails just after lunchtime and carefully hung them in the skinny wooden wardrobe in his room. He worked the gold and jet studs through one set of buttonholes on the crisply starched white shirt, and then inserted the gold-linked cufflinks into the French cuffs. He hung the shirt in the wardrobe and left the door ajar so that the clothes wouldn't crush. He attempted to finesse a strip of black silk into a tie. The first five or six tries were disasters; his fingers became even clumsier with subsequent attempts. Patiently, he smoothed the tie with his fingers, attempting to reverse the abuse. When some of the creases had relaxed, he gently lifted his hand as if he had just put a baby to sleep and stepped away.

If you asked someone to describe what Molly wore yesterday, they would have difficulty remembering. It was neither trendy nor dowdy, neither florid nor dull, but the consensus was she looked nice. 'Nice' being a euphemism for clean, neat and safe.

That is not to say Molly didn't love to look in shops and magazines to see the latest styles. When in the city she would stroll through the elegant arcades and department stores. She would muse about the day she would need to shop for something grand. That day was at hand. In the elegant flagship of stores, Buckley and Nunn, she saw a pink satin evening gown that the saleswoman

69

described as being 'very much of the moment'. Standing in front of
the three-way mirror, the assistant flitted around her picking at
ruffles that seemed to sprout everywhere. She felt like an oversized
Italian wedding cake. It may have been of the moment but it was
not a good moment for Molly. At Alice's insistence, the two of
them went to their sister Margaret, Snake, as she was known on
the farm. She was the one who mended and altered most of the
children's clothes. It was no surprise that later in life she would
make her way in the world as a dressmaker.

After thumbing through magazines for inspiration.
Margaret remembered something fabulous. "I saw this film. It was
set in Paris. There was this tall gorgeous woman about your height,
Bub, and with dark brown hair just like yours. Anyway, she wore
this fabulous black silk velvet dress with long sleeves and cut high
at the neck. Fabulous! And when she turned around, oh my God,
the back of the dress plunged all the way down to her bum. That's
what you should wear to the ball and I'll make it. Cheers!"

Molly sat on the edge of her bed and looked at her
fabulous dress. Snake was dead right: it was movie star material.
The drama frightened her a little but it was too late now. She
crossed to the chest of drawers and took a long strand of crystal
beads from the top drawer. When Molly was just a little girl, Nana
would hang her crystals around Molly's neck and they would have
tea. It was the only thing Molly wanted when Nana passed away
but she was too timid to ask. As busy as her mother was, she wasn't
oblivious to the significance of the crystals. They weren't talked
about for years but when Molly arrived in Melbourne the first
time there, in the bottom of her suitcase, and wrapped in a
handkerchief, were the crystals.

She hung the long necklace over the black velvet dress.
Lights danced through the crystals. Nana would have approved.

Chapter Twelve

The air wore a hint of spring the night of the ball. It had been a long dreary winter and the slightly sultry evening was welcome. Women chatted and laughed as they greeted friends on their way into the Town Hall. Men strutted back and forth, hale and hearty, and resplendent in their formals.

Paddy introduced himself to anyone and everyone who passed. This was, after all, the Publicans' Ball and he was now a publican. He checked his fob watch every few minutes and looked up and down Chapel Street for some sign of a Molly's taxi. He had wanted to pick her up but she insisted that she would meet him there. Somehow making her own way to the ball empowered her with a little more independence.

Bill came out to grab some fresh air. It was curious how, for so long, the expression 'going out to grab some fresh air' actually meant 'going out to smoke'. Once he had lit up he spotted Paddy. "She this is where you're hiding," he said. "Where's Molly?"

Paddy shrugged and looked down the street. He squinted as if it would help him recognize approaching headlights. "Dunno," said Paddy. "She should be here by now."

"Still early," said Bill. "Why didn't you pick her up, you miserable bugger?"

"I wanted to but she wouldn't have any of it. Once she gets her mind set it can be hard to budge her. She took off right after lunch to get her hair done."

Bill held out his silver cigarette case. Paddy took a cigarette, lit up. The two men watched cars approach and pass without speaking.

"She should have changed at the pub," said Paddy.

"Maybe she needed a break from you, mate," said Bill. "You can be tough going sometimes you know." He chuckled as he turned and walked back into the Town Hall.

Paddy turned back to the street as Molly's car arrived. She looked out, saw Paddy and offered a wave. Paddy quickly stepped forward, opened the door and offered his hand. Molly took a deep breath and accepted Paddy's hand. The transition from the back seat of the car to the street was a graceful one. None of the slipping or stumbling that had haunted her imagination, just a fluid graceful movement. Paddy was mesmerized. He held her hand and just looked at her. Molly smiled and waited patiently for some sign of approval.

"All right?" she asked modestly.

"All right?" said Paddy "Streuth, you look like a film star."

Molly gave a dismissive laugh that landed somewhere in between 'don't be silly' and 'go on, flatter me some more'. Paddy rummaged through his pocket for money to pay the driver.

"The lady already took care of it, mate," said the driver.

"Right," said Paddy.

"She's a real goodlooker, ain't she!" said the taxi driver with a wink.

"Yes, mate, she is," said Paddy. He shut the door and offered Molly his arm. Not a lot was said as they made their way into the foyer. There were a series of polite nods and greetings as they passed people. Paddy curbed his need to introduce himself to everyone who would listen. He didn't feel the same urgency now that he had the arm of this beautiful woman in the black velvet gown. For that alone, he would be noticed.

People were still mingling before dinner; a few were seated at their respective tables. Molly and Paddy surveyed the crowd.

"What do we do now?" asked Molly.

"Well, we can't just stand here. Let's see who we can find," said Paddy.

They moved through the crowd more as two people than a couple. From off to the side they heard a voice. "Paddy. Hey, Paddy, hold up there!" With that Bill appeared from behind a wall of black tuxedos. He turned to Molly, "Hello, Molly." he said, offering his hand. "I'm Paddy's brother, Bill. I've seen you a few times at the Junction but we've never formally met."

"I feel I already know you," said Molly. "Paddy has mentioned you often."

"I'm sure not half as often as he's mentioned you to me," said Bill. He let out a hearty laugh. Before Molly could respond, Bill's wife Elsie arrived with Esme Pratt in tow. Elsie was a cheerful broad-featured woman with tight waves of blonde hair.

"There you are," Elsie said to Bill. She turned her attention to Paddy. "Hello Paddy, I've been looking everywhere for you. Didn't Bill tell you?" Elsie smiled at Paddy and nodded a little excessively.

Paddy shook his head. "No," he said uncertain of Elsie's motive.

"Hello, Paddy," said Mrs Pratt. "Who's this?" she said with a cackle, pointedly referring to Molly and giving Paddy a naughty wink.

"This is Molly," said Paddy.

"Hello Molly, lovely to meet you at last," said Elsie. "Bill, don't just stand there, get Molly a sherry, there's a dear. I think we could all use refills here." Once again Elsie beamed at Paddy and nodded as if to share a message. Quickly tiring of Paddy's refusal to take the hint, Elsie took him aside and produced a corsage of white gardenias. "Did you forget about these? Not surprised. You were pretty flustered when you called this afternoon and begged me to pick them for you," she said.

"Bloody hell, I had totally forgotten," he said. "Thanks, Elsie, you're a lifesaver."

Esme clutched Molly's hand and held it tightly. "Nice to meet you, dear, I'm Esme Pratt, Alice used to work for me at the Eastern Hills."

"Pleased to meet you," said Molly. "Actually we have met before Mrs Pratt, once when I came to see Alice."

"Well, shame on me!" said Mrs Pratt. "I thought I was good, at remembering everyone but there you are. Never get old, dear, never get old!" She cackled and shook with laughter, tossing her lavender-tinted wig just a tad farther to the left.

Paddy resumed his place beside Molly and offered her the spray of gardenias.

"Sorry I meant to give these to you earlier," said Paddy.

Molly took the flowers and smelt the sweetness of their perfume. "Oh, I love gardenias," she said. "Thank you."

"Here, let me help you with those, dear," Elsie intervened, took the flowers from Molly and neatly pinned them on the left hand side of her dress a little below the shoulder. "They're lovely" said Elsie. "Just perfect."

Molly looked through the crowd to the ballroom. It was wonderful, just what she had hoped for. On most days the space was rather austere, a characterless cavern crowned with a ring of plaster fish circling a slightly stained ceiling. Now, with diffused incandescent light and candles on all the tables it became a fairy tale. Large bowls of pastel-coloured flowers centred the tables, which were dressed with large white tablecloths, silver place settings and crisp white linen napkins. The crowded quarters at the dairy farm in Gippsland's Yarragon never seemed so far away.

Alice arrived just before everyone moved to their appointed tables. She apologized profusely for her tardiness, explaining that she had been detained at church - an explanation that would only ring true if St. Francis had replaced the side altar with a stand-up bar. It wasn't so much the mild swaying motion or the slur, which some might have mistaken for a speech impediment. It was the glaze in her eyes that detached her ever so slightly from the world around her.

Alice rarely wore more than rouge and lipstick but that night was different. That night was gala. That was a night for eyebrows. Nature had bestowed her with very light eyebrows to match her fine copper-coloured hair. Unless the application of an eyebrow pencil was deft, the results could be tribal. Such was the case that evening. Two glassy eyes hovered between two hard tracks of ginger pencil and two large orbs of red rouge. Alice may not have had a pretty evening but she had a happy one. Molly took Alice in hand and sat her where she could keep an eye on her.

Dinner fulfilled the mandate of such functions: roast chicken, mashed potatoes, greens beans and carrots, the latter supplying colour more than taste or texture. Washed down with wine and it all tasted better than it had a right to. The dessert was a form of trifle that everyone thought was just lovely.

The seven-piece band took the stage, carefully positioning their ubiquitous glasses of beer so that were always within reach. The pulse of Duke Ellington's 'It Don't Mean a Thing If It Ain't Got That Swing' replaced the clutter of china as the tables had been cleared. Enthusiasm and energy made up for a few squashed notes and questionable synchronicity; it was after all their first number and there was little doubt that once their instruments warmed and their glasses emptied they would be fluid and mellifluous. Even if they weren't, with a few more drinks into them, the guests would cease to notice the difference.

Elsie returned to the table with drinks. "All right, time to round up the men," she said. "We should all be dancing! Where's Paddy?" she said to Molly.

"I don't know," she said. "I think he had people to see."

"I am sure he did," said Elsie. "He's going to shake every hand in the ballroom and that's just fine but he should have you up dancing."

"That's all right," said Molly. "I'm not much of a dancer."

"And you think he is?" replied Elsie with a laugh. "How about you, Alice, you want to dance?"

"What?" replied Alice. "Dance?" She grinned inanely. "Tell the nice man I'm not sure I can stand up," she said.

"What are we going to do with her?" Elsie asked Molly.

"She'll be right," said Molly. "I'll take her home with me."

Molly put her hand on Alice's shoulder and restrained her as she attempted to rise out of her chair. "Who wants to dance with me?" asked Alice.

"Sit down, Copper," said Molly.

"But somebody wants to dance with me!" Alice was becoming belligerent.

"Nobody wants to dance with you." Molly applied a little more weight to Alice's shoulder and she succumbed to the pressure.

Standing on the edge of a street drinking beer was a flagrant violation of the law; everyone knew that but nobody cared. The local disrespect for authority was deeply ingrained and universal so it was no surprise that the pride of Melbourne's publicans spread down the steps and into the street, every one of them with a glass in hand. Any police car that drove by would do no more than wave.

"All right, you're coming with me, young man." Paddy turned to see Elsie standing behind him. "You too, Bill," she said.

"Just having a beer with the blokes," said Bill.

"So I can see," said Elsie. "Well you're about to trade a beer with the blokes for a dance with the wife."

"You'd better do as you're told, Bill," said Paddy "I think she means business."

"Too right I do and that includes you Paddy Brennan. You bring this beautiful young woman to the ball and what do you do? You leave her sitting at the table while you spend the night out here. You should know better," said Elsie, quite enjoying taking charge. "If you'd planned to make the evening a job interview you should never have asked Molly to join you. It's time you did the right thing. There, I've said it." Elsie put a button on the scolding with the nod of the head. She took Paddy by the arm and led him back into the hall.

Paddy looked a little chagrined as he approached Molly. "Sorry I got caught up with things," he said. Molly didn't respond directly but smiled. "Elsie thinks we should dance," said Paddy.

"Elsie wants to dance with you?" said Molly being deliberately vague.

"She does?" said Paddy.

"That's what you said."

"No, I didn't"

"Yes, you did. 'Elsie thinks we should dance' is what you said."

"No, no, no, that's not what I meant." said Paddy.

Molly was quietly enjoying the game. "But it's what you said."

Paddy sighed and took a deep breath. "Let's try this again. Elsie was saying that you and I should be dancing."

"Is that what you want to do?" asked Molly.

"Yes, it is."

"I'm not a very good dancer," she said.

"Neither am I. I'm hopeless, but I'd still like to dance with you." Molly felt it was a genuine moment.

77

"Then I would love to," she said. Paddy took her arm and walked her to the centre of the dance floor as the band played the first few bars of 'When I Grow Too Old To Dream'. They eased their way into it as inconspicuously as they could. They didn't look at each other nor did they speak. Slowly, every so slowly, they relaxed enough to enjoy the moment. Their pleasure extended to a second song.

"Not so bad," said Paddy once the song ended.

"No," said Molly. "It was good. I think we did that very well," said Molly.

"I thought we were bloody brilliant," said Paddy with a smile. "But I think we should quit while we're ahead. Walk with me," he said and offered his arm. They slowly strolled around the edge of the dance floor.

"I made a point of seeing Griffith a little earlier. He's very happy with what we've done with the Junction. He said it was way more than he ever expected. Mind you, we may have worked ourselves out of a job. He's selling the Junction."

"Oh, that's too bad," said Molly.

"Yeah, it is," said Paddy, thinking about where he wanted to take the conversation next. Paddy stopped walking but held on to her hand. "But maybe it will all be for the best. You may remember me saying some time back that he'd guaranteed there'd be a healthy bonus for me if I could build the business and I have. Or should I say, we have. The thing is, I told him I wanted to have my own pub one day and he said he might be able to help me make that happen."

"You'd like that? Owning your own pub?" said Molly.

"My oath," said Paddy. "You don't get anywhere working for someone else all your life. I need to make something of myself."

"A pub would do that?" she said.

"I think so. I hope so," said Paddy. "You've got to want something, really want something. You gotta have a dream, something worth fighting for, you know what I mean?" Paddy had always seemed to be a man of the moment. It took Molly by surprise to know he had some far-reaching ambitions. "There got to be something you want," he said to Molly. "Do you know what it is yet?"

She had to think about that. There were dreams and fantasies but nobody had ever asked her directly what she wanted. "I don't want to milk any more cows, I know that." Paddy laughed at that but looked at her to continue. "There are little things, a new dress now and then, but that's not really important I know. I think I would like to have something, own something. A home. My own home. I think that's what I would like."

"Good for you," said Paddy. "I think we want a lot of the same things."

"Let's walk some more," said Molly. She took Paddy's arm and they slowly continued their promenade. "Where would it be, this hotel of yours?" she asked.

"Not real sure." He laughed. "Sounds funny to say I want something so much but have no idea where or exactly what it is. Doesn't make a whole lot of sense."

"I think it does," said Molly.

"Most likely it'll be some place nobody wants but me," he said with a smile. Griffith had mentioned some possibilities to Paddy. One of them, a country hotel, had fired Paddy's imagination. He wanted to share more of the details with Molly but was carefully measuring his steps.

When they arrived back at their table, Bill was holding forth on the state of the nation.

"Look," Paddy said to Molly. "If you'll excuse me for a minute, there is something I have to settle with Griffith before the gets away." He turned to his brother. "Bill, be a good bloke and get Molly a shandy would you?"

"Sure," said Bill. They watched Paddy make his way through the crowd. "What's he up to?" he asked.

"I'm not sure," said Molly.

Bill and Molly walked together to the bar and Bill got her a shandy and himself a beer. Molly sensed Bill had something on his mind and was taking a moment to compose his thoughts. "I hope you'll forgive me if this sounds too forward," he said, "but you've made a real difference to Paddy in the last six months."

That took Molly by surprise. She took a sip of her drink. "That tastes good, I was thirsty," she said, vainly trying to shift the focus of the conversation.

"Bloody hell, now I've embarrassed you," said Bill.

"It's all right, Bill," said Molly. "I think you may be reading more into it than there really is. Paddy and I just work together, that's all. "

"You think so? Well, you wouldn't know that from him. It's Molly this and Molly that. It's hard to shut him up sometimes. It's hard to shut him up most of the time, come to that," Bill said with a laugh. "

"He does like to talk," said Molly.

"You don't smoke, do you Molly?"

"No." she replied.

"Mind if I do?"

Bill used the time it took to take out a cigarette, light it and inhale a few puffs to think about his next tack.

"May I ask how old you are Molly?"

"I'm twenty-five," she said.

"And you know how old Paddy is?" he asked.

"Thirty."

"That's right. It's high time he settled down again," said Bill.

"With all due respect, Bill, shouldn't you be telling him, not me?" said Molly. She considered what Bill had just said "When you said he should settle down again, what do you mean by 'again'?" she asked.

Bill thoughtfully blew smoke into the air considering how to respond. "Well, I guess Paddy hasn't mentioned this and maybe I shouldn't, but what the hell. Did you know he'd been married before? "

"No," said Molly.

"Not surprised. Has a lot of trouble talking about it he does, even now. Her name was Theresa. She was just a little thing. Very tragic it was. She got sick. Cancer. Died six months after they were married. Shocking. I remember Mum saying the day we lost Tesa she lost Paddy, too."

Bill took a long drink of beer and Molly sipped her shandy. She felt that revelation began to explain a lot of Paddy's ways.

"The thing is, he's back now," said Bill. "And you've got more than a little to do with that. Can't tell you how good it is to see," he said with genuine affection. Bill looked up to see Paddy approaching. "There's the man, himself," he said. "Look, not sure I should have been the one to tell you about all that."

"No," said Molly. "I'm glad you did. Don't worry, I won't say anything."

"Good on ya," said Bill as he left.

"Did you see, Griffith?" Molly asked Paddy.

"Yes. Yes I did." He was pleased with himself. He obviously wanted to share some news with Molly but didn't want to do it standing in the middle of the floor. "Maybe we could sit for a while, talk, you know." Their attention was drawn to Alice who was loudly ricocheting between comedy and tragedy at a nearby table.

"I would love to but not with Alice like that. I think I should get her home."

"You're leaving?" Paddy was genuinely concerned that she should go so soon.

I think it's best if I do."

"Couldn't we just put her in a taxi?" said Paddy, eager to have her stay.

"She'd never get out of the taxi on her own." Molly laughed. "No, I can't leave her like this. It's embarrassing for her and uncomfortable for everyone else." Alice let out a shriek.

"What can I do?" asked Paddy?"

"If you could get her outside while I grab our coats that would be such a help."

"Of course," said Paddy.

"Thank you for asking me to come tonight. It was lovely." She started to leave but turned back to him. "I didn't want to forget to say thank you for the gardenias. I love them," she said.

"Good. That's good," said Paddy.

Paddy couldn't be sure if Alice was crying because she had laughed so hard of if she had just slid into a black hole of despair. At that moment, he didn't much care. He carefully but decisively got her to her feet. "She going to be alright?" asked a woman at the table.

"She'll be fine," said Paddy.

Alice looked up at Paddy through her moist, glassy eyes and asked, "Are we going to dance?"

"You bet," said Paddy as he steered her toward the exit. "We're going to dance right out to the street."

"Lovely," said Alice as her knees buckled yet one more time.

Molly was waiting for them on the steps outside the town hall. She wrapped Alice's coat around her shoulders. "Thank you," she said to Paddy. "Someone was good enough to call me a taxi so it shouldn't be too long." Paddy admired the way Molly handled Alice. It was firm but gentle.

"You've done this before," he said, indicating her slumping sister.

Molly smiled and shrugged. "We take care of each other."

"Good on you," said Paddy.

"Paddy, we're fine now. You don't have to wait here, honestly. Shouldn't you be in there charming Mr Griffith?"

"Right," said Paddy without moving. "Remember I told you that Griffith had mentioned some country pubs?" It was clear Molly didn't remember but that didn't deter Paddy. "Well, one of them is in Mansfield. I just have a good feeling about it." Alice slumped again and Paddy took charge holding her up. "The thing is, and I don't quite understand how it all works, I'd have to have someone look at this for me, but I could walk out of the Junction with a few quid in my pocket or I could keep just a little of it and put the rest into the Mansfield place. What do you think?"

"I don't know," said Molly. "It might be good. That's what you said you wanted. I just don't know."

Alice came to life and brushed Paddy aside. "I need a smoke," she said as she walked with disarming confidence toward the kerb.

"That's right. I did say that. This could be the chance to make that happen. If we could make a go of it, it would be like a dream come true, it would." He could barely contain his enthusiasm. He didn't have a clue about the pub itself or what condition it was in. Right then that didn't matter to him. It was a chance he thought he'd never get and that was enough. "What do you think?"

Molly didn't respond. Instead she turned away from Paddy and looked up the street for her taxi. Paddy was a little confused. "Is there something....did I say something wrong?"

Molly turned to face him. "You said 'if we could make a go of it'. We? Is that supposed to mean you and me?" She turned away from him again. "Where is that taxi?"

"Okay, maybe I didn't say it right and I'm sorry for that but I think we could make a go of it. I think it could be...."

"Just a minute. Wait!" said Molly. "I'm not going anywhere."

"I just thought...."

"No you didn't. You didn't think, that's the problem," said Molly, now feeling very flustered. "You shouldn't say that," said Molly, as she turned to leave.

Paddy hurried after her. "Say what?"

"We, us, things like that. You can't make assumptions about me. You can't do that. It's not fair."

"I didn't mean to do that," said Paddy.

"But you did it," said Molly. "Look, just forget it, please," said Molly.

Alice was rummaging through her purse and getting anxious. "I can't find my cigarettes! They must be inside." She started to make her way back into the hall.

"No! Stay where you are." Molly moved sideways to restrain Alice. "They must be in your purse, you just had one for heaven's sake!"

"Molly, I want you to come with me!" said Paddy.

"I can't find my smokes!" Alice shouted. "Someone took my smokes."

"Jesus!" said Paddy. He grabbed Alice's purse and rummaged for her cigarettes.

"What about what I want?" said Molly. "Did you take time to think about that?"

By now, Paddy had found Alice's cigarettes and shoved them in her hands.

"Lovely," said Alice as she lit up.

"Alice don't light that, we're leaving," said Molly. "Alice! Come on!" She put her arm around Alice and led her to the side of the footpath.

"I don't want you to go away like this," said Paddy. Molly took a step onto the street to look for her taxi. "Wait, please." said

Paddy. "We are good together. You can't deny that. Maybe I spoke too soon and I'm sorry about that. I guess I hoped you'd want this, too."

"Then you should have asked me!" She gave up herding Alice and confronted Paddy. "That's a problem with you, You don't remember to ask people what they'd like, Paddy, you tell them."

"I didn't mean it like that," said Paddy. "I meant…"

"I won't be told by anyone what's on for me," said Molly. She walked out to the middle of the street to look for her car. Paddy followed her. There was a crowd on the footpath closely following the unfolding drama.

"Listen to me…" said Paddy

"You don't have the right," said Molly.

"Bloody hell! Will you listen to me for a minute?" said Paddy. "What I am trying to say is I want you to marry me,"

He had many times imagined how he might say this once he summoned up the courage. Yelling it out loudly enough for everyone near and far to hear was not on his list.

"What?" It wasn't just that he'd said the words that shocked her. She looked into Paddy's eyes and saw that he meant it. He really meant it.

"I said I want to marry you." Paddy was suddenly conscious of the audience and attempted to bring the dialogue down to a calmer level. "I want to marry you," he said again, as simply as he could.

Whatever anyone else on the street was discussing had become secondary. Everyone waited for Molly's response.

Molly had her share of romantic notions of a proposal and how it should be. None of the fantasies matched that moment. It was too sudden, too shocking. There should have been a more gradual ramp up of obvious affection. How could she say yes standing in the middle of a street with a drunk sister on her arm?

This wasn't how it was supposed to be. She saw a taxi, waved it down.

"Please, Molly, don't go yet," said Paddy.

Molly took the cigarette out of Alice's mouth and threw it away. She stuffed her unwilling sister into the back of the taxi.

"Molly, please," implored Paddy.

"No, I'm sorry, I have to go now."

"I won't to go to Mansfield without you!" he shouted as the door of the taxi slammed.

Paddy stood there in the middle of the street as the black taxi pulled away. "Shit," he said quietly. He looked back at the audience to his drama. He wanted to tell them all to fuck off but didn't think that would help. Elsie was there. In her eyes he read a hint of sympathy although she shook her head slightly as if to say you silly bugger, you're timing was terrible. He already knew that.

He held his head high and calculatedly avoided eye contact as he walked back into the town hall. Griffith was waiting for him at the entrance.

"Are we still on for Mansfield?" he asked Paddy.

"My oath!" replied Paddy with a calm determination as he walked into the hall to where his brother, Bill, was waiting for him with a fresh glass of beer.

Chapter Thirteen

Alice was up early the following morning. No matter how late she had stayed up the night before, no matter how much Remy Martin she tucked away, she would rise early and the kettle would be on the stove by 7:00 a.m.

She didn't say much. She didn't do much. She just sat in the backyard in her dressing gown and drank a lot of tea. When her sisters left for mass at St. Monica's, Alice was still in her dressing gown. In order to make it to the last morning mass she had to take a taxi.

The eleven o'clock mass was filled to capacity. Hundreds of Sunday sinners assured their respective salvations in this impressive sandstone church, which was only just two years old. They started construction on St. Monica's in 1929 and it was officially blessed and opened by the venerated Archbishop Mannix in December of 1934.

The church with its blue lead-light windows, wide aisles and impressive thirty-feet columns did more than soothe souls; it had put bread on the table. The twenty-five thousand pounds it cost to build the church provided a critical infusion of wages that were desperately needed in Moonee Ponds during the Great Depression.

In contrast to her rush to arrive, Alice took the long way home. Most Sundays she would have walked from St. Monica's to Moonee Ponds junction and taken the tram, but on that particular morning, the late autumn air was brisk and the brilliant sun was invigorating. It was a four-cigarette walk to Moss Street Ascot Vale where Alice had spent the night with Molly and Anne at Margaret's house.

Margaret was naturally frugal; a helpful trait growing up in times like that. From her early teens she consistently looked for opportunities to earn a few extra shillings doing alterations. Although there was talk of a nascent economic revival, many people would still elect to alter and amend rather than pay the price for new. This was good news for Margaret; her days were full, those shillings grew into pounds and soon she had the down payment she needed to transfer the small Victorian bungalow on Moss Street from a rental to one she could call her own. It was a narrow semidetached single story bungalow with an oak doorframe and elaborate stained glass insets that were common in that period. Typically a long side hall was its major artery, travelling from the front door to the kitchen at the rear of the house.

Everyone who stayed with Margaret pitched in around the house, and when they had work they would contribute to the monthly payments. It was a boon to have a place in the city they could call home but all that would soon end. Margaret, a slim, blonde woman who was approaching thirty years of age, was to be married within the year. Anne, a.k.a. Tommy, when she heard the news of the impending nuptials summed it up with "Good on ya, Snake. 'Bout time."

Although a date had not been set, Margaret was to marry, Joe, a man they all adored. Joe was straightforward, honest, well educated and polite. He was a reformed drunk who pulled himself out of the grim times and started mending roofs and writing poetry. He mended Margaret's slate roof. She made him a cup of tea. He wrote her a poem. She mended his shirt. He fixed the gate, her fence, and cleaned up the yard. He was tall. She told him they called her Snake. He laughed a lot at that. She thought they should get married. He agreed.

Anne was shorter, stockier and a year younger than Margaret. She was already married to a Joe. They had a house in the country but Anne was staying in town while her Joe was away serving in the armed forces. He was an immigrant from northern England who liked to drink beer and chase snakes. When they moved into their home near Benalla, it had been deserted for almost ten years. It was in remarkably good condition but too many snakes now called the surrounds, home. Oblivious to their reputation as being among the most poisonous in the world, Joe relentlessly pursued them. Fleet-footed as a sheep dog he would get behind the snake and grab it by the tail. Then with a blend of razor-sharp reflexes and English madness, he would flick the reptile in the air and crack it like a bullwhip. Many watched in awe; few were tempted to try it. Joe worked at a lumber mill before he joined the army. He was short. They dubbed Snake's Joe, Big Joe and Tommy's Joe, Little Joe.

When Alice came into the kitchen, the three women were sitting at the kitchen table; a pot of tea had been brewed. Molly was looking out the back window, Margaret was copying a recipe from a magazine, Anne was smoking. Alice poured herself a cup of tea.

"Thought we'd lost you," said Anne.

Alice took her time to respond. She needed to sit and stir her tea and light up one of Anne's cigarettes first. "I walked," she said. That was the sum total of the conversation for some time, until Margaret put down her magazine.

"So how was the ball?" asked Margaret.

"Good," said Alice.

"That's it? Good? That's all?" said Margaret.

Alice thought about that for a couple of puffs. "I danced a lot," she said.

"Good on you," said Anne. "I love to dance. Joe took me to a lot of dances when we were courting. Who wants more tea?"

"Good idea," said Alice.

"I'll make a fresh pot," said Anne.

"You're quiet, Bub."

Molly just smiled in response and turned back to her view of the back garden.

"I'll bet Molly turned a few heads. I'd look good in a dress like that," said Anne, "If I was six inches taller and sixty pounds lighter," she added with a chuckle. "What about it, Bub, did you dance?"

"Yes, thanks," said Molly. "Is there any more tea?"

"Wait a minute," said Anne, "I'm making a fresh pot." For Anne, world peace was just a pot of tea away.

Anne and Alice nattered about the respective masses they'd attended, who they saw, who they didn't, how you can't beat Bushells for a good cup of tea, the price of tea, the weather. Anne read a brief letter from Joe saying he would be home soon and how he was looking forward to getting back to Benalla. Conversation lapsed when the kettle boiled and a fresh pot of tea was made and set on the table.

"There you go Bub, a nice fresh cuppa," said Anne as she filled Molly's teacup.

"Thanks," said Molly. "Mansfield's near Benalla isn't it?"

"Oh yes, not far at all, about thirty-five miles I think, why?" asked Anne.

"I was offered a job in Mansfield last night," said Molly.

That got everyone's attention, even Alice's, for although she was physically there to witness the exchange with Paddy, she had absolutely no recollection of the event.

"What sort of job?" said Margaret.

"Working in a hotel," said Molly.

"You got an offer to go and work in a hotel in Mansfield and you're just telling us about it now?" said Margaret. Everyone wanted more details: which hotel and for how long and what would she earn and how would she get there? Anne, although shocked, was not unhappy with the idea, as Molly would be so much closer when she and Little Joe returned to life in the country.

"I just don't know any more than that," said Molly attempting to placate them.

"Well, you haven't told us anything," said Margaret. "Who made you the offer?"

Molly hesitated for a moment uncertain whether she wanted to open that door. "Paddy did," she finally said. That was enough to stop everyone momentarily.

"But he doesn't have a pub in Mansfield," said Anne. "I'll bet you he's never even set foot in Mansfield. How could he offer you a job there?"

"Start at the beginning," said Margaret, "tell us what happened."

Molly told the story of Griffith and how he'd brought Paddy in to manage and how, because of the success at the Junction, there was an opportunity for Paddy to go to Mansfield with a view to one day buying the place. She went on to say how excited he was and how he'd asked her to go with him. There was sufficient implication of premarital conjugation for Alice to cross herself as a precaution.

"Wait a minute, just like that he asked you to go with him? Sounds like he's asking you to be more than a barmaid," said Margaret. Molly deferred and took a drink from her teacup. "Well, Molly? What did he say exactly?

91

"He said he wanted me to marry him," said Molly quite simply.

"Heavenly Jesus," said Alice.

"Bloody hell," said Anne.

"What did you say?" said Margaret.

"Just a minute," said Anne, "I'll be putting on the kettle. I think we're going to need a lot more tea."

"I said, no," replied Molly.

"No, you wouldn't marry him, or no you wouldn't go to Mansfield or both?"

"Just no," said Molly.

"I thought you said you liked him," said Margaret.

"You never told me that," said Alice.

"I do like him. Sometimes. Most times. I like the fact he won't just settle for things and he's not afraid to take a chance. I don't like it when he just bustles though without thinking of others and he shouldn't have made assumptions. That's what he did, he came out and said 'we'd' be good together."

"Well, wouldn't you be good together?" asked Margaret.

"That's not the point, he shouldn't have just assumed that," said Molly

"But it is the point. That's the heart of it all. Would you be good together?" asked Margaret.

Molly took her time to respond. On one hand she wanted to maintain her righteous indignation. On the other she wanted to concede Margaret's point. She chose a middle path. "I don't know," she said.

"What do you mean you don't know? Of course you know. Have you done well together at the hotel?" asked Margaret.

"I don't know what 'done well together' means?" said Molly.

"Don't come that with me, Molly Donahue, remember who you're talking to. You know exactly what I mean. Did you get on well? Did you work well together?" said Margaret.

"Yes. He does give me a lot to take care of though, and he just assumes I'll do it," said Molly.

"Why do you think that is? Because you do it well? Because he trusts you? Or is it because he can sense you want to be a part of it all?" Margaret was not about to let go.

"That's enough. Please. Where's that tea?" asked Molly. It was the end of a period and refreshments needed to be served. Molly washed dishes. Margaret prepared sandwiches for lunch. Anne made tea. Alice smoked.

Molly had thought a lot about the previous night. The vehemence of her response had surprised and somewhat disturbed her. What was it that she found so offensive? That was easy she thought. A man embarrasses you by making a scene on the side of a street in front of a crowd of people and asks you questions you're just not ready to answer. How could you not be angry? Or, she thought, you could look at it another way. A man buys you gardenias, dances with you, tells you that you look like a film star and then declares his love for you in front of the world. How could you be angry?

True, the unpredictability of Paddy was an issue. Molly liked it, but it scared her. Would she like to be with someone with whom she could anticipate every move or would she like to be living closer to the centre of the storm? She had grown up with conformity. Living in a family of over twenty people, there had to be structure and order. Anarchy would be intolerable. It wasn't that she didn't long to be more spontaneous, to chase dreams, it was just that, for now, it scared her. Finally the table was set and the group resettled.

"So where were we?" said Margaret, determined not to be put off.

"I've got a question for you," said Anne. "Does he make you laugh? If you can't have a good laugh there's no point in living with someone."

"Yes, he likes to laugh. And, yes, he does make me laugh."

"So what do you want to do?" asked Anne.

"I don't know. I really don't," said Molly.

"I think you should marry him," said Margaret.

"Really?" asked Molly.

"Absolutely. You can't sit around waiting for some other bloke to show up. I had just about given up until I looked up one day and saw Joe on the roof and I thought to myself, I could marry him, I should marry him. I'd be a fool to let him go. If you like Paddy and if you are good together and like Anne says, if you can have a good laugh, it's not bad," said Margaret.

"What do you think, Alice?" said Molly.

"I don't think you should marry him. He's not good enough," said Alice.

"That's a bit harsh Alice," said Anne, "Maybe you should say a rosary for him, make him a better man." Anne liked that and had a good laugh while she went to her handbag for a fresh pack of Turf cigarettes.

"Tell you what," said Molly. "I know you all want to know what's going on and that your hearts are in the right place but I think I have to work this one out for myself."

Molly gathered up her purse and slipped on a light woollen coat. "I'm going out for a walk. Maybe this evening we can play cards."

"Good, oh," said Anne. "We'll play euchre."

"Have a good walk," said Margaret, "and think about it. You'd be married to Paddy, I'd be married to Big Joe, Anne would be married to Little Joe and Alice would be married to Jesus. That could be one hell of a euchre night."

Chapter Fourteen

The window in Paddy's room at the hotel had a broken shade. At best it would cover half the window. Every morning the room warmed with light earlier than he wished. That morning it seemed earlier than ever. He rolled over and buried his head in the pillow in an effort to keep the morning at bay.

Having a hotel to call his own had become a driving ambition. It simply had to happen. If anyone were to ask him what he wanted most, he would answer without further thought that it was to have his own pub. Although he wanted to achieve this on his own merits, he didn't want to run it alone. He had worried about the aftermath: getting it was one thing, making it work was another. Molly had provided more than help just keeping the doors open. She gave him the confidence to believe he could make a go of it.

There was one day in particular. Paddy was doing what he did best: telling stories and joking with the crowd. He could endear himself to the patrons who would forgive the physical shortcomings of the Junction Hotel because now it had the personality that made them feel welcome and appreciated. It wasn't lost on Paddy that the men in the bar relished Molly's presence. He noticed how they loved it when she smiled and shared a moment with them and she genuinely seemed to enjoy them.

Most of all, Molly could see where Paddy was less adroit and she would quietly undertake additional responsibilities. One day over a beer, Paddy shared these revelations with Bill, declaring the place would collapse without Molly. Bill laughed and said it was about time Paddy noticed that; everyone else had known it for months.

After Molly's taxi had pulled away from the Prahan Town Hall after the ball, Paddy was disconsolate. He was seriously troubled about the outcome of the evening and the way he bungled an important moment with Molly.

It wasn't the first time Paddy looked for answers in the bottom of a glass. It hadn't worked then and it didn't work now. He knew the futility of it all too well but didn't have another solution at hand. Now, as the morning evolved he was dehydrated and tired. He wasn't surprised, he knew he would feel this way but that didn't dissuade him from going there.

There was no solace to be found in the hotel's kitchen. Over time the cream-coloured walls had become badly stained and scarred. There were no curtains at the one window that opened into a well of brick walls denying daylight much chance to brighten the place. The hotel seemed inordinately hollow on that morning.

He looked into the main bar. It smelt of stale beer and was never less inviting. It needed to be scrubbed clean but that would have to wait.

He made a cup of tea and a piece of toast and sat at the table in the kitchen wishing he had been more measured the previous evening. She was right, he thought. He was inconsiderate. Once he set his mind on something he'd mentally put all the pieces in place. His enthusiasm to make that mental blueprint a reality often outweighed his discretion. He'd have to work on that, he thought. In the mood of the morning he feared his future with Molly had evaporated in the heat of the moment.

He couldn't stay in the hotel. He'd go to his mother's house. She would cook him dinner and comfort him. It wasn't a cure for tomorrow but it would work for today.

He did a walkthrough of the hotel before he left, ensuring all lights were off and that doors and windows were appropriately locked. He noticed that there were coins on the floor near the front window. Closer inspection revealed there were two halfpennies slightly wedged under the chipped skirting board. He nudged them with his foot but they resisted the pressure. He really didn't want to bend down and pick them up; both cartilages in his knees had been spent playing football in his early twenties so they just didn't function as well as they once did. He looked at the two copper coins for a moment. Poor buggers, he thought, stuck in a hard place there. He could relate to that so crouched down to tug the coins free.

Suddenly, the large glass window above him exploded and long shards showered around him. He felt a sharp pain as glass pierced his back. In defence against the pain then he leaped up and arched his back; the puncture was shallow, the glass fell away.

It was as if a wall had fallen away and the bar was totally exposed to the world outside. Paddy looked at it in disbelief. There, on the other side of the street stood a man. Paddy could tell from the hat and coat that is was Jackie Dyson He had one hand inside his coat as if he were concealing a gun. He looked hard at Paddy and nodded.

Traffic entered the picture: two cars, a tram stopped almost opposite, and then three more cars. Once they cleared, the street was empty again. Dyson was gone. His grim warning was the pile of broken glass at Paddy's feet.

Chapter Fifteen

Griffith arrived at the hotel shortly before the police. Uncertain exactly what to do next, he had been the first person Paddy had called. Within minutes Griffith had assessed the situation and set wheels in motion.

Workmen would be there within the hour to board up the affected frontage. Monday the glass would be cut. Tuesday it would be installed. The gilt work to replace the Carlton and United Brewery logo was to start Wednesday morning. Griffith made it clear to Paddy that the doors to the pub would open on time the following day.

Griffith had decided that he didn't want any further vandalism or violence to devalue the investment so the property would be put up for sale immediately. Paddy objected to this decision, citing that there was six months left on the current lease agreement.

Paddy wasn't one to dwell on the fine print and would rather have worked on a handshake. It was to his bitter disappointment to discover that his so-called lease had more holes in it than a sieve. Griffith was not an unreasonable man but he wasn't Paddy's 'mate' and this was business.

"Look Paddy," said Griffith. "You've done a good job here and I think I've been very fair with you, but this isn't your pub, it's mine and I'm going to do what's best for me. I should let you know that I already have a couple of potential buyers lined up and a sale is imminent." He went on to say that Mansfield was still an option if he wanted it. He thanked Paddy for his hard work but made it abundantly clear that he shouldn't count on being at the Junction very much longer.

For now, Mansfield was not just a card on the table. It was the only card. That one bullet through the window changed many things.

The rain didn't help. It didn't help the men working on the replacement glass. It didn't help anyone inside the hotel feel more optimistic about the present or the future.

Molly, Paddy and Alice sat at a table in the lounge. The only thing to be heard was the rain beating on the corrugated tin verandas. The ever-present cups of tea sat in front of them. Molly took a sip from her cup and put it back on the saucer. Alice patted her hand and said she would make a fresh pot.

When the two women had arrived, all they knew was that there had been an accident and a window was broken. Paddy couldn't see how full disclosure would help anything or anyone at that stage. Later, they were shocked to see the actual damage and Molly was physically shaken when she learned that a bullet had been fired.

Paddy tried to mollify her by withholding the fact that it was Dyson who fired the bullet. That had come out when a police officer had stopped by earlier in the morning to let them know Dyson had been apprehended. Finding out that it was Jackie Dyson and that the shot was obviously fired at Paddy only made it all that much worse.

"You could have been killed," said Molly.

There was no point in denying it. He knew it was all too true. He just nodded his head. "I know."

He reached into his pocket to find the two halfpennies that he had found on the floor of the bar. He fingered the worn shapes on the flat faces of the coins. He took them out and examined them in his hand. Studying even the most insignificant details until the copper coins felt warm to the touch.

These two coins could not have been of less value but Molly knew that for whatever reason they were of grave importance to Paddy. Alice returned with fresh cups of tea. She placed teacups in front of Paddy and Molly and instinctively knew it would be better for her to retreat from that moment. She just picked up her cigarettes and matches and left.

"Just before he took a shot, I felt something under my foot," he said. "I looked down and saw these two little fellas stuck down there. I was going to just leave them but thought no, they may not be worth much but they're worth more than that, you know, just being thrown away."

He paused for a moment. This was more difficult than he expected. Molly could see the struggle in the man's eyes. In the cold light of morning he knew how close he had come to leaving it all behind. The dreams, the ambitions, all of it, just gone. Paddy briefly struggled with the emotion and cleared it with a cough and continued. "So, anyhow I decided to pick them up and that's when he fired the shot. If it wasn't for these," he said, fondly rubbing one coin in each hand, "I'd be dead I guess."

He placed the coins on the centre of the table between himself and Molly. "Guess I'm worth at least a penny, eh?" He reached out with his right hand and with one finger he moved the two coins side by side. "There. That's my life, right there."

Then with one finger he moved one coin over in front of Molly and the other half in front of himself. Molly looked at the coin in front of her. She could feel tears begin to well inside her and then before she could do anything they escaped her eyes and ran down the side of her cheek.

She looked at Paddy. He simply nodded as if to say yes this is the sum total of my life and I want to share it with you.

Ever so slowly Molly's hand reached out. She carefully picked up the coin in front of her and held it tightly in her hand. Paddy did the same with his coin. Finally Molly opened her hand to look at the coin. She traced her finger around the rim of the coin. She looked into Paddy's eyes. He looked remarkably innocent and vulnerable. Molly whispered thank you and Paddy responded with a trace of a smile.

"I suppose we should open the doors and get to work," said Molly.

"Yeah, guess we should," said Paddy.

Molly put the coin into the pocket of her dress and then picked up the teacups and returned them to the sink. Just before she left the kitchen she paused and turned back to Paddy. She pressed her right hand against the coin holding it secure in the pocket of her cotton dress.

"I hope I like Mansfield," she said.

"Me, too," said Paddy.

And so they went to work.

Chapter Sixteen

Mansfield, Victoria, marked a page in history when, back in 1878, three police officers were slain by the legendary bushranger Ned Kelly and his gang, at nearby Stringybark Creek. A monument standing in the centre of town reminds everyone of that memorable encounter.

The town was first named after Mount Battery but, proving to be unpopular, the name was replaced by Mansfield in 1856 at the prompting of a local station manager who apparently had fond memories of Mansfield, near Sherwood Forest, Nottinghamshire. Most days it was hard to imagine the similarities.

About one hundred and twenty miles northeast of Melbourne and thirty miles from Mount Buller, this was what they called the high country. As the locals put it, the weather ranged between 'bloody hot' and 'bloody cold'. January of 1938 was the hot end of the spectrum. Eddies of red dust swirled down the broad main street of Mansfield dancing in and out of the long, black ribbons the morning sun had cast across the street.

The train ride from Melbourne seemed endless to Molly. The steam engine wheezed and snorted through towns no bigger than the solitary train stations until, almost four hours after it left Spencer Street Station in Melbourne, the train pulled into

Mansfield station and the shriek of metal on metal brought them to a stop. There wasn't anyone to meet them. All they had was a key to a door and a sketchy set of directions. Not that one could get too lost in that town at that time.

Few of the twelve hundred residents were to be seen. A youth rode by on a lanky mare. From the edge of town the noisy clatter of a truck could be heard as it drew its way past the Imperial Hotel and along the street, leaving a cloud of dust in its wake. This was not the most encouraging introduction to their future life as a married couple.

The hotel itself did little to brighten the prospects. Paddy and Molly stood in the centre of the bar surveying the tragedy. The former hotel owners had simply deserted the place, leaving it dirty and in dire disrepair. Molly couldn't stand it any longer and walked away. She said she wanted to see the kitchen but what she really wanted to find some relief from the decay.

There was no solace to be found in the kitchen. Dishes were left in the sink; spores of life left encrusted on cups and cutlery. There was to be no concern or consideration for those who would follow. It was as if their time at the Imperial Hotel had not gone well and they purposefully left a trail of chaos to punish someone, anyone, for the disappointment of their own lives. It was utterly wretched.

"How's it out there?" came Paddy's voice from the bar.

"Don't ask." Molly could merely shake her head in disbelief that people could be so thoughtless.

It was all so recent: the wedding in white, the joyous reception, a Christmas where families came together for the first time. Life was light and brilliant. Where did it all go?

Standing there in the oppressive filth and neglect of this horrid hotel, Molly had difficulty holding on to the reasons they were there. It was neither the present nor the future she had envisioned.

Little more was spoken as they walked through the balance of the hotel. Just restoring the place to a state that was merely tolerable would be heroic. Paddy was the first to say it wasn't going to work.

"It's too bloody rough. I can't bring my wife into a mess like this. It's just not the way to start a marriage. It's not right." He spoke from his head not his heart, which was shattered.

"All right, here's what has to happen," said Molly. Paddy started to speak but Molly stopped him. "No, let me finish. This is, as you said, rough. Nobody can live here, not like this. As shocking as it is, I honestly don't know with the resources we have that we'll find anything better. If you think, and this is important, if you think that it could be good from a business sense, then we have to look at what might be not just what is. It'll take a month, minimum, just to clean and paint the place and make it decent. I'll round up Anne and Alice and anyone else I can get to come up here and help. We'll start in one corner and work our way to the other corner."

"I can't ask you to...."

"Paddy, stop, let me finish. Do you know of something better than this?"

He shook his head.

"Then I guess we'll just knuckle down and do what we have to do. Now, I want you to have a look at things like the electrical panel, the general mechanics and the foundation of this place. If it's solid and things that must work do work, we can take care of the rest. If you need to get someone in for things we don't understand, you should do it. It's worth spending a few quid up front rather than get caught later. Agreed?"

"Yes."

"And while you are checking things inside I am going to have a look around the outside of the place, get a feeling for it."

"I don't know what to say," said Paddy.

105

"Good because I really don't want to talk about it. I'll lose my courage if we do. You better get started."

Without another word, Paddy went to work performing a cursory inspection of the plumbing in the bar.

Molly walked to the rear of the hotel, sat on a step and cried for a full thirty minutes.

Chapter Seventeen

What they hoped could be done in one month took two. Fortunately the foundations of the hotel were sound and everything worked more or less the way it should. There were frustrating points of decay. A simple piece of tin flashing was missing from a gully in roof. It would have cost mere pennies to replace but it had been ignored and as a result water had seeped in and rotted a floor.

Both families pitched in to the project. Paddy's brothers helped replacing woodwork and any of the heavy-duty labour that was required. Molly's sisters scrubbed and cleaned and scraped mould off walls as they gasped and laughed and drank sherry to get them through the worst of it.

The first few nights everyone slept on the floors upstairs until Vince, Paddy's brother, arrived with some old but clean mattresses he had unearthed from where they had been stored in a church hall. The few original mattresses that remained in the living quarters were stained beyond salvation and had been jettisoned early in the restoration campaign.

Intermittent convoys ran between Mansfield and Melbourne arriving with care packages and hope. Every day seemed longer than the day before, even though the worst of the turnaround was behind them. The relentless heat exacerbated the fatigue and frustration; it sapped everyone's strength and enthusiasm and curbed how much could be done in a single day.

Bill and Elsie had spent the previous day helping to put the final touches in place. Molly hoped they could stay but it was a long drive back to the city and Bill had to be at work early Monday morning. For Molly, losing them was losing her link to the moderation of the city. Right then, she doubted that she would ever get out of Mansfield and back to Melbourne.

When she left the dairy farm in Yarragon, she thought she'd seen the end of country living. Now, married to a man five years her senior, she was back in the heart of the bush.

An animated conversation on the street outside the bar briefly caught her attention. Looking through the window, Molly watched a creased old man in a wagon talking to a younger bloke in shorts and work boots, Verbal exchanges were followed by bursts of laughter and then they were gone, evaporated into the heat of the day. Once again the street reverberated with silence.

She returned to the task of drying glasses for the day ahead. Very carefully and deliberately, she took the beer glasses, two in each hand, and transferred them from the towel on which they had been drying to a ledge over the bar. It was a ritual that was both clean and orderly, a pleasing contrast to the chaos preceding the pub's official opening. She was startled by a loud thud from somewhere below her.

"Christ Almighty!" was the muffled cry.

"Paddy? Paddy, you all right?"

Paddy entered from the cellar. "I dropped the whole bloody lot on my foot." He deposited a case of beer on the floor. "Those rickety stairs are going to kill a man some day. Gotta speak to Bill, get him to help me replace them." He carted the case over to the bar and started to stack the bottles under the counter. It was not even ten in the morning and already the sweat had drenched the back of his striped dress shirt.

"How you doing?" he said.

"I wonder if it ever rains here?" said Molly.

Paddy crossed to the window and looked out. "Hope we've got enough beer," he said.

"From the looks of this place, if the whole town turned up and brought their dead relatives with them, we'd still have enough beer," said Molly.

She looked at her husband standing there before her. He'd always wanted a pub of his own and now he had it. Mansfield was going to be a challenge. Lots of dairying and sheep grazing stations around and when the shearers were there the town really came to life. The other pub on High Street, the Prince of Wales, had been the centre of town for decades. The Imperial, which had never created a faithful following, had stood empty and long forgotten. There was local interest in the attempt to revive the old place but, despite their roots, Paddy and Molly were perceived to be city folk and would be treated with appropriate suspicion.

"You don't like it here do you?" said Paddy.

"I don't want to own it. This isn't where I want to stay," she replied.

"We've almost broken the back of this thing though," said Paddy.

"No, we haven't. We've just begun. Oh, I'm happy to see the end of all that work. I'm happy to be here with you, but look at it Paddy, no matter how hard we work this pub's no gem. It never will be. At least now it's clean. I think I'm just beginning to understand how tough this is going to be."

"I'm sorry I got you into this."

She crossed to Paddy and neatly re-rolled his sleeves up his arms. "Don't be. I made the choice. You didn't make me come. Besides, this is the beginning, not the end. Right? This is your pub, your first pub and I wouldn't have missed it for the world."

She fingered the thick strands of dark brown hair that had fallen across his temple and neatly set them off his face. She had never seen him quite so happy. How she loved this man. He clasped her firmly and pulled her closer into him. He gently kissed her on the top of her head and held her even closer. He was entranced with this young woman from the dairy farm, so trusting, loving and honest.

"Wouldn't be here without you." He whispered.

"So, let's get to work, Paddy Brennan. Call yourself a publican do you? Well, there are beers to pour and bills to pay."

"You watch, we'll do more business the first day than this place did the last six months."

"It was closed for the last six months."

"Well, then it should be easy." He said, with a laugh.

"It's almost ten."

"Just a few more minutes. I want to remember this." Paddy ran his hand across the smooth surface of the wooden bar.

"Oh I forgot something!" She hurried to the back of the bar and produced a small bunch of flowers. She held them up proudly. "Look what I got!"

"Aw no, love," said Paddy "We can't have flowers in here. It's not that sort of pub."

"We certainly can. They're for the Ladies Lounge. I think they're beautiful. That old woman who sits on the bench out there having a smoke every day, she gave them to me. I think she's crazy and I'm sure she stole them but I don't care, they're just what I needed and what the place needs. I'm going to try to have flowers every day if I can."

Paddy just looked at her. A slight smile creased his cheek. He shook his head and walked to the door and looked back at Molly. He levelled his eyes to hers.

"What?" said Molly.

"You're a bloody wonder you are," he said.

110

"Open the door," she said.

Paddy took a deep breath and rehearsed his opening line. "Welcome to the Imperial Hotel. My name is Paddy Brennan and the drinks are on me."

"Very good," she said, indicating the door. "Now, tell them."

Paddy nodded, turned to the door and swung it wide open and recited "Welcome to the Imperial Hotel. My name is Paddy Brennan and the drinks are on me." A wind had picked up and dust swirled through the open door, uninterrupted by any potential patrons clogging the entrance. Two men on the other side of the street stopped briefly to observe the movement at the door. They exchanged a few words and moved on. There was a shuffle and Paddy felt someone push past him. It was a stump of a man: short, dusty and in a faded blue suit jacket and a sweat-stained hat with half a dozen corks dangling from its brim. He headed straight for the bar and could barely see above the counter.

"G'day Missus," he said to Molly. "How about a nice glass of tawny port?"

Molly looked at the stunted, scrubby man in disbelief and then at Paddy, who was crushed. All she could do was laugh. Just when she felt she had it under control she looked down at the little man and his toothless grin and convulsed yet again.

"It's not that funny, Molly."

"Oh yes it is. It really is."

"Excuse me, Missus," said the man waiting at the bar. "Did you forget about me?"

"Oh, no I didn't," says Molly. "I don't think I ever will."

Molly poured a glass of port and placed it in front of the man. He took the glass and smiled broadly then sipped it as if to see it wasn't poisoned. Satisfied that it was safe he knocked back the drink and returned the empty glass to the counter."

"Thirsty work today," he said.

111

"Why, what do you do?" asked Molly as she refilled the glass.

"As little as I can." He replied with a breathy chuckle.

This time he savoured the port, smelling it and swirling it in his mouth as if he were judging the latest Bordeaux. Molly just watched him as he smacked his lips in satisfaction and then repeated the ritual a dozen more times. Paddy was still standing outside the front door looking left and right hoping to catch sight of any errant customers.

The solitary patron had now returned the empty glass to the counter once more. Molly poured a half glass this time.

"This is on us but the next one you'll have to pay for it. My name is Molly by the way, Molly Brennan. What's yours?"

"They call me Rabbit, Missus."

"So, Rabbit, are you from around here?"

Rabbit nodded as he sipped his port. He made small noises of pleasure as the port worked its way through his weathered body. Every now and then he flashed his broad version of a smile.

"Tell me, Rabbit, where is everyone?"

"Dunno, Missus."

Rabbit had a penchant for diving his hands into his jacket pockets as if he had just remembered something very important. Whatever he was looking for, it was never there and after a brief moment of contemplation he would return to his mission at hand.

"We were rather hoping to see a few more people down here for the opening."

"No, Missus. Not gonna happen. They don't like this pub. The people who were here before, well, don't want to say nothing bad about nobody, but they were miserable bastards, if you catch my drift."

"Hey, watch your language in front of the lady," said Paddy from his imposing position in the doorway.

"Sorry mate, sorry Missus, no insult intended."

"None taken, Rabbit. We're not the people who were here before. Perhaps when everyone gets to know us better..." said Molly.

"Perhaps," said Rabbit, carefully considering his next statement as he emptied his glass slowly. "But I'll tell ya something that's for sure."

Paddy and Molly both stood still in anticipation. As of now, this was the voice of their new universe. He might well be the only local to cast a shadow on the doorway of the newly cleaned and polished Imperial Hotel. Rabbit put his glass down precisely where he had picked it up and smacked his lips again. He looked up at Molly, whom it would appear he had now come to like.

"It's gonna be rough," he said, and with that he turned and headed for the door. "Thanks, Missus," he called out. He stopped at the door and looked up at Paddy. "What do they call you?"

"Paddy Brennan."

"Never heard of ya. Hooroo." He shuffled off down the street very possibly heading for the other, more-favoured, drinking establishment.

Chapter Eighteen

Wispy cirrus clouds tangled together and fingered their way down from Mount Buller and over the town. They were often predictors of warm weather and the locals endorsed the forecast saying that the current break in the weather was short-lived and the heat wasn't behind them yet.

Temperatures in Victoria usually averaged around seventy degrees in April, cooler on the coast, warmer in the centre of the state. Early that April the mercury had risen to ninety-four degrees; an unreasonable condition considering the unmitigated heat that had gripped the land since she and Paddy had arrived in Mansfield.

Bush fires were a perennial plague. There had been a spate of fires throughout the district; mainly grass fires but they skirted the edges of thickly timbered areas and often threatened to escape control. A runaway fire had already razed one small farmhouse just off the road to Merrijig.

One morning, almost a week prior, a wind whipped through the town and ushered in relief. The heat had finally abated and then there was rain. Blessed rain.

The first day of the rain was akin to a lottery win for the town. The population was mildly euphoric. The heat that smothered life had been lifted and people were out on the streets again laughing and chatting. Molly sat on the bench outside the hotel and let the rain shower the dust and frustration away.

There were two and a half days of rain in the week since the heat broke and the temperatures had slipped back to moderate levels so the relief seemed even greater. The idea of a return to unseasonably hot weather was consummately depressing.

While Paddy chatted and joked with the four men in the bar, Molly stood at the door of the hotel and looked up at the clouds moving slowly past.

"G'day Missus." The voice came from behind her. She turned around to see Rabbit tip his dusty hat. "Nice day," he said.

"Yes, it is," said Molly, looking back up at the clouds. "They say it may get hot again."

"Yeah, that's if you believe what people say the sky's telling ya," he said looking up and squinting. "Watchin' things, I think it's gonna be a hot and dry winter, that's the word, But what I says now is it's gonna rain first. Maybe cool off a little more, too."

"Really?" said Molly, delighted with the shabby little man's forecast.

"Yeah, but I may be the only one who thinks so," said Rabbit. "You can't just look at the clouds, you gotta look where they come from, too. You see that, over there, look." He pointed off far to the right. "See them?"

"Yes," said Molly not exactly sure what she should be seeing.

"Them's different clouds. They says rain to me, you wait and see," said Rabbit with quiet confidence. "Not a lot of rain, but some."

The two of them stood there for a moment looking at the clouds as though a message from the gods was imminent.

"Listen, what do you hear?" said Rabbit.

Molly listened intently to the sounds of the bush around her. Nothing leapt out as extraordinary in any way. "Maybe I'm missing something."

"No, you're not doin' it right. What are you listening to?"

"I don't know, Rabbit, everything I suppose."

If you listen to everything, you don't hear nothing. Listen to the birds, just the birds, okay?" said Rabbit.

Everywhere in the distance around her was the clear soprano chirp of the bellbirds. As she listened intently to them, a second flock swept into a tree near the water and sang in counterpoint.

The ubiquitous magpie chortled loud and strong to make its presence clear. Within the chorus, however, there emerged a regular sound, related to the tone of the magpie but more rhythmic. "There that's it," said Rabbit. His voice was urgent but hushed. He didn't want the birds to hear him.

"What is it?" Another volley of notes from these strange birds joined in, filling the air. "It's like a small dog barking."

"It's nothin' like a dog. That's a currawong, that is!"

"Really?"

"He talkin' to us. Telling us things."

"What's he telling us?" she said.

"He's telling us about the weather. What you have to know about the currawong is that they like to live in the higher country and they come down when it gets colder, you see. So, when I hear that many currawongs out there I know things are cooling off so I wouldn't worry about no heat for a bit," Rabbit said with conviction, nodding his head as if to underscore the absolute truth of the currawong.

"Wonderful. And what are the bellbirds telling us?"

"What do you think?" asked Rabbit.

"That there are bright and beautiful things out there if you just take the time to listen." She smiled at Rabbit. "Is that right?"

Rabbit just looked off across the street to an empty paddock where some birds had settled. "If that's what it means to you then that's what it means."

The two of them listened to the birds and the air and the trees until a rattling old Ford van swung around the corner scattering the birds and kicking up a storm of dust.

"I should get back to work," said Molly.

"Good oh," he replied and then pointed off to indicate something of importance happening in the clouds on the distant horizon. He nodded again as if Mother Nature had given him a personal sign. "Remember, you want to know what's going on, you just listen to what the land tells ya, the birds, the winds."

"I think it would be better news than what I hear on the radio," she said. Molly didn't think Rabbit had heard her. She wondered if he listened to the radio and doubted that he had one. She wanted to ask him but she didn't. He was so engrossed, so mesmerised by something out there she didn't want to crimp the moment.

"When I was a little bloke..." His voice trailed off. He turned to look at Molly as if he had just made a decision to share this with her. "When I was a little bloke, I used to go and sit by the creek and listen. Just sit, listen. You'd be surprised what you'd hear sometimes."

"What creek is this, Rabbit?"

"Jack Back Creek."

Molly just shook her head; that meant nothing to her.

"Not many knows it, that's why I like it." He grinned and looked thoughtfully down the road. "Do you want me to tell you where it is?"

The offer was not some trivial comment, it was a direct invitation into his world, and something she knew wasn't offered lightly. To accept would be to sign a personal agreement between the two of them, one that could not be shared lightly with others. "I'd like that, yes."

He quickly perused the street to further guarantee what he was about to say would be private. "You head back down the road past the railway station and there's a dirt track off to the right. You cross the tracks and keep goin'. You see three gum trees, big ones, standin' side by side, like soldiers. Well, you go through the scrub behind them and you gotta be careful 'cause it drops away, sudden like, into a gully."

Molly watched the little man lose himself on his journey. He was there as sure as life, standing on the edge of his gully. He could hear the water, feel the air around him, touch the shapes of the smooth stones that rimmed the waterhole.

"There's nothin' there now," he said, still fixed in his gaze. "Unless you get a big rain. Grounds so dry though the water don't last long." He glanced back toward the mountain to monitor the progress of the clouds he felt had promised him rain. He pointed to them as if to assure her that relief was looking closer. "When I was a little bloke, I used to go there and sit and read."

"What did you read, Rabbit?"

He turned back to her almost a little surprised that the answer wasn't obvious. "I've got a book," he said with a hint of pride.

"Of course," said Molly. "Lovely."

"No, nothin' there now, but when it rains. Sometimes. If it's a good one, the water rushes down from the mountain, the creek swells up. You can get in there and splash around." His voice trailed off into memory. "If it ever rains again, I mean really rains, I might go back. It's been a while. Too long."

"I've missed you, Rabbit, You haven't been around for a few days," said Molly and the two of them stood there and witnessed an eddy of wind swirl some dust high into the air a little farther down the street.

"Well, the truth is I'm a little bit broke right now," said Rabbit with surprise candour.

"How broke are you, Rabbit?" asked Molly.

"It could be worse, Missus. It ain't that I ain't got nothing. I have a little something set aside in case things get really crook one day, you know. I just ain't got nothing in my pocket this week. Things'll pick up."

"Let me fix you something to eat?"

"No, thanks, Missus. I've got some grub. No worries about that."

"A piece of cheese, you'd like that wouldn't you?"

"Thanks, but no, another time, maybe."

"You have to come in anyway, I'm going to pour you a glass of port," said Molly.

Rabbit thought about that for a minute. He took off his hat and rubbed his temple with the rough sleeve of his old wool jacket. "Thank you Missus but it just don't feel right," he said. "Not comfortable fronting up to the bar without a penny in me pocket."

"Fair enough," said Molly. "But you gave me something wonderful today and I intend to return the favour," said Molly. "You just wait right there."

Molly returned from the bar with a glass of port. "You were our first customer. That means you're very important to me," she said. "So, please do me a favour and enjoy this."

"If it makes you feel better, I'll do you a favour and drink it," he said, taking the glass. "Cheers."

"Cheers," said Molly.

Rabbit wasn't casual about drinking the port; he gave it his full attention, savouring each mouthful. He handed the empty glass back to Molly. "Thanks," he said simply. "Going rabbiting. If I'm in luck, might stop by with a fresh rabbit for you later." He tipped his hat and was on his way again.

120

"Excuse me, are you Mrs Brennan?" Molly's attention turned from Rabbit to a handsome young man in his twenties with dark wavy hair and intensely blue eyes. His clothes were clean but dusty and he held his wide-brimmed hat in his hand.

"Yes, I am."

"Pleased to meet you. My name's Barry. My family has a sheep station down toward Jameson."

They shook hands politely. "What can I do for you, Barry?" She couldn't help but think how more appropriate he would look on a movie screen than standing on the edge of High Street, Mansfield.

"I was wondering if you needed any help in the hotel. I have worked part time up the street in the bar there so I have some experience. "

"That's good to know but I'm sorry we can't afford to hire anyone just now."

He was obviously a little disappointed but smiled broadly. "Well, worth a shot. Perhaps you'll keep me in mind if something comes up?"

"Of course. Does Mr Scott have any work for you right now? They have most of the business in town."

Barry seemed to struggle to find the right response. "Well, to be honest, don't think he has a place for me right now." He smiled and gave Molly a respectful nod. He shuffled, showing some level of discomfort. "Well, problem is, I don't think he's too happy with me seeing his daughter, Maggie."

"Oh."

"Do you know Maggie?" Molly shook her head. "She's lovely." The simplicity and honesty of his statement made Molly smile. "I should be going. Keep me in mind," he said.

"I will. What's your last name?"

"Hutton."

"How do we get in touch with you, Barry Hutton?"

"I think in this town, Mrs Brennan, you can tell almost anyone you'd like to get in touch with me and I'll know it before the end of the day. Bye."

Molly watched him cross the street to where his horse was tethered. He had a pronounced limp; not the sort that would prompt you to ask if he'd just hurt himself, it was too much an ingrained part of him.

He deftly mounted the dappled horse, looked back at Molly and offered a wave as he rode slowly up the street.

Three of the remaining four customers walked out of the hotel. They were engrossed in conversation and barely noticed Molly as they passed. She walked back into the bar. Paddy was there, leaning against the bar and looking grim. Molly walked behind the bar and poured herself a glass of water.

"Who was that young bloke?"

"He was looking for work."

"He picked the wrong place here."

"I told him we'd keep him in mind."

"Did Rabbit pay you for the drink?" asked Paddy.

"No," said Molly. "It was my shout. We're not selling it so we may as well give it away." Molly thought about that for a minute. "I'm sorry," she said. "I didn't mean anything bad there."

"It's okay," said Paddy. "There's some truth to it."

Molly walked back to the door and looked up at the sky, hoping the clouds had shaped themselves into a less foreboding identity.

"What are we going to do?" she asked, as much to herself as to Paddy.

Paddy shook his head. "I don't know. We've hardly had a day when we've made enough to cover our costs. We can't put a bloody penny toward paying off the hotel and it looks like we'll lose the little money we came in with." Paddy moved to the far end of the bar and stacked crates. "I should go fix the floor in the storeroom so we can get all this out of here. I can't much see the point though." He propped himself against the bar and looked vacantly toward the street. "What the hell was I thinking?

Molly couldn't think what to say. There had always been risk attached. She knew that when she said 'yes' to the whole idea so she couldn't pretend to be shocked that Paddy felt defeated. On more than once occasion, she had found herself wishing they had never started on that road but, for her anyway, small moments like the one she just shared with Rabbit suggested that, just maybe, there was something there worth the fight.

"I'm sorry I ever got you into this," said Paddy.

"We can get through it," said Molly.

"I wish I could believe that," said Paddy.

She crossed the bar and stood in front of her husband. She reached up and straightened his suspenders and smoothed the wrinkles in his cotton shirt. "I believe in you, Paddy Brennan, I do." She slipped an arm around his waist. "I believe you can make a go of this."

"What the hell do you want me to do, Molly? I've tried everything I can bloody think of." There was more than a hint of anger mixed in with the frustration. She held him firmly. "You've done it before, you can do it again." Paddy wanted to interject, to tell her she was wrong but Molly wouldn't have any of it. "Listen to me! Remember the Junction Hotel? They didn't come to you so you went to them. You didn't sit around and feel sorry for yourself," said Molly.

"I'm not just feeling sorry for myself!" he protested.

"Of course you are. And that's allowed, you've earned the right, you've worked so hard. We've both worked hard getting this place together and we've done a pretty good job, but the answer isn't in here, it's out there. Come here."

Molly took his hand and led Paddy from behind the bar. He hesitated at first but soon followed her lead toward the door.

"Just take a look," she said pointing to the street outside. "You see those people over there, and that bloke in the truck going by? They're the answer. You have to get out there and round up them up one way or another. You did it before, you can do it again." Molly put her arms around his neck pulled him toward her and kissed him lightly on the lips. "Fair go," said Paddy lightly, "not in the bar."

"If we give this our best shot and it doesn't work, we'll survive, but we didn't come here to fail. I'll tell you one thing, Paddy Brennan, if you can't make it happen, nobody can. I believe that with all my heart. If I didn't, I wouldn't have married you."

She lay against his chest. He folded his arms around her and rocked her gently.

"When you two have finished, I'd like another beer," said the old codger at the end of the bar. There wasn't room for romance here, not for him when his glass was empty. He muttered to himself that he hadn't come here to see that sort of thing and can't a man get a quiet drink of beer when he needs one. He continued to mumble until Molly had filled his glass and placed it in front of him. One sip and his need to complain about the world had been quenched.

"I'm not exactly sure what time I'll be home," said Paddy as he made his way to the door. "You can handle things?"

"Oh, I think so," said Molly looking at the solitary patron.

Paddy just nodded and then walked out the door of the hotel. Standing there with his hands on his hips looking in both directions, he reminded Molly of a military general strategizing before heading into battle. Paddy turned back and looked into the bar. She waved to him and he was gone.

Chapter Nineteen

Paddy decided to cross the street and work his way to the other end of town. First stop was the grocery shop, a dusty edifice with a broad canvas awning that had seen better days. The stripes had bleached and the canvas had decayed sufficiently that on those odd days when it did rain, the water found little resistance.

"What can I do for you?" said the man behind the counter. He was polite without being friendly.

"G'day," said Paddy. "I'm Paddy Brennan, I run the Imperial Hotel across the street."

"Right, yeah, I've heard about you," said the man smoothing his unbleached cotton apron with his broad hands.

"Hope it was all good," Paddy said with a laugh. "Thought it was time I introduced myself." Paddy offered his hand.

"Fair enough," said the man as he shook hands. "I'm Archie, Archie Doyle. Mavis and me run the shop here. Been doing it for about twenty years now."

"Good for you," said Paddy. "My wife Molly is holding the fort over at the pub, right now."

"Yeah, we've met her a few times, Mavis and me. She's been in for groceries. Seems like a real nice lady," Archie said as he lifted boxes of soup from the floor and started stacking shelves.

125

"I think she is," said Paddy. "Haven't seen you in the pub yet."

"No," said Archie. "Well, we keep pretty busy, when we do get a break we go to the Prince of Wales up the street."

"Fair enough. Maybe you might give us a try some day," said Paddy.

"Maybe. I'll mention it to Mavis, see what she thinks."

Two women armed with shopping baskets came through the door and up to the counter.

"Can I get you anything?" asked Archie.

Paddy just shook his head feeling that Archie was missing the point of the meeting. "No, thanks, not right now," he said.

"Hello, ladies, what can I do for you?" Archie's interest had turned to the paying customers. Paddy began to ease toward the door. "Archie, ladies, have a good day." He raised his hand in farewell and addressing the two women, he said, "Paddy Brennan, Imperial Hotel across the street. First drinks are always on me."

The women said hello and smiled and looked at him with interest. They knew who he was before he ever said his name. Pleasantries were exchanged and in no time, Paddy was back on the street.

Next was the ice cream shop. Brenda Boyle, a large pigeon-breasted woman in a faded print dress, sat on a stool behind the counter. In front of her was an array of sweets; to the left was the ice cream in a refrigerated unit. There were four choices, vanilla, chocolate, strawberry and Neapolitan.

"Hello," said Paddy. "I'm Paddy Brennan from across the street."

"You want an ice cream?" said the woman looking quite attached to the stool.

"No, not really," said Paddy.

"You don't want an ice cream?" said the woman slightly incredulous that someone would walk into her ice cream store and not want ice cream.

"No, I just popped in to say hello," said Paddy.

"I know who you are. Everyone knows who you are," she said. "You sure you don't want an ice cream?"

"No, I just thought it would a good time to stop by, introduce myself, invite you over for a drink," said Paddy.

"I don't drink," she said. "And certainly not with the likes of you?"

"What's that supposed to mean?" Paddy was bewildered.

"You think we don't know," she said rolling her body to a superior position on the stool. "We know what you did."

"What?" said Paddy.

"Oh yes, play it like you don't know. Oh please! What you did. Terrible. What you did with that puppy?"

"What puppy?" said Paddy.

"Poor little thing, starving he was, good thing I found him" she said.

"I don't know what you're talking about," said Paddy.

"All he wanted was a scrap of food and you shut him out. Bastard!" she said.

"Now just a minute," said Paddy.

"Slammed the garage door on him. I heard him yelp clear over here, poor little bugger," she said.

"Wait a minute, wait. I'm not from the garage!" he said.

There was a pause while she considered that. "You're not? You sure?"

"I am bloody sure, I run the pub across the street," he said. "I've never even had a pup."

"Well, you could have done something about it," she said.

"I didn't know anything about it! The garage isn't even close to the pub; it's way down there." His voice was rising in frustration. "I'm Paddy, I'm from the Imperial Hotel across the street."

"Then what are you doing here?"

"I came to say, hello."

"So you don't want an ice cream then?" she said, rewinding the conversation.

"No!" said Paddy. "But if you ever jump the fence and decide to take a drink, you'll be very welcome at my pub."

"Don't hold your breath," she said, as she rolled herself into a fresh position. You sure you're not from the garage?"

That was when Paddy left the ice cream shop. He thought, If they're all going to be like this, I don't know what I'll do. Nobody will want to come to the pub if word gets around town that I abused a puppy.

Hans the blacksmith was a large German man with arms like anvils and a dazzling white smile. He was happy to meet Paddy, knew nothing about the pup atrocities and would be happy to come by for a beer, one day. No commitment, mind you, but a sincere smile amid the clang of metal and showers of sparks. This was more what Paddy had hoped for. Now that he was on a roll he thought he'd move on to the town's undertaker.

'Michael Talbot and Sons, Funeral Directors' read the sign. Paddy entered through the door. A bell on the door chimed. This was another world, one in stark contrast to the dusty and slightly shabby tenor of the town. The walls were covered in deep red, flocked, wallpaper, which looked almost decadent. The deep skirting boards were stained mahogany, as was the rest of the woodwork in the room. The lighting was incandescent bulbs in bell-shaped glass shades. It was very quiet. A door opened at the rear of the room and a man stepped into the light. He was in his mid forties, wearing a white shirt and dark-coloured pants with suspenders.

"Hello," he said cheerfully. "How can I help you?" There was an edge to the voice that said you poor thing I know what you have been though and I am here to lighten the load that hangs so heavy on your heart.

"My name's Paddy Brennan," said Paddy as he offered his hand. "I've got the Imperial Pub across the street and just thought I'd stop by and introduce myself."

"Pleased to meet you, Paddy. Michael Talbot," said the man shaking hands with energy. "Nobody's dead then?" he said with a smile.

"Not that I know of," said Paddy. He considered adding 'unless you mean the pup' but thought better of it.

"I don't get many social calls here, Paddy. People don't seem to want to drop by to see me," said Talbot. "I tell them they should be glad to see me. The day when they can't see me, that's the day they should be concerned." He laughed. "Would you like a beer?"

"Well, I'm here to invite you to have a beer in my pub," said Paddy.

"I'd love to," said Michael "but now's not a good time. You heard about old Jake, I suppose."

"Yeah," said Paddy, "terrible thing." He didn't have a clue.

"But when you consider his age," said Michael.

"Oh yeah, for sure, when you consider his age," said Paddy.

"Come on then," said Michael, "I just cracked a bottle back there."

Paddy and Michael drank their beers and a chatted while Old Jake just lay there, oblivious to the good times.

Paddy had stayed longer than he planned with his affable undertaker and the day was sliding away. As he left the funeral parlour he could hear shouts coming from the football ground over by St. John's Catholic Church. The sounds of the game were irresistible. He stopped at the edge of the field watching about twenty or so blokes loosely formed into teams, and informally kicking the ball around. Many years ago, in his early twenties, Paddy was touted as being an up-and-coming full forward for Port Melbourne. He went into training full tilt and played five games before he flew for an heroic mark only to come crashing down on his right knee. He swore he was all right. He wasn't. A severely torn meniscus took him out of the action. He faked good health and was back training with a vengeance six weeks later. Before he had a chance to put on a game jersey, he crashed on the other knee and that lay to rest his football ambitions.

As he watched, the ball bounced off the side of the field and rolled to his feet. The men on the field stopped to watch this stranger who had just picked up the football. Paddy looked around at the scrappy players in their shorts, dirty socks and torn sweaters. He could have thrown it back or even handballed it to show he had some prowess instead he kicked it. He kicked it long and high and hard and it felt good.

"Bloody good kick, mate," was the consensus. "You wanna play?"

Paddy was hardly dressed for the occasion but that didn't stop him. As restrained as he was, the players could tell that he knew the game. When they took a break Paddy introduced himself.

"We could use you on the team," said Blue, a tall man with a shock of red hair.

"Thanks, but I'm a bit long in the tooth," said Paddy.

"I dunno 'bout that, we've got more than a couple of broken-down old buggers on the team now," said Norm Clancy, the local butcher and coach of the football team.

"No, it's my knees, mate." Paddy talked about his days training with Port Melbourne and regaled them with football anecdotes The men had immediately warmed to him and when he invited them all over for a free beer after the next game he was further entrenched as a legitimate 'good bloke'.

He hadn't scored a goal with the people who sell groceries and was definitely not a winner with the crazy ice cream lady, but he had won over the man who buries people under the ground and the people who play footy on top of it.

It had been a good afternoon.

Chapter Twenty

When six o'clock rolled around there was no need for Molly to urge people to finish their drinks. The three customers who had defined the afternoon had long gone their own ways.

For almost an hour before closing Molly had sat on the bench out front of the hotel listening to the afternoon songs of the birds. Bellbirds, magpies, currawongs and rainbow lorikeets all had their moments, while and the occasional kookaburra mocked the content of the day.

There was simplicity to Molly's time on the bench. She could be in the moment and not worry about business, or the lack of it. On the dairy farm in Yarragon there was a tall hill to the west that marked the end of the property. A dilapidated barbed wire fence was enough to discourage the odd cow that strayed in that direction but hardly enough to deter anyone interested in crossing to the other side.

She was never sure to whom the property belonged. It bordered on three other farms, but never seemed to be used for grazing. What she did know was that once she stepped beneath the wire snared with barbs, the world behind slipped away and the soft wind and sounds of native birds enveloped her. A ten-minute walk brought her to a meandering creek that, in spring, was blessed with water, and thick with reeds. An old gum tree that had long ago given up hope and lay beside the creek bed, hid her from the world behind her while she pondered what might be.

Sitting on the bench on the edge of the strangely silent street in Mansfield reminded her of those days by the creek that now seemed so long ago.

"Do you know what time it is?" said a voice from behind her.

The voice startled Molly and she turned to see a man in a three-piece navy-pinstriped suit standing there. This very unlikely image of this formally-dressed and grim-faced man stunned her a little and she didn't respond immediately.

The man walked to the door of the hotel and scanned the empty public bar. "I said do you know what time it is?"

"I don't know exactly," said Molly. "It must be getting close to six."

The man looked at his watch ominously and said, "No, it's fifteen minutes after six."

"Really?"

"Really. Did you know you could receive a summons for violating the State of Victoria Liquor Licensing Laws by staying open past the legal closing hour?"

"Who are you?" asked Molly.

"My name is Jenkins. I'm the Liquor Licensing Officer for this region and right now you're in violation."

Nobody liked the liquor-licensing police and this specimen was a prime example of why. He was brusque and officious and puffed up with self-importance. Country pubs had their own codes of behaviour. The responsible publicans would close long enough to empty the bars and send the men to the respective homes for dinner. Other than that, you could get a frosty glass of beer most any time. Things were a little different in the city where laws were more stringently enforced. This man's attitude seemed gravely at odds with traditional country culture.

Molly stood up and took a deep breath. "Jenkins, you say?" She walked to the door of the hotel.

"That's right, James Jenkins, Licensing Police."

"Yes, yes, I got that, thank you," said Molly. "Well, Mr Jenkins, a pleasure to meet you, my name is Molly Brennan and my husband, Paddy, and I operate the hotel."

"Yes, I know that," said the man. "I've heard all about you."

"You have?" Molly thought that was the strangest remark. She couldn't imagine who would have been talking to this man about her or why.

"I think it would be better if I spoke with your husband," said Jenkins.

"He's not here at the moment," said Molly. "Perhaps if you came back when the hotel was open. I'm afraid that for now, you will have to deal with me, Mr Jenkins."

"This is a serious matter. When will he be back?" asked Jenkins.

"I can't say," said Molly. " As for the seriousness of the situation I think you may be mistaken. As you can see there are no customers in the bar; all the glasses have been washed and stored away; everything has been put to bed for the day. The lights have even been turned off. Not something you would do to attract business, don't you agree? The door is open only because I've been sweeping the floor."

Everything she said was true, up to a point. Things had been so depressingly quiet that Molly had used her time to thoroughly clean the bar. The chairs in the Ladies Lounge were upside down and resting on tables and the few stools in the Public Bar had been stashed in a corner. She had turned off the lights to save on the electricity bill.

Jenkins didn't speak at first. He walked back to the hotel and into the bar and looked around. There could be no doubt the hotel looked decidedly closed.

"The door should be locked, Mrs Brennan," said Jenkins. "I'll let it go this time but I'll be keeping and eye on you. We haven't had any problems in this town and we don't need them now. Like I said, I'll be watching you. Be sure to tell your husband I was here."

Molly was now angry with this nasty man. "I have to ask you to leave now Mr Jenkins. I need to sweep all the dirt out of here and close the door."

Jenkins took a final look around the bar and at Molly and left. Nothing more was said. Molly vigorously swept the wooden floor with her millet broom until all traces of dust and Jenkins were well out the door.

Chapter Twenty-One

Paddy was so happy with his foray into the town that Molly didn't tell him about Jenkins until the following morning. Paddy had some passing knowledge of licensing police from the Eastern Hills Hotel; he'd heard stories but had never witnessed their narrow justice first hand.

Jenkins insistence that he was going to keep an eye on them certainly indicated some premeditation. Why he would choose to target them in such a manner was a mystery to both of them.

Rob Scott was the owner of the Prince of Wales, Mansfield's established watering hole. He made one visit to see Paddy and Molly shortly after they first arrived. He was convivial and expansive in his greeting, but Molly always felt it was a reconnaissance trip rather than the community welcome wagon. Paddy was more accommodating and thought it reasonable that Scott should want to know more about them; they were, after all, intruding on his current monopoly.

Paddy decided that if anyone in town would know this Jenkins, his neighbouring publican would be the one; a visit to the Prince of Wales would have to be scheduled.

That morning had been a copy of the previous day with a few itinerant drinkers drifting by for a glass or two. Tom, a grey-bearded older man had become a regular. He could nurse a beer for an hour or more. He may have been dusty and dishevelled but had the distinction of clean boots. Tom said little but when he did it was at the least sincere.

Rabbit's fortunes apparently returned to favour as he stopped by for a glass of port before heading out to do whatever would put coin in his pocket on that day.

Rabbit nodded at Molly and then Tom.

"G'day, Tom."

"G'day Rabbit."

"How's it going, mate?"

"Pretty good, mate. No complaints," said Tom.

"Who'd listen?" said Rabbit.

"You got that right," said Tom as he raised the warm remnants of his beer in salute. They both considered the truth of that for a moment. "You think it might rain?" said Tom

"That's a good one," Rabbit said with a laugh.

"But you never know," said Tom.

"That's the truth," said Rabbit. You never really do know."

Another observations that warranted a respectful pause. "How's the wife, Tom?" said Rabbit.

"She's dead, Rabbit."

"When did that happen, Tom?"

"Almost five years ago now."

"Five years? Time slips away, don't it."

"Yeah, sure does, Rabbit." Tom nodded his agreement. "Thanks for asking though," said Tom.

"Good on ya, mate," said Rabbit.

Rabbit crossed to Molly at the other end of the bar, leaned across to her and whispered. "He's a good bloke, Tom. Misses his wife, he does. I think it's just polite to ask, you know. Something you may want to remember."

She placed the glass of port in front of him. "Thanks Rabbit, I'll make a point of asking from time to time."

"That'd be nice," said Rabbit.

Knowing who was doing what to whom was a characteristic of life in a small country town. This was no exception. Perhaps it was a by-product of his nomadic way, but Rabbit seemed to have a better knowledge than most of what made Mansfield tick.

"Let me top that up for you, Rabbit," said Molly as she primed his glass with port.

"Your good health, Missus," he said, as he raised his glass in thanks.

"So, tell me, Rabbit," she said, "What do you know about a man called Jenkins?"

"Jenkins? Which Jenkins did you have in mind?" said Rabbit.

"He's with the licensing police. He's been up here in Mansfield the last few days. I can't believe you've missed him," said Molly.

Rabbit thought about that for a while. He rubbed his stubbly chin, smacked his lips and offered his toothless grin two or three time before he decided to respond. "Think I know who you might mean. You want to buy a chook, Missus," said Rabbit.

"Excuse me?" said Molly.

"You want to buy a chook. I'm talking a big plump chook for two bob."

"Two shillings? For a chook?"

"Lovely and fresh. All plump and juicy, enough meat on her for three or four meals for sure." Rabbit's sale pitch was smooth; he might well have been selling a low mileage car. Molly thought about it for a moment.

"Where did you get the chook, Rabbit?"

139

"That don't matter to you, Missus, trust me. You see, I have this chook to sell, or I will have this afternoon," said Rabbit. "If I don't have to walk all around town trying to sell it, I'll have more time to hunt down this Jenkins bloke you want to know about and that's all I'm thinkin'. So do you want the chook?"

"Is this a live chook?" asked Molly.

"Do you want it live?" asked Rabbit.

"No, I most certainly do not, what would I do with a live chook? Is it plucked and cleaned?" she asked.

"Could be," said Rabbit with a wink.

Molly had decided it would be better not to ask too many more questions about the hen in question. Rabbit leaned over the bar and beckoned Molly to do the same. This was obviously a critical issue that was better not shared with the three other men in the bar. "Now you can't tell me Paddy wouldn't appreciate a lovely dinner when he gets back from walking the town, eh? I know I would."

"I take it you'd look into this Jenkins bloke for me?" she said sustaining the tension.

"Well, if I don't have this chook weighin' on me mind," said Rabbit.

Molly offered her hand. Rabbit took it, and in one firm shake, a wink, and a toothless grin, the deal was done.

While the poultry negotiations were taking place Paddy was courting the women who had gathered to play cards at the St. John's church hall.

Ethel Patterson, a stout woman in a felt hat, was the Treasurer of the Catholic Women's Guild, and was innately suspicious of anyone who was born more than fifty miles from the centre of Mansfield. She didn't trust Paddy. She didn't like him; partly because she didn't know him, partly because he wasn't from around here, but principally because he was a man.

Some fourteen years ago, Bob Patterson, another man and coincidentally her husband, went to Jameson to sheer a few sheep. He hadn't been seen since. Some said he found sheep more romantic. Some said he'd moved to the far side of the Snowy Mountains and remarried. Some said he was afraid to come back because of the many times Ethel had promised to cut his balls off.

"As God is my witness, I have never met a publican I could trust," said Ethel. She liked to preface most comments with 'as God is her witness'.

"Well, Mrs Patterson," said Paddy, "you've never met me before."

"You're just after our money," said Mrs Patterson.

"Not a bit of it, I'm after your company," said Paddy with all the charm he could muster.

She harrumphed and proceeded to shuffle the cards. The other ladies of the group were more receptive and welcomed the attention of a handsome man. A tall, gaunt woman with dry skin and dazzling blue eyes insisted Paddy sample her curried egg sandwiches. Plates of tiny sandwiches and nibbles appeared from all directions.

Paddy regaled them with stories of his life, many of which were true. He flattered them on their smart frocks and informed them of his surprise to find so many attractive women in a town this size. They laughed and fluttered and insisted he play a hand of bridge, a game at which Paddy had no skill. Subtlety, strategy and finesse were not among Paddy's stronger suits. His honest good nature and forthright approach married to his love of a good time were attributes that had endeared him most to others.

When pressured by the ladies to play, Paddy elected to divert attention to something with which he felt infinitely more comfortable. "No, don't have the time to play cards with you girls right now, but if you like, I'll recite a poem," said Paddy. The lack of logic in the leap from cards to poetry didn't seem to faze anyone in the room. There were comments of how lovely, and how they don't hear a good poem often enough. They placed their cards on the table and sat back with eager anticipation.

Paddy elected to perform his favourite party piece, George Essex Evans' bush poem Murphy's Brindle Cow. Mr Evans had titled it Murphy's Racing Cow, which had evolved through popular use to Murphy's Racing Brindle Cow. Paddy was in his element. He took the centre of the floor, hooked him thumbs into his suspenders and started the performance.

"Too much about Kanaka Bills, too much about the Chow. A headline for Matilda, Dan Murphy's brindle cow!"

The very idea of a poem about a cow was enough to captivate the women. Even Edith Patterson showed a modicum of interest. She had always liked cows.

"She'd grown up with the family as quiet as a mouse,
'Twas only with a spud bar you could keep her out of the house.

A fence could never stop her: if you put the top rail higher, she'd lie down sideways on the ground and kick through the bottom wire."

By now the ladies of St. John's were putty in his hands. Paddy had a devoted audience and he loved every moment of it. Line after line drew giggles and cackles and a smattering of applause, as Paddy worked his way to a big finish.

"She might pigroot off a dozen, but she couldn't sling 'em all.

In the early summer mornings, with the sweat upon his brow,
You could see the form of Murphy doing time upon his cow

She was on the track at daybreak, she was tried against the watch,

142

And she did a wondrous gallop with a clinker called Hopscotch,

And they proved her o'er the hurdles, and they knew that she could race,

So they made hot as ginger for the Fleatown Steeplechase."

He took a bow and the women burst into another round of applause. Ethel Patterson looked at him sternly with more than a hint of disapproval.

"You don't like the poem, Ethel?" Paddy asked her.

"I love the poem, but you didn't do it right, you skipped bits. And that's not the end, there's the whole race left. That's not nearly the end," she said.

"Ladies you have a fine patron of the arts here. Ethel knows her stuff. There's a lot more to the poem and if you'd like to hear it, I'll be glad to recite it when you visit us at our hotel."

"See," said Ethel, "he's only after our business."

The other women didn't agree with Ethel. They were uniformly unwilling to dismiss the only man who had come to visit them in the last two years who wasn't a priest.

"I think you're being hasty, Ethel," said one of the women. There was an echo of agreement.

"Ladies, ladies," said Paddy. "Of course I want your patronage. That's why I'm in business, but most of all I want you to have a good time. That's why, when you do come to the Imperial Hotel, the first drink is on me."

Paddy had made his mark. It was time to make an exit. He shook every hand at every table and smiled until his cheeks ached.

"Just one thing, Paddy Brennan," said Ethel.

"What's that?" asked Paddy.

"You don't fool anyone here. We're on to you. You don't know the whole poem and that the truth about that."

Betty Wright, a small skinny woman in the straw hat who had sat silently next to Ethel Patterson since Paddy first arrived stood up and spoke. "Oh, shut up, Ethel. I am so tired of your attitude. Nothing's right. Nothing's good. We like Mr Brennan. If we want to go there for a drink, we will. If you don't want to come that's fine, but we won't have you spoil it with your nasty disposition. "

The other women all applauded. Then, quite abruptly, the room fell quiet as everyone awaited Ethel's response. She sat there silent and stony-faced as she surveyed the women around here. None of the women were giving ground. If there was to be any conciliation, it would have to start with her.

"If I come, and I'm not saying I will, you'll do the whole thing. You can't skip bits. You've got to do the whole story, the whole Murphy's Racing Cow right through the Fleatown Cup."

"Fair enough," said Paddy.

"If you really know it that is," said Ethel.

"Don't start, Ethel!" said Betty.

Ethel sat down, picked up the cards and shuffled robustly. "Are we playing cards or not?" she asked.

"We're playing cards and it's not your deal, so hand them over," said Betty, who looked at Paddy and winked. "It was lovely of you to come and see us, Mr Brennan, now don't be a stranger."

A flurry of conversation quickly filled the room as the women settled back into their card games. Paddy left the church hall buoyed by his conquest of The St. John's Catholic Women's Guild, and wondering where next to try his luck.

If there was a hand to be shook on the main street, he shook it. Any woman with a baby was assured that she had to cutest, brightest baby north of Melbourne.

When Paddy made it to the sawmill, he was pleased to see Blue, Jocko and four of the other blokes from the football team. In turn they greeted him with a wave or a smile or both but this was not a time to chat. The foreman spotted Paddy and approached.

"What do you want?" he said.

144

"Just came by to see the boys," said Paddy.

"Well, you picked a bloody awful time to do it, mate. Nobody's stopping in the middle of shift."

"No problem," said Paddy, offering a wave and a drinking gesture to Blue, who returned the favour.

"I'm being nice now but bugger off! All this waving bullshit, someone's going to lose a finger or an arm."

"Right, sorry. If you feel like a beer...." The foreman glared at him. It was time to leave. No more waves, but a simple nod of respect, and he left the shrieking sawmill behind him.

There was a string of farmhouses down the road; Paddy took the lights appearing in windows to be his invitation to stop by for a visit on his way home.

Molly was cleaning up the kitchen in readiness for dinner when Paddy opened the door. It had long fallen dark and she was beginning to be concerned. "Paddy?" There was no reply. "Paddy, is that you, dear?" There in the lounge she found him slumped in a chair with his feet up on a small ottoman.

"I'm absolutely buggered," he sighed, closing his eyes. She knew what he needed and poured him a cold beer.

"How did it go?" asked Molly.

"Remind me when the next election comes around to give each of the politicians a free drink or two. They'll have earned it. I've kissed babies and old women with whiskers, I've joked, laughed, taken the hand of every old fart who ever drew breath. Oh, thanks love," he said as he took the drink.

"You just sit there. I have a couple of things to finish up in the kitchen. I'll fix a lovely supper, that'll make you feel better."

"I don't think I could eat a thing, love, if you don't mind."

"No, of course not."

"I've eaten little bits of this and that all day. Think I'm gonna just turn in."

"You go ahead and I'll bring you up a cup of tea."

"I don't think I can get out of the bloody chair," he laughed and held up his arm. Molly took his hand and helped him overcome gravity. They both laughed. He put his arms around her.

"I tell you, love, I was nice to everyone I met. And by and large, they were nice to me, but there are a few of them out there that, if they don't come to the pub, that'd be all right, too. Can't remember when it felt so good to come home."

They stood there for a minute, quietly appreciating the unspoken intimacy. "I'm not going to carry you upstairs, you know," said Molly.

"Bugger. A man can't be hanged for hoping."

She slapped him on the behind as if she was sending a small child on his way and returned to the kitchen. On the counter sat Rabbit's chook, now roasted to perfection. Keeping warm on the edge of the stove was a pot of potatoes waiting to be mashed; a small bowl of green peas sat to the side. She knew where he had been and why he had to be there. It was important to both of them. That did little to ease the disappointment. She picked up the potatoes and poured them into the sink; a dismissal of the dinner that almost was. Then she thought better of the gesture and scooped up the potatoes into a china bowl. Molly had been keeping a lean kitchen, no deeply stocked larders when money was this tight. She put the kettle on and watched it boil.

When she entered the bedroom with hot tea in hand it was already too late, Paddy was fast asleep. She pulled the blanket around him, covered him with a quilt and then kissed him gently on the forehead before she turned off the light.

Molly and the neglected chook kept company in the kitchen until it was time for bed.

Chapter Twenty-Two

A swirl of grey smoke rose from the chimney atop the Imperial Hotel. The town was waking slowly. What had initially promised to be bright and cloud free had quickly turned grey and wet. Puddles of red mud formed in the ruts in the road and the early morning traffic seemed to have retreated to take cover. Darker, sodden clouds loomed ever closer.

Molly stood under the verandah out front of the hotel, looking across the street to three children who were making their way to school.

"Come on!" shouted the older girl. "We're gonna be late." They were already over thirty minutes late. Her sister turned to the small boy who was slowly bringing up the rear; he was vastly more interested in stomping on water than hurrying to school. "Mom's gonna kill you," she said as encouragement. The small boy sprinted toward her and jumped into a puddle splashing his sister. She screamed and the three of them ran around the corner, and out of sight.

"What's happening out here?" said Paddy.

"Not much," said Molly. Paddy put his arms around her waist. "Thanks for lighting the fire, smells wonderful," she said.

"Just hope we don't burn the place down, God knows when the chimney was last cleaned."

147

"Yes, that would be terrible if the bar was full of customers," Molly laughed. The rain had picked up its intensity. "Now, I'm not complaining about getting the rain but it won't be good for business."

"I wouldn't be so sure of that," said Paddy

Molly looked at Paddy. He appeared to be very calm and assured. There was even a slight smile creasing his cheeks. "Why do you say that?" she asked.

"Think about it. All those blokes working at the mill or on the road down there; I wouldn't want to be outside on a day like this, would you?" You couldn't work on fences or anything much outside on the farm either, I suppose." Paddy smelt the air. "Love the way the smoke mixes with the rain. I tell you if I caught a whiff of that when I was out there getting drenched, the very thought of warm fire and cold beer might just get the better of me. No, I think it might be a fine day. Think I'll throw another log on."

Molly looked both ways down the empty street as the rain became even heavier. It was hard to imagine anyone wanting to be outside on a day like this. By mid morning they started to arrive: rain-soaked men who'd called it quits. Soon, a jovial buzz filled in the bar as they warmed themselves by the fire and comforted themselves with a beer or two.

If you asked any of the men there when is the best time for a beer, you would get a variety of replies. 'When your thirsty?' would rank near the top. "Anytime,' would be a popular response. On that day, at the Imperial Pub in Mansfield, the other most popular responses would range between 'when it rains' and 'when there's a lovely fire'.

So they came, three or four at a time, with odd stragglers bringing up the rear. Without exception they made their way to the bar via the fireplace. There was much rubbing of hands and appreciation of the bloody good fire as the crowd continued to swell. Both Paddy and Molly were beginning to wonder how many more men could there be out there; they felt the bar was working close to the limit already and it was barely noon.

"Hello, Bub," said the familiar raspy voice. Molly looked up from the sink of glasses to see her sister, Anne, standing there.

"Oh my goodness what a lovely surprise," said Molly. They laughed and hugged.

"Look who's here?" Anne stepped aside to reveal her husband Joe.

"Hello, Molly," said Joe with a broad toothy smile. He was a short man, a curious mix of joviality and depression. The more he drank the more outwardly jovial be became but internally there was a pervasive pessimism that would not be quenched. He had a swarthy Southern Italian look to him with black hair, thick black eyebrows and olive skin. Anyone who met him for the first time would be surprised by the unlikely North Country English accent.

Paddy glanced to the other end of the bar. "Bloody hell, look what blows in when you leave the door open."

"Where'd this lot come from?" asked Anne.

"It's a long story," said Molly. "Can I get you a cup of tea?" "Wouldn't say no but I can make it, you look like you've got your hands full here." Anne made her way toward the kitchen and turned back to Molly. "Molly, you got a minute?"

Molly cast her eye around the bar. She checked Paddy who simply nodded his head to say all was under control and the two women left for the kitchen.

"So what can I do to help?" Joe asked Paddy.

Paddy placed a glass of beer in front of him and said, "Sit there, drink this and don't piss anyone off." Joe thought that was very amusing. Paddy didn't. Joe annoyed him.

"I'll do you a favour then," said Joe, "I'll drink it."

Norm Clancy made his way through the door, still in his butcher's apron, his hair wet from the rain. "G'day Norm, there you go, mate," said Paddy; he placed a beer on the counter for him.

"Thanks Paddy, just shut the doors to get something to eat but I won't say no." He raised his glass in salute and promptly drained it. "Tell me, Paddy, you seen anything of Mike Talbot?"

"Not today, he often drops by a little later though. Don't tell me someone's dead,"

"No, no nothing like that," he said with a laugh. He wasn't at home and it looked like everyone in town was heading over here so just thought he might've dropped by. I should get going."

"Drop by later, I'll tell Talbot you were looking for him."

"No, don't bother, mate, not that important. Come and see the boys play, they're really doing well. Looks like a bit of a break in the rain, gonna make a run for it." It seemed the butcher and the undertaker were good mates.

Molly had filled the kettle and watched Anne settled at the kitchen table and light up a cigarette. "What's on your mind?" said Molly. Anne didn't answer right away but took another long thoughtful drag on her cigarette. "You didn't mention Joe was coming home," said Molly.

"Didn't know," said Anne. He wasn't due for leave and then without any warning he turns up. I dunno." She shook her head and focused on the ash on her cigarette for a moment. "I should be happy shouldn't I?"

"You tell me."

"Out of the blue I get this telegram to tell me he's arriving by train the next day. So, anyway, I got to Spencer Street station. Train's over two hours late. Now, I know that's not his fault but it doesn't help, if you know what I mean. Well, finally, the train pulls into the station. There were about a dozen of us there, and we're all waving. They all had husbands and the likes in the same army corps as Joe. I'd say the men started drinking somewhere north of Brisbane and didn't stop until the train did. "They were so drunk. The worst of them was what's his name, Hobbs, Can't remember his first name, an army chaplain, out of his mind drunk and using the worst language of the lot of them."

The kettle had boiled. Molly placed a cup of hot tea in front of Anne. "There you go, that should help," she said.

"Thanks, Bub," she sipped her tea.

"I'm sure he was glad to see you all the same," said Molly.

"You wouldn't have known it. He's mad as hell because I hadn't booked a train to Benalla. No, he doesn't want to stay in the city; he wants to go to Benalla and that's that. That's all he's been thinking about he says: our home in the bush. Rubbish. Anyway, there was a train leaving in three hours so I had to race back to Snake's and grab a few things, while he goes to the pub with his mates. He'd barely even said hello to me by this time. Well, it was a quiet trip to Benalla, I can tell you that. He's asleep most of the way. When we get to the house, it's cold and dark and there's no food to speak of. He tells me I don't appreciate all he's done and I should have made it nice for him, whatever that means, and then he falls asleep again. "I don't know. Maybe I'm expected to drop everything, and say hip-hip-hooray, but I have a life, too. Felt like that didn't matter. I wasn't important. I was so mad. I still am. So first thing this morning I got the truck started, thank God, and told him we were coming for visit and here we are."

"How long is he on leave?"

"Five days."

"What are you going to do?"

"What can I do? Oh, it'll be fine by tomorrow. If it's not I may have to hit him on the head with an axe."

Molly had never questioned Anne's devotion to Joe. It had been utterly consistent until the last six months when he had been away with the army. She had moved to the city and seemed to enjoy the creature comforts and the company that she had found in Melbourne.

"You know what?" said Anne. "It's a lot easier to leave than to be left."

The two women sat together and finished their tea. There was no need to comment; they knew each other that well.

"I should see how Paddy's doing," said Molly. "You coming?"

"In a minute. You go ahead and I'll make a fresh pot. Thanks for listening." Molly clasped Anne's hand. "I'm real glad you came over today."

"Me, too," said Anne.

As Molly re-entered the bar there were even more men than when she left. Paddy beamed at her, as if to say have you ever seen anything like this. "All right, all right, everyone!" He raised his hands to get attention. "Okay, okay, you lot, listen. Listen up now. The next round's on me!"

This brought forth a cheer from the men and they pressed closer to the bar. The first person to put his glass down was Joe. Joe was not one to help you pour or serve or clean up but would always cheerfully help you out by drinking the beer.

Molly and Paddy kept things flowing until every glass was refilled. When Anne arrived with two cups of tea she was shocked at how the crowd had grown. "Bloody hell!" she muttered, deposited the teacups and immediately went to work cleaning up and helping out wherever she could. There was another fresh surge of life when six young men who had been working on the roads turned up, absolutely drenched.

Molly brought in towels from the residence and helped them dry their hair. They of course protested and said it wasn't necessary but they loved the sense of a woman taking care of them.

"Thanks Missus," said the sandy haired youth as he handed Molly the towel. "Don't think anyone else around here would be kind enough to dry me down, that's real nice of ya."

"Dry ya down?" said one of his mates. "They're more likely to piss on ya." That brought a good laugh from the crew and by then it was time for another round of beers.

Hours passed and neither the rain nor the men relented. It was sometime around one-thirty in the afternoon when one of the men produced a mouth organ and songs were loudly sung as glasses were clinked. Rabbit was sitting in the corner grinning like a madman and clapping his hands in time with the song.

An hour later they were singing and dancing the Irish Jig outside the bar under the verandah. They wouldn't be restrained and all Molly could hope was that Jenkins wasn't in town.

Blue, Paddy's mate from the football team, elbowed his way to the bar, "One for the road, thanks Paddy."

"What are you talking about, it's still pissing down out there."

"Gotta get something to eat. This has been great, mate, but the blokes are real hungry. Hate to go but we gotta eat." ""No, no," said Paddy. "No, that's not on. After all," he said looking at Anne, "didn't Molly just go to the kitchen to make sandwiches? Isn't that right, Anne?

"Oh yes. Absolutely!" she said having absolutely no idea what he was talking about. She looked at Paddy hoping for more.

"Sandwiches, eh? Beauty," said Blue.

"What sandwiches?" she quietly asked Paddy.

"I've given away so many drinks this morning we have to keep them here to get our money back. Tell Molly we've got to have sandwiches. Now."

"Right," said Anne. "Lovely sandwiches coming up," she said to Blue. "I'll just pop out and see how Molly's doing."

Anne ran to the kitchen to find Molly who had simply taken a minute to go to the bathroom. "Sandwiches, sandwiches! Quick! We've got to make sandwiches." Anne was almost hysterical and started rummaging through cupboards. She told

Anne to stop what she was doing immediately. Anne quickly explained to Molly how Paddy had promised sandwiches so that they wouldn't leave. Molly said she couldn't make sandwiches. Anne said she had to. "Where's the bread? Got to get bread?" Anne insisted. Molly said she didn't have any bread. Anne said she'd get some. The race had begun.

Anne sprinted from the pub to the bakery and back in record time. She arrived with four loaves of bread under her arms. Molly had been looking for food of which there wasn't a lot. There was, of course, the plump roast chicken. Molly could only hope that the chook was given to her to fill a bigger, far greater, need than dinner.

As Anne sliced bread, Molly wrenched meat from the bird. She chopped it up to get as much distance as she could from the single bird. Two slices of bread, a little butter, a little chicken, some pepper and salt. Slice once. Slice twice. Sandwiches.

One of the men from the mill approached Paddy to refill a handful of glasses, "How long before we see the sandwiches, Paddy, I'm bloody starving."

Molly ran to the door of the bar and caught her breath. "Anne is just about to bring them in. Hope you like roast chicken," she said with a smile.

"Oh, yeah, I love chicken," he said practically salivating at the thought. "Me stomach thinks me throat's been cut!" shouted another man. More hungry mouths echoed the anticipation.

Molly ran back to the kitchen, "How we doing? They're making noises in there."

"This'll shut them up." Anne stacked another round of sandwiches on the plate and hightailed it to the bar. You could hear the cheer go up as she arrived. In almost no time she returned with an empty plate. "Bloody hell, I didn't even get the plate on the bar. Gone, just like a plague of locusts."

The pattern was repeated and repeated and repeated. By the end of the second loaf the butter was gone but Anne found a tin of lard and that did the trick. There was a little dried rabbit from earlier in the week and that was minced to cut in with the chicken. Some old cheese Molly was going to throw out found new life. Anything that could be called food found itself in the mix.

"Bloody lovely sandwiches!" Could be heard from the bar. "More sandwiches, Misses!" The music had struck up again, someone sang Danny Boy and there was peace in the world.

Whatever could be found was served until the crowd was sated and started to drift away. It was well after the regular closing time of six before they called it quits. Many of the drunks who had opened the doors were there to close them. It had been a glorious day for the men from the mill, those working the roads and anyone else who passed by and loved a good time.

It would seem that Paddy's persistence and God's precipitation were a potent combination. The locals would most certainly be talking about that day at the Imperial Hotel. Paddy and Molly had made a mark. "Bonzer couple they are!" Paddy was the best host in the district and Molly made the best sandwiches within a hundred miles or more.

Molly and Anne were having a cup of tea at the kitchen table when Paddy entered with handfuls of bank notes. "Look at this, will you! Just look at this." He put the money on the table in front of Molly. "I swear we took in more money today than we've taken in the whole time since we got here."

"That's good,"

"Good, it's bloody great. You could look a little happier about it."

"Sorry love, I'm just tired."

"You couldn't have come on a better day, Tommy. Don't know what we would have done with you?" said Paddy.

"It got hectic there for a while, I must say. Where's Joe?"

155

"He's still in the bar," said Paddy "Going on about some army bivouac up north."

"I thought everyone had gone," said Anne.

"They have. He's the only one in the bar."

"Does he know that?" she asked.

"No idea. He's been telling this story for over an hour now. There were a few blokes there when he started. All the same, don't think he should be driving a car right now." He looked around the kitchen at the chaos of the day. "Bit of a mess out here, but you were amazing, both of you." He noticed the chicken remnants. It was as if every trace of skin, fat and meat had been surgically removed. "Not much meat left on that. What are all these cans?"

"Soup cans," said Anne.

"That's what they were eating in the end, soup sandwiches," Molly started to laugh at the absurdity of it all.

"They loved them," said Paddy.

"Of course they loved them, they were drunk. I could have put a cat between two slices of bread and they would have loved them."

"I don't suppose there's anything to eat then?" said Paddy, "I'm starving."

"Of course, you must be," said Molly "I'm sure I have a couple of crusts here somewhere. So, what would you like a pea soup sandwich or a chicken soup sandwich?" That was too much for both of the women who collapsed at the table shaking with laughter.

Joe resisted every effort to get him into the car and shouted generally incoherent threats to any 'bastard who laid a hand on him'. Anne was not pleased. Molly had invited them to stay and share the eggs and potatoes that survived, only because there wasn't time to turn them into sandwich fillings, but Anne opted to drive home before it got too late.

Paddy was still mildly euphoric when they lay in bed that night. "We did it, didn't we? We got 'em in."

"Yes, we did."

"And they had a good time. They'll come back, I'm sure they will."

"I hope so."

"Oh, you can bank on it. I'll put money on the table they don't get treated that well at the Prince of Wales."

"Most of them don't get treated that well at home. Just remember, Paddy, no more free sandwiches. You can call that an opening special."

"But love...."

"But nothing. I'm not doing this every day. It would kill me. And we can't afford it; they'll eat all the profits. I'll make sure something tasty is available at a modest cost but no more of this free business.'

Paddy rolled over on his side, "You're right, of course," he said. "I'd like to have something on the counter now and then. How about cheese? Just a plate of cheese now and then to help the beer go down."

"Do we have to, really?" Paddy kissed her on the neck and pulled her closer to him. She started to laugh. "Fine, fine, you win," she said. "You can have your cheese. A mate of Rabbit's was around last week trying to sell me rounds of cheese for threepence."

"Sounds like rough cheese."

"Don't you worry, when I'm done with it, they'll love it."

"You're a bloody wonder you are."

There seemed no better way to end a day like that than in each other's arms passionately loving each other in the quiet of the night.

Chapter Twenty-Three

Within a week it seemed the rain around Mansfield was an illusion. It was unseasonably warm and windy. The earth had blotted up the moisture and turned mud back to dust. Anne and Joe had made two more visits to the hotel before Joe was shunted back to Queensland.

Nobody was dancing in the street but business had certainly picked up to a point where they were breaking even more often than losing money.

As promised, Molly had contacted Rabbit's cobber, Dodger, who was selling the cheese. She had learned from her naivety; when she got the first cheese she took it to the kitchen to cut into small cubes. Big mistake. To say the cheese had an odour would hardly begin to tell the story. A nauseous, rancid smell permeated the entire kitchen. It seeped into drawers and cupboards and nested there for days waiting to assault the senses of anyone foolish enough to open the drawer.

"G'day, Missus B, I brought you another cheese," said Dodger. "Rabbit said you was ready for another one."

"I don't think anyone is really ready for your cheese, Dodger."

Both Dodger and Rabbit had a good laugh at that one; they didn't quite know what Molly meant but she was 'a good sort' so it couldn't be bad.

"Think we might have a drink since we're here," said Rabbit.

"Bloody good idea," said Dodger.

"Step up to the bar, gentlemen, I'd be happy to serve you," said Paddy.

"I can take care of it thanks, Paddy," said Molly.

"I'm sure you can, my love, but I don't want to hold you up. You'll want to take care of that lovely cheese now, won't you?" Paddy stifled a smile, knowing full well how Molly hated the foul cheese.

The leathery skin of the cheese was a mottled yellow colour and had a coarse, waxy texture. Molly carried the large cheese to the back door. She placed it on the ground and wheeled it to the centre of the small yard. Skipper, a lean black and white border collie who adopted the hotel, looked on suspiciously. Normally placid to the point of a coma, the dog's ears pricked up as Molly went into the shed and returned with an axe. She wrapped a large white handkerchief over her nose and mouth and then raised the axe above her head. With one mighty blow she brought the axe down on the waxy round of malodorous cheddar and cracked it wide open. Molly immediately dropped the axe to the ground and ran to the door. Skipper leapt to his feet in terror, ran around the cheese several times, barking hysterically and yelping before fleeing the yard completely.

It was late the following day before Molly allowed the offending cheese back into the kitchen. By then the worst was over. She cut it into small cubes and placed it on plates and served it to the assembled masses in the bar.

"Lovely cheese, Missus B," said Tom, prompting the unanimous response of the crowd as they gobbled tidbits of stinky cheese and flushed them down with glasses of Victoria Bitter. She marvelled at the response to what she considered more of a death threat than a snack.

There was no argument business had improved. Nothing would match the day of the rain but the last two weeks had seen a much steadier flow of patrons.

"I think the cheese idea was bloody brilliant." Paddy put his arm around Molly's shoulder as they looked at a handful of scrubby locals having a laugh and a nibble.

Molly was happy to see their fortunes begin to reverse themselves but the idea of a future filled with putrid cheese sent a shiver through her.

"You all right, love?" asked Paddy.

"Fine," she replied.

"Someone walk over your grave?" he asked with a laugh.

"Something like that," she said as she indicated the door. "Speaking of which, look what just blew in."

Standing at the door was James Jenkins. He didn't speak; he just tucked his thumbs into his vest pockets and looked around the pub with his signature distain.

"You looking for something?" Paddy stepped forward.

"I hear you had quite a turn going on here a couple of weeks ago."

"Is that so?"

"Yeah, I heard the place was jumping."

"Don't know about that. Everyone had a good time, that's all."

The patrons raised their glasses to that comment and echoed the sentiment and said it was one of the best days they could remember, and maybe they'll have another party if it ever rains again."

Jenkins was unmoved by the enthusiasm. "I also heard that that beer was being served well after 6:00 p.m."

"Don't know where you get your information. Somebody obviously can't tell the time. It was all very proper. It wouldn't be legal to serve a drink after six, but you already know that, don't you. Can I get you a beer?"

Jenkins chose to ignore him. "People were outside singing and dancing in the streets. That doesn't sound very restrained or proper to me."

"On the contrary," said Molly. "I think what we all need is more singing and dancing in the streets. Have a piece of cheese Mr Jenkins." She took the plate from the bar and offered it directly to him.

"What?"

"Some cheese. It would please me if you had some cheese."

Jenkins eyed her with some suspicion. Molly smiled graciously and held the plate out to beckon him. Slowly the man moved toward the cheese. Molly didn't take her eyes off him. Finally he reached for the smallest piece he could see.

"Oh no," said Molly. "You must have a big piece; a man like you needs a big piece of this cheese." Molly turned the plate to display the larger pieces.

Jenkins didn't quite understand but felt his masculinity would somehow be impugned if he took a small piece. It was now a challenge.

The whole bar had fallen silent. It was akin to that moment in a classic western movie where they faced off at the local saloon. Jenkins took the largest piece of cheese on the plate and put it in his mouth, looking Molly squarely in the eye he slowly chewed it. For one fleeting yet decisive moment he abruptly stopped and stared earnestly ahead. The look in his eyes reminded Molly of Skipper the dog, just moments after the axe had fallen. With one mighty gulp James Jenkins swallowed.

"What did you think of that, Mr Jenkins?"

"Very tasty, thank you, Mrs Brennan. I enjoyed it."

"I thought you would," said Molly. "Now you must excuse us, we have work to do." Molly turned away and walked to the other end of the bar. She turned back to see Jenkins just standing there. "Good bye, Mr Jenkins."

The man was being dismissed but there would be no fond farewells. He turned and walked toward the door. "Next time you're in town, there will always be a piece of cheese for you," said Molly. He hesitated for the slightest moment and then continued to his exit.

"Your cheese does the trick, Missus B," said one of the codgers sitting next to Rabbit at the bar.

"Yes, doesn't it." As she looked at Paddy, the slightest smile of satisfaction began to crease her cheeks. She hummed to herself as she walked to the kitchen.

"So, Paddy," said Rabbit. "Your Missus was asking me about Jenkins."

"Yeah?"

"Maybe I should have mentioned this earlier, but there's something you should know about that bloke."

Chapter Twenty-Four

Hot and dry was standard fare for the summers. It was expected. Rain and a damp invasive cold was the stamp of winter. Not this year, however. The drought that choked the summer refused to release its grip.

Anne had been Molly's link to Melbourne and she'd been relied on for news from the city. Now that Joe was on leave from the army and they were ensconced in Benalla, Anne's world had much tighter boundaries. City news came principally by way of Alice, who would take the train from time to time, and one or the other of Paddy's brothers who had brightened the odd weekend.

Each day was preoccupied with making it to tomorrow.

Business in the hotel was sporadic at best. A core of the football team lead by coach Norm Clancy sustained their support for Paddy and some of the church ladies remained faithful in their dedication. Other patrons floated in and out of the bar and if there was any consensus it was that the going was tough and could get tougher.

One particularly lethargic day was brightened by the arrival of Barry Hutton smiling broadly as he walked through the door. "G'day Paddy, Mrs Brennan."

"You look happy," said Paddy.

165

"Well, what are the choices?" he said. "Being miserable takes work,"

"My oath!" said Paddy.

"So, here I am," said Barry.

"Paddy, I asked Barry to pop over. Have been feeling crook all day and thought I might lie down for a bit," said Molly.

"You should have said something,"

"I think I'm just coming down with something. Tummy's playing up a little that's all and I knew you wanted to go out."

"You should have told me," said Paddy.

"I didn't want to worry you."

"For heaven's sake, Molly. You got to take care of yourself. Go upstairs. Do you want a cup of tea?"

"No, I'll just have a drink of water and close my eyes for a bit. Thanks Barry." She looked at Paddy. "Go for your walk."

"Not if you don't feel well," said Paddy.

"You'll just make me feel worse if you stay in. That's why Barry's here. Now do as you're told, go for your walk," she said. Molly smiled at them as she turned to leave the bar. The two men watched her walk away, each wishing they could have said something that was meaningful.

"She'll be all right," said Barry. "I'll listen for her."

"Don't think I should go."

"Aw, I don't think that would go down too well with Mrs Brennan."

"I won't be long."

"Right."

Paddy has been looking forward to a break from the routine inside the pub. He walked the length of the town. When he reached the Prince of Wales Hotel he couldn't resist the urge to see how the competition fared, and possibly find some evidence to support Rabbit's claim. From outside the door there appeared to be an argument ensuing in the bar. He opened the door to see

166

almost a dozen men absorbed in animated conversation about who was likely to make the playoffs in the local football league. They were, by and large, Mansfield supporters. but there were enough cantankerous dissenters to stir up the pot.

It was clear that Robert Scott hadn't snagged the prime, business travellers or anyone with meaningful change in their pockets. The majority of patrons on that day looked like were the dusty survivors who talked far more than they spent. Scott looked up from behind the bar and saw Paddy at the door.

"What are you doing here, Paddy Brennan? Not enough happening down the street to keep you busy?"

On the rare occasion when Scott visited the Imperial Hotel, Paddy's first instinct was to pour him a beer and present it as a token of friendship. Robert Scott was not of the same inclination and simply leaned on the bar awaiting an answer.

"Just out for a walk, thought I'd say g'day, that's all."

"Oh yeah? Well, consider it done. And no, we are not doing great business either. Makes you wonder if there's room for two pubs in this town, doesn't it!" Scott delivered the line with a smile that was obviously at odds with his intention.

"You make it sound like a threat, mate," said Paddy, a little surprised by the bluntness of the comment.

"Just stating a fact. If you find facts threatening, I can't help that."

Before the men could take it any further, they were interrupted by the sounds of laughter as two women entered the room. One was Libby Scott, the publican's wife: a florid and slightly vulgar, big-busted woman with blonde hair. With her came a slightly shorter, younger version of herself.

"Well, you better get going if you want to get to Melbourne before dark. Robert, say good-bye to Glenda." Libby looked around the bar and spotted Paddy. "Oh, hello. I know who you are. You're Paddy...Paddy...I'm sorry, I can't remember your last name.

"Brennan" said Paddy with a polite nod.

"That's right," she said with a big laugh. "Glenda this is Paddy Brennan, he and his wife...."

"Molly," said Paddy.

"Right, Molly, he and Molly took over the Imperial. I told you about them didn't I?"

"Yes," said Glenda. "Jim's mentioned them a couple of times."

"This is my sister, Glenda," said Libby addressing Paddy. "She's up for a lovely visit."

"That's a treat I'm sure," said Paddy.

"Yes, Jim, her husband, he's here all the time mind you," said Libby.

Robert felt the need to interrupt "Shouldn't you get going?" he said sternly.

"Jim! Robert's giving you marching orders," said Libby with her indiscriminate laugh. "Time to go."

"I should get back to work, too." Paddy was about to use their exit when Glenda's husband entered. The "Jim" in question was none other then James Jenkins.

"Bloody hell, Rabbit was right," said Paddy. "The local licensing cop is your brother-in-law."

"That's right," said Scott.

"Better to have a policemen living in the family than knocking at the door," said Libby with her increasingly annoying laugh.

"Excuse me," said Paddy very politely. He smiled at the women and nodded respectfully again. "It's been a very illuminating meeting. Good bye."

Paddy was halfway down the street when Jenkins drove to the right hand side of the road and pulled up beside him. Paddy took one look and continued to walk. Jenkins got out of the car. "Just a minute Brennan," he said. Paddy ignored him and Jenkins pursued him down the street putting a hand on him to stop.

"Get your fucking hand off me or I'll drop you," said Paddy.

"Don't take that tone with me Brennan."

Paddy grabbed the man by the scruff of his neck. A yelp of horror could be heard from Mrs Jenkins in the car. "You bloody insect," said Paddy. "You come after me every chance you get, and I look up the street and I know he's breaking every rule in the book, and I can't figure out how he gets away with it. And it's you. It's you all the time."

Jenkins scuffled to break free. "You're not welcome here." He said. " We don't need another pub here, we don't need you."

Not one to shy away from a fight, it took every fibre in Paddy's being to resist punching Jenkins in the mouth. He knew that balanced against any fleeting moment of violent satisfaction was the likelihood that Jenkins would lay charges. Would he worry about that now or later? Just as Paddy raised his arm he heard Molly's voice.

"Don't do it!" she shouted from where she stood at the front of the hotel. Paddy was frozen in position. Jenkins eyes widened fearing that he was about to be injured.

"Do not hit him, Paddy. He's not worth it."

"You're bloody lucky this time, you little prick." Paddy dropped his fist, turned and walked away.

"I'm going to get you," shouted Jenkins from a safe distance.

"No, you won't, Jenkins," said Paddy with a calm certainty. "You don't have the balls, mate!"

Jenkins slammed the door of his car, crunched the gears and made an inglorious exit. Paddy watched the car melt into the swirling dust. He put his arm around Molly and led her back into the hotel. He felt angry at the games that had been played but now, at least, he knew the rules.

Chapter Twenty-Five

Any time of day the kitchen tended to be dark. In mid winter it was profoundly gloomy. Molly was cooking lamb chops for dinner and washing dishes that had accumulated during the day when, suddenly, the light bulb failed and the whole room was dark except for light bleeding in from the bar.

"Damn." Molly foraged in drawers for the spare light bulb but it was not to be found. Frustration was mounting. "Paddy?" Nothing. "Paddy!" She crossed to the bar where Paddy was chatting with some customers. "I was calling you," she said, blatantly intruding on the conversation. Paddy was mildly annoyed by her tone. He excused himself and crossed to Molly. "Sorry, what?"

"I was calling you." It wasn't the words that bothered Paddy. It was the delivery. Molly was admonishing him for not reacting fast enough. He was bewildered by her mood. "The light bulb has gone in the kitchen," she said.

"You want me to change it?"

"I'm perfectly capable of changing it if I can find the damn bulbs."

"Okay, okay, settle down," said Paddy.

"Excuse me, what did you say?"

171

"Nothing." He crossed to a ledge above the bar and took down a light bulb. "Here."

"What are you they doing up there?"

"You told me to put them there," he said.

Soon there was light in the kitchen but now there was another far more grave problem brewing. The chops she'd left on the stove were burnt. "Oh no," she said as if wounded. She instinctively reached for the iron frypan and burned her hand. She pushed it to the side of the stove. The frypan crashed to the ground scattering the chops across the floor.

"Thought I could smell something burning." Paddy appeared at the door just as Molly grabbed the frypan and burned her hand again. She let out a cry in pain and grabbed a dishcloth to protect her hand; she wrapped it around the handle of the frypan, which she then pitched into the sink smashing the dishes that were soaking in the dirty water.

"What's wrong?" It was too late to reason. Molly grabbed saucepans from the sink and hurled them at the stove. The furies that had been welling inside her were erupting. Every spoon, every pot, every lid, every pan was pitched in anger. Paddy had never seen her like that before. Molly fell to her knees and gathered up the chops. She tried to wipe them clean on her apron. The harder she tried to rub them clean, the more she cried.

"Okay, okay, come on, it's all right," said Paddy.

He tried to take the chops from her but she held on to them for dear life. "No. No! I only have three chops," she cried.

"I know."

"This is all we have!" She clutched the burned chops tightly against her breast while Paddy held her tightly in his arms.

"I'm sorry. I am so, so sorry." said Paddy as he rocked her back and forth until the pain subsided.

Chapter Twenty-Six

Mount Buller selfishly grabbed what little precipitation there had been in the sky. It was ironic to see the mountain flecked with snow while everything around it was gripped by drought. It may have been disappointment with the broken promise of rain coupled with the bitterly cold wind off the mountain that kept everyone inside on that afternoon.

Paddy walked across the bar and looked out at the street. He was oblivious to the chill. Barry was wiping down the bar. It was a ritual, not a necessity, as the bar was completely empty and had been for hours.

"Anything happening out there?" said Barry.

Paddy just shook his head slowly. "Pour me a beer," he said and walked back to the bar.

"How's Mrs Brennan doing?" asked Barry.

"I don't know if I thanked you for stepping in such short notice," said Paddy.

"Not a problem."

"She's okay, considering. The nurse stopped by this morning; seemed to think she was doing good."

A gust of wind rattled the door. Both men looked out onto the street to see if anyone out there reacted to the sudden force of nature. Predictably, there was nothing.

"Guess we can call the last couple of days our winter. They say it'll be bloody hot again by Sunday."

"If you want a drink, just help yourself, mate," said Paddy.

"No, thanks."

Barry had developed an affection for Molly. Although she hadn't been able to drum up much work for the young man, she had provided a safe haven for Barry and Maggie to meet.

One day in the bar, Molly had reported trouble with rickety shelves in the kitchen. She chided Paddy about his lack of carpentry skills. Barry immediately took the cue, said he could fix them in a jiffy. It seemed that whenever Barry came to work on the shelves, Maggie would arrive through the back door. Everyone knew Maggie Scott and everyone knew her father wanted her to marry well, as he liked to say. There were very few safe places in the town for them to meet - Molly's kitchen was one of them. True to his word, Barry did fix the shelves, but it took weeks.

"I had no idea she was expecting, Paddy. How far along was she?" said Barry.

"Three. Three months., mate Well, almost."

"Right." Barry walked around the bar and sat on a stool beside Paddy. "Does anyone know why, you know, how it happened?"

"Nope. The priest said it must be God's will." Paddy sipped his beer and thought about it for a minute. "Don't know why he's want to do a thing like that, do you?"

"She must have been looking forward to it, the baby.

"We both were, mate, we both were," said Paddy.

There was no consolation to be found in any corner. The hotel felt hollow. The light through the window was harsh and pale. There was no reason to think that day or the next day would be any more forgiving.

Paddy and Molly's bedroom was on the second floor of the hotel with windows looking out over the street.

The room was very simply decorated. Fresh cream paint covered the patchy old wallpaper; nobody had wanted to strip the walls. An iron double bed had been painted brown. In the head and footboards there were brass hearts inset into the cast iron. Molly polished the brass once a week.

There was an old wardrobe and matching chest of drawers that were in remarkably good condition considering they had been abandoned in another bedroom at the hotel.

Above the chest of drawers was a picture of the Blessed Virgin that Alice had given them as a wedding present. On the top of the chest were three cream doilies, crystal bowls and a glass tray. A tall vase containing a large bunch of white chrysanthemums and yellow carnations sat on the centre of the bedside table.

The room was simple but clean and there had been an attempt to soften the lines and make it a more personal space.

Molly lay on the side of the bed where she could see out the window. She was wearing a cardigan over her cotton dress. A blanket covered her legs. She didn't respond when Paddy entered the room.

He placed a glass of lime cordial beside her on the table and then took the blanket and covered her.

"You've got to keep warm," he said.

"When's it going to end?" said Molly. Paddy didn't answer, he couldn't. The wind crept in through the window beside the bed and the lace curtains shuddered. "I hate this country sometimes, it's so cruel."

Paddy tucked the blanket snugly around her body and rested one arm on her side.

"Come on, drink this." He offered her the glass. "Or would you rather I made you a nice hot cup of tea."

"I don't' want to stay here, Paddy," said Molly.

"Come on, have a sip, you'll feel better."

"I really don't, Paddy. I can't stay here like this." She didn't shout. She didn't cry. That had already happened. She simply said what was in her heart. There was a quiet resignation that made her sadness even more emphatic. They shared the silence for fully five minutes before Molly reached up and took his hand in hers. "Where did the flowers come from?" said Molly.

"Some of the women from the church. Ethel Patterson dropped them off."

"They're lovely." Molly sat up. She looked at Paddy and could see the sadness in his eyes. She didn't know if he had cried. She hoped he had found some release rather than bottle it all up as was his wont. She gave his hand a squeeze.

"Who's minding the bar?" she asked.

"Barry came right over."

"Such a lovely young man, I like him," said Molly.

"Good bloke. I should let him go soon. Think he's meeting his young lady."

"Good for them. I suppose I should start thinking about supper."

"Don't be silly, no. Anne will be over later."

"You called her?"

"Yeah. Tried to reach her yesterday but she was away. Oh and I think Alice is coming up on the train tomorrow."

"They shouldn't go to all that trouble."

"Of course they should," said Paddy. He offered her the glass and this time she took a sip and then a longer drink and passed him the glass. Paddy stroked her hair gently and then turned to leave.

"I'm coming down," said Molly.

"No, you're not."

"Yes, I am. It's no good lying up here feeling sorry for myself. That won't get anything done." Paddy stopped at the door and looked back at her. "Thanks for the drink," she said, "it was good."

By the time Molly had made her way down, the wind had abated and bright afternoon sunshine had warmed the place Rabbit, Dodger and Tom held up one end of the bar, as three strangers at the other end talked loudly and laughed.

The three regulars stopped their conversation when they saw Molly. They tipped their hats in respect. Molly smiled and walked around the bar to look out the front window.

"Do you want anything, love?" asked Paddy.

Molly shook her head and then turned to him. "Tell you what, I'd like a shandy." She approached where the men sat and took a stool beside them. She lifted her glass from the bar. "Cheers."

"Good on ya, Missus," said Tom.

"Cheers," said Rabbit and Dodger.

They sat there in silence while the men at the other end of the bar were oblivious to any of the circumstances, and continued to laugh, and have a good time. It was Tom who broke the silence.

"Sorry to hear about the baby, Missus."

"Thank you, Tom."

"You really don't know the little buggers before they're born do you, but that doesn't make it any easier," he said.

"No."

"Millie and me lost two that way, but ended up all right. Got our five in the end. But you mustn't give up hope. Cause if you do that, give up hope, you've lost everything."

"Okay Tom, why don't I buy you a fresh beer, that one's looking a little tired?" said Paddy.

Tom sensed Paddy's discomfort with his offering. "Did I say the wrong thing? I'm sorry if I upset you, Missus. Just wanted you to know you're not alone in it."

"Thank you, Tom, It's nice of you to say so." She placed her glass back on the bar. "Excuse me, I have to think about supper.

Paddy replaced the remnants of Tom's stale beer with a fresh glass.

"It's like having relatives with terrible breath, grief is." Tom's comment stopped Molly at the doorway. "Every now and then they comes to visit and it's bloody awful, Shockin'! You don't want 'em, but they're gonna turn up anyway, that's part of life, it is. But it's not something you should live with every day; it's just something you have to go through now and them. That being said, you know what relatives can be like, they won't go until you send 'em away and that's all I have to say about that. Cheers!" With that Tom raised his glass, drained it, placed it firmly back on the wooden bar and left

Chapter Twenty-Seven

Grandma Donahue stood in the doorway watching her granddaughter gaze out the window. Molly was tall. By the time she tuned twelve she had developed a penchant for stooping. "Stand up straight, girl," her grandmother would say. "Be proud." Molly would pull her shoulders back and draw herself up to her full height. "Is that better, Nana?"

"Much better. Now pay attention." She wiped her finger across a dresser and held up the dust-smeared finger as evidence. "You know what this is, my child?"

Molly knew the answer; this was a game they had played before. "Is it just dust, Nana?" she said.

"No, my child, it's not just dust. It's the ashes of yesterday. It's what used to be. Now, do we want to live with what used to be or do we want to live with what is? Is it yesterday or today for you and me?"

"It's today," said Molly.

"Exactly. So no matter how yesterday shaped up, it's still yesterday and there's no shine to yesterday, today. We're going to do something about that. What are we going to do?"

"We're going to make today shine."

To her grandmother's delight, Molly ran to the kitchen and returned with a small grey wooden box that contained well-used dust-cloths and a can of beeswax.

They set to in the front parlour bringing a rich dark shine to the simple mahogany sideboard and then moved around the room erasing yesterday one firm wipe at a time.

"What are you doing, child?" the grandmother would ask with each new item.

"We're making it shine."

For the mature Mrs Donahue, there was little distinction between bringing lustre to a sideboard and bringing brilliance to life. If Molly had an exam at school or was running a race on sports day, her grandmother never failed to give her a hug and whisper to her, "Make it shine, child. Make it shine."

With the lack of rain, the heat, the dust, and the struggle to survive the recent loss of hope, there hadn't been an excess of shine at the Imperial Hotel of late. On Monday, August 15, 1938, Molly decided it was time to change that. She waxed the counters and woodwork around the bar until everything glistened. Yesterday was dismissed from every corner she could reach. This was quite a shine. A shine of which Nana would have been very proud.

For that day at least, both Molly and the Imperial Hotel had distinctly happier dispositions.

"Back in a bit," she called out to Paddy. She didn't wait for a response but set off toward the railway line where Lorraine Lea winter roses grew wild along a decayed wooden fence. She could never quite figure out who would have planted them originally but learned to accept the gift for what it was and not to question how or why.

It seemed no matter how savage the drought those rose bushes could blot enough moisture from deep in the soil to hold on to their blooms.

She managed to find seven pink roses that still had life to them and arranged them with some stringy greens that also resisted nature. The three vases of flowers did wonders to brighten the Ladies Lounge.

Although the air was crisp and not really cold enough to justify a fire, Molly felt it was a necessary addition. The reaction of all who smelled the smoke, and saw the flames blazing in the hearth more than justified her choice.

The bar had never looked brighter or more inviting.

"What would we do without pubs I ask you?" said Michael Talbot. "Look at this, just look at this. It's welcoming and warm with sturdy walls to protect us from what's on the outside and beverages galore to warm what's on the inside. It's a thing of beauty."

"You can thank Molly for making it so inviting," said Paddy. "She did it all herself."

"Thank you, madam. You have created a sanctuary for us. I shall stay here until the world recovers its senses, or until closing, whichever comes first. I tell you, one and all, every day it gets a little more grey and more foreboding out there."

"It's not that bad, mate," said Paddy.

"I don't know, Paddy, it's not good I tell you. What I read in the newspapers...."

"Ah, now wait. That's your first mistake. Reading newspapers. They never tell you any good news. Newspapers are better used for wrapping fish and chips, Mike."

"Yes, well you do have a point there." Michael pressed on. "It's just not a happy place out there. There are too many crazy people in the world and if you don't' believe me, go and ask Hans how things are the Fatherland. He'll tell you all right."

"There's a few troublemakers here in the bar, too," said Paddy.

"What? You lookin' at me?" said Rabbit, who was perched at the bar, nursing his glass of port. Beside him sat his good mate and local purveyor of fine cheese, Dodger. "'You lookin' at me?" he repeated with even more enthusiasm. "Cause I'm lookin' at you." He nudged Dodger to say that was a good one, but it was clear from Dodger's hearty response that he didn't have a clue.

"All I am saying is, every day it gets a little more grim. That's all," said Mike. "And if that's not bad enough, somebody's been drinking out of my glass; it's empty."

"You can't let it get you down, Michael," said Molly as she refilled the glass. "Life's too short."

"You are so right, Mrs Brennan. That's why I was saying thank God we have pubs to protect us. Think about it. Where would we be without them? Where would I go if I wanted to meet people who weren't already dead? If you stay here long enough, you get to meet anyone who's worth meeting, and you hear all the news that's worth hearing. Catch up on the footy, speaking of which, where the hell is Norm? He should be here by now."

Michael Talbot had been there for an hour or two every day during the week. On that day, he'd been there for almost four hours and, as if to defend himself from the grim state of the world, he had taken the time to personally insulate himself from its pain.

Three men from Benalla had gathered in the corner and were a source or muted conversation and occasional laughter. Two salesmen from Melbourne had lingered for an hour and then left to drive home. Betty Wright, one of the women Paddy wooed at the church was there with Joanna, her decidedly-spinster sister. If Betty had said 'lovely flowers' once, she had said it a dozen times. There was nothing apparently special in the day itself except for Molly's passion to bring it to life.

Michael Talbot stood by the mantle mesmerized by the playful fire. He raised his glass to Molly in a salute. "It's a treat to be here today, Molly, I must say,"

"Thank you. It's not bad if I say so myself," said Molly.

"Not too bad at all. The world in here is blissfully at ease, the fire crackles, the beer is cold, the mood is warm and the company is delightful. If it could all stay like this."

"Perhaps it can," said Molly wistfully.

"Ah yes, well. Standing here like this I feel a need to say something profound, something from Aristotle or some of other Greek." He contemplated the options and sipped his beer. "I really am spending too much time with dead people."

"You need to find yourself someone to settled down with," said Paddy as he stacked bottles of beer into the refrigerator.

"Ah, yes, well," was his noncommittal response. "I think it's time for another glass of beer, thank you."

"Seriously though," said Paddy through the clink of bottles. "Isn't it time you thought about getting married, Mike?'

"Thank you," he said to Molly as he lifted his beer from the counter. "You see, Paddy, the problem there is that you have already snagged the only truly beautiful woman in town."

Molly laughed. "Paddy, I think one of the customers is flirting with me."

"As long as he keeps drinking that's allowed, love. If he's just flirting and not drinking, let me know and I'll turf him out."

Molly wagged her finger at Michael as a mock warning.

"It's a lost cause, I fear," said Talbot.

"Oh don't say that," said Molly, "someone will snap you up."

"I dunno Missus," said Rabbit from the other end of the bar. "Whichever way you slice it, he's still the bloke who spends his days diggin' holes and throwin' dead people in 'em. I wouldn't marry him."

"Well, there you are," said Talbot. "There's my second hope shot to ribbons."

Molly laughed heartily. "Oh, Rabbit, now see what you've done, you've broken the poor man's heart."

"You seem chirpy Mrs B. You win the Tatts lottery did ya?" asked Rabbit, as he raised his glass to Molly.

"I wish! Perhaps I should buy a ticket, Rabbit. Good luck may be on the way," she said.

"Didn't have ya pegged as a gambler," said Rabbit.

Molly wrapped her arm around Paddy's waist. "I must be a bit of a gambler. I married him didn't I?"

"Well, you can't win 'em all, can ya?" Rabbit underlined the humour of that observation with a toothless wheeze. Dodger just pointed at Rabbit as if to say what a funny bugger he was.

"Hello, it's me." The voice came from the kitchen, and Maggie Scott followed it into the room. "Hello, all."

"It's a miracle," said Michael Talbot offering a gentlemanly bow to the young woman. "Were you sent here to save me?"

"What?" Maggie smiled, amused by the game, but totally confused and a little embarrassed.

"They're all telling me it's time to get married and nobody wants me, I fear. Will you marry me, sweet girl?"

"Will I marry you?"

"Yes. Do you want me to go down on one knee? I will if you ask."

Maggie giggled; deep dimples formed in her freckled cheeks. "No, I don't want you to go down on one knee." She shook the red hair out of her eyes and stood very straight and looked at Michael. "Are you rich?"

"No."

"No? I hear stories that you take the gold fillings out of dead people's mouths and steal the personal jewellery everyone thought they were going to their graves wearing. Is it true?"

"What a horrible story!" said Michael.

"Looks like they're on to you," said Paddy.

"Who told you that?"

"Never mind, is it true?" Maggie was playing the game very well.

"No! Absolutely untrue."

Paddy turned to Molly, "Didn't he try to trade a tooth for a beer once?"

"So you're not rich and you don't have a drawer full of gold teeth and stolen diamonds?" asked Maggie.

"No."

"Hmmm." Maggie rubbed her chin and then walked around him as if she were inspecting cattle at an auction. "I don't think so. I'm sorry. Now, if you had the teeth."

Maggie turned abruptly to face the front door as Barry entered.

"Hello," she said.

"Hello," said Barry, looking a little embarrassed at the surprise meeting.

Nobody in the bar spoke. They all sat in expectation of the next move by the young couple. Even the sisters were peering into the public bar from their vantage point in the lounge.

"I thought you were working in the kitchen," said Maggie as she indicated the hotel kitchen, her eyes never leaving the young man.

"It was just a door on a cupboard. Fixed it, didn't see you come in."

"I came in the back way," said Maggie.

"Right," said Barry.

Neither could hide the pleasure of just seeing the other. They probably could have stood there for an hour or more simply looking at each other if it wasn't for Ethel Patterson bursting through the doors of the hotel as if propelled out of a canon.

Ethel stood stock still in the centre of the bar, jaws clenched and breathing audibly through her flaring nostrils. In her tightly clenched hand was an umbrella held at the ready to strike. Everyone was transfixed but the sight of her, snorting, quivering, on the edge of explosion.

"Ethel. Just a minute, now," said Molly. Ethel's head turned sharply toward Molly. The eyes narrowed as if to say, what did you say to me?" Is there something wrong, Ethel?" said Molly. The answer couldn't have been more obvious if Ethel has entered with her hair on fire.

She made a noise somewhere between a wheeze and a grunt and turned to scrutinize everyone in the room. Barry seemed to be her target of choice and she locked him in her sights. Maggie stepped forward and placed her hand on Ethel's arm. When Ethel looked at her, Maggie simply shook her head and silently mouthed the word 'no'. Ethel sucked air and then released Barry and moved to the bar. She looked up at Molly with a blur of desperation. Molly responded by taking down a glass and pouring Ethel a stiff shot of Remy Martin brandy. Ethel looked at Molly, looked at the glass, then grabbed it and downed the brandy in a single gulp.

She reached for her purse but Molly simply held up her hand to decline payment. Ethel gestured toward her purse. Molly persisted that it wasn't necessary. Ethel conceded and closed her purse. Ethel wilted like a slowly leaking balloon and flopped onto one of the bar stools. It was a tragicomic mime that begged to be directed by D.W. Griffith and underscored with piano.

Nobody spoke, nobody moved until Ethel finally turned and walked to the door in measured steps, sharply contrasting the fury of her entrance. She paused, smoothed her jacket and, without turning back, made her exit.

"What in God's name was that all about, does anyone know?" said Paddy.

"I've no idea." Molly crossed to the door and looked down the street to ensure her curmudgeonly visitor had not come to harm. "Oh, dear."

"What is it?" asked Paddy.

"She just took a swipe at Norm Clancy. Do you think I should go after her?"

"Hell, no," said Paddy.

"I think I know what's wrong," Everyone turned to Maggie. "I'm just not sure I should say."

"You may as well," said Barry. "Everyone knows."

"Veronica's pregnant."

There was an audible yelp from the Ladies Lounge as Betty and her sister strained against the bar to be sure they didn't miss a snippet of news.

"Bloody hell," said Paddy.

"What's happening? What did she say?" Joanna almost vibrated with anticipation.

"It's Ethel's little girl, Veronica. She's, preggers," said Betty.

I think Mrs Patterson just found out," said Maggie.

"Ever since Veronica got those breasts, I said watch out to Ethel, I told her, you're going to have to watch that girl, I said," said Betty.

"That's enough, Betty," said Molly.

"She flaunts them; brazen she is."

"That'll do, Betty."

"What's a fifteen year old girl doing dressed like that, all pushed up?"

"That's right," said Joanna. "All pushed up, flaunting them."

It took Norm Clancy's boisterous entrance into the bar to silence the nattering sisters. Norm was even more ruddy than usual as he stammered to find the necessary words. "What the hell are you serving in here?" He quickly walked out the door again and looked down the street to be sure Ethel had indeed gone. "I saw Ethel Patterson leaving here, must admit that was a bit of a surprise in itself, so I say to her, how's things with you today, Mrs

Patterson? I couldn't have been more respectful, I swear. She mutters something about 'men' and then tells me to keep it in my pants and wallops me with her umbrella! What the hell had she been drinking?"

"I think she's just having a difficult day, Norm," said Molly.

"You think? I think she's lost her bloody mind. You can't go around hitting people with umbrellas, that's just not on."

"Seems her daughter's pregnant," said Molly.

"Oh," said Norm.

"She's just what, fifteen?" said Molly.

"Yes," said Maggie.

"Oh, that'd do it," said Norm.

"No surprise though," said Barry." She's been, you know, doing it a lot."

"That's a terrible thing to say," said Betty Wright.

"It's no worse than what you said, Mrs Wright," said Barry, defending his position.

"It sounds awful, but I'm afraid it's true," said Maggie. "She's been a bit silly."

Veronica was always a little wild, partly in rebellion against Ethel's dictatorial home rule, and partly in defence against the ennui of a small country town. Her fantasy life was vivid and exotic, and she wasn't shy about sharing it with anyone who would indulge her. Maggie knew how to untangle Veronica's truths and fantasies and could name each and every young man on the football team who'd had his way with her.

Maggie believed that there was more to this new tale of rapture. This was not about a boy. Veronica rhapsodized about her 'man' and how he was mature and sophisticated and would take here away to exotic and mysterious places. But to give things the right perspective, Veronica thought Tasmania was exotic and mysterious.

"It must have been difficult for the poor girl to tell her mother," said Molly.

"She didn't. Mrs Patterson found out from Phyllis Henderson who was buying six cans of peas at the grocery shop; they had a special on. Phyllis overheard Gloria Morgan who works for Doctor Horton, she was talking to Archie and Mavis Doyle at the grocers and, anyway, Gloria said Veronica had been in to see the doctor and why, which was really rude of her to mention. So that's how Phyllis knew and she lives across the street from Mrs Patterson, so she asked Ethel over for a cup of tea and told her."

"So who's the dad, Maggie, do you know?" asked Paddy.

"No. I know she was seeing a couple of blokes on the football team, but..."

"Gimme the names," said Norm, "I'll soon find out who did it."

"I don't think it's one of them, not the way Veronica was talking," said Maggie.

"Well, what did she say?" Norm was pressing for details.

"Yes, tell us everything," said Betty.

Maggie never considered Veronica a real friend but felt she deserved more respect than to have her private life dissected in a public bar.

"I'm sorry but I have to go," she said. "We're having dinner at the farm tonight and I promised to clean up."

Along with the pub, the Scott's maintained a small farm on the road to Jameson. It was relatively low maintenance and reserved for grazing but it provided a welcome respite from life in the hotel.

"Fair enough, what was said privately between you and Veronica is best left that way," said Paddy. "There is one other thing I would like to ask you though. Has your uncle been in town, we haven't seen as much of him lately?" said Paddy.

"Oh, you will Mr Brennan. You're on his mind, I can tell you that much. He's here today so he'll show up all right. He's been acting strange lately. Don't know what that's about. Anyway, I should be going."

"I could give you a lift to the farm, if you like," said Barry.

"I am not going to sit on the back of your mare, if that's what you're thinking, Barry Hutton."

"No, I was thinking of a comfortable truck with windows and all." Barry looked hopefully at Norm who just shook his head knowing he could not deny the young man. "It's across the street. Keys are in it," said Norm. Don't take forever I've still got a lot to do."

"You're a good man, Norm Clancy, and God will repay you handsomely," said Barry. He took Maggie by the hand and they were off.

Seeing the two young lovers leave amid giggles and laughter made any other conversations in the bar seem inconsequential.

Betty and Joanna looked anxious. "You ladies ready for another drink then?" asked Paddy.

"I don't know," said Betty. "I am very fond of a good conversation. So I might stay if that's the case. What could we talk about do you think?"

"Well, I think the world is going to hell in a hand basket and I intend to expound on that for a while," said Michael.

"And I'm going to talk about the footy," said Norm.

The two women considered the menu and shook their heads. "Don't fancy any of that. I think we might go and see how Ethel's doing. I'm worried she might, you know."

"I don't think she'll doing anything foolish," said Molly.

"She's got a gun," said Betty. That got everyone's attention. "Oh yes, she has a gun and it's a big one." The two sisters gathered up their possessions and headed for the door.

"And it's a shotgun," said Joanna.

"And she can use it!" said Betty with a knowing nod.

"Brilliant," said Michael with a laugh. "Business could be picking up,"

"It really is too bad," said Molly. "She's so young. Maybe all she was after was a little more love."

"Love is a beautiful thing," said Rabbit. "We all have to learn to love each other no matter what, I say."

"I'll drink to that," said Paddy and the rest of the bar enthusiastically agreed. Molly crossed to Paddy and slipped her arm around his waist. He put his arm around her shoulder, drew her close against him and kissed her on the top of the head.

"A lot of crazy people out there." Michael raised his glass to the madness he perceived.

"She's a very silly girl and she's made some bad choices, no argument there, but she's having a baby. That should be a happy thing," said Molly.

There was a round of silent nods as the survivors in the bar acknowledged Molly's sentiment. Something stirred inside Rabbit who shuffled on his stool as he struggled bring his thoughts to words. "Did I tell you about the first time I was in love?' he said.

"No, but I'll buy you another drink if you promise not to," said Paddy.

"It's a beautiful story. You don't know what you're missing."

Paddy held up the bottle of port. "What's it to be? You want to talk or drink?"

"You're an insensitive bastard, Paddy Brennan, you know that?" Rabbit considered the option briefly, drained his glass and placed it on the bar for a refill. "Perhaps another day, you'll get lucky and I'll tell you. Until then, youse'll just have to imagine." He wheezed with amusement and raised his glass in a salute.

Chapter Twenty-Eight

Any time Jenkins had been in town since his altercation with Paddy, he had refrained from entering the Imperial Hotel. Instead, he chose to irritate from a distance. He would park his car on the opposite side of the street and monitor the hotel to ensure that the six o'clock closing was rigidly observed. Only when satisfied that the last patron had been evicted at six fifteen would he start the car and move on.

Anyone with less suspicion of his motives, would assume that was the end of surveillance for the day. Paddy knew better. He knew that Jenkins' apparent decision to abandon his watch was a ruse. Paddy knew he's still be lurking in the shadows hoping to catch Paddy selling someone a couple of bottles of Victoria Bitter after hours. Jenkins was driven to build a case against the Brennans.

Paddy decided his persistence shouldn't go without its just reward. The front door of the Imperial Hotel opened just far enough for Paddy to slip out of the light and into the dark of the night. It looked suspicious. It was intentionally so.

In his right hand he carried a large black leather bag, rather like an oversized doctor's bag. It was obviously heavy. He glanced to the left and to the right and furtively skulked off into the shadows that fringed the street.

He'd walked no more than fifty yards when the headlights of a car blasted through the black and pinned him against a storefront. From the darkness came a voice. It was measured and deliberate edged with an arrogant confidence.

"Where the hell do you think you're going with that?" said Jenkins.

"What?" Paddy looked dumbfounded and vaguely guilty. "What do you want?"

"Let's see what's in the bag, mister?" said Jenkins moving into the light.

"What?"

"You heard me," Jenkins reached for the black bag. Paddy withdrew it from his reach.

"Bugger off, this is personal property," said Paddy.

"No sir. I think you are attempting to transport alcohol for the purposes of selling it after hours."

"You think so?"

"Yes, I do. Hand it over Brennan."

"All right. I guess you got me." Paddy simple placed the bag on the ground and stepped back from it. He held his hands out to the side of his body as if in surrender. Jenkins could barely contain his glee as he grabbed the bag and dragged it to his side of the footpath and then snapped open the brass lock.

It was not quite as he had hoped. There were no bottles of beer or brandy. There was just a stack of old newspapers. Dirty, dusty old newspapers.

"I was just going to take them up to the hospital to see if anyone wanted something to read," said Paddy quietly relishing Jenkins' anger at being duped. "But look mate, if you see something you want to keep just say the word. I don't think anyone would mind."

Jenkins didn't reply. He simply retreated to his car and dove away.

Paddy repeated the act the following three nights, once leaving through the front of the hotel and twice through the rear entrance. Twice Jenkins called him on the action. Twice more he was equally frustrated. Jenkins had been in town for almost a week using Mansfield as his base to terrorize the district.

It was almost eight o'clock at night, and the town had fallen quiet. Paddy opened the front door of the hotel and walked across the street to where Jenkins was parked. He leaned against the front of the car while he finished his cigarette. He flicked the cigarette away from the car into an explosion of yellow sparks. Paddy indicated to Jenkins to wind down the window.

"You know the night you didn't stop me?" said Paddy. "That was the night you should have." He flashed a smile at Jenkins. "Look at you. Just look at you, sitting here in the night with one hand on your shiny badge and the other on your little dick hoping against hope that you can catch me with a couple of bottles in my bag. How pathetic is that?" Paddy took a couple paces back toward the hotel and stopped. "By the way," he said. "If you get cold out here and need a drink to warm you up, don't come to my pub. You're not welcome."

If Jenkins was in town and Paddy was bored or simply wanted to humiliate the man, he would play the suitcase game. It happened at least a dozen times and every time Jenkins would rise to the bait. Then, on a calm quiet night when Jenkins had almost had his fill of waiting, Paddy emerged from the hotel.

This was different. He didn't follow the same course as usual. This time he walked briskly toward the railway station and then doubled back. Jenkins waited as long as he could stand it and then turned on the headlights and drove quickly toward Paddy.

"Hold it, Brennan. Hold it right there," was the command as Jenkins leapt from his car.

"What is it?" Paddy had never looked more guilty.

"Just open the bloody bag!"

"All right," said Paddy. "You win this time, but just so you can see what you need to see." Paddy raised his arm as if to start a race and suddenly the street was flooded with light as the headlights from two cars and a truck lit up the front of the hotel. There in the light were most of the football team and a spattering of the locals, all with full glasses of beer.

Paddy picked up the bag and turned it upside down and papers fluttered and fell to the ground around him. This was the cue for the crowd to raise their glasses in a victory salute and cheer. It was a joyous moment of disrespect and defiance. Jenkins had no recourse but to swallow the humiliation, and drive away.

Jenkins seemed to have given up his vigil and although Paddy never played the bag game again, the retelling of the tale fuelled gales of laughter and filled many hours at the Imperial Hotel.

Chapter Twenty-Nine

To say the game against Benalla was pivotal would be an understatement. They'd won the trophy last year and had been a powerhouse early in the season. They looked like a certainty to repeat. As if in answer to the prayers of other coaches, Benalla began to suffer a rash of injuries. How inglorious the fall from grace! The previous season they sat at the very top of the pack; this season they struggled to stave off total elimination.

A win for Mansfield that afternoon would vault them to first place overall and give them home field advantage for the playoffs. A loss would boot Benalla outside the top four and totally out of contention. That spot on the wall where Benalla had planned to hang this year's premiership flag would remain naked.

You could debate whether the five hundred people who rimmed the field in Mansfield came to see a gripping do-or-die effort or whether they were looking forward to seeing the archenemy, Benalla, being drubbed.

There were some heroic marks and some fine play, but it wasn't a real contest. Benalla looked out of step and the body language spelled defeat. The scoreboard didn't disagree; by half time Mansfield had racked up a score of 10.8 (68 points) to Benalla's lame 4.11 (35 points). The outcome was inevitable and the Mansfield supporters had already crowded the corrugated tin

197

structure beside the scoreboard where the beer was stored in chests of ice.

Molly had insisted that Paddy should go to the football that day. "It'd be good for you to get away from the bar for a few hours," she said. "It'll just be the usual crowd listening to the races and if it gets really busy Barry will come over and help." It didn't take a lot of work to convince him. A chance to go to the footy, drink beer with his mates, and abuse the other team was just what he needed. He had worked hard to win over the players but being the one to supply the beer for the team on occasions like this was what he was after.

The Prince of Wales had what appeared to have a stranglehold on the football business. The social committee from the football club ordered the bottles from the hotel. Scott would deliver them to the football ground and then the club would, in turn, sell beer to raise funds for its operation. The same applied to St. John's Catholic Church. The grounds became one big beer garden and members of the church committees poured the beers and served an assortment of foods to raise money for the church and school. It was almost as widely anticipated as the game itself and had been dubbed by some locals 'the best post-game piss-up' in Victoria. If Mansfield made the playoffs the celebrations would run late into the night and the coffers would grow even fatter

As the third quarter neared conclusion the gap between the two teams widen even further. The fourth quarter would be a rout. "They're playing well today," said Paddy to Norm Clancy who was studiously watching, notebook in hand.

"Not bad," replied Norm. "Benalla's had the shit beaten out of it the last few games so I think they're ready to call it quits."

"Maybe but we've still got a good team out there."

"Bloody good, Paddy. Best we've had for years. Can't tell them that though or they'd slack off. Little Mozzie's really found his game, bloody ripper." Mozzie's real name was Morley, one reason why he was glad he'd been labelled Mozzie by his teammates. A tough, nuggetty young bloke with legs like pistons, he'd shown promise for two seasons without ultimately delivering the goods. Norm never gave up on him and felt a personal pride that the little bugger was now a terror on the field. "I reckon we can take it this year. Shepparton's come on strong, gonna be the one to beat but I think we've got the stuff."

The siren blared and those who hadn't already lost interest headed for the shed to get a cold beer. "Come on," Norm said to Paddy. "We'd better get a move on and I think it's my shout."

Chapter Thirty

Barry was holding down the bar while Molly kept an eye on the street outside the hotel. Molly was never careless with her clothes, but on that day she had taken even a little extra care. Her cotton dress was freshly pressed, her hair well brushed and she had taken time to apply a little rouge to complement her lipstick.

When the black Ford came to a halt outside the Imperial Hotel, she raised her hand in acknowledgement. From out of the car stepped Griffith. He took off his grey fedora and offered his hand to Molly.

"Very nice to see you again, Mrs Brennan."

"Good to see you, too. In your letter you said you would be here between two and three in the afternoon and you're right on time. I have no idea how you can plan that far in advance."

"I have to make good use of my time." His smile was genuine but made a point that there was little room for such casual dialogue. Molly took him on a short tour of the Imperial Hotel. They didn't dwell on the rooms upstairs but when they reached the kitchen and returned to the public areas, Griffith stood quietly in the middle of room and carefully surveyed any improvements or upgrades.

"I must say you've made a world of difference here."

"Thank you."

"I was a little concerned, well, to be honest, more than a little when you agreed to come here. I reiterated to Paddy how rough it was but nothing seemed to intimidate him. I don't know if I have ever seen someone so determined to make a go of it."

"It has meant a lot to him. Well, to both of us really. It still does. May I offer you a drink?"

They sat in the lounge. Molly had lemonade. Griffith had beer. She studied him for a minute or two as his eyes continued to dart around the hotel. He nodded a silent affirmation of his approval and raised his glass to Molly.

"Very nice," he said.

"A little elbow grease makes a big difference."

"It certainly does. Did you do some work in the kitchen? I seem to remember the cupboards literally falling off the wall," said Griffith, still somewhat awed by the changes.

"Oh yes," replied Molly with a laugh. "The kitchen was one of the first projects."

"Well, I am very, very impressed and congratulations to both of you."

"Thank you."

"Can I expect Paddy to be here shortly?" He took a gold watch from pocket of his vest and glanced at it.

"No, I'm afraid not." Molly was very anxious about how the next few minutes would unfold. She didn't fuss or fidget, she just sat a little more upright than before and took a very deep breath. "Paddy is out this afternoon. There is a football match and it was important for him to be there."

"I see."

"There are many people in town for the game and that's when Paddy is at his best: with people; getting people to come to the hotel, that's what it's all about. Getting new business."

"I see. That makes it a little awkward though." He reached into the inside pocket of his grey pinstriped suit and took out a neatly folded letter. He carefully opened it and scanned it again. "Are you aware that he wrote me a letter?"

"He says he wants to renegotiate the terms of our agreement. Now I understand that the football game is considered important but I question if it's more important than this. Paddy should be here."

"Well, Mr Griffith. "I'm here and I would be happy to discuss the agreement with you."

"You've read the letter?"

"Actually, I wrote it."

That obviously took Griffith by surprise. He took a white linen handkerchief from his breast pocket, exhaled on his glasses and cleaned them thoroughly as if seeing her more clearly would clarify his confusion.

"A question. Did you write this for Paddy, simply because you have better penmanship?"

"No."

He held up his finger to discourage her from going on. "One more thing. You say you wrote the letter?"

"Yes."

"Does Paddy know you wrote the letter?"

"No, he doesn't."

"I must say Mrs Brennan this is highly irregular, very highly irregular, and I'm not sure it's appropriate for us to be discussing this."

Griffith was obviously disturbed and his consternation eroded Molly confidence. Her hands trembled ever so slightly and she felt her throat closing. "I wrote the letter to you..." She stopped mid sentence to compose her thoughts. Her face was flushed with embarrassment and a modicum of anger. "I wrote that letter because that's what I had to do."

"What do you mean, you had to?"

Molly started to speak and nothing came out. She took a sip of her lemonade and tried again. "What you have to understand Mr Griffith is that this is a sort of partnership. Paddy takes care of the customers and I take care of the other things, like doing the books, writing the cheques, things like that."

"It has been my experience Mrs Brennan that partners share information of such import."

"Yes, I am sure, but there are times...there are times..." Molly moved her glass around the table as a diversion while she considered how to mollify Griffith and continue discussion of the agreement. "Tell me Mr Griffith, how well do you know Paddy?"

"How well do I know him? I would say I know him well enough. I wouldn't have trusted him with a property if I didn't know him."

"What do you think of him?"

"I'm not sure how that is relevant." Griffith took his time to consider this. He sat back in his chair and held Molly in his gaze. "You don't consider this to be extraordinary?"

"No, sir, I don't. What I think would be extraordinary and wrong, very wrong, would be for me to sit by and do nothing. Paddy is working his heart out in this pub. You know how terrible this place was when we moved in and, to be honest, I was a little shocked that, being in the condition it was, you would even offer it to Paddy. Oh I know we didn't have much and anything seemed like a bonus at this time but trust me Mr Griffith, this hotel was no gift."

Molly was suddenly very aware of Griffith just sitting opposite her with his arms folded across his chest. He wasn't attempting to speak He wasn't grimacing. He was just sitting there. Listening to her. It was too late to consider how he might react. She was too far down that road. She took another deep breath.

"We have worked hard to get where we are and we're barely putting bread on the table. If Paddy knew how bad it was, it would hurt him terribly, and I won't have that. I won't have him feeling like he failed because he hasn't. There are many good people in this town but it's suffering, from the heat, from the drought, you name it. So what it comes down to is this, Mr Griffith: we need to renegotiate the terms of the agreement. If we are to keep on living and working here we can't pay you any more than half of what we pay now. I know that may seem like I'm asking a lot but the truth of it is that we can't pay more and it's not worth more. If you choose to foreclose on us, the hotel will fall away to what it was before and you'll have nothing to sell. At least with us, we may be paying for this hotel for the rest of our lives, but it will be worth something."

"You make it sound like an ultimatum," he said after considerable thought.

"I don't mean to. That's just a the way it is."

Griffith rose from his chair and walked to the door leading back into the street. Molly felt totally conflicted. She had been expecting him for two weeks and had gone over and over in her head what she might say. She was glad she got it out but fearful that they would lose everything. How would she explain that to Paddy?

Griffith walked back to the table and stood looking down at Molly. She rose from her chair to meet him eye to eye.

"Can if freshen up that beer for you, Mr Griffith?" she said just as if he was a regular.

"No, thank you," he replied. "If I concede, would you tell Paddy of the new terms?"

Molly hadn't thought that far ahead, he'd caught her without a prepared response. "I honestly don't know."

"Don't you think he has a right to know? It's his name above the door after all."

Molly gathered up the two glasses from the table and walked back to the bar. "Barry, give me a fresh beer for Mr Griffith and I'll have a brandy, please." Barry quickly pulled the beer and poured Molly a shot of Remy Martin brandy and topped it with ginger ale. She took a glass in each hand and returned to Griffith. "Yes, Mr Griffith, I will tell Paddy everything he needs to know when it's right to do so, but I am not going to do it to make myself feel better or make you feel better. I'll tell him when it's in his best interests to know. In the meantime, there isn't anybody this side of Ayres Rock who can do a better job of making this pub into something than Paddy. And I'll be here working with him counting the pennies and making sure you get your monthly dues. I think between the three of us we can make a go of this, but it will take all three of us." She handed him his beer. "Shall we drink to that?"

Never in her life had she been so bold or forthright. She had spent many a sleepless night worrying about how to resolve the finances. Once she decided that maintaining the status quo was totally unviable she knew that the agreement would have to adjust to accommodate the realities. The dilemma was how. She didn't want to keep anything from Paddy but she also knew that he depended upon her totally to manage the finances. Making friends and drumming up business was his strong suit. The surplus or shortfall of money in the till would, of course, have been of real concern. How to manage that would be somewhat beyond him, she feared, and the knowledge would simply serve to distract him from doing what he did best: drumming up new business.

The decision to write to Griffith was not a hasty one but she recognized that immediate action was essential. Better to solve the problem and explain later, if ever, was her resolution. Now, with Griffith sitting opposite her she felt that the response she had hoped for, seemed unlikely. No matter what he said, she felt assured that what she had done was right. It wouldn't be her action that would cost them the hotel; it would be the lack of it. The deed was done. The terms were tabled. All she could do now was wait for an answer.

The look on Griffith's face was indecipherable. The look that was once locked on Molly had drifted into space. Whatever else could be said of Griffith he was first and foremost a businessman, and behind the glaze in his eyes he was no doubt adding up the numbers.

Molly wanted to look away and appear a little more nonchalant, a little less dependent on his concessions. She couldn't do that. She studied every twitch, every grimace, and every sigh. Griffith mentally re-entered the room. He looked toward the bar where two of the customers were laughing heartily. He moved his glass to the right. The condensation had formed a watermark on the brightly polished table. He took out a crisp, white handkerchief, blotted up the water and gently rubbed the table to restore the shine. The slightest smile creased his cheek. He quietly raised his glass and took a hearty drink. "You serve a good glass of beer, Mrs Brennan."

"Yes, we do, thank you."

"Do you ever come to Melbourne, Mrs Brennan?"

"Not often Mr Griffith, but I have sisters who live there and I hope to visit soon."

"Very good. When you are down why don't you call me and we can make arrangements for you to collect a copy of the revised agreement. Would that be suitable?"

"Yes, Mr Griffith, that would be most suitable.

He took out his fob watch and checked the time again. "Then if you will excuse me, I have a long way to go and I'm not fond of driving in the dark." He offered Molly his hand. She took it and they sealed the moment with one decisive handshake. Molly sat quietly at the table after he left the bar. She wanted to cheer. She wanted to cry. She wanted to buy everyone in the bar a drink to celebrate. When she glanced around she realized that the only person there was Barry who as drying some glasses.

"Barry," she said. "What you heard a few minutes ago. I mean, if you happened to overhear...."

"Overhear what?" said Barry, "I don't know what you're talking about, Mrs Brennan. I was too busy with the customers to hear anything. Was I supposed to hear anything?"

"No."

"Then it all worked out as it should, didn't it."

"Yes, thank you."

Molly knew if she stayed there the full realization of what she had accomplished would descend upon her. She felt emotion welling up inside her but didn't want to cry in public. So she went to the kitchen, made a fresh pot of tea and decided that crying should be reserved for joy and sorrow. This was business, just business.

Chapter Thirty-One

The following few weeks showed a measurable growth in business at the Imperial Hotel, largely due to Paddy working the crowd at the football. It still rankled him that the Prince of Wales Hotel got the biggest slice of the football club's business even though Robert Scott was never sighted at a game. Paddy determined that he would match Scott's apparent lack of interest with an obvious commitment to the club and everyone associated with it. He had even made a point of attending games away from home to help highlight the contrast between the two publicans and further insinuate himself into the club's favour.

Despite nature's nagging reluctance to honour the seasons and deliver the needed rainfalls, life in the hotel was relatively buoyant. This was due to a combination of things: Molly's relief that the financial burden had been eased; her dogged insistence on making the place shine; her continued ability to scavenge flowers; Paddy's natural good humour; and his sense that he was making greater inroads with the club.

The big day had arrived. Mansfield had struggled a little to retain its form but held on to top of the ladder by the slimmest of margins. As predicted, Shepparton blazed their way into the playoffs by soundly beating anyone in their path. Despite

Mansfield having home game advantage for the playoffs, the bookies had Shepparton a two to one favourite for the premiership.

The town was in high gear. The main street never looked busier as people came from all over the district to enjoy the day. The excitement reached as far as Melbourne and Bill and Elsie decided to take the train up on Saturday, and stay over that night before heading back to the city. Alice was not one to be left out and, once assured that the departure times didn't conflict with mass, she was in.

Anne had driven over from Benalla the previous evening; she had been more of a regular visitor over the past couple of weeks since Joe had been shipped north again. The transformation of the bar had not escaped her. On her first visit since Molly had gone to work on it, Anne just quietly walked around taking it all in with a brandy in one hand and a ciggie in the other. "It's grouse, Bub," seemed to sum it all up. She put her arms around her sister and held her tight. "Good on you."

Molly hadn't told anyone about the baby; living though it was bad enough, constantly reviving it would only make it worse. Paddy had told Anne. Anne didn't tell Molly that Paddy had told her but Molly knew he had and Anne knew that Molly knew but felt it was best not to mention it. It would be talked about over a cup of tea when the time was right.

Anne adored the whole pub experience and often stayed overnight. You didn't have to ask her twice to help out in the bar, particularly on a day like that when the place was busy from the time they opened the doors. She loved the socialization and the customers enjoyed seeing a fresh face.

Anne was quick to laugh and not easily rattled as long as she had her smokes handy.

More than once, Anne had suggested that Paddy and Molly take off for a weekend in the city. "You need to get away, you do," said Anne. "It'd do you both the world of good." She gave Barry a nudge. "We'd be all right, wouldn't we?"

"We'd be great, no worries," said Barry.

Anne called out to Paddy and Molly. "He's been after me for weeks now. He can't wait for you two to bugger off so he can get me on my own." She took a deep drag on her smoke and wheezed out a hearty laugh. "What do you say, Barry?"

Molly was amused to see the young man blush as he laughed it off.

"Hey gorgeous! Me and me cobber are dyin' of thirst over here. How about a little attention?" said one of the regulars from the lumberyard.

"You see," said Anne. "They're all after me."

"I'll tell you what," said Molly. "We might take you up on that in a couple of weeks. What do you say, Paddy? I'd love to get into the city, do a little shopping."

"I reckon we might be able to do that," he said as he adroitly juggled a handful of beer glasses. Standing in front of the tap he seemed momentarily lost in a thought. "Just a minute, mate," he said with a smile to the man in front of him waiting for a refill. He crossed to the far end of the bar, glasses in hand where Molly was standing. There was a glint in Paddy's eye as he quietly looked at her. "How you going? All right?"

Molly simply nodded, enjoying this surprisingly intimate moment. "How about you?"

"Couldn't be better," Paddy was unabashedly proud of the way Molly had rebounded from the loss of their baby. He had felt a deep frustration and disappointment that he had not been able to do something, anything to alter the outcome. Although that sense of impotence still plagued him they were both more committed than ever to have a family.

Molly wanted to kiss him but felt that sort of thing in the bar would only embarrass him. To her surprise, crowd or no crowd

Paddy placed his free hand on the side of her face and kissed her lightly. He smiled again, gave her a quick wink and quickly returned to the bar.

Molly felt that despite the struggle, despite the hardships and gruelling work, both of them being there together in that space, in that time, was just right.

Chapter Thirty-Two

It was settled, the women would hold the fort. Not an onerous task considering that once the game started the place would empty out, save for the few dusty survivors who religiously wagered a few shillings on the horse races every Saturday.

Elsie had taken charge of the kitchen and made sandwiches for Barry, Bill and Paddy before they were shunted out. "Oh, what a lovely chook that is!" said Elsie; it didn't take a lot to please Elsie. "Look at that Bill, look at the chook. We can't get a chook like that in the city. Look at it Bill, isn't that a lovely chook."

"It's lovely," said Bill, not really caring.

"You're lucky to find a chook like that," she said to Molly as she picked it up to check its heft, as if she was judging at an agricultural show. "Where did you get a beauty like this?"

"You just have to know the right people," said Molly, returning the celebrated chook to its platter. "I thought we might roast it for supper."

"Lovely. Be sure to save the carcass and I'll make some soup."

"Here we go," said Alice as she placed three glasses on the table: a brandy and dry for herself, a sherry for Elsie, and lemonade for Molly. "They're waiting for you in the bar, Bill. Paddy's getting impatient."

"Bill, where the hell are you?" came the voice from the bar.

"Told you," said Alice.

"Off you go, have fun," said Elsie.

"You don't want to come with us?" said Bill. "It should be a bloody ripper.

"I'm sure, but I'll enjoy a visit with the girls just as much."

So the stage was set. The boys were off to the footy and the girls stayed home. Everyone seemed content but none knew that a bigger drama than the football final was about to unfold.

Chapter Thirty-Three

Almost exactly a week prior, emboldened by her meeting with Griffith, Molly decided to tackle Robert Scott. She told Paddy she was going to get some groceries but instead, she headed straight for the Prince of Wales Hotel. As she approached the front of the hotel her bravery wavered. She walked past the hotel and up the street appearing to look in windows. If she walked past the hotel once, she did so five or six times and was about to call it off when Scott left the hotel with a short, balding man by his side.

"Mr Scott!" Molly called out.

Scott turned to see her approaching. "Mrs Brennan. How are you, today?" He tipped his hat to her and opened the door of his truck.

"Fine, thank you. I wonder if you could spare me a moment, please."

"Of course. What can I do for you?" His words were courteous enough but his demeanour was that of a man who would much rather be somewhere else. He didn't bother to shut the door, a clear indication that he intended to keep the meeting brief.

Molly was momentarily stumped. She hadn't mentally rehearsed what to say with a stranger present. She looked at the inconvenient man who was obviously disinterested in this intrusive woman. Scott sensed her distraction.

"Mrs Brennan do you know Clive Barlow?" Molly shook her head. "Molly Brennan, this is Clive Barlow. Clive was president of the football club until he moved to the city."

"Pleased to meet you, back for a visit?" said Molly.

"Business actually," said the short man in the too-tight three-piece suit.

"Molly and her husband, Paddy, are trying to make a go of the Imperial Hotel."

"Really. Good luck." It wasn't said without obvious malice, but it was clear that the 'good luck' comment implied that he thought the Imperial Hotel was a lost cause. "Look, Robert, I've got a couple of things to take care of, why don't I catch up with you a little later," said Barlow.

"Sure." The two men shook hands and Barlow walked briskly up the street.

"Clive still takes a very active interest in the club. He's a good man. Now, what was it you wanted?"

"It's a coincidence really, him being with the football club. That's what I wanted to talk to you about. Well, about the finals, to be precise."

"You want to talk about football?" He was confused about what this woman wanted.

"Well, more precisely about supplying the beer for the events."

Scott was surprised to hear this and folded his arm in a defensive pose. "What about it?"

"Well," said Molly. "It's about the Prince of Wales supplying the beer to both the football ground and to the church hall after the game."

"Go on."

"Well, I was wondering if you would perhaps consider sharing the responsibility."

"Sharing?"

"Yes, you would still supply the beer during the game which I am sure is by far the larger part of the order, and I though we could supply the activities after the game."

"I see." Scott's apparent reluctance to offer more than that made Molly uncomfortable. "And why would I want to do that?" he finally added.

"Because it would help us enormously and because the football game and everything around it is a community event, and it seems to me that it would be nice if we could all share it, sort of like partners in the community."

"Mrs Brennan." His tone was that of someone reprimanding a small child. "Do you have any idea what you are asking?"

"Yes, I think I do."

"No, I don't think you do. I've been here a long time and I intend to be here a lot longer. Listen to me." He took a deep breath as he assembled his thoughts. "I admire your courage in coming here to ask this, but the reality is that the town is not doing well right now and I don't think there's enough business to share, not if we both want to keep the lights on. So, the idea of giving away a prime piece of business just doesn't make good business sense. I am sure you can appreciate that. Now, if you'll excuse me."

He tipped his hat again and stepped into the truck. Molly put her hand out to stop the door from being closed. Scott did not appreciate the gesture.

"I'd like to think that if things were the other way around and we had all the business and you were struggling, we'd find a way to make it work."

"You're dreaming, Mrs Brennan. I'm running a business, not a charity."

"We don't want to fight you for our share, Mr Scott, but we're here to make a go of it, make no mistake about that."

Scott bristled and stepped a little closer to Molly. "Is that a threat, Mrs Brennan?"

"Just think about it, please," said Molly. "It would mean a lot to us."

"I'll think about what you said, all right." He got into his truck and pulled the door shut.

"Thank you," said Molly.

The truck engine sputtered to life, Scott slapped it into gear and without looking back drove off down the street. This would be one more thing she wouldn't tell Paddy for now. She didn't like the way the list was growing.

Chapter Thirty-Four

Somehow the larger the crowd, the later the football game started, and the more protracted the breaks between quarters became. Nobody was surprised. Nobody cared. There were more things to do than watch your watch. This was a day for young and old, rich and poor, tall and short, to gather together and meet friends they perhaps hadn't seen since last year or last week. It gave everyone a chance to shout and cheer and jeer and tell lies: a true community celebration with exciting footy to break up the drinking.

The game itself was everything everyone hoped for. The score continually bounced back and forth, leaving Shepparton with a five-point lead at half time, only to see Mansfield claws its way back to head into the fourth quarter with a seven-point advantage.

Paddy, Bill and Barry had hooked up with Michael Talbot and they were keeping one eye on the game as they edged closer to the beer pavilion. "I almost didn't make it," said Michael. "You'd think people would know better than to die right before the grand final."

"Bloody inconsiderate," said Paddy.

"No kidding, Two of them. If the coffins hadn't arrived from Melbourne this morning, I'd be sitting there waiting for them now."

"Shocking," said Bill. "All this talk of coffins is making me thirsty. Come on." There was general agreement that a cleansing ale was needed, and they moved through the crowd toward the refreshments.

"Paddy Brennan! Mr Brennan!" The woman's voice was urgent and loud enough to cut through the cheering and yelling. Paddy peered into the melee of people that surrounded him but there was no clue who had sought him so urgently.

"Mr Brennan! Here! Please!" Paddy turned around quickly to see Ethel Patterson erupt through the crowd. "Thank God, I found you." She clutched her breast and fanned herself with her handbag while she attempted to catch her breath.

"What's up?" asked Paddy.

"That's what I want to ask you!" She placed her hand across her chest as if to steady her heart and then took a deep very breath. "Betty Wright went to the hotel to see you but the woman in the bar told her you were at the game. So we came right over here to find you. I don't know where Betty is now mind you, I've lost her somewhere in the crowd. Trying to find anyone here is impossible. Anyway, Robert Scott dropped off a few dozen bottles so we'd have something just in case, thank goodness."

"Okay Ethel, calm down, calm down." He clasped her arm firmly to help steady her. "Now, what are you talking about?

"The beer. That's what I'm talking about. The bloody beer! I asked Mr Scott if he'd seen you but he said he was sure you weren't at the game, which surprised me because the woman at the hotel was sure you were."

"That's rubbish! I've seen Scott here today and I know he's seen me."

"Well, it was when he was bringing some beer to the church that he said you weren't anywhere to be found, and I know that's what he said because I was there when he said it but that's not the point. What really matters is where's the beer?"

Paddy was completely confused. This was obviously critical but Ethel made absolutely no sense to him.

"What beer?"

"What beer?" she said, incredulous at his response.

"Yes, you keep saying 'the beer, the beer' and I don't know what the hell you're talking about. What beer?" said Paddy.

"The beer you're supposed to send to St. John's. For the dinner. After the game. The tents are up and the women in the Guild have been cooking for days, everything is ready to go and they expect a record turnout this year, hundreds of people. What are we going to tell them if there's no beer? What?"

"I'm not supplying the beer."

"You certainly are. Of course you are. Robert Scott said so."

Paddy looked at Ethel as if she was speaking in tongues. There was a moment where everyone stood in stunned silence, checking each other in the hope that one of them could unravel the chaos. Although she didn't understand why, Ethel sensed she'd have to spell it out for Paddy.

"All right. Listen. Mr Scott told us that this year, he was doing the game and you were doing the rest. It was all set up with Mrs Brennan. All arranged. Didn't she tell you?"

"That's impossible," said Paddy, in utter disbelief.

"Well, Clive Burrows, a man I never did like or trust for that matter mind you, but he says he was there when Mrs Brennan spoke to Mr Scott, and that he'd witnessed the conversation. His very words."

Paddy turned and started to walk away, the other men followed him picking up the pace step by step. "Molly never agreed to this," he muttered.

"Where are you going?" shouted Ethel.

"To get your damn beer!"

"You've been set up, you know that don't you," Michael had moved up beside Paddy. "He's set you up. Cunning bastard."

Indeed Scott was cunning. He had planned this well. "I think it's only fair," he said to the committee the morning of the game. "It would help the Brennan's enormously and because the football game and everything around it is a community event and I just think it would be fitting if we all shared it, sort of like partners in the community." He had used Molly's words almost exactly.

Everyone commended him on his generosity. Granted this change in plans seemed to be made at the last minute but it didn't adversely affect any of the festivities and his motives certainly seemed admirable.

Just in case it hadn't occurred to anyone that Paddy Brennan might not come though, Scott added "Don't worry, I'll keep an eye on things just in case. The Brennans are still very inexperienced and if it looks like they're going to let us down, I'll make sure things are taken care of." Indeed he had already begun to paint himself as the saviour by supplying a few dozen to keep them going in light of Paddy's projected delinquency.

The plot thickened as the men approached the hotel. It was now 5:40 p.m. and by the time they got the order together it would be after the legal closing. There, perched outside in his car, was Jenkins waiting patiently for Paddy to attempt any after-hours delivery.

"Bastard!' said Paddy.

"He's set you up good, he has," said Michael.

"Looks like he's got you by the short and curlies, Paddy," said Bill.

"Be damned if I'll let him do this to us. We'll get the beer there or die trying." Paddy stopped abruptly. His eyes widened. Thoughts flashed through his mind so quickly he could barely get words out. "Okay, okay, okay, I've got it. I've got it."

"What? What is it?" said Bill.

Out of nowhere Paddy gave Mike a huge hug. "God bless you!" The other men were now even more confused. "Barry, you go with Mike, Bill you come with me. This is the plan." There was a quick and muffled exchange between the men. Michael muttered "Brilliant!' Then they split and hurried off in opposite directions,

Bill and Paddy headed directly for the hotel. On the way they passed Jenkins in his stationary car outside the hotel. Without missing a step Paddy pounded his fist on the roof of the car. There was a muffled cry of "shit" from inside the car as Jenkins leapt in his seat and jammed his leg into the steering wheel. The men never looked back and entered the hotel.

"How was the game?" asked Anne from behind the bar. The men ignored her and marched through to the kitchen. "Molly? You there?"

Molly was peeling some vegetables and Alice and Elsie were seated at the kitchen table with the ubiquitous cups of tea in their hands.

"Molly, did Scott tell you we were supplying all the beer at St. John's?"

"What?"

"You heard me." His was now discernibly angry. "Did he tell you that?"

"No."

"So you never talked to him about it?"

Molly felt she had been caught red handed. What should she do? She didn't know exactly what had happened to disturb Paddy but she knew it was serious, very serious. Her confused silence seemed to answer his question. "My God, you did, you did talk to him."

"Yes."

"Woman, what were you thinking? Jesus!"

"I'm sorry."

"You're sorry? Well, that's bloody great that is."

"Go easy, Paddy," Alice had never seen Paddy quite so angry.

"Stay out of this Alice! It's none of your business," said Paddy.

Molly stood there unable to defend herself; hey eyes welled up with tears of hurt and frustration. Elsie wanted to comfort her but Bill gestured to her to sit and be silent.

Paddy braced himself, hands on hips, and took deep calculated breaths in an attempt to steady himself. "What did you say to him? Exactly."

"I just said, I met him on the street that's all..."

"Tell me what you said!" he insisted.

"I just asked if he'd consider sharing the job and that it would mean a lot to us that's all."

"What did he say?"

"He said he'd think about it."

"And?"

"And nothing, I never heard from him again."

Paddy paced around the kitchen propelled by frustration. "Why would you do that and not tell me about it? You shouldn't have been talking to him about business in the first place, damn it."

"I am so sorry. I just thought I could appeal to his sense of decency."

"Decency? Jesus! He's using that conversation to screw us out of here. That's his idea of decency."

Molly crossed her arms and held on to her shoulders to try to stop physically shaking. She couldn't speak. She didn't know what had happened or what to say that would calm Paddy. She had never seen him like this before. "Paddy, I swear he didn't say anything to me about sharing anything."

Paddy looked at Molly. The sight of her standing there in such distress moved him. "Don't worry, love. I believe you." He put his arms around her. "It's okay. I'm sorry. I didn't mean to upset you. It's okay. It's not you." He could feel her trembling and pulled her even closer. Molly was about to say she was sorry again but Paddy put his finger on her lips. "You've got nothing to be sorry for. You're not the first person he's used like this."

Alice blessed herself. "I'm going to personally see the man goes to hell."

"Good. Well, I guess we learned another lesson. But now it's time to teach one. Bill, we got a delivery last week so there's a lot of beer in the cellar. We need to start bringing it up."

"I'm going to help," said Elsie. "Anyone want to tell us what's going on?"

"Bill will fill you in," said Paddy. "We have to move quickly."

There was a lot to be done in a very short time, not the least important of which was to take a quiet moment for Paddy to hold Molly tightly in his arms and begin to repair the damage of the day.

Chapter Thirty-Five

In contrast to the thunderous energy at the football ground as the game roared to a conclusion, High Street was deadly quiet, save only for the muffled clip clop of hooves on the dirt as a horse-drawn funeral hearse briskly paraded down the street. The very few people who observed its passing, stopped and looked and wondered who had died and why hadn't they heard about it already.

The hearse finally came to rest in front of the Imperial Hotel. Alice was standing out front and looking bereft with a rosary in one hand and glass of brandy in the other. Beside her stood Anne dabbing mock tears from her eyes with the handkerchief in her left hand and holding a smoke in her right hand,

Michael had moved promptly to the rear of the hearse and opened the back door. He and Barry swiftly slid the coffin out the hearse and hoisted it to their shoulders as they resolutely marched to the front door of the hotel.

This bizarre incident was too much for Jenkins who had left the security of his car to investigate more closely. "What exactly is going on here?"

Without missing a step Michael replied with studied calm "Somebody died, asshole." Jenkins was left slack-jawed in their wake as he watched them disappear through the front door of hotel. He knew something was afoot and confronted the wailing women, "All right! Who the hell died?"

Alice's response was a decided increase in the volume of her Hail Mary; Anne just flicked her handkerchief at him as if he was a pesky fly. Then they, too, were gone.

Inside the hotel everyone was geared for action. "Christ, it took you long enough," said Paddy.

"Forgive me," said Mike. The coffin was placed on the centre of the bar and the lid slung open. "I thought a galloping hearse might look conspicuous."

Under any other circumstances, a coffin entering the room would put the kibosh on any celebration. Not so that night at Mansfield's Imperial Hotel. This silver-handled mahogany coffin was a symbol of hope. Elsie was pone to nervous laughter at the best of times; the sight of this elegant coffin so inappropriately yawning open in a public bar sent ripples of giggles through her. Anne laughed at Elsie and the absurdity of the whole thing and Alice poured herself a brandy and finished her Hail Marys, not quite sure if all this would fit in God's Plan, but convinced that under the circumstances he'd be on side.

"Okay," said Bill. "Let's do it."

Paddy passed the bottles to Bill who passed them to Elsie who passed them to Molly and Anne who stacked them in the coffin. Alice was a silent supervisor. "Do you reckon the beer will stay cold in there," said asked.

"Everything stays cold in there," said Michael.

The laughter was large; far larger than the joke deserved. Elsie nearly dropped her bottles. Alice almost snorted brandy out her nose. Outside the hotel, Jenkins skulked from window to door to window trying to catch even a glimpse of the goings-on inside. He was convinced that they were far too happy to be coping with death.

In the corner of the bar sat Rabbit and Dodger totally in awe of the situation. "So, Paddy," said Rabbit. "Why'd you ask us to hang around? I'm not saying I'm not having a good time just watchin', but if there's something you want me to do."

"Alice, a couple of fresh ports for the two gentlemen if you please. Your time will come, mate," said Paddy.

Alice proceeded to pour two glasses of port and propped them in front of Rabbit and Dodger who still had no idea what was going on but couldn't have been happier to share the moment.

"That's a pretty flash coffin," said Rabbit. "Bet is costs a few bob."

"You're not wrong there, Rabbit, it's pretty expensive for sure," replied Michael. "But look at it this way, it's yours for life."

Elsie and Anne laughed so hard they had to be relived of their duties and Molly finished packing the coffin. Any fuller and they wouldn't have been able to lift it. Michael carefully closed the lid and bolted it in place.

"Okay, let's move it," said Bill.

"You want us to help you carry that?" asked Rabbit.

"No, mate," said Paddy. "I need you out of the way for a few hours though so here's a thought. Why don't you and Dodger take that fresh bottle of port upstairs and make yourselves at home."

"Tell you what, I'll do you a favour and drink your port for you," Rabbit cackled at his own good humour. "One thing though, when can we come back down?"

"When I say so."

"Fair enough," said Rabbit and the two of them shuffled off, bottle in hand.

"Okay, let's do it," said Paddy and the men hoisted the coffin to their shoulders. "Bloody hell, that's a load. Everyone okay?"

"Molly, think we'll need you to open the hearse door for us," said Michael.

First out the door were Alice and Anne assuming the grieving positions. Next followed Molly, followed by the men bearing the coffin. Jenkins was standing right beside the hearse. "What the hell are you up to, Brennan?"

"Show a little respect, mate," replied Paddy as the men carefully lowered the coffin taking care not to rattle the cargo.

"So, who's supposed to have died?"

"Poor old Rabbit," said Paddy. "Very sudden."

"Very sad," said Molly.

"What are you talking about? Rabbit couldn't afford to be buried in a potato sack let alone a coffin like that. Open it up."

"Piss off," said Paddy.

"You'll open that now or I'll have you all up on charges!" said Jenkins.

"For what?" said Michael, who was now angered by Jenkins' petulant insistence. "You're out of our depth here, mate. You're a lousy licensing cop. You don't tell me who I bury and who I don't. If you really want to see the poor man's body be at St. John's Church the day after tomorrow. Now excuse me, I have a job to do." As Michael berated Jenkins the other men slid the coffin safely inside and closed up the hearse.

Michael mounted the front of the carriage and slapped the large black mare on the rear end and was on his way.

"You can't do this!" shouted Jenkins.

"We just did it," said Paddy. "And there's nothing you can do about it. If you caught the poor bloke drinking after six you might have a case, but dying after six? I don't think so. Don't embarrass yourself; go sit in your car, it's what you do best."

Jenkins stuck his chin forward in defiance and refused to move.

Molly crossed to him. "Don't you ever, ever dare to even speak to us again, you hear me. One more episode like this and you'll be the next one to leave here in a coffin."

"Is that a threat?"

"Damn right it is!" She stared him down until he retreated to his car. He'd been beaten and he knew it. He sat through the arrival and departure of the next coffin. That time the procession was dedicated to Dodger, whom they said, this time with a laugh, died of grief, brought on by the loss of his best cobber, Rabbit.

There was an alchemy of shock surprise and delight when the first coffin of Victoria Bitter arrived at the church. Michael spun a yarn and told them 'it was all an allegory' for they way Mansfield buried Shepparton in the final quarter. That brought a cheer from the crowd and any concerns that may have lingered about the supply of beer totally disappeared.

There were four 'deaths' in total before the crowds' seemingly endless needs for libation had been sated. It was one hell of a night.

With all deliveries successfully completed and the coffin safely returned to its resting place, it was time to join the festivities. Elsie insisted on providing relief for the Church Ladies' Guild in the kitchen and eventually took total control of the food and the cleaning. Anne sat and smoked and laughed and loved every moment of it. Bill told stories and sang 'I'll Take You Home Again Kathleen' to Sister Kathleen who taught Grades One and Two. Alice met the older brother of the full back from the Mansfield football team, disappeared for over an hour and seemed very happy when she returned. Michael insisted this was how every funeral should be: a good laugh when you pick up the body and a party when you get to the church. Molly held Ethel's hand for a long time and Ethel talked at length about Veronica's transgression. Paddy was Paddy: he laughed and joked and flirted and always had a poem our two ready for any occasion.

Scott did not attend the celebration. Nor did Jenkins.

As word of the evening's drama filtered though the town, as it inevitably would, there was a discernible shift of business from the Prince of Wales to the Imperial Hotel. There was also serious talk among members of the football club about giving all the business to Paddy if the club made the finals next year.

It was that Rabbit and Dodger who had the final words when he met Scott and Jenkins on the main street two days later. Robert Scott's anger was still simmering as he saw the odd couple approaching. "You don't look very dead to me," he said.

Rabbit came to a sudden stop and patted his hands over his coat and pants, feeling his body as if to confirm it was still there. Satisfied he was whole, he flashed his tooth-deficient grin at the men, tipped his dusty hat and proclaimed, "Praise the Lord, I'm alive again."

"Hurrah!" said Dodger. It's a bloody miracle,"

They were still laughing when they reached Paddy and Molly's pub.

Chapter Thirty-Six

The Melbourne Cup is an extraordinary horse race. It was first run at Flemington Race Course in 1861, and four thousand people were on hand to see Archer record the first of two successive Cup wins. The concept of Captain Frederick Standish, a member of the Victoria Turf Club and former Chief Commissioner of Police in Victoria, the Melbourne Cup filled the club's perceived need for a good race of handicap conditions over two miles.

In 1925 the Australian Broadcasting Corporation broadcast the race for the first time, and the excitement of the Melbourne Cup was ignited nationally. Shops would shut and factories would come to a halt at 3:00 p.m. on the first Tuesday in November, so that everyone could listen to the broadcast. It is said that even parliament would suspend the business of government for the three minutes plus it took to run the race. All over the country people were huddled around their radios, but in Melbourne itself, being a live witness to the race was the answer.

Even in the bleakest times of the depression there were never less than seventy thousand people at the Flemington Race Course on Cup Day. In 1937, a total of one hundred and eighteen thousand, two hundred and twenty-six punters were on hand to cheer The Trump to victory.

233

For the millions who couldn't be there, there were bookmakers aplenty, but it was sweeps, more formerly known as sweepstakes, that were the chances of choice in every Aussie household. Anywhere that two streets crossed there would be a sweep. Sweeps, which were also illegal, were run by clubs, churches, choirs, and, on occasion, by the local police stations. Mansfield was no exception.

Ever since the football final, business at the Imperial had picked up considerably. When word of the fiasco and deceit got out, some who had been loyal to The Prince of Wales for years, got up from their stools, left and never looked back; in their eyes, lines had been crossed that could never be forgiven. For many, they found the tale too incredible or were simply too entrenched in their routines and so remained faithful to Robert Scott.

The bottom line was that the Imperial Hotel was a very busy place on November 1, 1938. The drawing of the sweep that morning attracted a relatively large crowd, most of them clutching the newspaper guide for race day. There were twenty-two horses heading for the gates, twenty-two chances for lucky locals to get into the race. If one sweep was oversubscribed a second or third sweep was opened until every man woman or child who had the money had a horse. The Imperial held two sweeps that year, forty-four chances sold at one shilling each. The sixpenny sweep offered by the Catholic Church was a standard fixture that crossed all religious boundaries. The fact that Paddy had upped the ante by doubling the stake to a shilling had people talking. The armchair jockeys who rode the winner each received a whopping twelve shillings, the second, six shillings, and four shillings for the third place horse.

Neither Paddy nor Molly would enter the sweep but it was fair game to everyone else in the family. Joe, who was home on leave, and Anne drove over from Benalla and were two of the first to sign up; Alice, who had come up on the train from Melbourne for a few days, garnered the last spot on the second sweep.

When it was only a few hours until post time, excitement began to take over the crowd. Paddy had deliberately held back the draw closer to the race itself to encourage people to stay once they got there. It seemed to be working. Those who drifted in to see which horse they had drawn decided to stay and ordered more than a couple of beers to help pass the time.

When time came to make the actual draw. The consensus of the crowd was that Alice should draw names and Michael should draw the horses. "All right, everyone," Paddy called the pub to order and beckoned Alice and Michael to take their places at the front of the bar where two large tins had been set up; one with the names of the horses and the other with the names of the patrons. Alice would draw two names and they would share the saddle on the horse Michael drew.

Alice, primed on Remy Martin and giggling for no apparent reason, appeared incapable of completing the most basic function without convulsing into laughter, such as drawing a name from one of the large tin cans on the bar.

"Come on, Alice, draw the first name for God's sake." Paddy was becoming a tad impatient.

Alice turned to Paddy as if to explain, but her struggle to speak resulted in a loud snort. The crowd in the bar voiced their wish as one, exhorting Alice to 'get a bloody grip and get on with it!' With supporting words from Michael she took a deep breath and set herself behind the tin in which rested the names of the players and the other tin containing the horses.

In went Alice's hand as she stirred up the papers. "Got to give them a good shuffle here," she said. With an enormous sense of ceremony, she completely withdrew her empty hand and held it poised for a moment before she took a dive for the first.

"And...the first name in today's sweep is Michael." There was a roar from the crowd; someone shouted it's rigged.

"Oh, shut up," snapped Alice as she waved the paper as proof. "And...the second name is ....." It was no good. Alice was lost in voiceless spasm of laughter. Michael took the piece of paper out of her hand and looked at it.

"Blood hell,' he said with a wide grin. "What are the odds of that? It's Alice."

Amid the gentle derision and catcalls was a warning from the back of the bar. "You draw the Royal Chief now and we'll take you out the back and do youse." A sentiment endorsed by all.

"All right now," Paddy's voice of authority brought matters back to order. "Draw the horse, Michael. The bloody race'll be over if we don't get a move on."

Michael held the paper high. "The very first horse out of the gate is...St. Constant."

Alice shrieked with delight. "It's God's will!" she cried and raised her glass of brandy high to the heavens.

"And Jesus is our jockey! We can't lose!" shouted Michael and a cheer went up all around the bar.

"He's right, Alice, you might be on a good thing there," said Archie. "St. Constant's second favourite."

"About six to one," chimed Mavis, nodding to Alice to confirm her good fortune.

Alice may have been slow out of the gate but she picked up speed; names almost leapt from the can and in no time half the field had been drawn.

This surge of enthusiasm was due in part to the sheer excitement of the day, the assurance that God was in the saddle of her mount and because Paddy had threatened she couldn't have another brandy until she got the job done.

"All right you lot, pay attention," said Alice. "We are heading into the final turn for home. Let's see what we've got here." Alice fluttered her hand inside the tin and retrieved a piece of paper. "The next lucky person is Maurice McCarthy.

Maurice was a regular in the bar, often there when good sense would have ushered a less-committed man home. It was Cup Day and a celebration of this nature warranted a critical break in tradition: he brought his wife with him. Iris was a meek, chicken-necked woman, diminutive in size and nature and the mother of five scrappy children; to see her in the bar was indeed an oddity.

Maurice nervously drummed his fingers on the wooden bar. Gambling didn't come easy to Maurice. It all came down to options: how many beers did he know he could have, no risk involved, as opposed to how many beers he could have if he hit the jackpot.

"Riding with Maurice will be... Anne, it's you."

"What'd we get, Mike? Make it a good one," said Anne.

Michael put one hand over his eyes and with his other hand dipped into his hat full of horses. "Royal Chief! Isn't that the favourite?"

"Too right," said Anne. "You beauty!" She planted a big kiss on Michael's cheek.

A loud groan went up around them. That was the horse they had all hoped to draw. Maurice hooted with delight, untold glasses of larger danced in his head.

"You've got a good chance there, Anne," said Archie Doyle, the grocer and probably the most educated punter in the town, save only for his wife, Mavis.

"E. Bartle's on board," said Mavis to further assure Anne.

"Bloody good jockey, Bartle," said Archie. The Doyles fancied Royal Chief but knew the real odds of winning were not always in the favourite's favour.

As the draw continued, Ethel Patterson quietly appeared in the doorway. It took a minute before Molly spotted her. Ethel surveyed the crowd, standing somewhere between making a full entrance and retreating into the street. Molly waited for some indication of Ethel's intention but there was nothing so she crossed to the door, gently slipped her arm around Ethel's shoulders and led her to the relative quiet of the Ladies' Lounge.

"Can I get you a drink?" asked Molly.

"It's a bit early isn't it?" said Ethel.

"I don't think so." Molly walked briskly to the bar where Barry was wiping some glasses. "Pull me two shandies, Barry."

Barry complied and placed the drinks on the bar in front of Molly. "You're not going to tell her, are you?"

"Why do you ask?"

"I don't know, It's just...I don't know."

Molly took the drinks and settled in beside Ethel. A roar erupted in the bar.

"They seem to be having a good time."

"Yes, the Melbourne Cup's always a fun day. Did you get into a sweep?"

"No, couldn't see the point."

Ethel was not wearing well. The stress of Veronica's position had taken its toll on her. She always had her hair pulled up and tightly pinned into a bun with nary a stray strand but lately every day saw a little more dishevelment creep in. She was also known to cry a lot; at church, at the bakery, at the grocery store, or just standing on the side of the street waiting to muster up enough mettle to cross to the other side.

Ethel looked around the room feeling dramatically at odds with the lightness and laughter. "Why'd you ask me over?"

Molly had thought long and hard about whether to do this and if she did do it if she was doing it for the right reasons. She decided that it was information that Ethel had a right to know and the potential outcome could have its own rewards for Molly. "Well, I know who got Veronica pregnant."

Ethel looked at Molly, first in shock and disbelief, and then a quiet intensity settled over her. "How do you know?" she said with a challenge, suspicious of how Molly could know this so surely. Another roar went up in the bar followed by howls of laughter that momentarily interrupted the drama in the Lounge. "Go on," said Ethel.

"All right," Molly took a deep breath. "Veronica told Maggie, Maggie told Barry, and Barry told me. He asked me not to say anything as Maggie had told him to keep his mouth shut and he did, except for telling me that is. Maggie was certain Veronica had been honest with her." Ethel remained unreadable, static. "They said not to say anything to you but I think that's why they told me, because they knew I would."

Ethel took a drink to brace herself and turned back to Molly. "Well, go on. Are you going to tell me or not?" A resounding cheer from the bar filled the room. What Molly had to say was not something to be shouted so she leaned over and whispered the name to Ethel. Unsure of how the woman would respond, Molly watched her closely. Finally Ethel shook her head then looked at Molly. "Are you certain?"

"Yes," said Molly.

Ethel shook her head again and finally nodded slowly as if to affirm her understanding and unspoken decision.

"Thank you, Molly, I appreciate your consideration," she said as she rose and buttoned her woollen coat. "If you'll excuse me, I have things to take care of."

"Ethel, are you all right?"

"No, I'm not, but I'm all the better for knowing what I now know and I thank you for that." Ethel moved through the crowd in the bar. She paused only once to look at Barry who had been silently studying the action in the lounge. She gave him a nod as if to acknowledge his role in bringing the truth forward and to say thank you. Barry nodded to Ethel and she left.

239

"Well, two names left," said Alice. "The first one is..." Alice played up the moment. "It's Iris McCarthy."

It shouldn't have been a surprise to anyone but it was. Iris had spent her life being overlooked. Of everyone, it was Maurice who was most surprised to hear his wife's name called. "Where'd you get the money to enter?"

"I saved it," she said.

"How the hell'd you save it?"

"I just did," she said as she sat there staring at the floor. There was a real tension erupting but Alice was to have none of that. "All right, you lot, let's see who up there in the saddle with Iris. I wonder who it could be?" This time everyone knew exactly who it must be. They all looked at Rabbit who was sitting there clutching his glass of port and chuckling noiselessly. "And the last one out of the starting gate is Rabbit!"

Hoorays were sounded and glasses were raised.

"Hold on, not quite finished." Michael held his paper in the air "And the lucky horse is Catalogue."

There, it was done. The draw had been made. Now it would be the tension leading up to race that would sustain the crowd. The banter began to gain volume as everyone could crow or bitch about their prospects.

"Bad luck, mate," said Archie with a grin to Rabbit. "Looks like you could be last for real."

"Catalogue's not a bad horse," said Mavis.

"You crazy? Have you lost your mind, Mavis?" said Archie. "Never seen anything so plain; should be pulling a bread cart."

"Rubbish! You don't know what you're talking about. Don't listen to him," said Mavis. "He's more of a miler, but ran a promising third to Spear Chief in the Hotham Handicap."

"Lovely," said Iris, just as if she understood. "Could I have the piece of paper?"

"What's that?" asked Paddy.

"The piece of paper. The one with the horse's name on it."

"Of course you can, love," said Paddy who rummaged though the shreds of paper on the bar and found the one that said Catalogue. "Here, you go" he said. "Someone pass this over to Iris."

"Give it to me, I'll do it," said Mavis and she passed the slip of paper to Iris who studied it for a moment, smiled and closed her hands around it. "Don't worry about him," she said indicating Maurice. "You're having a day out, aren't you?"

Iris simply smiled and nodded. Mavis never liked Maurice. She thought he was a piss pot and wouldn't hesitate to say so. Now, to thwart him by indulging Iris gave her great pleasure.

"Let me buy you a drink, dear, what'll you have?" said Mavis. "You want a sherry?"

"A beer, please." This had indeed turned out to be a grand day already for Iris. The children were all at school and she had arranged for them to go to a nearby farm after so that she could stay at the pub for the big race. She didn't even care that Maurice kept looking in her direction, still befuddled as to how she got her hands on the stray shillings.

Archie loved to argue and if it was about horses he loved it even more. He also had enormous respect for Rabbit and was not about to let this moment to gently jibe him slip away. "I'm telling you Rabbit, that gelding is as plain as the day is long."

"Sort of like me then?" Rabbit's wheezing retort brought forth another reason for the crowd to raise their glasses.

"And if you weren't in enough trouble, Catalogue is trained by a woman. Fair dinkum, a woman trainer!" In those days the idea of a woman trainer was not only improbable, it was unacceptable to any racing establishment. So inappropriate was it, Mrs A 'Granny' McDonald could not be formally listed as the trainer and her husband's name was entered into the records.

"I think a woman trainer would be a good trainer," said Mavis. "We had to train you blokes and that hasn't been easy but we did it, didn't we Iris? And another thing, that horse is owned by a woman, too," said Mavis. "Woman owner, woman trainer. It's about time we showed you men how it's done."

"You're doomed, Rabbit," said Archie. "The horse'll never last two miles with two sheilas on its back!" Mavis didn't think that was nearly as funny as Archie did. "You're last, mate. Dead last!"

"No worries," said Rabbit as he stood up and offered his glass to Paddy for a refill. "It'll all work out for the best, I reckon."

"Good on you, Rabbit, that's the spirit," said Anne.

Rabbit responded with his breathy chuckle and raised his glass to the crowd in a toast and everyone responded appropriately. "So, the last shall be first, and the first last: for many be called, but few chosen," said Rabbit with unusual precision.

"Lovely." Alice was now primed to offer her own favourite excerpts but Rabbit wasn't finished.

"And Jesus going up to Jerusalem took the twelve disciples apart in the way, and said unto them, Behold, we go to Jerusalem; and the Son of man shall be betrayed unto the chief priests and unto the scribes, and they shall condemn him to death. "

The bar had fallen silent, amazed that this door to Rabbit's world had so unexpectedly opened. The little man stood there transfixed by his own musings. "Ah, them was the days," he said.

As quickly as he went to that place, he returned. "Last, eh? We'll see." He flashed his trademark grin and gave them all a knowing wink as he settled back onto his barstool. "Cheers!" he said and raised glass to the heavens.

And so the race began.

Chapter Thirty-Seven

Excitement was beginning to peak and everyone pressed hard against the bar to get their glasses filled before the horses leapt from the gates. If you didn't have a drink in your hand before the start you certainly wouldn't have one until the race was well and truly over.

Snippets from the radio announcer seeped through the clamour. "The starter is calling them up...." Then, a bluster of noise swirled through the bar as some attempted to hush the crowd while others raised their voices even louder to finish a story or a thought.

"Shut up, all of you!" demanded a voice from the back.

"They're off!" said the crackled voice on the radio. Everyone in the bar roared as if on cue and then, as one, fell silent, intent on hearing how their horses fared.

They crouched, they leaned, they sat. They all listened intently as the announcer rattled off progress reports with astonishing accuracy and detail. There were odd mutters and groans as horses fell behind or made their moves. Two miles was a long race but the announcer's voice never flagged, indeed it became more fervid with every furlong. The horses were about to turn for home and in every bar of every hotel in every town and every city of the entire country, the same hushed tension was about to explode.

"Come on, come on." The chant began to swell. "Move it."

"Come on Royal Chief, let's go," shouted Maurice McCarthy.

The favourite was bravely holding ground but not looking like a winner. Alice shook her hand high in the air as if beckoning God to spur on St. Constant, who now appeared to be going backward. Then, as if out of nowhere, loomed Catalogue. He made his move coming out of the final turn into the straight with a 'slashing run'. What the sturdy little gelding lacked in glamour he made up for it with guts, as he continued to leave the field in his wake, and he won the 1938 Melbourne Cup by an impressive three lengths.

Three minutes and twenty-six seconds after it began Rabbit was hoisted into the air shouting, "The last shall be first!" He was the hero of the day, as celebrated as if he himself had ridden Catalogue to glory.

"Just a minute," said Mavis. "Have you forgotten we have another winner here, too? Stand up, Iris!" A fresh volley of cheers resounded through the bar.

Everyone was happy except Alice who told the crowd to collectively piss off when anyone reminded her that St. Constant finished third last.

Paddy handed out the winnings. Iris didn't say a word but just held the coins tightly in her hand.

"That's a lot of money," said Maurice.

Iris's eyes narrowed and she looked at him unflinching. "And it's mine." She took her half glass of beer and retreated to the lounge. Anne and Mavis followed to see how she was holding up.

"That's lovely, that is, Iris," said Anne. "I'm glad you won, dear."

"Thank you," said Iris.

"What would you like to do with your winnings?" asked Mavis. "Any plans?"

"I'd like to put everything I have in a bag, catch the train to Melbourne and never come back." Nodding her head as if to confirm it would be a wonderful thing.

"Are you going to?" asked Anne.

Iris shrugged, "Don't know."

Her co-winner, Rabbit, couldn't stop grinning as he accepted his winnings. He loved the very feel of the coins, the weight, the undulations. He looked at each of the twelve shillings as if each was a minor miracle. He took a cream linen handkerchief from the inside pocket of his suit coat and laid it on the bar.

"Your shout, Rabbit!" said a voice from the back. That brought forth a cheer. Rabbit just ginned a little wider and shook his head. "No, afraid not, mate." He carefully laid the stack of silver coins on their side and rolled them inside the handkerchief. "This is me 'one day' money."

"You hang on to that money, Rabbit. These buggers will drink it up real quick if you let them," said Anne."

"I will for sure, Mrs Rae." He chuckled. "I reckon it might be handy one day." He turned his attention to the bar as he stowed his newfound wealth safely inside the pocket of his jacket. "Tell you what, Paddy, I'll do you a favour though. I'll let you buy the winner a drink."

"You're a tight fisted bugger, aren't you?" said Paddy. Rabbit laughed and nodded in agreement as Paddy placed the glass of port in front off him.

Chapter Thirty-Eight

The race itself may have been over but in the Imperial Hotel it was being rerun with every round of drinks poured. Nobody seemed to tire of the repetition. Rabbit relished the attention and would stir the pot from time to time by waving his winnings in the air and then stowing them safely back in the breast pocket of his shabby jacket.

"When you are gonna buy us a drink, my miserable bastard?" was the stock response.

"One day," wheezed Rabbit. "One day. Maybe."

The crowd that had remained in the bar held on to the celebration and winning or losing had ceased to matter. They came for the ritual and would stay until the doors had closed and the horses and stories of races past had long been put to bed.

Suddenly a loud crack silenced the bar

"What the hell was that?" said Archie as he swung around on his bar stool. The bar fell abruptly silent. Everybody just looked at each other uncertain of what had happened or was about to happen.

Crack! "Bloody, hell," said Michael. "That's a gun!" The sound was clearly coming from the street.

Half a dozen customers rushed to the door and peered outside. Alice and Anne, along with a handful of others sought shelter behind the bar.

"She's got a gun, all right!" said Archie. "Bloody hell."

"Molly, get back here!" shouted Paddy. Molly ignored him and forced her way through the knot of men at the door.

It was as if she had a premonition of what was awaiting. "Oh, my God, it is her," said Molly. "It's Ethel."

This was not the repressed, demoralized Ethel Patterson of earlier this afternoon. This was a woman on a grim, determined mission: to track down the bastard who impregnated her little Veronica, namely a Mr James Jenkins. Ethel slowly marched down the centre of the street, peppering the dirt with bullets as Jenkins dived behind drays, barrels, benches or trucks, anything that might provide even meagre protection.

Ethel raised her Lee Enfield .303 Service Rifle to her shoulder and took a bead on Jenkins. Molly shouted from across the street "Ethel! Don't Ethel. Don't do it."

Oblivious to Molly, Ethel quietly squeezed the trigger and released another shot.

Crack!

The dirt spat up dangerously close to Jenkins feet.

"For God's sake, woman, stop!" he cried as he danced on the spot. "Jesus! Someone help me."

Molly turned to Paddy. "You have to go out there and stop her."

"You're joking. I'm not going out there. She's crazy."

"Right then." Molly was in no mood for his trepidation. "I will." And she was off, shouting for Ethel to stop as she ran across the street.

"Bloody hell!" Paddy was hot in pursuit.

"You bastard," muttered Ethel as she snapped the bolt back and raised the rifle one more time.

"Sweet Jesus!" shrieked Jenkins as he fell to his knees in the dirt.

"Ethel, don't!" said Molly.

"Stop right there!" shouted Paddy.

Just as the drama was building to a crescendo, a new character emerged, running, screaming, ranting and crying from the other end of the street. "No! My husband. Please. Dear God. Aaaggghhh!"

It was Glenda Jenkins, the distraught wife, making throaty, unintelligible noises that edged the drama every closer to farce. Her whole body quivered and shook as she sprinted toward Ethel. She clutched her cotton dress in her fists as if that would make her more fleet of foot.

Spectators began to crowd the fringes of the melee. This was not to be missed.

Ethel turned to see Glenda almost upon her and instinctively raised the rifle in defence against the hysterical woman. " Aaaggghhh!" cried Glenda who abruptly stopped in her tracks no more than ten feet from Ethel.

"You hold it right there." Ethel raised her rifle a little higher to underscore the warning.

"Stop!" said Paddy.

"Ethel!" said Molly.

"Sweet Jesus, don't kill me!" Glenda clenched her hand as if in prayer.

"Go away, you stupid woman," Ethel spun back to get a fix on Jenkins who was up on one knee and ready to sprint away. "Don't you think of moving, you insect!"

"Give me the gun, Ethel," Paddy held out his hand to take it.

"You all right?" said Molly. She reached for Ethel but was brushed aside.

"Come on, Ethel, hand it over." Paddy insisted.

"She's a crazy woman!" shrieked Glenda who was now on her feet again. "She's crazy!"

"Knock it off, Glenda." Paddy didn't want this woman getting in the way. Her wildness was not helping matters.

"She's trying to kill my husband. Why would she do that? Why? She's crazy, that's why. She's a crazy person!"

Ethel turned abruptly to Glenda and growled at her. Glenda made an odd high-pitched squeal and flinched. "Are you going to kill me, too?"

"If you don't shut up I will." She swung around to centre Jenkins who was now a snivelling, sobbing mess, assured that any minute a bullet would pierce his skull. "You want to know why? Is that what you want to know? I'll tell you why. I'm shooting at him because he got my daughter pregnant. That's why."

"You liar," growled Glenda. "You bloody liar. He wouldn't do that." She made a grab for Ethel who elbowed her out of the way. Glenda responded by pounding her fists on Ethel's back.

Things were not getting better.

"Stop it! I can't aim when you do that!"

Molly forced her way between the two of them and grabbed Glenda by the shoulders. "Glenda, stop it, just stop it."

Glenda implored her husband to deny the charges. "Tell them you didn't do it. Tell them!"

"Glenda, listen to me" said Molly forcing Glenda to face her.

"He wouldn't do that. He wouldn't," said Glenda.

"But he did!" said Molly. She had to physically shake Glenda to get her attention. "Listen to me, it's true. It's all true. He did it."

"No, it can't be true. Please. No"

"I am so sorry Glenda, but he did get Veronica pregnant. I know for a fact it was him."

Glenda, blanched, stared slack-mouthed at Molly. It was as if the life had been drained from her body.

"I am so sorry, Glenda."

"No, no, no, no, no." What started as a groan soared into a roar. "You bastard!" She turned back to Ethel and made a grab for the rifle. "Not again. You promised me." Glenda was flushed with a new injection of rage.

"Let go!" shouted Ethel as the women wrestled for the gun.

"I'm gonna shoot your balls off this time you lying bastard." Glenda grabbed the stalk of the gun and attempted to wrench it from Ethel.

"Bugger off!" said Ethel, and she spun around to shake Glenda's grip. "If anyone shoot's him, it's me."

"I'm gonna get you, you bastard," cried Glenda as she tugged on the gun. "Give it up, Ethel! I'm gonna kill him!"

"Okay, that'll do!" Paddy attempted to mollify the wrestling women as they swirled around, the gun lodged between them.

"Give me the gun." Molly tried to get a hand in between them before Paddy wrenched her away.

"You stand back," he said, forcing his way into the eye of the storm; the gun went every which way, women shouted, grunted, swore. Paddy shouted. Molly begged. The women swirled and twisted until the inevitable happened.

Crack!

As if from nowhere, a bullet splintered the wooden awning over the grocery store. Ethel fell backward and released her hold, which sent the gun flying over Glenda's shoulder.

There was a stuttered second of shocked silence, then cries of 'Holy Jesus' and 'Look out' erupted across High Street as people ducked every which way for cover.

Paddy's reflex action was to make a move to get possession of the gun but he was no match for Glenda. "Don't anybody piss me off," she said as she waived the gun high in the air. "Now, don't anybody move! "This was a warning to be taken seriously. This was not a woman to be ignored. Everybody froze in their tracks.

She slowly and deliberately stepped closer to her perfidious husband who still hadn't mustered the courage to make a run for it. "You promised me," she said.

"It's not true, Glenda, I swear."

"She loomed over him. "You can't keep it buttoned up can you?"

"I didn't touch her!" he implored.

"Just like you didn't touch all the others, I suppose." She stood over his squirming body and looked at him in utter disgust. "You little shit!" She slammed the stock of the rifle into his chest.

The impact winded him and sent him tumbling backwards, and then with one swift and decisive blow she brought the butt of the rifle down full force on his crotch.

It was said his scream could be heard on the far side of Benalla.

"That'll do," said Paddy as he took the gun from her. Glenda slumped to the ground, sobbing. "Give me a hand here," Paddy said to the women.

Molly and Ethel hauled Glenda to her feet and led her across the street toward the pub.

Paddy crouched so close to Jenkins he could whisper in the man's ear. "So, how did it go, mate, your plan to keep an eye on us? Isn't that what you threatened Molly with, that you'd keep an eye on us?" Paddy took Jenkins' collar in his fist and squeezed. Jenkins wheezed. "Another thing I remember: you telling me we're not welcome here. Funny how things change." He drew the collar tighter and the man gasped for air. "The worm has turned." Paddy drew even closer. "If you so much as cast a shadow in this town or anywhere near it, you'll be a dead man. I won't take the gun away from anyone next time. You got that?" Paddy cuffed the back of the man's head for punctuation and then got up and followed after the women.

As Molly, Paddy, and the two women reached the hotel, men tipped their hats in respect as if they were returning from the war. "Okay, give the ladies some room, that's it." Paddy outstretched his arm to shepherd them through the crowd.

A respectful chorus of 'Good on ya' followed their path through the front door and into the bar. Paddy glanced back at the battle site. All that could be seen was a shadowy figure limping into distant darkness.

Catalogue stole the headlines in morning papers all across Australia the following day. The brave little gelding was the talk of the every town in the county large and small.

Except for one.

Mansfield.

There were other things to talk about there that day.

Chapter Thirty-Nine

Just standing on the side of the street outside the hotel Paddy could feel the perspiration trickling down his back. His striped cotton shirt couldn't blot any more sweat. Such had been most days in December.

Rabbit and Dodger were sitting on the bench outside the hotel with Ginger, Dodger's dog, stretched out beside them.

The men acknowledged each other with nods. It was too hot to speak. The 1920s through the 1930s proved to be the driest period in Australia over the previous four centuries. According to measurements at the Mansfield Post Office, November of 1939 yielded less than a quarter inch of rain in the whole month; December followed suit. Add to that temperatures that constantly hovered around the century mark and the earth became so hard-baked that any precious precipitation that did land ran off before it had a chance to seep into the ground.

Eventually, Paddy broke the silence. "You know what?"

"What?" said Dodger.

"Think I'm in the wrong business. If I'd learned to make rain, I'd be rich by now," said Paddy.

"My oath," said Dodger.

In 1938, the Australian Bureau of Meteorology established a special research division to develop long-range forecasts. In

Mansfield anyone interested in long-range forecasts generally turned to Rabbit.

"What do you think, Rabbit?" said Paddy. "This gonna last?"

Rabbit looked to the edges of the horizon as if he could somehow see beyond. Then he cocked his head, listening to the sound of the earth or anything that dwelt upon it. "You know what I reckon?" he said finally.

"What?" asked Paddy as he watched a truck recede down the street into a pall of red dust.

"Gonna be hot," said Rabbit.

"You reckon?" said Dodger.

"Bloody hot."

"It's already bloody hot," said Paddy.

"He's got a point there," said Dodger as he casually stroked Ginger's dusty coat.

"Tell me something I don't know," said Paddy.

"It's gonna be hot for quite a while yet."

"When are we gonna see rain do you reckon?"

"Don't hold ya breath," said Rabbit.

Dodger looked toward a swirl of black smoke off to the west. "Don't like the look of that. More than a few acres goin' up in smoke there. Don't know if that's this morning's or hanging over from last night." The dog raised her head and looked at him.

"What are you looking at, Ginger? Eh?" She was panting; her long, pink tongue lolled out the side of her mouth. "I think you need a drink, old girl."

"There's a water bowl over by the door," said Paddy.

"It's empty," said Dodger.

Paddy pointed to the black smoke lingering in the western sky. "I think that's from last night," The three men quietly studied it as it rose and slowly dissipated into the muddy sky. "Not as bad as it was earlier this morning."

Rabbit crouched down and picked up some red dirt that he rubbed between his hands like an herb he hoped to savour. "Remember the terrible bushfires we had back in the nineties, remember them?" he said.

"My oath," said Dodger.

Rabbit cupped his hands around his nose, sampling the scent. "This one could be worse. A lot worse."

"We should pray for rain," said Dodger.

"Worth a shot," said Rabbit. "We'll make that your job."

The three of them fell silent watching for whatever stirred on that oppressive Sunday morning.

"What's happening out here?" said Molly.

"Not a lot. Getting Rabbit's weather report," said Paddy.

"Needn't have bothered, I could have told you as much. It's hot. It's hot now. It'll be hot later. And tomorrow, it'll be hot again. Never anything else here."

Paddy studied her standing there. It hadn't been a good day for Molly. She grew up on a dairy farm so she knew what it could be like but this stretch had challenged her resistance. Molly crouched down and gestured to Ginger. "Come," she said.

With the grace of a small foal Ginger struggled to her feet, walked to Molly and flopped back down. Molly cupped Ginger's face in her hands and stroked the dog's face with her thumbs.

"You should take better care of her. She needs a drink." The remark was not blatantly directed at Dodger but was more of a general admonishment to the three men.

"The water's gone," said Dodger.

"What?" said Molly.

"The bowl you set out for the dogs, it's empty," said Paddy.

Molly had little patience for that. "When did the three of you lose the use of your legs? If it's empty, fill it. Honestly."

Paddy looked back at the empty doorway and then to his two companions. "Think we've been told, haven't we."

Rabbit chuckled and nodded. Paddy picked up the bowl and headed back into the hotel. "I'll get some water."

"Getting you a drink, he is. He's a good bloke, Paddy is." Dodger rubbed the stomach of his skinny Kelpie. "Yes, he is, my girl."

Rabbit had rescued Ginger from an abusive owner. She had been so neglected and mistreated that she couldn't walk. Rabbit found her lying on the side of the road where she had either fallen out of or been thrown from a truck. He carried the dog in his arms for almost two miles before Norm Clancy happened upon them and brought them home.

Paddy returned with a full bowl of water and placed it in the shade.

"Come on, girl. Look what he brought ya, eh? You're a lucky one, you are," said Dodger gently patting her as she lapped up the water.

"You've changed your tune, Dodger. Remember you saying a dog was too much trouble, didn't want one, bloody nuisance, and all that."

"Nah, doesn't ring a bell."

"Wasn't she your dog anyway, Rabbit?" asked Paddy.

"Kind of. Just for a while though."

"Well, you're never going to get her back now. She's taken a shine to Dodger." Paddy smiled at the obvious affection the old codger had for the dog.

Rabbit had nursed the emaciated dog back to health and seriously thought about keeping her. He liked dogs, but he ultimately decided his mate, Dodger, had a greater need.

A couple of months ago, Dodger's best mate, Tom, was chopping wood as a favour for Nettie Kelly, a frail widow who lived nearby. It was unreasonably hot. Not a good day to be exerting that sort of effort. Tom had a heart attack and although Nettie called the hospital straight away, the damage was done.

Dodger was with Tom at the hospital that afternoon. When he asked if he could do anything. Tom said yes there was something. So Dodger left the hospital to finish chopping the wood for Nettie.

He went back to see Tom shortly after dinner and took a pack of cards with him. He asked Tom if he felt up to it. Tom said yes as long as Dodger didn't cheat. They had a good laugh about that.

Cards had been a ritual in their lives for as long as they could remember. They would sit for hours playing cards, having a beer or two and swearing at each other. Dodger felt a game of euchre would lift Tom's spirits; it was his favourite. Tom was a canny player and generally had the best of Dodger. Not so much that evening. He was tired and had trouble staying focused on the game.

"I really should go, you need your rest." It was not the first time Dodger had said that.

"No, don't go, mate. One more hand."

"That's what you said last time and you fell asleep."

"Didn't."

"Yes, you did, mate."

"Silly bugger." Tom settled back and closed his eyes again.

"One more then, then I'm gonna go for sure," said Dodger.

"I just..." Tom's thought hung in the air. He shook his head slightly, a little annoyed that his senses had betrayed him. He raised his hand to see if it could somehow grasp the sentence from the air. "Sorry."

"No worries, mate."

Dodger gathered up the cards. It was odd to see his friend from that angle in that light in that sterile place. It was odd to see him so passive. Any other day, when Tom squinted through his bushy silver brows there was a spark, a curiosity, and an interest in how things were and how they got to be that way. That night just holding cards was a challenge. How Dodger wanted Tom to look at him in that way and call him a silly bugger one more time.

"Tom?" said Dodger.

"What?" It was more of a whisper than a word.

"Nothin'."

Tom looked older than Dodger thought either of them would ever be. "You want me to deal?" Tom responded with the faintest smile and a hint of a nod. "Right. I'll deal. I'll give 'em a good shuffle, too. You always tell me I don't know how to shuffle. Let's see how I do this time, eh?"

He did what he promised. He gave them a good shuffle and dealt out two hands. "Look at that, mate," said Dodger with a laugh. "A right bower. Dealt myself a right bower and you said I couldn't shuffle."

Tom didn't reach for his cards. The air had become very still.

"Tom?" Dodger said, in a faint hope that his friend was still there.

Dodger stayed by Tom's bedside until a nurse came by on her rounds. He didn't want his mate to be alone.

It was shortly after that that Rabbit felt Dodger should have a dog.

Dodger wasn't too sure.

Rabbit said it would help.

He was right.

It did help.

Chapter Forty

Paddy entered from the street and closed the door behind him. The old electric fan in the corner clicked and hummed and stuttered as it vainly attempted to simulate a cooling breeze. Molly sat at the table in the lounge, rationalizing the week's receipts. She rubbed her eyes with the palms of her hands and looked at the columns of numbers again.

"How are we doing?" he asked.

Molly glanced at him but didn't respond. Paddy did a circuit of the lounge straightening chairs that didn't need to be straightened, generally killing time, and hoping Molly's mood was better than it seemed.

"You going to mass this morning?" It was more about making conversation than asking a real question.

"Of course."

"You think there will be much of a crowd coming to the pub after church?

"How would I know?" She gave him a look, and Paddy retreated to the bar, and made himself busy cleaning and organizing glasses to be ready for the late-morning crowd.

Technically, hotels closed on Sundays but it was part of the local ethos to satiate your thirst after you'd cleansed your soul. Following the eleven o'clock service, the faithful would assemble at the pub of their choice for an hour or two; sometimes the local police officer would stop by to share a beer and chat a while. The trick to keeping the local constabulary happy was to ensure everyone was booted out in time to be home for dinner.

"I expect some of the firefighters might stop by," said Paddy.

Between the blistering heat of the fires and the blazing sun, it was often too exhausting to fight fires during the day, so the teams of volunteer firefighters tackled the blazes at night. Tired, blackened, and frustrated they would frequently stop for a beer of two to clear the ashes from their throats before attempting to catch some sleep.

"Do me a favour, will you?" said Molly.

"Sure."

"If they do stop by and they offer to pay for their drinks, as they will, let them."

"I think a beer or two is the least we can do to say thanks," said Paddy in mild defence.

"I agree but it's not the odd beer or two that I'm talking about. I don't think you've let them pay even once. Listen to me Paddy, we simply can't afford to give away the profits like that." She looked long and hard at him to underscore the gravity of the situation.

"Sorry." Paddy didn't know what else to say.

Molly gathered up her papers and stacked them on the end of the bar. She looked at the clock on the wall. "I have to change my dress."

December, with its holidays and boundless good cheer, was anticipated to be a very good month for the hotel. Nature had other notions. The land was tinder dry and with the spontaneous outbreaks of fires, large and small, farmers were reticent to leave their properties for too long. The heat and constant threat of fires had dramatically depressed any fresh logging. As a result, work at the mill was sporadic and without money lining their pockets the men who worked the mill were anything but regular.

Molly returned briefly to the bar. She had slipped on a crisp new cotton dress, freshened her lipstick and combed her hair.

"I'm off," she said.

"You look nice." Paddy may have often thought it but didn't always remember to say it.

"Well, thank you. Hope I don't look wrung out by the time I get to church." She looked in the mirror and adjusted her wide-brimmed straw hat. "One other thing."

"Yes?"

"Christmas is exactly one week from today. Are you aware of that?"

"Of course."

"Sorry, but I have to ask because you keep avoiding the subject." She looked at Paddy to say something but he didn't have a response. "You seem to want to pretend it's not happening." It was true; he had been avoiding the subject of Christmas. Any time Molly brought it up, Paddy dissembled and deferred, simply adding to her frustration.

Molly nursed her own litany of reservations and regrets about the impending holiday season but she was ultimately more pragmatic and had actively sought some relief. She had called her sisters, hoping to rouse interest in someone coming to visit, but without success. Those who were in town were staying in town. Even Anne, whom she hoped would drive over from Benalla, was in Melbourne because Joe would be on leave there before he shipped out. There was a flush of hope when Alice declared that she would love to visit for at least a couple of days. However, on two separate occasions prior to her departure, the train from Melbourne was cancelled because of fierce fires blazing near the tracks. Alice always wanted to be close to Jesus but not that close and not that soon.

Molly even called Paddy's brother, Bill. Although all the brothers were having dinner with their mother on Christmas Day, he was keen to drive to Mansfield for a day or two prior. Elsie totally rejected the idea. Molly could hear her in the background berating Bill and declaring they would both be incinerated on the highway.

More than a few Christmas wishes went up in smoke that year.

"Let's agree that we will talk about it after Mass. Okay?" She needed assurance she had been heard and understood and didn't make a move until Paddy responded.

"Okay."

One look at Paddy and she knew he was just as much at sea as she was. She felt badly for putting him in a corner but it had to be done,

"Tell you what," she said. "I'll make a deal with you."

"Okay."

"If the firefighters come in, you can shout them the first drink but they pay for rest. Fair enough?"

"You bet. Thanks." His voice stopped her at the door. Molly."

"Yes?"

"I do love you."

"I know. And I love you. I've got to run." She paused. "Christmas, think about it."

"You bet."

Think about it? He had thought about almost nothing else since the beginning of the month. This wasn't the way he wanted their first Christmas to be remembered: astray in a Promised Land that was parched and predatory and so, so far from home.

"You gotta have a dream," he had once told her, extolling the romance of their adventure. She had believed him. She had trusted him. Now, he felt as if somehow he had betrayed her.

His guilt was overwhelming.

"What the hell," Paddy muttered and poured himself a beer to aid constructive thought. He considered bringing Rabbit and Dodger in from outside and plying them with free drinks to serve as a distraction but decided that would be a bad move on every front.

He turned his eyes to the heavens. "Listen, mate. Molly's up at your place praying for something good to happen. If you have any thoughts on the subject, let her know will you, 'cause I don't have a bloody clue. Thanks." He raised his glass. "Appreciate it."

Chapter Forty-One

Father Dolan was old. Very old. None, not even the most senior parishioner, could remember when he first came to Mansfield. Some said it was in anticipation of the birth of Christ.

Time, however, had taken its toll. Father Dolan's frailty had become increasingly acute. These days, simply scaling the pulpit safely could be celebrated as a minor miracle.

The countless years he had spent as a priest in Australia had done little to moderate his Irish brogue. If anything, it had thickened and distorted into a muddied confluence of dialects, totally unintelligible, save only the frequent, and crisply punctuated interjections of 'Virgin Mary' and 'Hell'.

Despite his dotage and persistent pressure from the Monseigneur, Father Dolan staunchly resisted retirement. The ecclesiastical hierarchy, however, would not be denied. At the eleven o'clock service five weeks ago, Monseigneur Murphy made a personal appearance to announce to the congregation that the following Sunday would be Father Dolan's last mass as parish priest of St. John's.

Poor Father Dolan looked lost. He was a little crumpled child whose toys had been taken away. Looking at the little man hunched in disappointment was pathetic. Despite his quirks and incoherence, at that moment everyone wanted him to stay.

267

The nostalgia was short lived once the Monseigneur introduced Father Dolan's successor, Father Thomas, a young man brimming with pious zeal who could be both heard and understood.

The Lord be praised. A new day was born at St. John's. Regrettably, that honeymoon didn't last. Father Thomas may have fulfilled the promise of being both articulate and audible, but that simply begged the question, did they want to hear what he had to say? After all, he didn't imbue the gospel with insight or revelation; he simply injected it with evangelical fervour. Worst of all, he looked intensely at every person in every pew to ensure they had heard every word. It all became a blur of glory and redemption to which everyone was compelled to listen to even if they didn't want to. At least when Father Dolan had preached, listening wasn't an issue. It wasn't expected. Parishioners used the time fruitfully to mentally resolve personal issues, work a crossword or, in the case of old Mary O'Shea, finish shelling the peas for Sunday dinner.

Things got done.

Molly was distracted. She was infinitely more interested in how each of the people around her might be spending Christmas than the passion from the pulpit. There was nothing premeditated about it but when she left the altar after communion she continued walking past her pew and clear out into the street,

She didn't want to be there. She wanted to be strolling though Melbourne's Queen Victoria Market. It was all so vivid in her mind. People jostling down the shaded aisles, excited and happy to be out for the day shopping, surrounded by life. Coats and suits hung in rows; shoes were stacked six feet high; tables overflowed with neatly trimmed gloves in enough colours to dazzle and confuse.

Her mind drifted to a different day, one moist and soft as spring. She mentally crossed Elliott Avenue in Royal Park, and followed the path they had taken as children on their way to the Zoological Gardens. The air pressed softly against her skin. Fragrant grass, painted the young green that belongs to spring, fell into soft folds on either side.

A car horn blurted loudly! "You okay there, Mrs Brennan?" shouted a man.

Molly stopped abruptly, startled by the voice. "What?"

"You gonna cross? Don't want to run you down," said Archie Doyle, with a chuckle.

"He would, you know," said Mavis, sitting beside him in the truck. The old Ford sputtered and shuddered as it waited impatiently.

"You all right there?" said Archie.

"Yes, yes, fine thanks. I was daydreaming, sorry." She started to cross the street.

"No worries," replied Archie. The truck crunched into gear behind her.

Mavis called out "You going to be here for Christmas, love?"

Molly stopped in the middle of the street and waved to Mavis. "Yes, looks like it."

"Lovely, we'll get together and have a chat!" Mavis shouted as they vanished into the trail of dust.

The bar almost felt cool compared to the raw heat of the street. "You back already," said Paddy as he rinsed some glasses. "The blokes fighting the fire up by Merrijig have come and gone. Sounds bad up there. Nobody's turned up from church yet."

"They'll be a while. I left early. Just couldn't stay there any longer."

"You okay?" She nodded. "How about I make you a nice, cold shandy?"

"Sounds good but think I'd rather have a lemonade, please." She sat at a table and fanned herself with her straw hat.

"Oh, and you needn't worry, all the blokes paid for their own drinks. They even bought me one," said Paddy.

"There you go."

Paddy pulled back a chair and sat beside her as he placed the glass in front of her. "So, I thought about Christmas."

"Good. And?"

"I'm sorry."

"For what?"

"For dragging you up here."

"No, you mustn't feel like that."

"I just didn't think it would be this rough."

"I know."

"I just wanted us to have a place of our own."

Molly took his hand in hers. "We both wanted that."

He lightly squeezed her hand, and they sat together in silence for a minute or two. "Truth be known, I think I was pretty selfish about it," said Paddy. Molly wanted to interrupt, but Paddy shook his head. "No, no, I've thought about it a lot. This was all my idea. You supported me but it wasn't on the top of your wish list, I'm sure. Mind you, if you hadn't been with me, well, I wouldn't have lasted this long, there's no doubt about that. I wish I could make Christmas better for you, you deserve a treat, something good to happen."

"We can't beat ourselves up," said Molly. "Did you know there were going to be such frightful droughts? No. It wouldn't matter where we had gone, Paddy, this terrible heat would have been waiting for us."

"This isn't what I'd hoped for." Paddy suffered sincere regret.

"It's not that bad."

Paddy just looked at her as if she'd lost her mind. Molly laughed a little. "All right, the pub is rough. Better than it was when we first got here. Remember? If you can look past that, there are some nice people here."

"Does it feel like home though?"

"Well, no, not yet anyway. But I am here by choice, Paddy. Don't forget that."

He leaned across the table and kissed her. They sat there comfortable in the silence of each other. "I wish they wouldn't come today and we could just close the doors," said Molly.

Paddy stood up and moved toward the pub door. "Do you want that? Seriously? Because if you do I'll gladly do it, shut them out for a change."

"No. Thank you, Paddy, that's very sweet of you, but no. It's not bad; they don't stay too long, and we can use the money."

"You sure? It could be one of your Christmas presents," said Paddy. "It might be your best offer, afraid we're going to be a little shy on Christmas presents this year."

Molly laughed and took a sip of her drink. "We're not going to worry about things like that this year. We have other presents that mean much more. Just being here, together."

They sat for a while thinking about the time ahead. "How about we reconsider locking the doors," said Paddy. Molly smiled. "Let me get you a little more lemonade?" said Paddy. He crossed to the bar. "I remember when I was a lid, wanted a new bike for Christmas. Wouldn't shut up about it. It had to be blue."

"Why blue?"

"No clue," said Paddy.

"Did you get it?" said Molly.

"Yeah," said Paddy. "Terrible bike, fell apart in about six months. Blue bikes aren't all they're cracked up to be." He placed Molly's lemonade in front of her.

"I had to have a new dress. Think I was about seven," she said. "Didn't care what it looked like as long as it was new. Seemed that everything I had had been passed down from one of my sister. Nothing was shabby, mind you, but nothing was new."

"Did you get it?"

"Yes. It was pink with yellow flowers. And it had this cardboard tag that said Fine Quality Dresses for Young Girls. That was maybe more important than the dress."

"So, do you want a new dress for Christmas this year?"

"No, not really. She leaned across the table and kissed him lightly. "Thank you for asking though. What about you?" she asked.

"I don't need anything," said Paddy.

"Okay, put need aside for a moment. Is there something you would like, something that would just make you happy?"

"Matter of fact there is," he said.

"Oh, really?"

"You bet. If you'd go to Melbourne for a few days, that'd make me happy."

"What?"

"I know it's not as good as rain, or a new dress, but I think it would be a good thing for you to do."

"I can't go to Melbourne!"

"Why not?"

"I can't leave you here alone."

"I'm a big boy, Molly. I can take care of myself for a few days, you know."

"But, what about the business?"

"I can get Barry to pitch in. There's no problem getting help. I do expect you to come back, you know," he said with a smile. "Just a few days away from this place should do the trick. See what the girls are up to. Look at the shops, that sort of thing."

"I can't."

"Course you can."

Molly was forced to think about it. It was not something she had ever considered, but the idea of escaping the dust and isolation was beginning to captivate her. "Can we really afford it, what with the train and everything?"

"No, not really but it's not like I was planning to pay bills this month anyway."

Molly was momentarily speechless. She just sat there, her mind racing ahead of her. "Oh, my!" She looked at Paddy; he just grinned and nodded. She wrapped her arms around his neck and kissed him. "Thank you. Thank you so much." She beamed at him and her cheeks flushed. She walked away to the bar and turned back to Paddy. She looked very alive and excited as if she had a wonderful secret.

Paddy studied her for a moment. "What?"

"I have an early Christmas present for you."

"Yeah?"

"Oh yes. It's something I think, I hope, that will make you very happy. She pulled him closer and whispered in his ear. There was a pause before he responded. He needed to replay it in his head to be sure of what he thought he 'd heard.

"Fair dinkum?" he said.

Molly nodded.

"Oh, my God." He swept her into his arms. "That's bloody brilliant."

"You happy?"

"Happy? Are you kidding?" Paddy's eyes glistened. "There's nothing in the world, nothing that could even come close. How long have you known. I mean, when?"

"Toward the end of May. I'm just over two and a half months now."

"Bloody hell, I'm speechless!" Paddy reached out and softly stroked her cheek. "We're going to have a baby," Paddy picked her up spun her around as he let out a mighty "You bloody ripper!"

"Are we interrupting anything?" said Norm Clancy. He was, standing at the door; the crowd from church was close at his heels.

"Matter of fact you are,' said Paddy. "Stand outside the door and I'll whistle when it's time to come in."

In no time the place buzzed with chatter as people lined up for drinks. "Go call your sisters, give 'em the good news," said Paddy.

"Mum's the word," said Molly. Paddy nodded and gave her a wink. "And you don't have to buy everyone drinks," She blew him a kiss and left.

Paddy couldn't stop smiling as he turned his attention back to his customers. "All right you lot. No pushing. You just came from church, didn't you? You should know how to behave."

"What's the big grin, Paddy?" said Norm. "You win the lottery or something?"

"Matter of fact, I did," he said as he placed a beer in front of Norm. "This one's on me, mate. Just don't tell the misses."

Chapter Forty-Two

There were no immediate fears of fires along the tracks for Molly's trip to Melbourne. Every now and then, acres of black stubble and charcoal stumps that were once proud gum trees would come into view as reminders that danger was never far away. Even so, it could not completely quell her excitement.

As promised, both Margaret and Big Joe were there at Spencer Street Station when the train pulled in. Margaret was thrilled to see Molly. Big Joe was, as always, charming and gentle. Molly liked him. He could build a roof, have beer with mates, and then write a poem for his wife. How could anyone not like him?

Margaret and Molly chatted briefly about the train, the heat and the prospect of being mothers. Although Margaret was a mere eight weeks shy of delivery she was spry and flushed with good health. Joe walked four paces behind carrying Molly's case.

"We're going to go home and give you a chance to freshen up," said Margaret. "Joe's got some work to take care of but thought we'd all head up to the Eastern Hills Hotel a little later if that's all right with you. Expect to see a lot of the family there." Alice got on the phone to round them up. Probably the only chance we'll have to get together before Christmas,"

"Sounds good," said Molly.

Did you know Jimmy was real crook?" said Margaret.

"No, nobody mentioned it," said Molly.

"Well, you know Jimmy, he wants to keep things quiet but it doesn't look good. Cancer, you know."

"When did this happen?" said Molly.

"Remember when he had surgery a couple of years ago? That's when it first struck. Now it's come back with a vengeance."

"I thought that was just to remove his appendix."

"Don't feel bad. None of us knew," said Margaret.

By the time they had reached Spencer Street and there were steady streams of traffic in both directions. "We're just parked across the street, the green car. Come on."

"Margaret! We are going to cross at the corner." Joe's voice was tinged with an edge of reprimand.

Margaret looked over her shoulder at him and smiled. She took Molly's arm, and stepped off the footpath into the confusion of the street. "Margaret!" Joe's voice was urgent. He was about to take her by the arm and pull back to safety when Margaret turned to the oncoming line of cars and waved. As if on command they dutifully stopped and let the pregnant women safely make her way to the centre of the street where she repeated the performance. "There," she said as they reached the car. "One of the perks of being really pregnant, everyone's happy to stop for you."

Molly spotted Joe at the corner waiting to cross the street safely. "You watch," said Margaret. "He won't speak much 'til be get home. Really annoys him when I do that."

"Why do you do it then?"

"Don't know. When you're as big as I am and you get to a point you have to do something for excitement, and please don't tell me it's irrational." She laughed. "I know he only gets mad because he loves me and wants to protect me. I like that." She waved at Joe as he approached. "He looks pissed off doesn't he," said Margaret. "I'd be so disappointed if he wasn't."

Chapter Forty-Three

A fan that Joe had set in the kitchen window hurried cooling air though the house. "Tea is ready," called Margaret. Molly had changed her clothes to freshen up. Margaret smiled broadly as Molly entered the room. "What are you grinning at?" asked Molly.

"You. I can see your bump. It's lovely."

"I don't think I could have kept it a secret much longer."

"Why did you want to?" said Margaret. "Keep it a secret, that is?"

"Just a little cautious, I guess," said Molly. "It's just with what happened last time. I wanted to be absolutely sure." Molly sat at the kitchen table. She loved the calm and quiet of the kitchen. "You look wonderful, by the way," she said.

"Joe keeps feeling my stomach trying to feel how many feet are kicking. I don't want to spoil his fun by telling him there's only one baby in there. He is so funny and sweet," said Margaret. "Here, a little more tea."

"Is he joining us?"

"No, He's working for bit. He'll meet us at the pub. Oh, while I think of it, I left some maternity dresses in a bag in your room. They'll be handy."

"Thanks." Molly fell silent. There was a wonderful peace and sanity to just being there. She slowly sipped her tea. "I think this is so good because all I can smell and taste is tea. There's no dust or smoke. Sometimes there is grit in the air from ashes that have blown into town. You can taste it."

"It's not as bad here, but there are days. Not long ago, huge ashes fell right in the heart of town."

The silence resumed. They enjoyed the comfort of sharing time together. "It's been tough up there?" said Margaret.

"Yes," said Molly but it was clear she didn't want to pursue that conversation.

"How was Paddy when you called him?"

"He was relieved I got here safely. Said he missed me."

"He called here, you know," said Margaret.

"Really? When?"

"Yesterday. He worries about you."

"I know."

"He was very funny, like a school kid. He kept fishing to know if I knew about the baby. I finally told him I did. He was very excited. We should get moving, I guess."

"Yes. It will be good to see everyone. Although going to a pub wouldn't be my first choice tonight." Molly gathered up the teacups, took them to the sink and rinsed them. It'll be lovely, though, seeing everyone," said Molly.

Margaret crossed to her sister and put her arms around her. "Look Molly, I know times are tough right now, but you're going to be okay. We're both making babies and we both have men who love us, so I think we're doing pretty well, don't you?" Molly nodded. "Now let's call a taxi, go to the pub, and drink lemonade 'til we can't walk straight."

Chapter Forty-Four

The Eastern Hills was in fine form by the time they got there. Margaret and Molly's entrance was greeted with a rowdy cheer.

Alice was seated with Anne and Bridget, an elder sister who had moved to Geelong. Tillie and Elizabeth found themselves in Melbourne for a few days and joined the party. Her brothers Jack and Morris were at the bar. More siblings were slated to arrive as the afternoon gained momentum.

Already the din had blurred any hope of real conversation. Molly didn't want to chat trivially in shorthand, she wanted to talk, really talk. That obviously wasn't going to happen. Alice and Anne had obviously had a head start on everyone else. They were jolly and unquestionably happy to see Molly but, on that night, they simply annoyed her.

If she said 'Everything is fine, thanks' once, she said it a hundred times. 'Yes, Paddy's great. Yes, we love it up there. Yes, we'd love you to come visit.' Everyone just wanted to know things was fine. Nobody really wanted the details, the dramas. This wasn't the time or the place and Molly simply wasn't interested in someone's bung knee or noisy neighbour or a plugged toilet. That wasn't why she had gone there.

At one point she considered standing on a table, telling them all she was worried about how they would get through next week, how she was frightened to sleep some nights when the fires drew close, how it would hurt Paddy if they failed at the pub, and how she resented the many reasons she couldn't feel completely joyful about the baby she was carrying inside her. She didn't do that. Instead, she slipped outside to catch her breath.

"Is it that bad in there?" Big Joe smiled broadly.

"I think I'm just tired, that's all."

He took out a packet of cigarettes and lit up. "You don't mind do you?"

Molly shook her head. It was a relief just to hear the distant clatter of the tram and the occasional car passing by. She didn't feel a need to speak and fortunately neither did Joe. Molly finally broke the silence. "How was work?'

"Okay, as work goes." He took a long draw on his cigarette and slowly exhaled the grey smoke into the night air. "It'll be good to have a few extra bob in my pocket when the baby comes." His eyes wrinkled and his smile drew even broader when he mentioned the baby.

"Tell me something, Joe. What does the baby mean to you?"

He didn't respond immediately. He leaned back against the brick façade, looked up to the sky and took a deep breath. Nobody had ever asked him this before. "Streuth, I don't know." He shrugged. "Everything, I guess."

He thought about that for a minute or two. "Bad shit can happen, you know. God knows, there was a time there when I couldn't find anything else. I was real unhappy. With myself. With everything. Then I said, no, stuff that, I got to get a life. If I'd stayed the man I was, I never would have found Margaret, and even if I had she wouldn't give me a second look. Look at me,'" he beamed. "I'm happy now. I made a life. Well, we made a life,

Margaret and me. Look at us, we're having a baby. A baby! Who'd have thought? That trumps all the other stuff, don't it?'

"Yes, it does. It certainly does."

"You coming back in?" he said.

"Honestly, I don't think so. I've seen everyone. I'll just hop on a tram and go home."

"You certainly will not," said Joe. "I'll run you home." He flicked his cigarette into the street. "Back in a sec."

"Joe, no, I don't want a fuss. I just want to go home. Margaret's having a good time, let her be."

"No worries. I'll be back before she knows I'm gone."

All right, thanks. Oh, my bag's inside," said Molly.

"You get your bag and I'll pull the car up. I'll be quick as a wink," said Joe.

The moment Molly opened the door she was convinced she'd made the right decision. She picked up an almost empty glass from a ledge; without it someone would insist on buying her a drink.

She made her way to where the sisters sat and picked up her bag. "Where you off to?" asked Agnes. Molly just pointed vaguely toward the toilets and slipped away before they all decided to join her.

In less than fifteen minutes she was home. The quiet inside the house was a perfect contrast to rowdiness of the pub. She filled the kettle and sat at the kitchen table waiting for it to boil.

How odd she thought it was that she had so longed to get to the city, to see everyone and yet, when it did come to pass, it was so much less than what she hoped for.

Her grandmother had often told her. "There can be far more passion to be found in the longing than the doing."

Molly never quite knew what she meant. Until now.

Chapter Forty-Five

The pub felt eerie at night when Paddy finally gave in to the day. There were no sounds of taps or kettles, no muffled footsteps on the stairs. The tiny incidental noises that breathed life into a home were suddenly absent.

Although he knew that leaving town for a few days was a good thing for Molly, He didn't like the fact that is was necessary and he determined to make important changes.

When Molly came home, the hotel would brim with Christmas cheer. The plan stirred in his brain as he lay there in the dark. "A tree," he thought as sleep threatened to overtake him, "We have to have a tree. Decorations. We have to have decorations." He could see it all and it was wondrous. "A crèche," he muttered, his mind spinning into darkness. "Molly would love that. I'll build...a crèche."

Now there was a plan. It would have to happen quickly and it wouldn't happen without help.

If Paddy were to be Santa, then Rabbit and Dodger would be his elves. This Mansfield Christmas would indeed be one to remember.

Chapter Forty-Six

The morning was freshened by a soft, cooling breeze off the bay. Just walking to the tram without sweat dripping off her after five minutes was an exhilarating change. She sat in the middle of the tram where the fresh air rushed around her body. Almost too soon she arrived at St. Vincent's Hospital on Victoria Parade, ironically no more than two blocks from where everyone partied the previous night.

Molly paused at the impressive entrance to St. Vincent's. She watched people flow in and out as nuns shuffled back and forth. She had never been comfortable with hospitals; they were foreboding and never free of implication.

When she was very young, her brother Alistair contracted meningitis and was rushed to the local hospital. He was in relative isolation; his mother could visit only if she was capped, gowned and masked. Molly had to wait outside. She would sit on a hard wooden bench in a hallway, listening to the echoes of feet on hard, tiled floors, distant hacking and wheezing, or someone crying; it was rare to hear laughter.

Hospitals never seemed like good places to come if you wanted to get better. Alistair's death supported that notion.

The fresh air of the outside world temporarily gave way to the stale air inside the hospital. She stopped at a desk and was directed to the fourth floor. The fist thing Molly noticed when she got off the elevator was that windows had been opened to beckon in the sweet air from outside. She felt better about the place already.

"Excuse me," Molly said to the nurse shuffling folders at the nursing station. "James Donahue. Is he on this floor?"

"Yes," she said as she looked at the watch pinned to her uniform. "Straight ahead. You have about an hour left."

The ward was large with a wall dividing it into two units each accommodating eight patients. Molly quietly walked from bed to bed looking for her brother. Obviously a mistake had been made, he wasn't there. The nurses' station was empty so she slowly retraced her steps.

This time she found him. The chart hanging on the end of the bed was proof. "James Donahue" it said in bold letters. Molly looked at the man again. Could this really be her brother? The tall, happy, handsome man who survived the war and would tuck her in at night, tickle her and tell her stories. Can this really be him?

His complexion was sallow; his cheeks hollow, the skin on his arms hung loosely over the bones. He was alarmingly thin, emaciated. He looked as if the breeze through the window were even a tad stronger it could carry him away.

Someone touched her on the shoulder. It was a nun who had brought a straight-backed chair over for Molly. She placed it by the bed and gestured for Molly to sit. "You'll be more comfortable. It's easier for him not to have to look up all the time." Molly sat in the chair still in some degree of shock that this could be Jim. "He should wake in a few minutes." The nun put her hand on Molly's arm as if she was dispensing a blessing.

"Thank you," said Molly. The nun smiled. She brought a sense of comfort and reassurance to Molly. There was nothing to suggest that Jim would be all right, but there was a certainty in her eyes that suggested this was a part of life and we all go through it so don't be afraid.

Molly sat there for about fifteen minutes before Jim stirred. He studied her sitting there for a minute. "Bub? That you?"

"Yes."

"Been a while," he said.

"Way too long."

"What are you doing here?"

"I found myself in the city for a day," said Molly. "Thought I'd come and say hello."

"Good on ya." His voice was unusually soft. "You're looking good."

"Thanks. I'm having a baby in May."

"That's lovely. Don't think I'll be around to see the little bugger."

"Don't say that, Jim, you never know," said Molly.

He didn't have to speak; the look in his eyes said it all. Molly took his hand in hers. She wanted shout that this was so unfair but she couldn't do that. Jim had enough to deal with; he didn't need her outrage. Shouting or crying would just have to wait. "Why didn't you tell us, Jim?" she said.

"I dunno. Never did like bad news, I guess. Anyway, always thought it'll be better tomorrow. Story of my life really, thinking tomorrow's gonna make things right. Stupid. You miss too many things that way. Know what I mean?"

Molly nodded. "Yes."

"Big mistake. Lying here, where you can see the end, you can also see where you come from, what you missed. Didn't do it right, Bub." Jim squeezed her hand a little tighter. "Tell me something," he smiled at her. "Is there anything you really want to do?

Molly had to think about that for a minute to be sure her answer was an honest one. "Yes."

"Then get on with it. You hear me."

The nun returned to the bedside. "How are we doing? Having a good chat?"

"Yes, thanks," said Molly.

Jim had closed his eyes. "Anything I can get you, James?" she asked. "Almost time for your medication." She looked at Molly to be sure she understood that the visit was coming to an end. I'll pop back in a couple of minutes."

Jim opened his eyes again. "It's for the pain. Knocks me out though."

"Is there anything I can do?" asked Molly.

"I'm real glad you came." He tapped his temple with his finger. "I got you up here now. It's good." He closed his eyes and breathed deeply. "You can do me one favour though."

"You name it," said Molly.

"Don't come back. I probably won't be here if you do but that's not the point. I don't want you to remember me like this. All right?"

Molly understood, but that didn't make it any easier to say goodbye to her brother. "Right."

"You got to promise," said Jim.

Molly didn't want to mean it but had to say it anyway. "I promise."

"Now, give us a kiss before you go."

Molly leaned across, hugged him tightly and kissed him on the cheek.

"Real glad you came," said Jim. "Lovely surprise. Now off you go."

"Good to see you, Jim"

He waved his hand lightly. It was clear there were to be no long goodbyes. Molly picked up her handbag and slowly made her way to the exit.

Her nun walked toward her. "On your way dear?"

Molly nodded.

"I haven't seen him look that good for a long time. You were a tonic." She reached out and placed a healing hand on Molly's shoulder once again. "God bless you, dear."

Molly walked into the street. She was numb. It was all such a tragic waste. Traffic buzzed every which way but it was a blur. All she could see was the broad smile of a young man in love with life. All she could hear was his joyous belly laugh as he tickled and teased her whenever he was home. How excited she was to see him then.

Where did he go? Who was that man she saw today. There was no joy, no laughter there, only deep sadness and a cancerous regret that life had been forfeited for the wasteful hope that tomorrow would be better than today. That happy, brave soldier had completely lost his way.

That's when Molly cried. She cried not just for the imminent end of her brother's life but also for the total loss of the life he had hoped to live.

Chapter Forty-Seven

The four sisters were seated around the table finishing a dinner of fresh lamb and vegetables. "Who'd like some more wine?" asked Margaret.

"Lovely," said Anne, holding up her glass.

Alice drained her glass. "That's a good drop," she said.

"Well, I guess you two will have to take care of this." Margaret placed the bottle on the table between them.

Good-oh," said Anne. "You're not pregnant, are you Alice?"

"Don't be disgusting."

"Well, you've been seeing that bloke, Jack, or whatever his name is and I hear he's a bit, you know." Anne enjoyed getting a rise out of Alice.

"No, I don't know what you mean."

"How was Jim, Molly?" asked Anne. "I went a few days ago. He slept through the whole thing. Left a note but don't think he knew I was there."

"I had a mass said for him Sunday," said Alice.

"We talked a bit. Hardly recognized him. It's all very sad. Look. I have a change of plans, I'm getting the train home in the morning."

"Anything wrong?" asked Alice.

291

"Did you get any shopping done?" said Anne.

"No, no, nothing wrong. I did have a walk around town and looked in the windows. It was all very pretty, but I miss being home. I miss Paddy. In some ways, that's been the best part of the trip, realizing that's where I want to be right now."

"I am sure he'll be glad to get you home. It'll be a lovely surprise for him when you turn up a day early," said Margaret.

"Well, it won't be a surprise, I phoned him this afternoon. He seemed a little stunned, but happy." Molly started to clear the table. "Now, who's ready for a cup of tea?"

Chapter Forty-Eight

Paddy looked up from the list he was making to see Barry walk into the bar. "Thank God you're here. You're free for the whole day?"

"Yeah. What's the panic about?" said Barry.

"Molly just called. She's coming home a day early."

"And you've got to clean up the place. All those sex parties."

"Yeah, there's that," said Paddy. "And I have to get the place decorated for Christmas. It's a surprise for her and now I've lost a whole day." He picked up the list and started checking items. "Christmas tree." Rabbit knew where everything that could be found would be found. "Where am I going to get a Christmas tree around here, Rabbit?" said Paddy.

Rabbit scratched his head and looked at Dodger for inspiration. "I dunno," he said. "There was a big stand of pines up the other side of the Paps.

The Paps, large hills the shape of giant breasts, were local landmarks on the outskirts of town.

"Didn't they burn down?" asked Barry as he cleaned up the bar.

"Nah. Not all of 'em anyway. We'll find something," said Rabbit.

293

"Right. Remember, it's got to be up and decorated by the end of day."

"All right, don't get all aerated!" said Dodger.

"What?" said Paddy.

Dodger turned to Rabbit. "I don't have a good axe any more."

"I do," said Rabbit with a wink and a canny cackle you would expect from a serial axe murderer. "We'll need a base to hold it up?"

"No worries," said Barry. "I'll take care of that."

"Right, Just go, Please," said Paddy. "There will be drinks waiting for you when you get back." Another wink and a nod and they were off, all the while debating what lay on the other side of the Paps.

"Okay, Barry, you're in charge here, I've got people to see and things to do." He studied his list. "Got most things covered I think. Where do you think I can get some snow? "

"Easy. Just take a couple of bottles to the hospital and they'll give you loads of cotton wool."

"Brilliant. If you get a minute, make a couple of calls and see if you can scrounge some decorations, tinsel, that sort of thing."

"No worries. I'll get Maggie on it. She's good with stuff like that. Do you want her to get the cotton wool, too?"

"Beauty. The more she can do, the better. I'm going to have my hands full with this crèche."

"You still gonna build that, eh?" said Barry.

"My oath. If I can ever figure out where to start."

"Why don't you ask whatshisname over at the school?" Paddy shook his head. "Who?"

"The Irish bloke. They say he's that way inclined."

"What's that supposed to mean? Said Paddy.

"You know, artistic like," said Barry.

Ronnie Mulhair, the third and fourth grade teacher was considered to be artsy and good with his hands. Barry felt sure he could give Paddy some pointers on how to get started.

"Worth a shot, I guess," said Paddy.

Back in the woods, there had been a fire behind the Paps and a large number of pine trees fell victim. The ones that had been spared were either way too big or way too small, with one exception, Pinus Rigida pine that stood some distance away from edge of a track. Pinus Rigida was never a truly gracious species of pine. It had a kind of scrubby, scruffy quality. The particular tree in question was no exception. It was hunched to one side as if cowering away from the flames. The needles we surprisingly sparse in places, as were branches. It was not blessed with what people liked to call 'a good side'. That being said, it was green and it was a tree, and that was better then anything they'd found.

Chapter Forty-Nine

The children had all been released for the Christmas holidays but fortunately for Paddy, Ronnie was one of two teachers who had come in to mark papers and tidy up their rooms.

"Paddy Brennan? What are you doing here?" said Ronnie as he approached. Ronnie was a man in his early forties with a shock of curly red hair, a mass of freckles and the lilt of Dublin in his voice. He often described himself as being tall for a leprechaun. He may have been one of the few parishioners who had actually understood any measure of Father Dolan's sermons.

Most of the women in town said he was sweet. Most of the men at the club said he was more interested in tight shorts then tight games.

"I need a little help," said Paddy.

"God knows, don't we all," said Ronnie with a laugh. "In any way in particular, Paddy?"

"I need to get a crèche built." Ronnie looked at him somewhat askance. "I don't mean a real one. Sort of like a model that can be in the lounge of the hotel."

"Cutting it a little tight aren't you?" said Ronnie.

"Tighter than you think. It's a surprise for my wife and she comes home tomorrow."

"Let me get this straight. Are you asking me to build you a crèche?"

"Hell, no! This is something I want to do. I just don't have a clue where to start."

Paddy was maybe the last person he would have expected to walk in the door wanting help with a crèche. It made Ronnie laugh. "Okay," said Paddy. "This was a mistake, sorry to have bothered you." He turned to go.

"No, no, stop. Wait! I'm just a little surprised. You? A crèche? It's not how I had you figured. You're not what one might call a regular churchgoer are you now?" Paddy wasn't enjoying this but didn't feel he had any options. "I'm sorry, I shouldn't have laughed," said Ronnie. "Come."

Paddy was somewhat reluctant but conceded. He really needed help on this one. Ronnie ushered him into his classroom. He asked Paddy for some details like where the crèche would go, how big should it be, what exactly did he have in mind. Paddy was responsive but it was all very vague, more guesswork than concept. Armed with the little he could glean, Ronnie sketched out a plan.

It was simple in its rendering but comprehensive. There would be a background that represented earth and sky. Ronnie indicated how a simple piece of string could stretch stars across the make-believe sky. Then, there was a simple stable structure, and he sketched all the characters and indicated how to cut them out with extensions on the bottom that would fold behind them to make them freestanding. He was very adept as throwing colour on the sketches to bring them to life.

"Is this getting complicated?" he asked.

"Yes," said Paddy.

"Do you want to do something else?"

"No."

298

"Have you ever done crafts before?" "Paddy seriously tried to think of something that applied. "Never mind," said Ronnie. "Have you ever done any creative things with your hands."

Paddy just grinned.

"Other than that," said Ronnie.

"I used to play a good trick with dead snakes that..."

"Don't finish that sentence. Here, what do you think? These are like mechanicals, how to build it, how it should look, sort of.

Paddy held up the drawing. "You're very good."

"Thank you."

Ronnie had drawn a simple structure with Mary, Jesus and Joseph standing within it. The Baby Jesus was centred. The three wise men in the background were slightly to the right. The animals of the field fleshed out the scene. It looked perfect.

"Maybe I could just stick this on the wall," said Paddy.

"No," said Ronnie. "This is a guide, not a god." Ronnie summarized instruction where to start, how to cut, what to bend, when to glue. He then packaged a generous supply of coloured cardboards and craft papers, both scraps and full sheets. Paddy listened earnestly, nodded and prayed it would still be clear when he got back home. Ronnie could sense Paddy's trepidation. "You sure you don't want me to help you build it?"

"Struth, of course I want you to but I'm going to take a chance and say no thanks You see, mate, it's sort of personal. This is a big part of my Christmas present to Molly, you understand?"

"Yes, I do, and I can't think of anything nicer." This was a side of Paddy that Ronnie or, indeed, most people had never seen. "I could give you a big hug right now," said Ronnie. Paddy just stared at him. "Don't worry I won't." There was a moment when neither of them knew what to do next.

"What the hell, it's Christmas." Paddy gave him a manly hug and patted him vigorously on the back. "Thanks mate, you've been a big help."

"My pleasure entirely. I'll walk you to the door." Ronnie put all the materials in a large portfolio. "This will make it easier to carry. You can hang on to my bag and I'll pick it up when I come to see your handiwork. Do you want to know why I decided to help you?"

"I don't know. Is it important?" said Paddy.

"I think it is. First of all, the fact that it's a present for your wife was a good enough reason by itself but...." Ronnie became a little reticent to continue. "How can I say this delicately? Maybe I can't. All right. Some blokes, a lot of blokes, are very quick to call me a poofta or look at me that way, but you never did."

Paddy couldn't think was to say and so he responded with a smile and shrug."

"I appreciated that," said Ronnie.

"Right. No worries. Not an issue, mate. Next time you come over to the pub, the first beer's on me."

"Thank you. Now, don't just stand around here, you've got a lot to do. Merry Christmas, Paddy."

"Merry Christmas, Ronnie"

The two men shook hands and Paddy went on his way to build a new home for Baby Jesus.

Chapter Fifty

There had been a minor transformation to the pub by the time Paddy made it back. Barry had come though with a base for the tree and Maggie had decked it with tinsel and decorations. Seems there was a surplus of Christmas supplies stored at the Prince of Wales that she could pillage. Barry had added a unique, personal touch by stringing beer bottle tops. The tree now looked considerably less mutated and quite jolly.

There was cotton snow on the edges of the windows and the mantle. There was even a slightly tattered but colourful wreath over the mantle in the Ladies Lounge.

Paddy had a beer while he reviewed the progress. Then it was time to tackle the piece-de-resistance: the crèche.

He was never noted for his fine motor skills but that didn't deter him. He cut long strips of brown cardboard to build a superstructure, which he glued. He meticulously studied Ronnie's blueprint but, try as he may, it looked increasingly less like a crèche and more like a bomb shelter.

The Virgin Mary came together brilliantly. The face was pink. The robes were blue. The trim was white. Stunning. The hard bits were things like eyes and mouths. The first mouth was unsuccessful. The lips were actually larger than the head. Subsequent attempts were fraught with their own quirks. Finally,

301

after many, many tries he had lips that were appropriate in both scale and proportion. "There" he said to himself. "That'll do the trick." He made the final commitment and glued them in place. The Virgin Mary had lips. Finally, something to be proud of, even though the lips were narrow and taut, leaving Mary with a curiously strained expression that suggested she was still in labour.

The baby Jesus came together quickly. His small pink face was swaddled in thin strips of cream cardboard. He looked a little like he'd been holding his breath for several hours, but that was very acceptable under the circumstances.

Paddy felt Joseph should be wearing brown robes and have facial hair. He was running short of brown cards but, undeterred, he held firm to his vision. "Pretty good," said Paddy, genuinely pleased with the fact that Joseph had both a beard and mouth. Later, when he assembled the characters, he'd discover that Joseph was a midget. For the life of him, Paddy couldn't imagine how Joseph got to be so small.

There was a stable, there was straw, there was a Virgin Mary, there was a Baby Jesus, and there was a Joseph. Pretty good. But there were no animals of the fields. There were no wise men. There were no gifts and it was 2:00 a.m.. He was also running out of materials and none of his characters had eyes. He stretched out on the floor of the bar to take a break. "Just for a minute," he said to himself. An hour later his snore, or rather snort, woke him abruptly.

He sat up and shook his head. Both his body and mind were crying out to go to bed but he refused to be beaten. He knew full well that if he gave in to those urges that would be the end of him. He may have been willing to accept a few compromises, but the could not accept defeat.

'Animals.' he thought. 'We need animals, like a lamb to rest at the end of the cradle. Typical to earlier efforts that evening, the lamb took forever. Unless there were drastic changes, it would be New Year's Eve before he finished.

Time to accelerate the process. Armed with a pair of scissors, a copy of Australia's rural newspaper, The Weekly Times, some string and a little glue he had all the animals he hoped for plus some he'd never thought of. Instead of gathering curiously around the cradle, cows, bulls, horses, sheep, pigs, rabbits and chicken now floated miraculously in the sky.

The three wise men fell victim to the lateness of the hour and the depletion of supplies. Those benign, richly-robed guests were now shadowy, faceless figures lurking ominously in the background.

Eyes had became Paddy's true nemesis. Misshapen lids and rejected eyeballs littered the floor around him. Just as he felt it would never happen, he had two good eyes. They were a little reminiscent a ring-tailed possum that had just woken up after a bad night, but they were the best eyes he had ever made.

There was, however, one small problem: they were a little too large to fit on to any one face.

It was way too late to start again and even if it wasn't, he was utterly exhausted and knew he couldn't conjure a better pair of eyes, so he made a creative decision. Mary got one eye, Jesus got one eye and Joseph got eyebrows.

The sun would soon peak over the horizon but no matter, it was done. The holy crèche, according to Paddy, had been rendered.

Chapter Fifty-One

Paddy was at the station almost twenty minutes before the train was due to arrive. The withering weather had moderated to what could have been described as just another hot day. Paddy slouched on the bench at the railway station, legs stretched out, arms folded. He peered down the track but the train was nowhere to be seen. He closed his eyes and felt the warm sun play upon him.

There were many more people than usual at the station on that day. Filled with thoughts of Christmas and what it might bring, children laughed, shouted and ran back and forth along the platform. Their unbridled excitement chastened only by mothers calling out that if their children get too close to the tracks they would be run over by the train and where would they be then?

The sound of the whistle and the train finally coming into sight created a flurry of excitement. People gathered up children and lined the platform in anticipation. The train snorted, rattled, and came to a clattering halt. As passengers filed off, they were hugged and kissed and whisked away with promises of frosty glasses of beer or some other beverages of choice.

In mere minutes the platform had emptied, save only for the young woman in the cotton dress and straw hat who sat on the bench next to the man who was lightly snoring. Molly leaned toward her husband and whispered, "Paddy?"

Nothing. He remained oblivious to the world. Jake the stationmaster walked passed the bench and looked at them. "He looks pleased to see you, don't he?" said Jake.

Molly could only smile. "He put on one his best ties."

"Oh well, that's all right then. He's been working hard while you've been away."

"Really?"

"Yeah, but I better shut up now, don't want to spoil the surprise."

Before Molly could ask what surprise, Jake kicked the sole of Paddy's shoe. "Come on, Paddy, you can't sleep here. You make the place look untidy!"

Startled, Paddy immediately woke and leapt to his feet. He stumbled forward, temporarily blinded by the flash of sunlight. "What?" he said.

"Move along, young man," said Jake. "Or I'll have to call a copper."

The first thing Paddy noticed was the stationary train. "Bloody hell!" He looked up and down the platform. "Did you see Molly?" he asked Jake as he peered into the window of the deserted train.

"Oh yeah," said Jake. "She left with a shoe salesman from the city?"

"What?"

"She's right behind you, you big mug," said Jake with a huge grin.

Paddy spun around to see Molly sitting on the bench. She waved at him. "Hello, love. Did you miss me?"

"Did I ever!" I must have dozed off. Sorry."

Molly just laughed. "You snored."

"Oh, no."

"Oh, yes. It was very funny."

"Welcome home." He kissed her.

"Thank you. It's good to be home," said Molly.

"Yeah?" said Paddy.

"Yes," said Molly.

She looked into his dark eyes. There was a cautious excitement there. Of the many things Paddy wanted from life, there was perhaps nothing more important than building this woman he loved a home. This past year had more than its share of challenges. Molly was more inclined to give voice to her frustrations with the relentless heat, the enduring sense of isolation, and the paucity of money that they could truly call their own. These were not imaginary battles; they were very real, and she knew they would all be there when she returned from Melbourne. But now, however, the shades and shapes of these torments that had haunted her were eased by the knowledge that she wasn't just going back to Mansfield. She was going home.

"For all its warts and wrinkles, this place gets under your skin." A smile, almost shy by nature, creased Paddy's face. This was a minute that mattered deeply. Molly's hand followed the angular lines of his handsome face. "I have to tell you Mr Brennan," she said, as she refined the knot of his best silk tie. "What makes this home is that you are here, you know that?" Paddy gently kissed the palm of her hand and then held her hand over his heart.

"Now," said Molly, "What's this big surprise I hear about?"

Chapter Fifty-Two

Molly wanted to tell Paddy about the odd sense of displacement she felt in Melbourne, how life there seemed trapped in time. Walking from the station to the hotel wasn't the time to do that. Paddy obviously had other things on his mind. Just before they entered the hotel, Paddy had a fleeting moment of insecurity "Remember, we didn't have much time."

"You didn't have much time. Yes, I understand."

"It was a bit of a rush to round up everything we needed so some of it's not quite finished the way I'd hoped." He paused for a moment and looked at her. "You don't know what I'm talking about do you?"

"Not a clue." Molly laughed. "Can we go in now?"

Paddy nodded and graciously ushered her through the door. As they entered, the bar itself seemed empty except for Barry. "G'day Mrs B. Good to have you back."

"It's good to be back. Oh, my," she said as she spotted the tinsel. Her eyes followed the tinsel's journey around the walls and over the top of the bar. She gave Barry a look to imply that she knew he was complicit in this; he just smiled and shrugged.

Finally her journey came to rest on the arthritic Christmas tree in the corner, looking very reminiscent of that very special old uncle one never talked about, standing proud in a borrowed party dress. Molly clasped her hands over her mouth to refrain from gasping, laughing or crying. She moved closer to revel in the glorious detail of hand-strung bottle caps, weathered or chipped ornaments and lush silver tinsel now gilded with age.

Paddy was anxious, unsure of how to read her reaction. He knew it was a far cry from the romantic image on Christmas cards, but it had a rugged, unabashed character of its own. "Do you like it?" he said.

"Like it?" said Molly, still mesmerized by the Christmas package she never expected. "I think it's the most beautiful tree I've ever seen in my life."

She wrapped her arms around Paddy. "It's perfect. Thank you."

Over Paddy's shoulder Molly looked into the Ladies Lounge. Dodger, Norm, Michael, Ronnie, Archie and Mavis had lined up in front of the Holy Family. They stood there, gleeful in anticipation, looking back at Molly and grinning foolishly.

"What's this lot up to?" asked Molly.

"We're not up to anything," said Mavis with a giggle.

"Come on you lot. You've got to take it seriously," said Ronnie. His focus shifted to Molly. "Paddy has worked very hard on this. I think what he achieved in such a short time is remarkable."

Molly looked at Paddy. She couldn't imagine what lay ahead. It was like unwrapping a present and having no idea what it might be.

"I'd just like to add..." said Ronnie

"Dear God, Ronnie, no, enough," said Paddy. "Just get on with it."

And with that, the human shield stepped aside; Paddy's interpretation of the Christmas story was revealed in all its glory. Molly was awe struck by the images assembled before her. "Oh my goodness," she said. "It's a crèche!" Where on earth did you get it?"

"He made it," said Mavis, with a certain reverence. "He was up all night. "What's more, he did it all to show Molly how much he loved her," said Mavis.

That's beautiful," said Dodger, wiping a tear from his eye.

"I think he did a fabulous job." Ronnie lead them in a round of applause. "What do you think, Mrs Brennan?"

"I think it's the best Christmas present ever." Molly moved closer, exploring all the details. "There is Mary and the baby Jesus." She turned to Paddy. I can't believe you made this, it's wonderful." Paddy was thrilled. "Thank you," she whispered and then turned her attention back to the crèche. "Where is Joseph?"

"He is right there," said Paddy as he pointed to wee Joseph.

"Right, right, right. There he is," said Molly. "Is he kneeling?"

"No," said Paddy. "That's just how he turned out."

"He's just a little fella isn't he," said Molly with a smile.

"Actually, it's very accurate," Ronnie stepped forward acting as something of a tour guide. "It's clearly noted in Deuteronomy, Just after the bit about Joseph being sold into slavery by Ishmaelites. And he shall marry Mary and he shall not be tall."

"Really?" said Molly, laughing. .

"Really," said Ronnie, nodding profoundly.

"Did he say anything about Mary only having one eye?" she said.

"Well, Jesus only has one eye and she's his mum," said Paddy. It had all made sense to him in the early hours of the morning when he was groggy and exhausted.

"Just a second," said Ronnie. "If I remember Exodus, and I think I do." He pointed to each of the characters as he spoke. "He said in chapter eleven, verse twenty-one - And there they stood in the stable surrounded by the beasts of the fields." His hand rippled across the fluttering cut-out animals on the string. The one-eyed

Virgin Mary and the one-eyed Baby Jesus." Then Ronnie started to giggle as he pointed at the creature at Mary's feet. "And their seeing-eye cat."

"That's a bloody sheep!" said Paddy.

"Sorry, their seeing-eye sheep."

There was a cheer of approval from the crowd and they all raised their glasses in tribute. Paddy had to wipe the tears from his eyes before he could speak."

"What are you lot so happy about?" Rabbit was standing in the bar looking at them.

"Come join us Rabbit." Molly beckoned him to come closer. "Barry, pour Rabbit a drink will you, love?" Rabbit moved slowly into the room still uncertain of what lay ahead. He took a long hard look. "What have we got here?"

"It's a crèche, Rabbit. Paddy made it for me for Christmas."

"Did ya now?"

"Can't deny it," said Paddy. "All my own work."

Rabbit quietly took it all in. Thoughtfully he pointed at the animals on strings and looked at Paddy. Paddy smiled and nodded. Barry handed Rabbit his glass of port. Rabbit took a sip, smacked his lips and returned to the Christmas scene. He pointed at the Virgin Mary as if to say this is yours too? Paddy nodded. Rabbit studied Joseph for minute, pointed, looked at Paddy, who, in turn, nodded. "You made all this?" he said. "All of it? On your own?"

Paddy nodded and smiled broadly.

Rabbit took a closer look at the characters. "And this," he said, "this little bloke here with only one eye, this is the baby Jesus?"

"Yeah, that's him all right," said Paddy.

You know what?" said Rabbit. "You're gonna go to hell."

Chapter Fifty-Three

Molly woke first on Christmas morning. The faint breeze of the previous evening had evolved into parched and oppressive gusts of hot northerly wind. She closed the window and sat on the edge of the bed contemplating what had to be done.

Paddy grabbed her around the waist and pulled her back beside him on the bed. "Merry Christmas,' he whispered.

"Merry Christmas" she replied. "Thank you."

"For what?"

She kissed him and lay close to him with one arm around his neck. She brushed the thick dark hair away from his face. "Everything," she said. They kissed again, this time with passion. Whatever else the day would be it would have to wait while they made love and then lay silent in each other's arms.

"What was that package on the bar," said Paddy.

"What package?" said Molly.

"I don't know," said Paddy. "There was a package down there with your name on it. Sitting right on the bar."

"No, there wasn't. I wiped down the bar last night."

"Well, maybe it was the Christmas fairy." A huge smile creased Paddy's cheeks.

"What have you done?" she said.

"Nothing."

313

"Tell me," Molly immediately put her fingers to work tickling him. "Come on, tell me." Paddy yelped and giggled and begged her to stop.

Finally he got clear and jumped out of bed. "Don't touch me! I'm just a messenger. Go check the bar. "Molly hurried down the stairs and into the bar. Yes, indeed, there was something for her

It was a brown paper package tied with string. Written in pen was her name and address, Molly Brennan, Imperial Hotel, High Street, Mansfield, Victoria, Australia.

She unfolded the paper and there it was, a new dress, hand-sewn by her sister Margaret. It was a pale shade of blue with small yellow and pink flowers. Tied around a button was a slightly crude cardboard tag that read Fine Quality Dresses for Young Women. The enclosed note simply said, "Dear Bub, thought you might like this." Margaret knew how tough it had been in Mansfield, and she sensed her sister's longing for something fresh and bright. She did what she had done those many years ago that made Molly so happy. She made her sister a dress.

Christmas Day was shaping up to be perfect.

Any fears that this would be bleak and lonely were quickly dispelled once Paddy opened the door, inviting guests in to celebrate with them. Neither Rabbit nor Dodger had social conflicts and leapt at the invitation. Rabbit volunteered to bring a chook. Dodger said he would cook something.

Ronnie was still glowing from the crèche event and rather invited himself and promised to bake all manner of things. Michael and Norm both found themselves at loose ends, Paddy insisted they come. Michael insisted nobody would want to eat what he could cook so he'd put money on the table for beer and refreshments. Norm promised at least one leg of lamb. Maggie heard about the communal dinner and said she would pitch in with the cooking. Barry would serve the drinks. Mavis and Archie

314

brought two Christmas hams. Molly felt this would be a tough Christmas for Ethel and daughter, Veronica. They shouldn't be left alone. Ethel was thrilled to be invited and brought fresh peas. Her sinful daughter would bake a pie for penance. The day had gained a momentum of its own.

Tables were lined up in the lounge and dressed with crisp white butcher's paper. Maggie brought her touch to bear; candles set in glasses and held firm with tiny pebbles decorated the length of the banquet table. There were enough white plates in the hotel kitchen to accommodate all the guests. Sprouts of artificial holly, remnants of tinsel, ribbons and crepe paper pulled everything together. This makeshift moment, this spontaneous gathering of assorted people could not have looked more elegant and festive.

Perhaps it was the spontaneity that helped spark the day. Nobody was there because of obligation. Everybody was there because that was precisely because that was where they wanted to be on that day. The food was abundant, the libations flowed freely, the laughter never really stopped. Of all the Christmas dinners being served that day in Mansfield, all of Gippsland and beyond, it would be hard to find one that more innocently or abundantly embraced what Christmas should be.

Ethel played the piano with gusto. Songs were sung, poems recited. Even Veronica, so shy and awkward by nature, sang and danced and laughed and cried. It was as if she has been released from her social solitude and didn't want to miss a moment.

There was one moment of caution for Molly. Everyone was about to find a place at the table for dinner. Rabbit, who hadn't stopped smiling since he arrived, was about to take his place. Mavis joked that he couldn't sit down at the Christmas table with his hat on. Rabbit just nodded and smiled and elected to pretend he didn't hear Mavis's comment about his hat. Mavis wouldn't let it rest. She was good-natured about it but insistent. It was Dodger that tugged on Molly's arm and whispered to her. So, the next time Mavis made a dig at Rabbit, Molly chimed in that this was Rabbit's finest Christmas hat and she insisted he wear it for the evening. Mavis laughed and said that in that case maybe she should have worn a hat, and the issue or Rabbit and his hat was never raised again.

Molly found a moment to take Dodger aside and ask him why the hat was so important to Rabbit. It turned out that Rabbit had become self-conscious of mysterious lumps that had formed on his head; one above his left ear and another more toward the base of the skull. Even with the hat on, if you knew where to look, you could see the irregularities.

Molly asked if Rabbit had seen the doctor. Dodger said he had been once some time ago but didn't like what the doctor told him so he hadn't gone back. Recently, the lumps had become significantly more pronounced.

Rabbit had always been prone to headaches. He never really complained about them but, upon reflection, they always seemed to be there. Once Molly had offered him aspirin. Rabbit declined, saying he had some herbs he could gather in the bush that he would grind for tea. He said they always did the trick.

Dodger made Molly promise not to say anything because his mate was having a corker time and he'd be upset if he knew he'd told her. Molly agreed. She would not forget what she had been told but that was not a time to focus on what might be. It was a time to focus on what was, and that particular day was a very good day for everyone.

Chapter Fifty-Four

It was 6:10 a.m. on the morning of Friday, January 13, 1939. Technically, the sun was up but the morning was black as pitch; a dense pall of smoke denied any light access to the scorched earth below.

Maurice McCarthy was sleeping in the back of the house. He had been up that night fighting fires that were overtaking the ridge just five miles outside Merrijig. He hadn't made it home until four in the morning.

Nothing was usual. Nothing was normal. Schools had been closed and the children had been confined to the house. Iris couldn't sleep soundly that night until Maurice was safely home. The children were restless. Three of the children stirred when they heard their father arrive. They wouldn't go back to bed; they wanted to sit in the kitchen with their mother. It wasn't even close to dawn but already the day had been shaken upside down. Iris decided a treat was needed. That would be her happy distraction. She would bake a cake.

The anticipation of a freshly baked cake excited the children. The children chattered in anticipation. "Hush," said their mother. "Don't wake the babies." Dawn and Jacob, the youngest of the brood, were still sleeping soundly in the bedroom next to the kitchen.

"Too late," said David, the oldest boy, as Jacob came to the doorway and looked in. "What are you doing?" he said, rubbing the sleep from his eyes.

"Mom is making us a cake," said Judith. She was thirteen years old and slight of frame like her mother.

"It's for all of us," said Iris, "including daddy."

"I'll tell Dawn," said the little one.

"No, no, no. Let her sleep." Maurice appeared at the kitchen door. "Oh, I'm sorry, dear, did the children stir you?" said Iris.

"Thought the smell of smoke was getting stronger," said Maurice. He went to the door of the house and looked outside.

"I've probably just burned the cake," said Iris in an attempt to allay fears.

Winds had shifted abruptly. The sky was a frightening fusion of scarlet and orange. "I don't like the look of this," said Maurice. "Get the kids dressed."

"Yes, of course," said Iris. "Come on you lot. You heard your father." Just as Iris opened the oven door to check her cake, a ball of fire crashed though the back bedroom window and exploded like a bomb.

"Oh, my God," said Iris.

"Out! Out! Everyone out!" shouted Maurice.

It was instant pandemonium. The children barely knew what happened before fire rushed down the hallway toward them.

"Out! Out! Everyone out now!" shouted Maurice.

The children cried and screamed in fear as the parents grabbed them and threw them through a doorway rimmed with fire and into the dark of day. In less than a minute the whole house was consumed by fire.

"You got everyone?" Maurice was shouting to Iris to be heard above the roar.

"Yes. Yes. I think so."

"What do you mean you think so?"

Iris spun around trying to the children behind her. "Oh, God. Maurice! I can't find Dawn. Have you got Dawn?"

"Jesus." Maurice ran back to the house shouting out for his daughter. "Dawn! Dawn!" He put his arms over his head to shield himself and ran back into the kitchen.

"Oh God. No, no, no." Overcome with despair, Iris sank to her knees.

"Mum, mum," said David, clutching at his mother.

Iris pushed him back. "No, get back. Everyone stay back."

"But it's Dawn. She's here. She fell into the ditch."

"Oh, God. Dear God, no!" She sprinted toward the house calling out for Maurice. "She's here! She's safe, Maurice. She's here!"

With a giant crack the old house snapped in two and roof collapsed over the doorway. There was no way out. Fire spat from the house and ignited a small stand of trees beside them.

"Come, everyone, quickly. Into the car. Quick," said Iris. "Dave, carry Dawn over to the car." The door handles were almost too hot to touch but that didn't matter now. The family scrambled into the car.

It was common practice to leave the keys in the car in case anyone needed it in a hurry. Iris fumbled and found them in the ignition, pumped the accelerator pedal, and slowly turned the key. "Please, God, start." The engine growled reluctantly. The stand of eucalyptus tree to the left of the house suddenly exploded in flames. Ashes and burning embers rained down around them. The children screamed in terror.

Iris cranked the key again. This time the engine caught and the car rattled to life. She rarely drove, she always deferred to Maurice, but that wasn't an option any more. She crunched the car into gear. It lurched forward and immediately stalled. Iris tried to screen everything else out and focus on the one thing that mattered: starting the car and keeping it running. She grabbed the key and turned it again. The car obediently complied. She pressed hard on the clutch and forced the car into gear. Slowly they gained speed. "Mom, the fire's closer. Hurry." The voices around her were urgent; the fire seemed to be chasing them. Iris slammed the car into the next gear, pressed the accelerator as hard as she dared, and urged the car up the little hill to the road. The gate was open. Acrid black smoke belched around them. It was more memory than sight that let Iris make it around the next curve. She planted her foot and the car picked up speed. They had left that fire behind but they were far from safe.

As they passed the next farm, Judith wound down her window and yelled. "It's coming, the fire's coming!" A man hastily acknowledged her as he and a boy scrambled to open gates in the feint hope that the sheep could make it to the creek and not be incinerated.

"Where's daddy?" said Dawn in a whisper. Iris was so focused on the keeping the car on track and running that she couldn't speak. She had no answer for the child.

"Where's daddy?" Dawn persisted. "Where's daddy? Why isn't he here?"

"Shut up," said her brother, Dave.

"But why isn't he here?"

"'Cause he went back into the house, that's why."

"But why...?

"Because he's dead, Dawn." Judith yelled at the child. "That's why. The fire got him. Dad's dead. Now, shut up."

Nobody spoke again before they reached Mansfield.

Chapter Fifty-Five

Molly looked blankly at the ceiling and listened to a fierce northerly wind stir the early morning world outside. Her thin cotton nightgown was already wet with perspiration. Molly had closed the windows when they went to bed in a vain effort to evade the smoke-saturated air.

That Friday was predicted to be the hottest day on record; there was talk of 114 degrees. That wouldn't be a total surprise. January had already recorded temperatures of 110 and 112 degrees.

It wasn't just the smothering heat that unsettled her. The whole town had been restless. Bells from the Fire Station were not unusual these days but that particular morning they were alarmingly regular. The frequent sounds of cars and trucks, both on the street outside and in the distance, also heightened the sense of foreboding. Everybody in Mansfield knew they had been living near the edge of tragedy. That edge was becoming defined.

Molly sat bolt upright in bed. She listened intently. On the edge of the wind was a voice calling out. A muffled knocking sound emerged, then ebbed away.

"Paddy? Are you awake?" she whispered. Paddy was sprawled out beside her. She shook his shoulder. He sat up in bed startled but not totally awake. "I think there's somebody at the door," said Molly as she clutched her dressing gown around her.

"Who's at the door?" Paddy was struggling to grasp what had happened.

"I'm going down to check on it." She hurried downstairs. The knocking had grown faint but there was definitely somebody out there. Molly briefly fumbled with the lock and opened the door.

Kneeling on the ground, crying and gasping was Iris, surrounded by five terrified children. Her bloodshot eyes were awash with tears. Molly crouched down. "What is it, Iris? Tell me what's wrong."

Iris was barely coherent, exhausted, unable to remain upright. Molly held her around the waist and half carried her, half dragged her to a chair in the lounge. "What happened?" she asked the children.

"Dad's dead," said David.

"What?" said Molly.

"He went back into the fire, and the house blew up," said Judith.

"Dear, God. Come inside," said Molly.

The relentless reports of fires across the state had been disturbing but this was different, this touched her personally. Maurice McCarthy was a man who had been in her bar. She knew where he liked to sit, what he liked to drink. He was a friend.

Molly stood in front of the stove watching the kettle boil. She felt she should return to the McCarthy's but needed time to let the gravity of the event sink in.

"What's up?" said Paddy as he entered the kitchen. He was dressed in pants and a shirt.

"It's Maurice McCarthy. He was killed in the fire. The whole house has gone."

"Jesus." He shook his head in disbelief.

"What do we do?" said Molly.

"I dunno. Whatever we can. I'm going to get cleaned up."

Molly made tea. Her hand trembled uncontrollably when she took down the teacups. She grasped the edge of the table and inhaled deeply until she felt more in control. She placed the pot on a large tray with teacups, some sugar and milk and returned to the lounge.

Nobody spoke. The hurt and horror of the last hour had numbed everyone. Some drank tea. Some started ahead without saying a word. Paddy returned. His hair was brushed and he was clean-shaven. "I'm going to open up the pub," he said. "I know it's early but blokes will be coming back from fighting fires. They might need a beer, somewhere to sit down."

Within two hours the bar was crowded. There was none of the usual lively banter. The fury of the fires had beaten down the men. Barry had turned up to give Paddy a hand.

Iris had stretched in a corner and her children lay on the floor around her. All the children were asleep, except for Judith who held the two youngest in her arms. Judith's face was streaked where muddied tears had trickled. Molly wiped the girl's cheeks and eyes with a warm facecloth. Judith didn't respond. She couldn't.

Molly went to the kitchen to take a quick inventory of supplies. The day was already a challenging one and it wasn't going to get any easier.

Chapter Fifty-Six

Noojee is an aboriginal word for 'place of rest". That's not why Rose, Molly's oldest sister, chose to live there. In 1919, the rail linked Noojee to Warragul, and this sleepy little town from the gold-rush days sprang to life. Sawmills could now operate in the area; work became plentiful. More than 120 miles of tramlines were built to link the many mills to the railway station. Wally, Rose's husband, saw this as a great opportunity to finally bankroll a few quid and build a home.

The work was tough, the money less abundant than hoped. That being said, they got by pretty well. Then came the summer of 1926. Fierce bushfires ravaged the region and Noojee was all but destroyed. 'Emoh Rou', as they had christened their cottage, was miraculously spared. Sadly, though, Wally went to help fight fires at the mill and was never seen again.

Catharine, the next oldest sister remained unmarried and went to stay with Rose who was then over fifty and suffering from crippling rheumatoid arthritis. There was a phone on the kitchen wall. It was dusty. It wasn't that nobody rang so much as they rarely chose to answer it. The two women became increasingly reclusive.

Anne became concerned as the fires in Gippsland grew more virulent. Joe was away and, as she was loathe to drive, she

325

took the trains from Benalla to Noojee via Melbourne. She had hoped to encourage her sisters to flee to the safety of the city. She knew the task would be a difficult one, Rose and Catharine were never what one might call compliant, and so Anne recruited Alice to make the journey with her.

Anne and Alice had only been in Noojee for one day and they were already fearful. When Anne stepped out of the house early the morning after they had arrived, fires that had seemed quite distant the previous evening now flared in every direction. This was far worse than anything Anne had seen before and she knew how treacherous the fires could be. Alice said little but prayed a lot. She had been terrified from the moment they had arrived. There was a train scheduled to leave for Warragul that afternoon at three o'clock; Anne was determined they would all be on it.

When Anne raised the subject of moving to safer ground, neither Rose nor Catharine seemed the least interested in leaving. "You are fussing about nothing, Anne," said Rose. "You're just trying to get us upset."

"Nothing? Just step ut of the house and take a look. You can see the fires. I mean you can actually see them, and the ones out west are moving closer and closer as you look at them."

"Can't be worse then the fires of twenty-six and we got through them. Alice, what do you think?" asked Rose.

Alice was sitting quietly at the end of the kitchen table, her hands clenched in prayer. "I'm terrified. I can't wait to get out of here," she said.

"What rubbish," said Rose. "I certainly am not giving up my good home. We're going to be fine."

Anne clasped Catharine's hand. "Cath, say you'll come with us."

Catharine thought that was almost amusing. "I can't do that, Anne. You know Rose can't get around without me."

326

"I should have stayed at home. I was safe there. "What if the train can't get through?" Alice was increasingly agitated. "Dear God, what will we do then?"

"You should say a rosary," was Catharine's offering.

"That won't put out the fire, Cath," said Anne.

The four women sat there in the kitchen. Rose reading a book, Catharine crocheting a doily, Alice quaking and praying and Anne with her head in her hands wondering how she could have been so naive to have come here in the first place. The phone rang. Catharine and Rose paused briefly and then resumed their tasks.

"Well, aren't you going to answer it?" said Anne.

"Never had good news over the telephone yet," said Rose, condemning the object with a curl of her lip.

Anne hurried to the phone and answered it. "Hello? No, it's her sister. What? Yes, Right, Right. Yes. Right away." She hung up the phone. "Come on, we have to get out now."

"What are you talking about?" said Rose.

"We have to evacuate the town. There are fires closing in all around us. We can't stay here."

"Where would we go." Catharine finally showed concern.

"They said, the river," said Anne as she hurried out to the front porch. She could see houses off to the edge of town that were already in flames. "Sweet Jesus."

"For God's sake, Rose, the town's on fire we have to go!"

"No," said Rose stubbornly. That's how Wally died. He went out there into the fire. Look what happened to him. I stayed here in this house and the fire didn't touch me. God will take care of me again. You watch."

"She's right," said Catharine. "It's safest here."

"No, no, no, that's not on." Anne gathered up her handbag. Alice didn't need to be asked to leave; she was already at the door. Anne turned to her sisters one more time. "Please. For the love of God, please come with us."

"No," said Rose with a chilling calmness. "If you feel you've got to go, you should go. We'll pray for you."

Anne could hear a truck getting closer. If they could get a ride, she thought, that might be their best chance. She ran out on to the porch just as the truck rushed by oblivious to her waves and shouts. She watched the truck stop abruptly as a flash of fire blocked the road in front of it.

They had to get to the river. Anne took Alice by the hand. They both cried and gasped as they ran as fast as they could toward Toorongo River. It was close to one hundred and fourteen degrees and north winds of over eighty miles an hour were whipping the fire into a rage. It was no more than a few hundred yards but it was almost more than they could endure. Alice stumbled and fell to the ground. A man hauled her to her feet and carried her toward a track heading down river.

"Alice!" Anne called out to her sister.

"Get in the river!" The man carrying Alice called out the warning again as he hurried away. Within moments they were out of sight. There was nothing Anne could do. She stood at the edge of the river, her heart pounding as she sucked for air. She looked at the water; there was nowhere else to go. This would be a leap from one danger into the arms of another. Anne couldn't swim a stroke.

A couple with a baby were already wading into the waters ahead. Fifteen or twenty people had crowded the deepest section at a narrow bend in the river.

Anne stumbled upstream a little to where it looked less deep. She kicked off her shoes and waded in. Immediately, her feet slipped on rocks and she fell backward. Water rushed over he face, into her mouth, her nose. She thrashed helplessly until hands grabbed her and hauled her out. "You okay, lady?" Anne gasped and sobbed unable to give the man a real answer. "Come on, up river a bit," said the man. "Less rocks. Better footing."

"Thank you," she said and gasped his arm as she followed him. He was right, when she waded back into the waters she felt much steadier, less panicked.

"When the fire comes, go right under. Just squat down."

"All right," said Anne.

"Practice it now," said the man as he hurried further downriver. "It's gonna be here in a minute." Anne looked upriver. It was terrifying to see fire ravish the banks and leap the very river itself.

There were more than people escaping to the water: dogs, cattle, bush creatures, even snakes had come out of the gully to find refuge. None of them bothered her. None were more frightening than the reckless fires forging toward her.

The heat was utterly fierce and the smoke so thick that when she surfaced she had to hold the sodden skirt of her dress over her face so that she could breathe. She submerged, she hid, she surfaced, she gasped, sucked air and then did it all again. Time and time again, she diligently observed the ritual until the fires abated. Gasping and sobbing, she had survived.

When it finally appeared safe to leave the water she waded upstream and clambered onto dry land, Her leather handbag still hung on her arm.

Further upriver in a pool of rocks she found her shoes. They were hot and soft as if they had been boiled, but they were still shoes.

Grasses were black stumps, stands of trees still burned but, if she was careful, she could make her way through the charred remnants of Noojee. Nature had savagely betrayed this fragile place of rest.

A team of firefighters descended with burlap water packs on their backs, rakes and other primitive tools to help save any shreds of life that survived but it was too late. Talking to one of the men was the man who had rescued Alice. Anne rushed to him. "My sister, Alice. You carried her away. Where is she?"

The man's face was frightening, blackened by soot; his eyes edged with blood. "What?"

"My sister. What happened to my sister?"

He was vague and unresponsive. For a moment Anne was uncertain that this was indeed the same man. Her heart sank.

"Your sister?" There was a moment of clarity. "The road south opened up. I got her on a truck. She'd be in Jindivick or Longwarry by now. No fires there right now."

Before Anne could respond, the man had turned and walked back into the remnants of the town. But Noojee was no more.

Anne slowly followed him until she turned the corner to Rose's cottage. She could barely believe it. There it stood: scorched, smudged and blackened but still intact. Every other building in the town had been razed but though some miracle the fire danced clear around Rose's cottage.

She hurried forward, but stopped when two men came out from inside. They spoke to her as they passed. "This your place?" said one. "It's a bloody miracle it's still there," said the other.

"No. My sisters," said Anne.

"Your sisters? Sorry about that, lady," they said as they went their way.

Anne pushed back the door.

Rose and Catherine were still there. They survived the fire but not the smoke. They had asphyxiated and lay slumped on lounge in the front room, as if asleep.

It appeared they had been holding hands.

Chapter Fifty-Seven

"Hello?' The voice came from the other side of the door to the lounge.

"Come in," said Molly. Perhaps the last person she expected to enter was Libby Scott. Libby rarely lacked confidence or bluster, but on that occasion she was more than a little subdued. There was no flashy smile, no insincere laughter. Molly had too much on her mind to be concerned about this apparent shift in attitude.

"Am I interrupting something?" Libby's question was almost an apology.

"What can I do for you, Libby?" Something was obviously out of order. "What is it?"

"It's Robbie, he's missing. Just wondered if you'd heard anything."

"No, nothing," said Molly. Robbie's disappearance was hard to figure. He wasn't the sort to be on the front fighting fires. How could he just go missing? Noise from the bar filtered into the kitchen.

Paddy entered. "What are you doing here?" He had little time for Libby or her husband.

Molly was quick to respond. "Robbie's gone missing."

331

"Oh," said Paddy. "Sorry about that." He turned to Molly. "Look love, I've got these two blokes in the bar. They came up from Yea to help fight the fires here. They're exhausted. I said we'd put 'em up."

"Right," said Molly. She couldn't argue with the sentiment. It was the logic that challenged her. "Where are we going to put them?"

"We've got some rooms upstairs," said Paddy.

"Yes, but they're totally empty rooms, Paddy," said Molly. "I've already got Iris and her five kids lying on the floor in the lounge.

"You don't have any beds?" said Libby with surprise.

"No, Libby. No beds, no sheets, pillows, nothing." Molly's reply was curt. She didn't appreciate Libby's interjection.

"Just thought I could help," said Libby.

"Sorry Libby, didn't mean to snap at you,"

Shouting from the bar caught everyone's attention. "You should get back in there," Molly said to Paddy.

"Just a minute, Paddy, before you go," said Libby. "If you need beds, I've got a bunch stored in the back of the pub. They're no great shakes but they're beds, some old mattresses too if you want."

Molly was taken off guard by Libby's offer. It was totally unexpected and seemingly out of character for someone Molly considered to be so self-obsessed. "Are you sure?"

"Of course I'm sure. Come on Molly let me help. I want to do something."

Molly nodded. "All right. Thank you."

"I'll need help getting them here," said Libby.

"No worries," said Paddy. "Some blokes in the bar will do the job."

"I'll go with them. Sure I can find linens, too."

"That would be wonderful," said Molly.

332

As Libby and Paddy headed for the bar, a woman pushed past them into the lounge. "You gotta take care of us?," she shouted.

Paddy suggested she take it easy, lower her voice a little.

"Don't you fuckin' tell me to take it easy." Her voice was grating. It was hard to put an age on the woman; she had become distressed by the fire in particular, and life in general. She wasn't old, but didn't look like she'd ever been young. Her hair was wildly unkempt, exposed flesh was smeared with dirt and charcoal, eyes were angry. Her three children were similarly wretched.

"That for us?" she said when she saw Molly with the tea.

"No," was Molly's succinct reply.

"Don't we get tea? Someone's got to take care of us," said the woman.

"Oh really?" Molly was by nature a nurturing soul. Her compassionate nature was rarely tested. That day was an exception.

The sudden, cruel and wasteful death of Maurice had devastated Iris yet, when she arrived, she demanded nothing and was grateful for any measure of kindness. This crude, offensive woman was the opposite: selfish, demanding and oblivious to everyone else's needs. "What's your name?" said Molly.

"Dolly. You gotta take care of us, my kid's broke her arm."

Dolly was from one of the forestry camps. Unholy places in the hills, some so impenetrable there was not even road in or out. The children were almost feral. Everyone one of them was filthy with matted hair and fingernails like pitch. It would be a fair bet that the dirt on their bodies had been there since birth. Molly felt for their plight but had neither the means nor the passion to have them in her home any longer.

So," said Molly in measured tones. "Who said we'd take care of you?"

"My girl broke her arm. It's gotta get fixed."

"Then you should go to the hospital."

"They didn't want to see us."

"I don't believe that."

The children ranged in age from about ten to fourteen. It was the oldest, a skinny leggy girl with bad skin who nursed her arm in a torn strip of fabric. Molly crossed to where she was sitting and knelt down. "What's your name?" The girl remained mute and suspicious. Molly pointed to the arm pressed against her chest. "Is this the arm you hurt?" Again the girl was unresponsive. If anything she flinched and moved away every so slightly. "Let me have a look at it." Molly gently moved her arm forward. She wanted to see if the girl could rotate her wrist and move her fingers. The girl did not want to be touched but Molly persisted and lightly manipulated the wrist. It seemed fine. She slowly bent the fingers. The girl leapt to her feet.

"Piss off!" said the girl.

"What did you say to me?"

"Stupid cow." The girl spat the words at Molly.

"You hurt her," said the mother. "You're not supposed to hurt her."

"Don't ever speak to me like that, you hear me?" Molly was furious.

"You gotta feed us, too," said the mother.

"No, I don't," said Molly.

Dolly glared at Iris and her children, obviously resentful that they had the tea. It was enough to terrify Iris. She gathered her brood around her.

"We had to sleep in a wombat hole last night."

"That's terrible," gasped Iris.

"At least you're alive today," said Molly,

"I held a wet blanket over the front to keep the fire out. All of us crammed in there. That's how she broke her arm."

"It isn't broken."

"It is!"

Paddy appeared at the door to the bar. "My young blokes from Yea. I've given them a couple of beers but they really need some grub, can we do that?" Before Molly could respond Paddy had vanished back into the bar.

There was a faint knock on the door from the bar and a mature man and his wife entered. "Excuse me." They'd obviously dressed in great haste. He had boots, no socks. He wore pants with suspenders, a jacket but no shirt. She was still in nightgown and slippers with a blanket around her shoulders. "We lost our home and wondered if you had a room we could rent for the night, please," said the man.

Molly's response was guarded. "I'm not quite sure what's left."

"We was here first," said the woman from the hills.

Would you mind if we just sat down for a bit? My wife's awful tired," said the man. "

"Od course you can. Come in. We'll see what we can do."

"Thank you," said the woman.

Dolly grabbed Molly by the arm. "We got here before them, remember" Molly shook herself free. Dolly grabbed her again.

"Stop that," said Molly.

Dolly was not to be put off and got right in Molly face. "You gotta take care of us."

"That's it," said Molly, pulling free. "I want you out of here, right now. Go! Take them and yourself to the hospital and if you don't like it there go to the old Coffee Palace up the other end of the street. It's been set up to help people and if they give you anything, say thank you. Lastly, and this is most important thing to remember, never, never come into this hotel again. If you do I'll have you arrested and thrown in goal for neglect."

"You're a cold-hearted bitch, you are."

"Hey, you, watch your language," said one of two young men standing in the doorway to the bar." You've been asked to leave," said the young man, as they closed in on the angry woman. "Get going."

Dolly spat at his feet, glared at Molly, then roughly grabbed her children and forced them out the door, almost knocking Libby Scott to the floor as they left. Libby placed a stack of sheets and pillowcases on a table. "There's more of this coming and the beds are on their way. I told the men to take them right upstairs, is that okay?"

"Thank you so much," said Molly.

One of the brothers stepped forward. "Paddy said we could stay for a while, rest up." They could barely stand they were so tired.

"Of course. We don't have any beds right now, but soon."

"No worries. We could just lie down over there." Leo, the elder brother, nodded in the direction of the corner.

"Of course," said Molly. "Are you're hungry?"

The men were too tired to reply; a light snoring sound began to grow. It wasn't just the physical fatigue that was debilitating. It was the feeling that, try as they may on that day, they simply couldn't win. The two young men sleeping in the corner had stood alongside many other brave men, working with nothing more than rakes, axes, shovels, crude burlap beaters, slashers or crosscut saws. If they were lucky they had knapsack pumps that could be refilled. Collectively they sought to hold an indiscriminate inferno on a thirty-mile front. Any victories forged were small ones and almost inconsequential. The whim of nature dictated the play. The entire day would be mired in chaos and uncertainty.

Libby had proven to be unexpectedly good to her word and delivered enough beds for the rooms upstairs along with two more to sit in the hallway. Her hotel, The Prince of Wales hadn't opened its doors, partly in deference to her husband's disappearance. Libby seemed to genuinely enjoy the shift from publican's wife to public benefactor. She dispensed food and care and shuttled people back and forth to the hospital and to the old Coffee Palace.

Molly was pleased to offer whatever help they could but wanted the hotel to be a way station, not destination. They simply didn't have the supplies to properly take care of everyone. She couldn't replace a home or possession so she willingly gave the most valuable gift she could, her time. She listened. Paddy manned the bar. He gave away far more beer than he sold and he did the most important thing he could. He listened. They both gave friends and strangers alike a place to hang their grief.

There was a numbing sameness to the stories. Each was gripping. Each was moving, fascinating, transfixing. Yet almost without exception each moved inexorably to the same tragic end. The charred stumps that were once homes. The slivers of cinders that had been snapshots of babies. The twisted metal that had once been a bed. So many times they wanted to look away, to stop listening, to find some respite from the horror outside the door but as long as someone needed to speak, they listened.

Six o'clock came and went. The doors stayed open. The frenetic energy had been numbed. The shock had subdued but the threat still hovered over everyone. The heart had been burned from Mansfield that day.

Iris came downstairs into the lounge. "I put the kids to bed."

"You all right up there?" said Molly.

"Oh, yes, I've got three of them top to toe on a mattress on the floor. The little ones are in my bed. It was a blessing Mrs Scott came up with the beds. We'll all say a prayer for her tonight."

"Yes, we will," said Molly. Libby had gone to the kitchen over half an hour ago to make a fresh pot of tea and hadn't been seen since. "Iris, keep an eye on the place, will you?"

"Of course."

There was steam rising from the spout of the kettle when Molly entered the kitchen. Libby was sitting at the table; her hands were clasped as if she had been praying. Molly lifted the kettle, it was almost dry.

"You're going to burn the bottom out of this in a minute, if you're not careful," said Molly as she refilled the kettle.

"I'm sorry," said Libby. "I wasn't paying attention."

Molly sat opposite her. "You've been a huge help today, thank you."

"It's been good to think about others for a change. Spend most of my time worrying about myself."

"Any news about Robbie?"

Libby tipped her head back and laughed without even a hint of humour. "Any news? Well, I'd say Robbie is dead for sure."

"You know this?"

"Oh, yes."

"You mean they found him?" said Molly.

"Not exactly."

"I don't understand." Molly waited patiently for an explanation.

"Can I tell you something?" said Libby. "Just between us girls." Libby didn't wait for any commitment from Molly. "I needed some money today, just a few pounds to be sure I could get groceries and things we needed here. They were going to close the bank early on account of everything that was going on but I made it. Problem was, there was almost no money. The account had been pretty much cleaned out. They told me Robbie had been in yesterday, withdrew a large sum of money. He took everything."

"Oh, my God," said Molly.

"Hang on, it gets better," said Libby. "So, I went and called the main branch in Melbourne where we keep most of the cash. Or should I say, where we used to keep most of the cash. Nothing. All gone. Every bloody penny. Robbie took it all and, wait for this, he took it all the day before yesterday. So, add it up. All our money in Melbourne, gone. All our money in Mansfield, gone. Trusted publican and husband, Robbie Scott, gone. So, you tell me, Molly, is he dead or not?"

"Libby, I don't know what to say." Molly was genuinely in shock.

"He's using the fire to take a flit. Bastard. He's got a little slut in Melbourne, don't know if she's got anything to do with it."

"Are you going to be all right?" said Molly.

"Me? Sure. I'm no fool. I have money put aside he doesn't know about; the pub's in my name and it's insured to the hilt. Be too bad if it caught fire wouldn't it."

"Don't do anything foolish," said Molly.

Before Libby could respond Iris popped her head inside the door. "Mrs Brennan, it's the phone. Paddy said to get you. I think it's your sister."

Molly hurried into the bar where the phone was on the wall. She looked into Paddy's eyes for some sign, some clue as to what might be waiting for her. He was unreadable. He held out the phone and said, "It's Anne."

"Anne? You all right? I was worried when I hadn't heard from you. What? Rose? I don't know, I phoned her about a week ago I guess. Why?" She listened intently and slowly closed her eyes. "Both of them?" There would be the occasional, perfunctory 'yes' and 'right'. Paddy already knew the gravity of the news. He put his arm around Molly's shoulder. "How will you get here then?" Molly asked Anne. "No, of course. No, you shouldn't stay there. We'll work it out. Right. See you in a few hours then. Right. Bye."

She stood there motionless; Paddy took the phone from her and hung it up. "Anne got a ride, she's coming to stay tonight."

"Good."

"Rose and Catherine...."

"Yes. I know. I'm so sorry, love," said Paddy.

Molly shook her head in disbelief at what had happened.

"Do you want to talk about it?" There was no response. She looked at Paddy. There was s sadness in her eyes so grave that it had left tears far behind. She struggled to find words to tell Paddy what she felt inside but they wouldn't come. "I just don't know...." She vaguely gestured toward the street.

" Go for a walk," said Paddy. She looked at Paddy, hoping he would say, wake up it's all a dream. "I mean it," said Paddy. "Get out. Go for a walk."

Chapter Fifty-Eight

Molly walked to the edge of Mansfield and just beyond.
Slowly the sounds of the town began to dissipate in the hot wind.

She couldn't quite comprehend that her sisters were gone.
She had never been close to Rose or Catharine but they were real,
they were precise, they weren't just one of the vague but harrowing
stories others told. They were her blood, her family, touchstones
in her life.

And what of the rest of her family, many of whom still
lived in pockets of the bush? They must be fine, she thought, or I
would have heard. Somehow bad news always makes its way
through the clutter.

An old gum tree had fallen by the side of the road many
years ago. Molly had retreated there before whenever she needed
to leave the town behind, sit and find her thoughts. She looked
up at the sky as the sun, eager to retreat from its complicity in the
day, sank quickly to the west. The deadly conflagration continued
to smoulder and flare in every other direction. The darker the
night became, the more astonishing the sky. Ribbons of yellow and
orange edged ashes floated high on the strong wind.

Molly remembered standing on the porch, as a young girl,
watching the very same thing far off to the south of the farm.
Then, it was one of the most beautiful things she had seen. She

341

hurried inside to tell her grandmother. "Nana, hurry look, there are magic lights in the sky."

Her grandmother walked back to the porch with the child to see these magic lights that had the little one so excited. She looked off to the horizon for some time. "No, my child, they are not magic lights. God is unhappy about something. He has hammered on his anvil and sparks have filled the sky. They are not happy lights. Now stop looking at them and come inside at once."

Later, from her bedroom window, Molly could still see the faraway lights. She wondered how anything so pretty could be so bad.

She promised herself that one day she would find out exactly what her grandmother meant.

Now she knew and wished she didn't.

The following morning winds still blew, fires still raged, smoke still tainted the air. Although the very worst it seemed was over, danger levels were extreme until, on the evening of Sunday, February 15, it rained.

In one day, that Black Friday, seventy-one people died, one thousand three hundred homes burned to the ground; several whole towns were entirely scorched from the face of the earth; a total of three thousand seven hundred buildings were destroyed, including sixty-nine sawmills; just shy of five million acres of land lay blackened and burned. Ashes fell as far away as New Zealand and contaminated local water supplies. It would take a decade to recover from the hell of a single day.

No one in the state of Victoria or even Australia was untouched by the tragedy.

Chapter Fifty-Nine

"I am naturally very sorry about how difficult it has been for you both over the last few weeks but we are at a juncture where we must take the appropriate action to resolve the continuing problem." Paddy stopped reading the letter long enough to top up his beer. "Why doesn't he just say what he means?"

"What does he mean?" asked Rabbit, the only customer in the bar at that early hour.

"We're months behind with the rent," said Molly.

"Streuth!" said Rabbit. "Is he gonna chuck you out?"

"Looks that way," said Paddy.

"He can't do that, can he?" said Rabbit.

Paddy continued with the letter. "Okay here we go...as a result of being three months in arrears, I have no option but to kick your sorry arses into the street."

"He said that?" Rabbit was appalled.

"No, I made that bit up," said Paddy attempting to lighten the moment. "He's going to be here later this week. Thursday," said Paddy. He folded the letter neatly and placed it on the bar.

Paddy and Molly had been living a fantasy. There had been too many months when they couldn't cover all the operating expenses and still pay the rent. The problem was that if someone had a serious thirst and didn't have a shilling to ease the pain,

343

Paddy would shout them a beer or two. Molly would scold Paddy for giving away profits and then do the very same thing herself. They banked many good feelings but little money.

The consequences of those decisions were never discussed. They didn't need to be. Both Paddy and Molly were silently aware of what might happen but in their hearts hoped and prayed that something, somehow, somewhere would make everything right again. That letter coldly spoke the unspoken. The costs of their omissions were most grave. They were to lose the home they had fought to save. There was a time for Molly when leaving this bruised, sunburned place didn't seem like a bad idea. Now, it broke her heart. Paddy had said little but Molly knew that even now he couldn't accept the idea of failure. It was Monday. Griffith would arrive on Thursday. There were only three days to construct a miracle and he didn't have a clue where to begin.

"Well," said Rabbit, "It all seems pretty cut and dried, don't it."

"Doesn't sound good, mate," said Paddy. "Have to say, the idea of just walking away sticks in my craw. Worked too bloody hard to give up."

"What are you gonna do?" Rabbit asked Paddy.

"Don't have a clue?" Paddy read the letter again in the feint hope that there was something less dire to be found between the lines.

"I had a thought," said Rabbit.

"Yes," said Molly.

"Is it dry in here or is it just me?" said Rabbit clutching his throat.

"Would a drink help?" asked Molly reaching for the bottle of port.

"Worth a shot." Rabbit savoured a sip of port and smacked his lips. "Much better, thanks Misses. So, I'm thinking, why don't you buy him out?"

"What was that?" said Paddy.

"Rabbit just said he thinks we should buy Griffith out," said Molly.

"Good thought," said Paddy. "How much have we got in the till?"

Michael Talbot entered the bar and looked around at the crowd of three: Paddy reading the letter one more time, Rabbit gazing thoughtfully into his glass of port and Molly totally lost in her own thoughts. None of them said hello, none of them even noticed he was there.

"Who died?" he asked.

"Looks like the pub did," said Rabbit.

"What?"

"Did you want something, Michael?"

"Well, I just popped in to say hello but if it's a wake of sorts, I guess I'll have a beer."

Rabbit went on to explain in remarkable detail how Griffith was coming in a few days and how, short of a minor miracle Paddy and Molly, would get the boot. He reiterated his suggestion that Paddy should buy the hotel and noted that Paddy dismissed the idea without giving it any real thought. Mike expressed his profound disappointment and regret and went on to say that it would be a terrible loss for the town. Rabbit agreed that the town would suffer and that something should be done, which brought him back to his starting position of buying out Griffith.

"For the love of God, Rabbit, don't you think I want to?" said Paddy. "I just don't have the money, it's as simple as that, mate."

"There's no-one you could borrow from out there? Any rich relatives?" asked Michael.

"No, we agreed we can't do that," said Molly. "The only one with money is Paddy's brother, Greg, and everyone turns to him to bail them out. I know he'd help but it's not fair to ask and so we won't. We have about a hundred pounds we could scrape together but that won't do it."

"I could probably lend you another hundred, if that helps," said Michael.

"Thanks, mate, I don't think so." said Paddy.

"Wait a minute now," said Rabbit. "There's my one-day money. Time we put it to good use, I say."

"Thanks mate, but that's to keep you alive."

"I don't know about that, Paddy," said Rabbit. "When the fires were raging there I thought that could be it. If me house goes up in flames, there goes me savings, I thought. A lotta good it would've done me then."

Molly told Rabbit he should keep his money in the bank where it's safe. Rabbit expressed his disdain and mistrust of bankers and how the potato sack he'd had since a child was his bank and how he could trust it not to run off with his money.

"How much have you got tucked away there, Rabbit?" asked Paddy.

"Paddy!" Molly scolded him for even asking even though she wanted to know the answer herself.

"Don't know. Never counted it," said Rabbit. "Tell me, Paddy, how much does this bloke want for the pub?"

"Well...I don't exactly know what he wants," said Paddy.

"Well, how do you know you can't afford it? Something's only worth what someone's willing to pay for it. What other offers does he have?"

Molly didn't even wait for Rabbit to ask and refilled his glass. She then topped up Mike's beer and poured drinks for herself and Paddy. There was nothing to be said at that very moment but there was a lot to speculate. They still only had one hundred pounds, two hundred if they took Mike up on his offer. Although they didn't know what Griffith would consider a reasonable offer, they knew two hundred pounds would be nothing more than a futile insult.

The future of the pub became a second thought when Rabbit attempted to get off his stool and fell hard to the floor. Rabbit was disoriented and confused. He had no idea what had transpired or, indeed, where he was. Mike propped him up and rested his head in his arms, Molly held a cool cloth to his temple. Paddy tried to get the doctor on the phone but without success. Rabbit gasped, his eyelids fluttered as the last flush of blood retreated from his gaunt face. Then, as suddenly as he lost control, he regained it. What had happened was a fog to him. He was flustered and disturbed by the attention. He insisted on getting up despite the protests of everyone. Once on his feet he couldn't wait to take his leave. Paddy told him that he had called the doctor. That only served to make Rabbit more determined to get out of there. He insisted that a pot of his special herb tea would fix him up, no worries. Nothing could dissuade the little man from this determination to leave. No, he would not talk about it. No, he would not allow anyone to walk him home, but he did promise to return later in the day when he was more himself.

The balance of that day was sleepy and uneventful but there was more drama yet to unfold. It was around 4:00 p.m. when Libby arrived.

"Hello, you lot," said Libby. "Paddy pour me a brandy, there's a dear. Molly, I got your message about the beds and everything and it's sweet of you to worry about them but I don't want them back. They're yours to keep."

As Paddy placed the brandy in front of Libby she clasped his wrist to hold him close. She glanced around the bar and then beckoned Molly to join them. It was all very conspiratorial. "Molly, I told you to keep the beds and all that. Well, there's a lot more treasures in the storage room. There are a couple of quite useful chests of drawers, a few tables and side chairs, there are even a few table lamps and there is a huge stack of linens and curtains. I've no use for them but they could make a big difference here. My point is, dear, you should make time to move everything you fancy from there to here." She nodded slowly at Molly as if there was a code shared between them.

"Paddy, in the back storage room you will find some boxes that I'd like moved. Remember, the door's not locked so anyone can get in there now. In two of the boxes are Robbie's private collections of fine Scotch whiskies. They cost a bloody fortune. I don't drink the stuff and he's certainly not going to get them now, so I'd like you to have them. All right?"

"I don't know, Libby..."

Libby held up her hand to halt Paddy's protest. "Listen to me! This isn't just for you; it's what I want. In the other boxes are some recent shipments of spirits for the hotel. I don't need them either." She anticipated Paddy's concern and held up her hand one more time. "I know what you're thinking but, trust me, it's for the best. You'll make much better use of them."

"I don't know what to say."

"Then just say you'll take care of things like I asked. There's just one thing, make sure everything's out by the end of next week."

"I don't understand," said Paddy.

"You don't have to understand." Libby looked at Molly. "He's a bit slow on the uptake sometimes isn't he. Let me put it this way Paddy. It would be terrible if anything happened to the pub but these days with the fires and all that, who can tell? It would be a pity if, I don't know, the pub caught fire or something like that and all those lovely things you could have used went up in smoke." She touched her lips to seal the secret. "I have to run. Glad we had this little chat." She drained the last of the brandy from her glass. Remember, everything out by the end of next week." She glanced around to confirm that no interlopers had heard the conversation and then left.

When Rabbit pointed out they didn't know they couldn't afford the hotel because they didn't actually know what it would cost he planted a tiny seed of hope. It wasn't much to hang on to but it was more than they had at the top of the day. Now, if something were to happen to the Prince of Wales as Libby inferred, that would make the Imperial the only pub in town and then its real value would certainly double or triple.

Just maybe, they began to feel, just maybe there was a way to get out of this mess after all. There was still one huge obstacle to overcome: the lack of any real money.

Chapter Sixty

The doors had been closed for just over an hour when Dodger and Rabbit arrived with Michael in tow. Turned out that Rabbit was still feeling wobbly when Dodger came to call. Rabbit told Dodger to get Michael who would drive them back to the pub and help them handle the bag in which Rabbit had stowed his life savings.

There was no pomp or ceremony. The bag was placed on the middle of the kitchen table and everyone sat around it in respectful silence. They just looked at it. How big should a bag be to hold a life? It was bigger than a handful of banknotes and smaller than his calendar of years. There were enough remnants of writing on the coarse brown burlap to confirm it had been a humble potato sack before Rabbit found a better use for it. There it sat, a holy grail, grubby and coarse and tied up with string. Finally Dodger shattered the awkward silence.

"How much do you think is in there, mate?" he asked.

Rabbit shrugged. "Dunno."

"You never counted it?" asked Michael.

Rabbit just shook his head. "Didn't see the point."

"Right," said Paddy. "First things first. I think we all need a drink." That idea struck the right chord with everyone; glasses were filled and the mood lightened.

351

Molly noticed that Rabbit's attention has returned to the sack on the table. She put her arm around his shoulders. "You don't have to do this, you know."

"Not doing it because I have to. Doing it because it's the right time to do it."

"You sure?'

"Yeah." He grinned broadly. "I want to know what's in there now."

"Then let's do it," said Molly. She took his hand and led him to the table. "If anyone's interested we're going to get started."

The three men stood back and watched as Molly untied the sack and began to tip the contents onto the table. Money tumbled everywhere; it was like a pirates booty being discovered. Some coins rushed from hiding and scurried and rolled across the table and onto the floor in an effort to escape.

Skinny strips of tattered newspaper fluttered around the mound of loose coins. Paper money appeared to be more organized. Ten shilling and one pound notes had been neatly straightened to minimize the creases and then neatly rolled. Some wads were fat, some were skinny. Rabbit never sorted them into specific amounts; it was more of less governed by what was on hand when the mood struck him. The wads may have been random but the treatment was consistent. They were all tied with strings that were remnants of other times.

Coins that had once been sorted and rolled in strips of newspaper had generally broken loose, as the papers had given in to age. Everything rattled in the bottom of the bag, halfpennies, pennies, three and sixpenny pieces, shillings and two shilling coins. Crowns, five-shilling coins, were stashed in envelopes that once carried birthday cards for or letters. Everyone had chattered and joked as the money tumbled from the bag. Now they were silent. This was, after all, a man's life.

"What do we do now?" said Michael.

352

"We count it," said Molly. "I'll get a pencil and paper and keep tally."

The men sorted and counted and stacked the coins while Molly concentrated on the paper money. One envelope lay to the side. It was unique, unlike any others. Molly picked it up. There was some scratchy writing on the front that she couldn't discern.

"What is this?" she asked Rabbit.

He took the envelope in his hands and gently felt the gain of the paper and smoothed out the edges that had been crushed. It was not as he said, "Aw, it's just an envelope." Molly knew it was much more than that.

"There's ten quid in there," Rabbit grinned as he handed the envelope to Molly.

"Ten pounds is a lot of money," she said. "Where did you get it?"

Rabbit searched for an answer that would skirt the truth but satisfy Molly.

"Rabbit?" Molly persisted.

Finally the little man relented. "It was from my Aunt Addy. It was to get me started when I left school."

"Then you must keep it." Molly's tone was absolute. This was nothing to discuss.

"No. I don't need it now. Just chuck it in with the rest. Be better off there."

"We don't want it, thank you, Rabbit," said Paddy.

"Well, I don't need it now." Rabbit was willing to push in the other direction.

"Please," Molly said very gently. "I think this is important and it would make me happy if you would keep it safe. Perhaps one day we may need it, but until then..."

Rabbit conceded and slipped the envelope into the pocket of his jacket. Despite his protestations, there was a small satisfaction to be discerned in Rabbit's eyes. Finally the job was done. All sat around as Molly added the numbers. "How many times you going to count that Molly?" said Paddy.

"Shush," said Molly as she went through the numbers yet one more time. She put he pad on the table in front of her, took a deep breath to compose herself and said. "There's four hundred and twenty-eight pounds, fourteen shilling and eight pence."

"Bloody hell," said Paddy. "That's a lot of money."

"You think it's enough?" asked Rabbit.

"Don't know, mate." Paddy shook his head. "For a pub? It's a reach for a sure but, I mean, you never know."

"I can still lend you a hundred quid if you need it," said Michael.

Paddy smiled and shook his head. "Thanks, mate, but we're so far below what I reckon he'd expect, I don't think it will make a difference."

"When's he coming?" asked Michael.

"Thursday," said Molly.

"Then I'd better get cracking," said Paddy.

"What are you gonna do, Paddy?" asked Rabbit.

"Don't know exactly, Rabbit."

"But you're going to buy the pub, right?" said Rabbit.

"We're going to buy the pub. You're a partner now," said Paddy. Rabbit chuckled at that and said that wasn't on. Paddy jovially maintained his insistence but Rabbit looked Paddy steadfastly in the eye and saying, quite simple, that he didn't want that. The matter was closed.

"Fair enough," said Paddy. "We want you here with us on Thursday. He's coming about one o'clock. Okay?"

Molly suddenly felt a need to protect Rabbit. He looked overwhelmed and a little lost. She put her arm around him. "You all right?'

He looked up at her. "I don't know if I can make it Thursday." For reasons that couldn't be explained he was genuinely concerned about his ability to be there.

"Don't worry about it, Rabbit." Molly squeezed his shoulders a little tighter. "If you can, we'd love to see you here."

"It's been a big day," said Rabbit.

"Yes, it has, mate," said Paddy.

Rabbit nodded, thought about everything for a moment and turned to leave. Molly noticed that the envelope from his aunt was back on the table. "Just a minute." She opened Rabbit's jacket and slipped the envelope into his inside pocket. "This is yours." She closed his jacket and pressed her hand against where the envelope would be. Ever so faintly she felt his heart beat.

"Thursday," said Molly.

"Thursday," said Rabbit. He smiled and then was gone.

Chapter Sixty-One

Molly was in the kitchen making sandwiches to get a head start on the lunch crowd. The mill that been quiet for weeks had restarted operations and the men would be thirsty and hungry. As she turned to get a fresh loaf of bread, she saw Rabbit standing there in the kitchen. Molly gasped and clutched her hand to her chest.

"Oh! You startled me."

"Sorry, Mrs B," said Rabbit softly. "Didn't mean to frighten you."

Just seeing Rabbit in the kitchen was a shock. He was very reticent to venture anywhere in the hotel other than his habitual place in the bar.

"It's all right. I just didn't hear you come in," said Molly.

Rabbit just smiled and nodded. He quietly watched Molly carefully measuring out the ham and cheese.

"Did you want something, Rabbit?" Molly asked as she arranged some of the sandwiches on a large plate. "We don't meet with Griffith until tomorrow."

"I know. Just thought I'd say hello, that's all."

Molly wiped her hands on a tea towel while she looked at the little man who seemed more wizened than before.

"Are you all right?" asked Molly.

He smiled and nodded.

"Would you like a sandwich?"

"I'm going for a walk," he said.

"Right," said Molly. She was becoming increasingly uncomfortable for reasons she couldn't quite understand. Rabbit was by nature enigmatic but on this occasion he was even more difficult to read. The deep hazel eyes didn't twinkle, and his face didn't crease with lines of laughter or thought. Life was momentarily suspended.

"Then you'll be hungry," she said. "Let me make a sandwich for you to take on your walk."

"You don't have to do that, Misses."

Molly sliced the bread and made Rabbit a hearty ham sandwich, which she wrapped in wax paper. "There you go, and I'll wrap a thick slice of cheddar cheese for you. It's your favourite."

She handed him the sandwich and cheese and as she did he took her hand and shook it. "You're a good sort, Missus, you are. The sandwich'll be good." He carefully tucked the sandwich into one pocket of his jacket and the cheese into another.

"I should get going," he said.

"On your walk?"

"Yeah. Think it will be nice after the rain we just got."

"Yes," said Molly. "Everything feels better after rain."

She didn't want him to go. "Tell you what, why don't you sit down and eat your sandwich here with us." She crossed to the door from the kitchen to the bar. "Paddy, pour Rabbit his glass of port will you, dear. He's going to visit for bit."

"What?" said Paddy. "He's not here. I think he left."

"Just do it, please." She turned to Rabbit. "You'll have plenty of time to go for a walk later. A lovely glass of port. A sandwich. We'll have a good chat."

"No, I gotta go," he said with simple assurance.

"Your glass of port is on the bar." Molly could think of no stronger hook to hold him but Rabbit just shook his head and gave her a toothless smile. "Well, it'll be there on the bar for when you come back from your walk," said Molly. "Don't you forget that."

"Fair enough." He shuffled a little then turned for the door. "Hooroo."

"Just a minute," said Molly as she walked to where he stood. "I gave you a sandwich, don't I get a hug?"

"If you like," said Rabbit.

Molly put her arms around him. She could feel the bones in his skinny frame. It was time to let him go.

"You have a good walk," she said.

"I will." He left through the door into the bar on his way out of the hotel. Molly could hear Paddy call to him.

"Here's your drink, mate. Rabbit? You hear me? Here's your glass of port, mate."

There was no response. Rabbit was gone. There, on the sideboard, was the envelope from Aunt Addy with the ten-pound note still safely tucked inside. "Rabbit!" she called out. "Paddy, is Rabbit still there?"

Paddy poked his head around the corner. "No, he's gone."

Molly returned the envelope to the sideboard. "Make sure he gets it when he comes back."

"What's up with him, anyway?" said Paddy.

"Nothing," said Molly.

"Funny little bugger he is," said Paddy.

"He's just going for a walk."

"We're getting busy in here, how long you going to be?"

"Not long." Molly closed the door to dampen the shouting and bluster coming from the bar. She sat at the table in the empty kitchen and thought about the little man with the ham sandwich in his pocket and all he had meant to them.

Chapter Sixty-Two

It was a quarter to six and a few locals who should have gone home hours earlier still lingered in a corner of the bar. Down at the end of the bar sat a glass of port. Paddy wanted to clear it away; Molly insisted it stay.

"I need to get some air," she said. "Can you close up without me?"

"Of course," said Paddy. "You gonna lie down?"

Molly's pregnancy had been very uneventful but now at six months she was often prone to be tired. "Don't think so," she said. "Just need to get up and stretch my legs. I'll do the till when I get back. All right?"

She didn't wait for a response; she needed to go. The heavy rain had settled the red dust that most days had lined her throat. By contrast the humidity of that afternoon pushed against her skin; she could almost grasp it as it rose from the ground.

There were puddles on the edge of the road as she made her way back past the railway station and soon her shoes were spattered with mud but she didn't care. A skinny, mushy track led her over the railway lines and soon she came to the three sentinels of which Rabbit had spoken. There seemed to be no path to follow through the scrub but Molly forged on. Dried brambles scratched her legs and snagged her stockings; mosquitoes descended upon her in a cloud and she thrashed around in frustration until miraculously, the dense brush cleared.

There it was, the gully, and Jack Back Creek was enjoying its injection of life. The narrow creek led to a small pond where water eddied near a clump of gum trees. It was very quiet save only for the sound of the water and the magpies that had come to rest across the creek. Molly listened intently for a minute of two as a flock of crested bellbirds joined the chorus and settled near by.

"Rabbit?" Molly called out but only the magpies responded.

She carefully made her way to the water's edge and stepped around the stones and scrubby bushes to where the land cleared. This was, indeed, where Rabbit had come for his walk.

He lay there still and silent on the edge of the creek, shaded by a big red gum tree. He had obviously taken off his clothes to bathe in the waters. The remnants of a small bar of pink, carbolic soap sat on a stone beside him. His silver hair was combed straight back and cleaner than Molly could ever remember seeing it. A ragged yet clean white towel had been rolled as a pillow on which to rest his head.

His eyes were closed and she felt there were still traces of a smile at the corners of his lips. It looked as if his hands had been lightly clasped on his chest but one had fallen to the side. Arms and face had become crusty, taut and brown from all the sun they had endured but the skin on his body was very white and almost translucent as it sagged on the ribs that rippled on this strangely subdued man.

Molly leant to touch him, and as if in protest there was a rage of squawking from the magpies and bellbirds. "Leave him be!" they seemed to say. There was no life to discover; that much was clear. He was gone. Molly simply lifted his right hand and placed it back on his chest. That seemed to satisfy the birds that guarded him. She picked up his coat jacket with the intention of covering his naked body but decided against it. This was how he should be. This is how he entered life. This is how he chose to leave it.

There was no wailing. There were no tears. This was a place of peace and resolution and Molly felt lucky that, in some way, she could share this brief time with the odd little man she had come to love.

She knelt beside him and prayed for him and thanked God for letting Rabbit find his peace here beside this creek that he'd known as a boy. As she stood, she noticed that the wax paper in which she had wrapped his sandwich and cheese had been neatly pressed and folded. Beside it was a book. Molly gingerly reached over and retrieved it.

The lovingly frayed leather cover had mellowed to the texture of velvet. It felt warm and comfortable in her hands. Tom Brown's School Days by Thomas Hughes, it said, subtly embossed and still sporting traces of gold. If Molly had to pick a book for Rabbit, it wouldn't have been this, but somehow now it felt totally right.

This book was worn but in a way a book should be worn: with respect and with love. She tentatively opened the cover. Inside, on the right-hand page, there was a simple note, hand written with a nib pen and ink.

Dear Peter. To celebrate your twelfth birthday. Congratulations on winning the school race. You run like a rabbit, my dear. Bless you,

Aunty Addy

1878

So there it was: Rabbit had a name after all, and it was Peter.

Chapter Sixty-Three

Thursday was steamy. Molly could feel the sweat on her back when she first went into the bar to spruce up the place before Griffith arrived. She was determined to wax the bar so brilliantly that a person could see himself well enough to shave. She had just started at one end when Paddy entered.

"What are you doing?" he said, somewhat disturbed to see her so hard at work.

"I want the place to look its best, that's all," she said.

Paddy took the polishing cloth out of her hand. "Good on you, love, but we don't want that do we?" Molly was confused. "I'm going to be telling him the place is going to the dogs and he's lucky to be getting just over four hundred quid for it. The nicer you make things look the tougher it'll be to convince him."

This rationale made perfect sense but it went against everything she had been taught. Special occasions were made more special with elbow grease and a good wax. "Can it at least be clean?"

"It's always clean," he said.

"You're right. I know you're right," said Molly. Reluctantly she gathered up her tools. "I wish Rabbit could have been here."

"He's here, love. He's with us and I won't let him down, don't you worry about that." Paddy held out his hand for the polishing cloth. Once it's ours, you can polish it every day.

Strategies were operating on a number of fronts. The last thing Paddy wanted at this time on this day was a bar full of thirsty patrons. Anyone with a beer on his mind was being diverted either to the Prince of Wales hotel or to the undertaker. Michael had been stocked with bottles of Victoria Bitter to act as an offsite bar that would help keep parched patrons away from the real pub until Griffith's Ford had receded into the horizon.

The weather had been fractious; days of oppressive heat momentarily interrupted by occasional squalls of rain. On that Thursday the heat hung heavy with soaring humidity.

Griffith looked curiously out of place in a dark three-piece suit as he entered the hotel. He glanced around the empty bar as Paddy came around to greet him. "Good to see you, Griffith."

"Hello Paddy. Mrs Brennan." The stiff collar of his white shirt was stained with perspiration.

"For God's sake, take off your coat. The heat'll kill you," said Paddy.

"Yes, I think I might." He took off his coat, hung it on the back of a chair and then unbuttoned his vest and sat. This was not Griffith's usual decorum. He had always seemed impervious to the conditions. Paddy hoped this would be a good sign.

"Let me get you a cold beer."

"No, thanks Paddy, not while I am working and I have to drive back to Melbourne."

"How about a cold lemonade then?" said Molly.

"That would be lovely, thank you. He looked around again. I seem to be your only customer."

"Well, business isn't what it used to be before the fires. We've had a couple of people in, two or three anyway."

366

Griffith took a moment to consider that and then opened his briefcase. "Well, to business. I am sorry that we have come to this point, Paddy but the lease agreement was very clear about how much latitude you had."

"There you go," said Molly as she delivered lemonade for Griffith and beer for Paddy. "Mind if I join you?"

"No, not at all." Griffith opened his leather briefcase and extracted a copy of the agreement between himself and the Brennans. "I am sure you're familiar with the agreement but let us go over it one more time, shall we?"

"No, thanks. I don't think so," said Paddy.

Griffith was surprised by Paddy's response to what was obviously meant to be a rhetorical question. "I beg your pardon?" he said.

"No, we don't want to go through that again. It's not going to get us anywhere. You like to get straight to business, don't you?" said Paddy. "So do we." Paddy reached across the table and, to Griffith's surprise, took the copy of the agreement out of his hands and looked at it. "Yes," he said. "I've got one of these." He crossed to the bar and opened up a folder filed with papers. He held the two agreements side by side. "Yup, same thing. Tell you what. These are useless right now, let's leave them here and talk about something else."

Molly felt proud of Paddy for remaining calm and doing exactly what he had rehearsed earlier in the day. He was off to a good start and staying focused. Paddy had a penchant for sometimes creating circular arguments embellished with side-tracks and invectives. They were always charming, engaging and ultimately wise, but they required others to be willing to take the journey. Today he was not offering the scenic route; this train was heading directly toward the station.

"You see," said Paddy. "Those agreements over there once had us believing that we could finally own this place. I can't remember all the expensive words and the way it was all put together but, in the end, it doesn't mean a damn thing, does it?"

"Now, Paddy, I wouldn't say that," Griffith was surprised by Paddy's tack but was not about to concede points in the lease agreement.

"Let's cut to the chase, shall we? We missed a few payments and you're here to tell that, basically, if we can't put the money on the table, we're out of here."

"I wouldn't put it like that."

"No, of course not, but that's about it isn't it?"

"Well, yes I suppose it is." Griffith said, rushing to rationalize such actions. "We did have an agreement."

"Right, but look at it this way," said Paddy. He picked up his beer glass and headed back to the bar for a refill. It was all a ploy to buy time while he got himself back on track. "You see, it's like a game of footy and you're two goals down in the fourth quarter...." Football was not an analogy upon which he and Molly had agreed. Obviously he had lost the thread of his argument. Molly knew it was time to intercede.

"What Paddy is getting at, Mr, Griffith, is that if this was a game of footy, it's not one you'd want to win. Isn't that right, Paddy?"

"Right. Yes, For sure, that's it." He looked at Griffith. "You understand what I'm saying?"

"Frankly, no."

"I think you'd better have a beer after all," said Paddy as he poured one for Griffith. "Bottom line is you don't want this place. It's a losing proposition. Think about it for a minute. What are you going to do with it if you chuck us out? While we were here you got at least something out of it. Okay, there were maybe a few months where that didn't happen, but on the whole you did pretty well. But when we're gone, mate, nothing. That's what it will be every month, nothing. Seriously, nobody's going to take this pub on. It's a physical wreck. The economy's shot. Everyone up here's broke. The talk is that if and when things do pick up, there'll be two more pubs up here in no time. What little business there is here now goes to the Prince of Wales. I mean, look around, you can see how busy we are."

Griffith sipped his glass of beer. "Go on."

"So, we thought about it long and hard and decided we could do you a favour and buy the place outright. Cheers." Paddy raised his glass and Griffith slowly reciprocated.

"Let me see if I have this right. You want to tear up the agreement we have and start afresh but this time with an agreement to purchase?"

"That's about it," said Paddy.

"That's not quite right." Molly held up her empty glass. "If you don't mind, Paddy. I'll have a beer now, love." She moved her chair around to face Griffith more directly. "Just want to clarify things a little, Mr Griffith, what we are talking about right now is not that we want to pay you so many pounds a month to someday own it. We want to own it now, today, and to do that we're willing to make you a cash offer. You get to walk out of here cash in hand and you are free of any liabilities attached to the hotel. It's a clean, profitable break."

This was hardly what Griffith had expected. He rose from the table and walked to the bar. He tossed back the remains of the beer and tapped the glass with his finger. Paddy took the cue and refilled his glass.

"Help me understand. If this is such a wretched business, such a millstone, why would you want to buy it? Why would anyone in their right mind want to put money into it?"

"Fair enough," said Paddy. He had anticipated that important question. "It's pretty straight forward really. Right now we can't pay you rent and continue to put bread on the table. It just can't be done. We got to choose one or the other and if we

don't have to pay you every month I think we might just make a go
of it."

"Paddy is right," said Molly. "It's all about choices. Even
without having to pay you each month it'll be a hard life. We
know that. We've lived it." Molly took a deep breath and
repositioned her chair slightly to underscore her next point. "At
some point, Mr Griffith, you have to decide where you want to live
and I want to live here. This is my home. I'm going to have a baby
and I want my baby be born here. In my home."

"All right," said Griffith as he made his way back to the
table. "Let's see your offer."

This was not a number to be blurted out or scribbled
hastily on a piece of paper. That would not impress Griffith's sense
of propriety. No, Paddy had gone all the way and had a formal
offer typed up by the town's solicitor. It included full property
description, lot numbers, title details, most of which had been
gleaned from the comprehensive lease agreement. There, nestled in
the legalese, sat the offer. Four hundred and twenty-eight pounds.
It seemed less money now than when they had planned everything
the previous day.

Molly and Paddy sat in dead silence. The only sound was
Griffith's breathing. There was no clue to be found there. He
didn't huff in disgust or gasp in horror. He remained remarkably
in control as he worked his way through the entire document. The
formality of the presentation confirmed that this was not
frivolous. He had to take it seriously. Finally he looked up at each
of them.

"May I ask how you came to arrive at this number?"

There was a momentary pause as Paddy and Molly looked
at each other unsure of exactly how to handle that question. "Are
there precedents? Did you look at other sales in the area?" he said.

"Fair enough. How did we get to that number? Truth is,
it's the most money we can come up with," said Paddy.

"I see."

Griffith thoughtfully fingered through the papers. "And if business is wretched, how did you come by this? This four hundred and twenty eight pounds?"

"We have someone who wants to invest in us, in the pub. He's going to be a partner."

"Well, where is he, this partner? I'd like to meet him."

"He couldn't make it today," said Paddy.

"He couldn't make it? That seems a little casual, don't you think? His lack of real interest doesn't speak too well of your business," said Griffith.

"No, mate, it speaks very well of our business. Very well indeed. You just don't know...." There was a clear hint of anger in Paddy's response, of which Paddy was not fully aware. Molly gently placed her hand on his arm. He took a deep breath. "What I am saying is you just don't know the man."

Griffith acknowledged Paddy's position with a simple nod. He stumbled to find an appropriate response but decided that silence was his best ally at that time. He returned to the papers. "I just want to say I am taking this very seriously. I believe it is a genuine offer."

"Thank you," said Paddy. "It's for real, no worries about that."

"It's just...."

There was no need to wonder what would have come next. The money was going to be tough to resolve. Paddy knew that. He had to play a new card. "There was another pub here in town," said Paddy.

"The Grosvenor," added Molly.

"That's right. The Grosvenor," said Paddy. A very nice establishment or so I'm told. Anyway, it burned down. The insurance payout was very close to what we put together for you, today."

"Really? And when was this?"

"Well...It was about twenty years ago," said Paddy.

"With all due respect, Paddy, don't you think this place is worth more than something that burned down twenty years ago?"

"No, not really." The bluntness of Paddy's reply took Griffith by surprise. "Have you had a good look around here?"

"Here?"

"Yeah, here. How well do you know the place? Do you want to know a good way to turn off the overhead light in the kitchen? Plug in the toaster. Do you know that if you step on the wrong boards in the storeroom you'll go right through to the cellar? I've got a list of things if you'd like to see it. Strictly speaking since you're our landlord, it's up to you to fix all this. Safety, you know. But we've moved past that, haven't we. Come on, I've got something you gotta see."

This was to be the trump card Paddy had up his sleeve for just such an occasion. "Have you ever taken a leak here?"

"I beg your pardon?" said Griffith.

"Didn't think so," said Paddy. "Come on."

Paddy walked to a rear door off the bar. Griffith was still sitting, watching.

"Come on."

Griffith followed Paddy to the door marked, somewhat ironically, 'Gentlemen'. The men's toilet was little more than a shanty. The corrugated tin roof was rusty and leaked through holes where nails used to be. It sloped down to and slightly beyond a weathered wooden wall that supported the urinals. Urinal was a generous description. It was a run of galvanized eavestrough crudely hammered to the wooden wall and angled slightly so that the urine would run off and vanish into another downspout. It was, at the very least, primitive.

Beyond the urinals were two stalls with doors.

"What do you think?" asked Paddy.

372

Griffith was obviously shocked at the shabby conditions. "I had no idea. I didn't do a physical inspection of the hotel. It was all transacted on paper." He shook his head. "I don't think I have ever seen anything like this before."

Paddy took a step toward the eavestrough and reached down to unbutton his fly. "Just a minute, I'll show you how it works?"

"No, no, no." said Griffith, lunging forward and reaching for Paddy to stop him. He looked up at the broad grin on Paddy's face. "You had me for a minute," said Griffith. "We can go back to the bar now,"

The first thing Griffith did upon his return was look to reclaim his position. He buttoned his vest and put on his jacket. He then spent an inordinate amount of time holding on to the offer and gazing out the window. Molly began to worry that he would spot the beer wranglers who were heading off potential customers and shepherding them to the funeral parlour. She looked up at Paddy for some clue, some sign of how things were going. Paddy simply shrugged; he really didn't know.

"All right," said Griffith turning back into the room. "I am comfortable with most of the conditions in your offer."

"Great," said Paddy feeling that they were close to a deal.

Griffith held the papers "This has been well put together. Mind you, it's all quite straight forward really, no real conditions, now if we can settle on a price.... "

Paddy's moment of confidence dissolved when it all came back to price. There was no more money to put on the table.

"Four hundred and twenty eight pounds. Four hundred and twenty eight pounds." Griffith kept throwing the number into the air. "And you say that's the most you can offer?"

"That's right. We don't have a penny more than that."

"Do you have a separate float?" said Griffith. "Tell me you have a operating budget over and above this four hundred and eighty pounds."

"Of course we do." Molly could sit still no longer. "It may not be much but it would be an absolute folly to give you every penny and not hold back something to stock the shelves or keep the lights on."

Griffith nodded. "Quite right." He turned back to the window to consider the situation one more time. "All right, I have made a decision. I will agree to everything you ask but we must adjust the price. I am going to change it on all three copies." He sat at the table, took out his fountain pen and proceeded to make the necessary changes. He signed and dated every copy including a separate signature to confirm the change he had made.

"Paddy, you will have to sign this as well. The bottom of each page and again to confirm agreement of the revised sale price."

Paddy wanted to say just a minute or hold on or something to keep the conversation open, but he couldn't find the words. Griffith made it all seem so settled. Paddy sat at the table and looked at the offer. The price had indeed been changed from four hundred and twenty eight pounds to four hundred pounds. He had lowered the price! "Yes, it's four hundred now," said Griffith. That was enough provocation for Molly to quickly reach for a copy and see it for herself. She was stunned. "You see," said Griffith. "I am not above taking a loss for the company, that's part of how it goes. Four hundred is not a serious figure. It suggests that there are extenuating circumstances and the property needs to be disposed of for more than obvious reasons. If I leave it at four hundred and twenty eight pounds, it all looks petty and miserly, as if I screwed the last penny out some poor people. I say that with respect. Four hundred is clean and efficient. There are no nasty implications. I trust that you will grant me this one indulgence."

Paddy sat slack-jawed, pen drooping in his hand. Griffith may as well have spoken in tongues. All he could see was the number on the paper.

"Go on, dear, sign it." Molly's voice was superficially calm.

"What?" said Paddy.

"Sign it, dear, Mr Griffith is waiting."

"Yeah, of course, of course." Paddy immediately put pen to paper. Griffith stood over his shoulder pointing Paddy in all the right places to sign.

"Well, I think we're done here." He said as he slipped his copy of the sale into his briefcase. This will be filed first thing in the morning; titles and such will be forward to you as soon as is possible." He held out his hand. Paddy grasped it and shook it heartily. "Congratulations, you own a hotel." He turned to Molly "Mrs Brennan." Molly stood and took his hand.

"Mr Griffith," she said.

"Good luck," said Griffith. He tipped his hat, turned and left the hotel.

Paddy and Molly walked to the street, watched him get into his car and then drive away.

"You've got a pub," said Molly.

"We've got a home," said Paddy.

"Just like that," she said

"Just like that," He slipped his arm around her waist. "A pretty good day's work, I'd say," said Paddy. "Still hard to believe."

"Yes it is." Molly cupped her hand over his. "Our Mr Griffith turned out trumps, didn't he?"

"Yeah, good bloke," said Paddy. "Bloody hell, love, we own a pub."

Griffith's car had reached the end of town and disappeared behind the hill before The Paps. Molly squeezed Paddy's hand.

"Can I wax the bar now?" she asked.

"Yeah, I reckon." He kissed her lightly on the top of her head. "I've got a feeling it's going to get busy around here."

"I think you're right." She smiled at him and walked back into the bar.

Two blokes across the street waved to Paddy; he returned the greeting. It felt good to be standing there in the sun out front of their pub, their home,

Very good indeed.

Chapter Sixty-Four

It was a shock to everyone when the Prince of Wales caught fire just over a week later. None of the surrounding buildings were damaged but the hotel was a write off; another unfortunate victim of the bushfires. Curious though, there hadn't been a bad fire around town for at lease five days. The local fire chief summed it up as "shocking," and went on to say, "but these things do happen."

There was constant chatter about new pubs coming to town, which would be inevitable, but the economy was still rough so there would be quite a lag before anyone broke ground. Long enough for the Imperial to become firmly entrenched as the place to go in Mansfield.

Business boomed and Molly had to wax the bar a lot more frequently over the next few months. The Imperial Hotel felt more like home every day.

Rabbit's ten-pound note from Aunt Addy had been framed and hung above the bar, just beside a bottle of his favourite port.

On May 4, 1939, at 6:48 p.m. Molly and Paddy had a son.

They called him Peter.

Born in Moonee Ponds, Australia, Terry now
lives in Niagara-on-the-Lake, Canada, with his wife,
Donna. Terry has written extensively for the stage,
television, film and print. His passion for relationships
is evident in his novel, **the printer, the actress
and the cat she couldn't mention,** a romantic comedy
set in Buffalo, NY, and New York City. **Matters of
Kindness,** his anthology of short stories, anecdotes, and
memories, was described in reviews as "Touching
moments interspersed with hilarity,all crafted
with eloquent insight". His new novel,
Painted Tongues, is slated for release in 2017.

45603631R00212

Made in the USA
Middletown, DE
08 July 2017